SUNASTARA & THE VENUSIAN

A SPACE CRUISE ROMANCE

JESS K HARDY

This is a work of fiction. Names, characters, places, and incidents either are the product of the author's imagination or are used fictitiously. Any resemblance to actual persons, living or dead, events, or locales is entirely coincidental.

Edited by: VB Edits

Published by Pinkity Publishing LLC

A NOTE TO MY READERS

Five years before the events of this story, the main character lost her child. She continues to process this loss and her grief throughout this book. I tried to approach this loss with as much respect, care, and love as I could. But please take care of yourselves.

This book is for my mom, who raised me on Star Trek and made the mistake of telling me I was too young to read Dune when I was ten. Mentat-level reverse psychology. Love you.

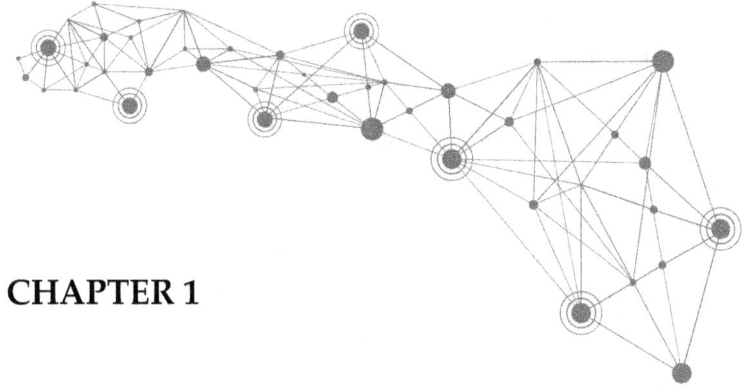

CHAPTER 1

My eyes flew open as the ceiling tilted and the ship dropped out from under me. Only it wasn't the ship. It was me, rolling out of bed and landing hard on the floor. My head throbbed like a stubbed toe. I frowned down at my half-buttoned blouse, black lace underwear, and the red heel still clinging to my foot. Wincing, and as quietly as possible—even though it was unlikely any overnight guest would have slept through my ass hitting the floor—I peeked up at my bed. *Empty, thank the stars.*

<Where are you?> Elanie barked through my viewChip comms.

<In my pod,> I groaned, turning the volume down on my neural implant. <Why? Where are you?>

<Outside your door. I've been knocking for five minutes.>

Sitting up, clutching at my head, I commed, <Elanie, what in the worlds did I do last night?>

<I'm going to assume that was rhetorical,> my assistant replied flatly. <Open the door. Your shuttle to the City of All Knowledge arrives in twenty minutes.>

I tried to remember what I'd had to drink last night, and how much of it. But I'd never been good at math. <I am not

going to the CAK. I'm sick. And I hate Deprogramming and Reprogramming week. It's the worst.>

<You are not sick, Sunny. You're hungover. And you don't have a choice. D&R week is mandatory if you want to keep your job. *And* there we go.>

My door slid open, and Elanie strode in, her long, tanned legs stopping at the foot of my bed. "Stars above, Sunny," she said, staring down at me like she'd just walked in on a crime scene. "What *did* you do last night?"

"Did you hack my lock?" I started to pull my blouse closed, then decided *who cares*. "And I had fun. Loads of it." This might have been true. I couldn't remember. The last thing I recalled with any clarity was meeting Co-Captain Isla Jones for drinks at the Blurvan tavern on deck eighteen. There might have been some karaoke later. Possibly a ride around the tavern on a Blurvan's tail. A sloppy make-out session in a bathroom rang a hazy bell. With whom was anyone's guess.

Elanie held out her hand, and I took it, letting the perpetually scowling bionic haul me to my feet.

"Why is the ship rocking?" I asked, listing on my way into the bathroom.

"It's not." Elanie rolled her eyes while she plucked my other red shoe from the lamp, where it hung by its heel. Where I—*or someone else*—had apparently flung it last night.

Peeling off my blouse and shimmying out of my underwear, I stumbled into the shower.

<I've started packing your bag,> Elanie commed while I turned the water to near scalding. <And set clean clothes on your bed.>

<Thank you, darling,> I replied, holding my hand under the shampoo dispenser and waiting for it to squirt.

<Don't thank me yet.> My D&R itinerary popped into my VC files. <Quite the week they have lined up for you.>

I perused the itinerary she'd sent me while I rinsed the shampoo and waited for the conditioner squirt. <I have to go ziplining?> Forgoing my typical three-minute conditioner routine, I rinsed quickly, turned off the water, and stomped out of the shower. "Seriously? Wait, is this a prank? Did you corrupt these files?"

"I'm afraid not."

I scanned the rest of the itinerary. "Caroling? And an ugly sweater contest? What is *wrong* with these corporate assholes?"

She shrugged. "It's not their fault your D&R coincides with Vorp's Winter Revel. I suppose you'll have to figure out how to be festive. Do you even have an ugly sweater? Or anything with a cat on it? You know how much Vorpols love cats."

"No. No to both," I insisted, ducking under the quikDri. I waited impatiently as a dehydrating film made of microscopic sand guppies dropped from the device. It clung to my head and sucked before peeling itself off with a satisfied sigh. "And I refuse to participate in anything that features the word 'ugly.'"

"Suit yourself. You have ten minutes."

As the hospitality specialist aboard the *Ignisar*—the premier interstellar pleasure cruise in the Juniper-13 star system—I knew my yearly D&R week was unavoidable. But that didn't mean I had to enjoy it. The coming week at Luna-Corp HQ would test my skills for perma-smiling while saying things like: *All I've ever wanted to do is make other people happy*, and *I'm so excited to learn from my cohort's skill sets and experiences.*

Puke.

"How entrenched is your precept to do no harm?" I asked Elanie after closing the file.

"For the last time, Sunny, I will not dislocate your shoulder to get you out of this training. No matter how much you beg."

"Killjoy."

A bright-red banner flashed: **Your shuttle has arrived. Your shuttle has arrived. Make your way to airlock C-14,** directly over my central field of vision.

"Your shuttle has arrived," Elanie repeated unnecessarily.

"Right." Accepting my fate, I blew a stream of air between my lips, crossed my pod to give Elanie a kiss on her cheek that she promptly wiped away, and then got dressed.

THE SHUTTLE PILOT, a handsome green-skinned Aquilinian male with impressively broad shoulders, strafed me head to toe with an irritated glare as I ducked through the docking bay fifteen minutes later.

"You must be Sunastara Nex," he said, a brow sharply arched. "You're late."

"My apologies," I replied, quirking a brow of my own. "But believe me, I'm well worth the wait."

When he only glowered at my attempt to butter him up, I shrugged. "Can't win them all, I suppose—"

"Buckle in," he snapped. "I'll need to break some speed records to get us to the CAK on time."

As the pilot steered the shuttle away from the *Ignisar*, my ship gleamed back at me through the flexGlass. I so rarely saw her from the outside, and despite the debauchery that took place inside her, she truly was a marvel. A kilometer long, encased in white titanium and embellished with diamonds and rubies mined from one of LunaCorp's mega-asteroids, she was a shimmering queen in the blackness of space. A drag queen, but still.

I'd just pressed my hand against the window separating me from my ship when the pilot accelerated away from her, shoving me back into my seat. Dizzy—and still very hungover

—I closed my eyes, searched for reality TV shows on my view-Chip, and waited for the shuttle's velocity to level out.

"SHUTTLE PASSENGERS," the pilot said, interrupting the episode of *Kuiper Worm Chasers* I'd been watching. "We're, uhhh, making our final approach on, uhhh, the City of All Knowledge."

Why did all pilots sound the same? Did they teach pilot-speak in flight school?

"Please return to your seats, buckle in, and, uhhh, prepare for landing."

Through the shuttle's viewport, the CAK—a seventy-kilometer-long wonder of high-tech engineering and obscene credit expenditure—hovered. Towering skyscrapers reached into the blackness of space like the sparkling points of Miss Known Universe's tiara, while countless orbiting satellites created a twinkling veil cast over the city. The CAK was positioned at the border of the wormhole linking Juniper-13 with the Solar System of New Earth, acting as the port of entry and customs for travel between the two. It was also the home of LunaCorp's HQ, and one of my least favorite places to visit.

The shuttle landed with a whisper-soft *thud* that was completely at odds with the gravity tugging on my shoulders. Stepping onto the tarmac, I winced and shielded my eyes against the garish glow of the red and blue Winter Revel lights strewn across the surrounding trees.

Since the accident, holidays were, to put it mildly, challenging. But considering the countless species the *Ignisar* catered to—all with their own unique customs and celebrations—I'd learned to shoulder through them with a grim determination. I had no choice. A full week at the CAK during a holiday, however, was a different story entirely. A week cut off from the comfortable, numbing routine of my work. A week of mandatory fist-bumping, corporate ego stroking, and enthusiastically feigned interest during team-building bullshit. A week spent being bombarded by holiday music everywhere I went… All I knew for certain was that my mini bar had better be fully stocked.

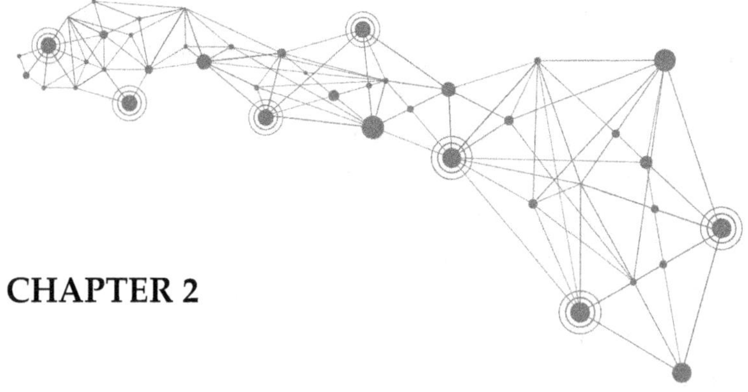

CHAPTER 2

The first few days of D&R week were, predictably, a boring, tedious slog. The only break in the monotony came from a terrifying and extremely uncomfortable ziplining tour through the LunaCorp Fun Zone—a fifteen-kilometer-long green space in the center of the CAK, fashioned after Old Earth's Central Park.

Feeling like I'd more than satisfied my team-building quota when I let a freckle-faced Mercurian teenager strap me into a harness and shove me without mercy across the abyss, I was determined to avoid the evening's ugly sweater contest come hells or high water. Instead, I showered, slid into my favorite little black dress, and staked a claim to a stool at the hotel bar.

These days, I felt most at home in places like this—loud, dark, anonymous. But after I'd spent the last three days fighting so hard not to roll my eyes or groan in boredom that I think I sprained something, even the dim bar couldn't calm my nerves. I was antsy, out of sorts, unsettled. And there was only one sure-fire cure for that.

After ordering a glass of dry Delphinian red, I opened *Squee*, my favorite VC dating app. A group of empaths from the ocean planet of Portis developed *Squee* using an algorithm that connected individuals based not on who their perfect partner would be forever, but on who their perfect date would be at that precise moment. Immediate gratification—a heady sensation that evidently made Portisans exclaim, *Squee*! Hence the name. I, myself, had never *Squee*ed after using the app. But I'd definitely had some phenomenal one-nighters. And that was exactly what I needed now.

Taking a sip of my wine, which was surprisingly good, I set my desired search parameters: Age, *thirty to fifty*. Gender, *any and all.* Fur, *no* (allergic). Tentacles, *no* (shit *always* got weird). Horns, *hmm, why not.* Multiple partners... I considered this briefly, ultimately marking *no* when I realized that at forty, I was too old for that amount of work.

While I tapped my foot against the barstool, the app—reading my biorhythms and hormone fluctuations—lit up my VC with recommendations for a partner within a two-kilometer radius of my hotel. Which came to a whopping total of 4,152 beings. Apparently, I wasn't the only antsy tourist looking for a little CAK strange.

While *Squee* was designed to whittle my choices down to a handful of optimal matches for my current mood, occasionally, I liked perusing bios for my own entertainment. For instance, there was Martin, an accountant with a medium build from my home planet of Tranquis. Martin was recently divorced. He loved classical piano and downhill skiing, and he used to perform as a contortionist at the Gala Galaxia Extravaganza.

That might be interesting.

No sooner had the thought crossed my mind than *Squee* flashed a **12% match for current mood** warning over Martin's dimpled chin. *Fair enough.*

After a few more minutes of being scolded for considering partners *Squee* deemed unsuitable, I allowed the app to find my match. It presented me with three choices: two Venusian men and one stunning Portisan woman, her skin as blue as the oceans of her planet.

I considered sending the Portisan an in-app message, but with the Revel lights twinkling over the bar and the table of Vorpols behind me singing (*meowing, more like*) their planet's bizarre, cat-themed holiday music, my mood was far too precarious to share it with an empath.

The Venusians were both handsome, but one of them, Joshua, had piercing gray-blue eyes that reminded me of a thunderstorm. There was no weather on the *Ignisar*, and sometimes I missed the rain.

He was funny too. His bio read: *Intermittently interesting. Passably presentable. Very Venusian,* and that was all. And Joshua was staying in this hotel. Aside from self-deprecating humor, convenience was my second biggest turn-on.

When I asked *Squee* to inform Joshua that I was interested, I received an **Excellent choice, Sunastara** message. Inclined to agree, I downed the rest of my wine, tapped the glass for a refill, and awaited Joshua's response.

FIFTEEN MINUTES LATER, he walked into the bar, slid his hands into his pockets, and glanced down the line of stools. When his gaze snagged on mine, his instant smirk pulled a happy little hum from somewhere deep in my throat.

Dressed in an impeccable black suit and tie, he weaved effortlessly through high-top tables and serving drones, devouring the distance to me in long, fluid strides. His dark-brown hair—that I imagined had been expertly styled all day—was happy-hour mussed now, a few strands falling over his forehead. His cheekbones rode high above his strong jaw and freshly shaved chin. And in the middle of all this apparent perfection, his nose was a bit crooked right over the bridge, like maybe he'd broken it once.

When he reached the bar, he stood over me, so close the tip of my shoe ran up against his pant leg. Staring down at me with those stormy eyes, his lips curling into a fantastic smile that was fifty percent suggestion, fifty percent hope, and one hundred percent working for me, he said, "Phoebe?"

While my foot floated up enough to trace along the muscles of his calf, I replied with, "Joshua?"

Nobody used their real names on *Squee*. Phoebe was a name I'd read in some romance book. Where Joshua had come from, I could only guess. Maybe it was his college roommate, or that one uncle who showed up blitzed to every family function. It didn't matter.

Joshua, or whoever he was, continued to aim that suggestive smile at me as he slipped off his suit jacket and folded it over his arm. As he loosened his tie, as I imagined tugging it the rest of the way off with my teeth, he tilted his head toward the corner of the restaurant. "There's an open booth back there. Care to join me?"

I turned to look. Indeed, there was. A small booth. Intimate, dark. *Yes, please.*

The hand he extended was warm, and his grip was gentle yet firm as he led me away from the bar. I felt every ounce of wine I'd just guzzled while trying to follow in a straight line behind him. But my attention kept slipping to his backside, which was round and firm and more than a little biteable.

Would you like to rate this match? *Squee* asked, the message popping over his bum in my vision, five empty stars awaiting my evaluation. I certainly would. I rated all my matches, but never until the night was over. So I closed the app while Joshua slowed a step.

Busy wondering if he'd received the same message, if he'd submitted a star-rating for me, and, more importantly, what it might have been, I tripped over my own feet. Getting my shit together, I refocused my efforts on making it from the bar to the booth without falling face-first into his spectacular butt.

Joshua released my hand to let me slide into one side of the booth, then he slid smoothly into the other. The upholstery was soft and plush, velvety. I wanted to wrap myself inside it.

"This is nice," he said, brushing a long-fingered hand over the soft black fabric. "Feels like kitten fur. I wonder if they're always like this, or if they reupholstered them just for Vorp's Winter Revel."

Running my fingers along my cushion, I murmured, "Hmm, you're right. I can almost hear it purring."

Vorpols had, in my personal opinion, a ridiculous obsession with cats. After LunaCorp ships first traveled from New Earth's single moon through the wormhole to Juniper-13 over a thousand years ago, several animal species were exchanged between the star systems in a campaign entitled Peace Through Pets. PTP was largely unsuccessful—many animals were eaten outright, and trestals (ten-feet-long raptor birds used for hunting on Gorbulon-7) still terrorized the New Earth Americas. But there was one glowing exception to the PTP disaster. As soon as the first Vorpol felt the fuzzy tail of a cat wrap around its singular leg, the entire species went off the rails for the furry little felines. Now they wore cat clothing, lived in cat-shaped houses, visited cat-themed amusement parks, and owned an inordinate number of actual cats.

Joshua leaned in close and rested his elbows on the table. His grin was conspiratorial. "As marketing strategies go, these booths are pretty fan*cat*stic."

Having never met a pun I didn't love, I grinned back and replied, "Meowsively brilliant."

His rich, warm laughter poured over me like honey. Breaking eye contact, he glanced around the bar. "I'm surprised more Vorpols aren't dressed up tonight."

Spotting only one set of kitten ears perched on top of an exceptionally drunk Vorpol's head, I said, "You're right. They rarely miss a chance to dress up for the holiday. That reminds me. Wasn't there an Old Earth musical where people sang and danced dressed up as cats?"

"I have no idea," he said, brushing the soft strands of his bangs back into place. "But I wouldn't be surprised. There was an Old Earth musical for just about everything."

"There was. I'm certain of it. In fact, I think it was called"—I leaned back, spreading my hands out before me as I announced dramatically—"*Cats*."

"No." He laughed. "Really? It was just called '*Cats*'? If this is true, how has *Cats* not been revived on Vorp?"

I gasped. "We should do it. We'll be stinking rich. Finally able to leave this life of corporate drudgery behind us and live out the rest of our days drinking mai tais on Portisan beaches and refusing to wear any clothes."

He sighed, staring wistfully at the ceiling. "That's the dream, isn't it?"

"This is so much better than an ugly sweater contest." I said this mostly to myself, mostly because Joshua was more magnetic than Jupiter's core.

"Wait. You too?" His eyes flared. "It was on my itinerary, but I ditched. Even though I do have an exceptionally hideous cat sweater a Vorpol I worked with on my last ship gave to me."

"Ah. You could have been a contender," I said, and he burst into laughter. Then his eyes narrowed, like he was about to tell me a secret. "It's interesting, don't you think?"

I crossed my legs. "What's that, darling?"

"You and I were due at the same party. We might have met tonight either way."

That is interesting, I thought, more intrigued by this stranger than I'd been by anyone in years. "Has anyone ever told you that you are very charming, Joshua?"

"Has anyone ever told you that you are very beautiful, Phoebe?"

"Charming *and* smart. Gorgeous as well. Almost too perfect." I cocked my head. "Are you a serial killer?" And suddenly, I forgot how tired I was, because Joshua's broad smile was starlight in the dark bar, his hand brushing through his hair a gentle breeze stirring something deep in my belly.

A serving drone floated by our table, but we were so intent on each other that it had to bob in place several times and make a *bleep-bloop* noise before it pulled our attention.

"Drinks?" Joshua asked.

I nodded.

He ordered whiskey, and I switched from wine to a holiday cocktail the serving drone suggested called a Meowtini. It was tasty, if not a little tart, and it had candy rocks I didn't notice right away at the bottom of the glass. When they caught my attention several sips later, I was worried—and mildly horrified—that they were meant to replicate kitty litter.

"So, what brings you to the City of All Knowledge, Phoebe?" Joshua asked, sipping his kitty-litter-free whiskey, his gray eyes sharp as diamonds.

"Work, of course. And you?"

"Same. What do you do?"

Meeting his penetrating stare with one of my own, I said, "Whatever I want."

His laughter was a low, two-note rumble that hit me right in the spine. With a hint of a smile, he asked, "And what is it you want?"

It was only then that I noticed his slight Venusian accent—like a hint of an Old Earth Scottish burr—growing thicker with every sip he took of his drink. It was somehow adorable and scorchingly hot at the same time. I licked my lips, ready to tell him exactly what was on my mind. But then my stomach growled. "Right now," I said, "I'd like some food.

Later?" I raised and lowered my shoulder. "Anything's possible."

"Anything?" he repeated with mischief in his eyes. "Well, then, let's get you fed."

He was gorgeous and sexy and delightful, and I was so in the mood for something delightful. "One moment," I said, holding up a finger while I opened *Squee* again, breaking my own rules of waiting until the end of the night to give him a five-star rating.

"What was that?" he asked, his brow furrowed.

"Just leaving *Squee* a rating for this match."

Sitting back against the booth with an amused tilt to his lips, he asked, "How did I do?"

"I'm not sure yet," I said, leaning forward, letting my gaze travel down his throat, dip into the notch between his collarbones. "But I have a feeling you'll do just fine."

The serving drone returned, breaking the charged silence that had settled between us.

"Are you ready?" Joshua asked.

Was I ever.

After the kitty litter garnish mishap, I declined the Winter Revel special of Calicoq au Vin and decided to stick to steak. Joshua ordered scallops. And then we ate, talking and laughing and flirting shamelessly between bites.

Maybe it was the drinks, or maybe it was the way he listened to me so intently, leaning in, tilting his head a little, like he didn't want to risk missing what I might say next. But I could hardly be bothered by the heads turning my way when I laughed out loud at his story of almost losing his pinky finger when he'd stuck his hand into a sleeping ballont's mouth. His grandfather had told him that if he touched its tongue, he'd be able to see the future. The ballont—a reptilian creature native to Venus that resembled a poodle-sized dragon—woke up a split second before tongue-contact was made and bit the tip of Joshua's pinky straight off. And the punchline: "If only I'd seen it coming," almost made me spit out my drink.

Like most Venusians, Joshua was a natural storyteller, drawing me in like light to a black hole, like a Vorpol to a humane society. Which was how I found myself, an hour later, sharing a dessert called chocolate-covered cherry hairballs with him, my cheek resting in my hand while I imagined what his tie might feel like sliding through my fingers.

When I popped one of the bourbon-soaked, chocolate-dipped cherries into my mouth, twirling the stem until it broke free, Joshua asked, "Are they good?" his eyes trained on my lips.

"They are." I winced after swallowing the boozy little fruit. "But strong."

"Strong?" he asked, plucking one of the cherries from the plate, still meeting my stare. "I like strong." When he dropped the cherry into his mouth, my toes curled in my shoes.

We reached for the next cherry at the same time, and as his fingers brushed over mine, tiny electrical impulses popped and crackled across my skin. Leaving the dessert behind, he ran his fingers gently over my knuckles, tracing the side of my hand, his thumb and forefinger sliding from the base of my pinky up to the tip.

"I hope I'm not being too forward," he said while heat swirled between my legs. "And please stop me if I am, but I spend a great deal of time studying planetary cultures." He watched me, his attention rapt as I licked a bit of chocolate from my fingertip. When he spoke again, his voice was half an octave lower, his pupils half a centimeter larger. "I have a feeling, considering your accent, your fair skin and hair, and the way you hold your fork between your middle finger and thumb sometimes, that your home planet is not actually Delphi, as stated on your *Squee* profile, but Tranquis."

I grinned, too drunk off the cherries and the color rising

into his cheeks to care that he'd breached this bit of my anonymity. "How did you know that?"

"It's kind of my job," he said with a sheepish shrug, his fingers still running over mine in a reverent sort of way that made my eyelids heavy. "Anyway, since Tranquis and Vorp are about as far away from each other as two planets can get, how much do you know about Winter Revel?"

"Aside from cat sweaters and yowling holiday mewsic?"

"Did you say *mew*sic?" When I snorted, he shook his head and said, "I'm stealing that one."

Try as I might—and I did really try—I couldn't remember the last time I'd smiled this much in one evening. It wasn't that I didn't smile in my day-to-day life aboard my ship. I had to. It was part of my job. But the expression never felt like this, impossible to hide, making my cheeks ache. "It's all yours."

His eyes twinkled, and I traced the lights reflecting in them the way I used to trace my finger over the constellations at night. Only instead of horses or serpents, Joshua's stars made the shape of full, kissable lips, a necktie draped over a bedpost.

"There's a Winter Revel custom I think you might not know about."

"Is there?" I asked, my heart picking up an extra beat as he intertwined his fingers with mine.

"Well"—his voice dropped low—"on Vorp, when two people meet for the first time on Revel, it's custom that they must see each other naked before parting ways."

"Custom?" I peered up at him through my lashes. "Really?"

He held up his free hand. "I don't make the rules."

"Of course not."

"In fact," he went on, making a show of looking around like what he was about to say was of the utmost importance, "Vorpols believe that if this custom isn't observed, then somewhere, sadly, tragically, a kitten won't find its forever home."

Sinking my teeth into my grinning lower lip, I asked, "Joshua, would you like to see me naked?"

With his eyes locked on mine, he replied, "More than anything in the Known Universe." While I laughed, he tugged at his collar. "But only if you're finished with your dessert."

"I'm done with this one," I said, pointing my chin at the cherries. "But I think I'm ready for the next."

After a heavy pause that spun me up like a faster-than-light jump drive, he grasped my hand more tightly, slid out of the booth, and pulled me to my feet.

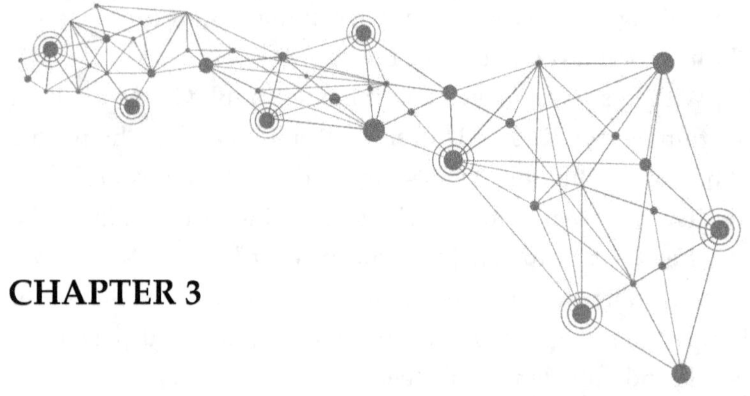

CHAPTER 3

THE ELEVATOR WAS ALMOST at capacity when we raced through the doors, wiggling our way through a pack of tipsy, ugly sweater–wearing LunaCorp execs. I hadn't let go of Joshua's hand since we'd left our booth. And as the elevator rose, his thumb brushed over mine. Ripples of sensation spread out from the spot in perfect, overlapping circles until I felt his touch everywhere at once. It wasn't enough, though, only his thumb. I wanted every part of him. I wanted his lips, his hands, his tongue. I wanted him the way I wanted sunshine after weeks of rain. But I had to wait. My room was all the way on the forty-eighth floor, and it wasn't until the doors opened on forty-five that our final fellow passenger bid us a slurred good night.

"Thank fuck," Joshua rasped, his hand gripping mine.

I didn't wait for the doors to close again before I turned, fisted his tie, pulled him close, and moaned in relief at the feel of his lips against mine. They were just as full and soft as I'd imagined they'd be. His hand slid across my low back, warm and firm as he urged me closer, groaning when I brushed my tongue over his. He tasted like cherries and chocolate.

When the elevator *ding*ed, and the doors slid open on my floor, he slipped his arm low around my hips, hoisting me up.

While I wrapped my legs around his waist, he cradled my thighs and stopped kissing me only long enough to ask, "Room number?" as he carried me out into the hallway.

Burying my hands in his hair, I licked a meandering trail up his neck. Then I took his earlobe between my teeth and slurred, "4810."

He spun around, pushing me up against a door I was pretty sure wasn't mine, and kissed me with such blind hunger it was almost indecent. Pressing my hips against his thick, rigid length, I sighed. Then I laughed when whoever was in the room that definitely wasn't mine shouted, "Hey! Who's out there?"

"It's...down the hall," I managed while his teeth grazed over my neck where it met my shoulder, making my vision go hazy. "Last room on the right."

I clung to him, digging my fingers into his shoulders, and I thought I'd lost a shoe. Not that I cared. Who the hell cared about shoes when he'd unzipped my dress and unclasped my bra before we'd made it halfway down the hall. I was half tempted to skip the room entirely and beg him to fuck me on top of the ice machine. But then he pushed me up against another door and said, "This one's yours," against my lips.

Reaching back, I fumbled blindly to touch my thumb to the security panel. Then I wrapped my arms around him again as he flung the door open, carried me through, and kicked it shut again after it banged off the wall.

I yanked his tie off and unbuttoned his shirt in a frantic dash as he walked me to the wall, working my dress up over my hips. While I slid his shirt over his broad shoulders, he reached down to unbuckle his belt.

"Do we need protection?" I asked, panting like some sort of wild animal in heat as he slid my panties to the side.

"No," he said, his lips skimming the sacred spot behind my

right ear, his finger sliding through the wetness between my folds, slipping easily inside me. "I'm on the pill."

"Good," I praised, arching my back as a second finger joined the first. "That's really good."

His soft kisses along my exposed throat, his hand cupping my ass, his fingers moving inside me, were superb. But it wasn't enough, and I'd never been called a patient woman.

Pushing his pants and boxers down over his hips, my legs trembling from holding on to him, from the pressure and friction of his fingers, I said, "I need you, Joshua. Now."

"Yes," he ground out, pulling his fingers free so he could take himself in hand, notch his round head into place at my entrance, and push.

My breathing turned into ragged little moans as finally, like a child standing in line for ice cream on a hot summer day, I got that first lengthy lick of him. And *it was delicious.*

"I should have taken your panties off," he said, grasping my thighs, his fingers digging in enough that I felt them, though not enough to hurt. "But I couldn't wait. And now it kind of chafes."

I laughed, then gasped as he thrust into me again. "They're not my favorite pair. Do whatever you need to do."

I'd had several pairs of panties ripped off me in my lifetime, but never with such speed and finesse. Did he practice on mannequins? Or was this some innate skill that was bestowed upon him at birth, like a royal title: the Prince of Perfectly Torn G-strings.

With nothing but skin between us, he became an artist. He was fast when I needed him to be fast, and slow when I wanted him to be slow. It was like he could read my mind, or my G-spot. Like he was a G-spot psychic. And he was just *right on top of it.*

"Joshua!" I cried out, clinging to him, hanging on for dear life as I tensed and pulsed and came apart in waves. *Squee* flashed a firework emoji in front of my eyes with **Orgasm Achievement Badge attained!** scrolling underneath.

Joshua made this contented, purring sort of sound against my neck. Then, with such ease I wondered if he might be some new model of bionic, he pulled out, spun around, and tossed me onto the bed.

With my dress still rucked up over my hips, and while tiny aftershocks of pleasure pulsed through my core, I scooted back toward the pillows. Kicking off his pants, he stood above me, his gaze skimming over my body, studying every curve and contour like a sculptor might study a vase.

"Come here," I said, letting my bent knees fall open.

Despite the heat in his gaze, his smile was almost shy as he moved toward me, naked, delaying only long enough to remove my remaining shoe. When he crawled onto the bed, prowling over my body until he towered above me, I took his face between my hands and kissed him.

No longer quite so out of my mind with need for him, I took a moment to appreciate his lips, his tongue. Joshua was a phenomenal kisser. Especially when those soft, warm kisses slid down my throat, between my breasts as he slipped the straps of my favorite little black dress over my shoulders and removed my bra. Even more when the tip of his tongue traced a warm, wet circle around my belly button as he pulled my dress down over my raised hips. When he draped my dress carefully over the edge of the bed, the small act of courtesy shook me. Who was this person? Nobody was this perfect. "*Are* you a bionic in disguise?"

As he kneeled between my legs, staring down at my naked body, his voice sank deep. "Phoebe, do you have any idea how long I've been searching for the perfect breasts? My whole life, I think. And you've hidden them from me until tonight."

My exhale was more laughter than anything else. "These

breasts are a treasured heirloom the females in my family have handed down through generations."

He leaned forward, his eyes locked on mine, holding my gaze as he flicked his tongue over the tip of my nipple. "Absolutely perfect," he whispered over my wet skin. And when he took my nipple into his mouth and sucked, I shuddered.

As his mouth moved to my other breast, I threaded my fingers through his hair. When his hand settled between my legs, his finger stroking, pressing, circling, sinking into me, I wondered if the simulated gravity on the CAK had malfunctioned. Because I was levitating.

"This isn't your first time, is it?" I joked breathlessly while his mouth and fingers carried me to the brink of another climax. So close, almost there... But just as ecstasy gathered in my belly, brisk and electric like a sudden summer storm, he reared over me, slung my legs over his shoulders, and fucked me until I saw stars, constellations, entire galaxies swirling into each other, colliding, becoming something new.

"Oh...*Phoebe*," he grunted as we came together. At the same time. No, for real.

Simultaneous Orgasm Achievement Badge attained! Ultra-rare! flashed behind my closed eyes as Joshua collapsed over me. While I tried to hold him, encircling him with my arms and legs with whatever paltry strength I had left, he raised his head from my shoulder enough to kiss me, a small brush of his lips on mine. And then he rolled to the side, flopping onto his back.

The ceiling swam above me, my body warm and loose and buzzing. "That... It was—"

"Yeah," he agreed, winded. "It really was."

Aside from our breaths slowly evening out, the hotel room went silent. But before anything got awkward, he turned toward me, slipped an arm around my waist, and pulled me close. Tucking a stray strand of my hair behind my ear, he said, "I can't believe I have to leave tomorrow. I've just finally found you."

My heart did something weird inside my chest, like a *whump*. "Tomorrow?" I asked, sounding a bit too desperate for my liking, which was...also weird. "So soon?"

"Today," he said. "Technically. It's after midnight."

Brushing my fingertips over the straight line of his jaw, I admitted, "That's a shame." And it was. Because I wanted more time with him, more than one night. And I *never* wanted more than one night. This wasn't me. This wasn't normal. I was always the first to leave after sex, slipping out before I'd even put on my shoes.

"Well," he said, yanking me so close he pressed against my thigh, half-hard again. "Since I have to leave in a little less than four hours. What do you say we make the most of it?"

Almost ashamed of it for some reason, I buried my grin into his smooth, hard chest and said, "Isn't that what we just did?"

"Oh no." He rolled over, flipping me onto my back, and settled between my legs. "We're only getting started."

Reaching down, guiding him into me again, I let myself smile as the word propelled itself out of my mouth. "Squee!"

In the bed, on the floor, bent over the table, standing under hot water streaming from the shower... We didn't leave each other alone for hours. After racking up seven orgasm badges from *Squee*—shattering my previous record of four in one night—I fought to keep my eyes open while I watched Joshua sleep.

Whisper soft, I traced my fingers over his eyebrows, down the crooked line of his nose, across his full lips, charting the course of his face, memorizing each curve and contour, not wanting to forget. Because I'd probably never see him again, and I knew more than anyone how easy it was to forget. But even though I tried, even though I fought it, eventually I lost, and sleep claimed me.

STANDING at my door an hour later, his dress shirt buttoned but his tie loose, he furrowed his brow. "I don't know what to say to you."

"Thank you should suffice," I said with an airiness I didn't feel.

Giving me a small laugh, he said, "Fair enough." Then he grasped my hand, bringing my knuckles to his lips. "Thank you. I will never forget this night, Phoeb—" He stalled out, meeting my gaze. "Tell me your real name."

I smiled at him, then shook my head. "No."

He clicked his tongue. "Worth a shot. Mine is—"

Flipping my hand over so it covered his mouth, I said, "No. No real names." I might have gotten carried away last night, and this morning, and even right now as I considered making him miss his shuttle. But I had my boundaries. Excellent boundaries. Firm. Solid. I just needed to find them. *They're definitely around here somewhere...*

He kissed my palm, holding my hand in both of his, making it warm. Then he let me go.

Resting my head against the door frame, I reached back up to stroke his cheek. "I think I'll miss you."

Without another word, he slid his arm around my waist and pulled me into what was quite possibly the most passionate kiss of my entire life. With his arm holding me flush against him and his other hand gripping the back of my neck, he pressed us together so tightly I could hardly breathe. But breathing, I realized while my body decided all it needed to live was this kiss, was highly overrated.

When we pulled apart, he stared down at me and sighed. "I have the strangest feeling that I'll regret leaving this hotel room for the rest of my life."

While my heart gave another weird *whump*, I slowly loosened his tie and slid it from his neck. Then I wrapped it around my hand. “I would like to keep this.” It was silly, and probably a bad idea, but I wanted something of his, something to remind me that this night had actually happened. That it wasn’t just a chocolate-cherry-hairball-induced fever dream.

Kissing me one last time, he said, “It’s yours,” against my lips. And then he smiled, a devastating little thing, and walked away. About halfway to the elevator, he stooped down to swipe something off the floor. When he turned back, he held the shoe I’d lost last night by its heel. The look he gave me was a question, and after swallowing the lump rising up my throat, I nodded an answer.

“And this is mine” were the last words Joshua said to me as he walked away with my shoe dangling from his fingers.

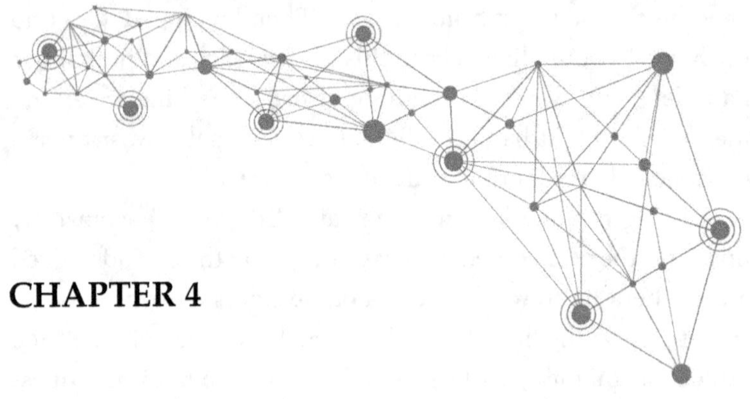

CHAPTER 4

THREE MONTHS LATER

The Argosian took up most of the bed, his massive arm slung over my waist, pinning me in place like a nova beetle on its back. And I thought, while staring at his gargantuan and extremely naked body, that there was no way in hells I'd had sex with him last night. None. Physically impossible.

This was a mistake. I had made a *terrible* mistake. But when a being spent the last several months chasing after the high of the best one-night stand of her life, mistakes were bound to be made. And while this was, admittedly, the biggest mistake I'd made so far, it didn't change anything. I wouldn't stop. I couldn't. Because no matter what I did, or who I did it with, nothing erased the feel of his hands on my body, the taste of cherries on his lips, the way he looked at me like I was the only—

<Where are you?> Elanie barked through my VC. <You're late.>

I groaned, froze as the Argosian stirred, then commed, <Wrong number.>

<Don't start with me.> Elanie, per usual, was in no mood. <I've laid an outfit out for you on your empty, unslept-in bed.

We have a staff meeting to welcome the new languages and customs expert in twenty minutes. Please get your ass to your pod directly.>

<I don't appreciate your tone, Elanie. I'm hungover.>

<Really? Because you sound like you're still drunk. And I did say please.>

Gingerly, I scooted back toward the headboard and tried to sit up. The room spun. My temples throbbed. I guess I was still drunk. Argosian ripple took no prisoners. <What if I can't move?> I asked, peering down at the arm now slung across my thighs.

Elanie's sigh was deep, long-suffering, and entirely too dramatic for a bionic. Which filled me with pride. I was training her well, like my half-robot little sister.

<Please,> she commed. <For the love of all the stars in all the skies, bid farewell to whatever disaster you've wrought upon yourself and make your way to your pod. You do not want to miss this meeting.>

<Roger that,> I replied, relenting. Because, enormous Argosian mistakes or not, I did have a very busy day ahead of me. Pinching the purple arm squishing my thighs, I cleared my throat. "Ahem, darling? Wakey, wakey."

A deep and resonant grumble was his only response.

"Hellooo," I said a little louder. "Although last night was"—I stalled out, having no idea what last night was—"memorable, I'm sure, if you wouldn't mind, would you please move your arm? I'm running late." I'd be lying if I said I wasn't a little worried I might not be able to walk out of this room if we'd somehow made the impossible possible, but first things first.

When the Argosian rolled onto his back, taking his tree trunk arm with him, air flooded my lungs. "Much better." Without much grace, I slid off the bed, thrilled that all my pieces and parts seemed to be functioning normally. "I'll just find my clothes and be on my—"

"You will not find them," he rumbled with a sleepy smirk. Golden tattoos embellished his broad chest and firm stomach —a scythe, harvest moons glowing over a field of grain, exquisitely detailed seeds—images meant to pay tribute to the agricultural life that drove his planet's economy.

"I can see that," I said, looking around his room. "Happen to know where they are?"

"You do not remember?" His smirk stretched into a full-fledged grin. "They got...messy. We sent them to the laundry."

I blinked. I did not, in fact, remember. And didn't particularly want to. "Super."

Scratching his chest between his stunning pectorals, he said, "Argos makes a strong drink. Do not be ashamed."

"Did we...? Did I...?" I forced down a swallow.

He shook his head. "You and I had much fun times, but we did not join. We were not *worthy* of each other."

A profound relief buckled my knees. *Worthy*, on Argos—where males tended to outweigh females by one hundred kilos or more—referred to the way body parts might or might not fit together between two partners. I offered a silent prayer of gratitude to the gods of fermentation for blessing me with complete amnesia of the evaluation of our *worth*.

"I guess anatomy strikes again, eh?" I said, snatching his yellow coveralls from the bed—the preferred outfit for all Argosians for reasons I've never quite understood—and wrapping them around me like a robe.

"Those are mine." His deep voice reverberated through my ribcage.

"Well, I can't walk back to my pod naked, can I? I'm sure you understand. I'll have my assistant return your...*garment* to you straight away. You have my word." I reached out awkwardly to pat his big toe, which he wiggled under my palm. Then I straightened, tied his coverall arms into a bow around my chest, and recited my customary closing remarks. "I trust you are enjoying your stay aboard the *Ignisar*. And I sincerely hope you will look no further than LunaCorp for all your future holiday and interplanetary travel needs."

Giving him a curt nod, I scampered from his room while he chuckled, shaking his gigantic, golden-tattooed head.

HOLDING up the too-long legs of the Argosian's coveralls, I tried my level best not to trip over them on my way into the staff elevator. Never empty when I wanted it to be, the elevator was packed full of two exhausted-looking, sunglasses-wearing Ulaperians who'd likely just finished their shift at the Voyager Club, one quad-armed room attendant from Gorbulon-7—two of those arms busy teasing his hair up to the ceiling—and one way too good-looking Blurvan, who I was fairly certain worked at one of the bars on deck thirty-six. The Blurvan, leaning his humanoid torso against the back wall of the elevator while his gelatinous lower half jiggled, took one look at my outfit, arched his brow, and asked, "Rough night?"

Mashing the button for deck twelve, I muttered, "No rougher than usual," and wished for the thousandth time that I had more privacy on this ship. Yes, I knew my life choices were sometimes questionable, but why did everyone else have to know it too? Maybe if that Blurvan had been through a fraction of what I'd been through, he'd understand. Maybe he'd be ashamed of that smug, judgmental expression on his face. But then he popped his pecs, twice, and I realized...probably not.

Scurrying out of the elevator toward the staff quarters, I smiled stiffly at a duo of hopping Vorpol maintenance technicians. When one of them asked the other, "Is she wearing Argosian coveralls?" I ducked my head and double-timed it toward my pod.

Scowling deeply, Elanie stood in front of my door, her arms

crossed under her perfect bionic cleavage. "Staff meeting is in ten minutes. I hope it was worth it."

Artificial intelligence with DNA spliced between the wires, all bionics were designed to emulate the peak physical characteristics of their particular species. Elanie, for example—with her silky brown hair, straight nose, and big brown doe eyes—always looked as fresh as spring rain. While I, on the other hand, probably looked like the refuse compactor on jettison day. It was certainly how I felt.

"Is that a pair of Argosian coveralls?" A look of pure horror overtook Elanie as she realized what species I'd shacked up with last night.

Always endeavoring to project the appearance of having my shit together, even though I rarely did, I replied, "It is, and it was *completely* worth it."

"An Argosian? Sunny, you could have been killed."

Blowing air loudly through my lips—even though she was right—I waved her off.

She placed her hand on her hip. "You are not a sex worker, Sunny. You are a hospitality specialist. You do not need to sleep with all these males—"

"And females," I interjected with a raised finger, sliding past her into my room.

"—to be good at your job."

"At the risk of shocking your bionic sensibilities so thoroughly you'll need a full factory reset, I will only say this." Throwing off my coveralls robe to put on something more appropriate for a work meeting, I winked. "Life is far too short not to do what you love as often as you can."

Her eye roll was monumental. "You have nine minutes."

Slinging on a pair of kitten heels, I tucked a white button-down into a black pencil skirt, pinched my cheeks, then waved a hand over my body. "Yes?"

Elanie frowned. "No. Your hair looks like a trestal's nest."

"Right." Running water over my hands, I wetted down my short, jagged blond hair, then ducked underneath my quikDri. "Better?"

One of her shoulders rose a fraction, the gestural equivalent of *I can't begin to tell you how little I care.*

"Elanie?" I squinted at her, suspicious. "Are you all right?"

"Fine," she replied flatly. "Why?"

She didn't seem fine. Even for a being as universally annoyed by my antics as she was, she seemed...moody. "It's just, you're a bit pricklier than usual. What's it been, three months since LunaCorp released the hormone upgrade for generation twenty-six bionics? Any chance you finally decided to install?"

Her entire body shuddered. "No."

"Why not?" I waggled my brows. "Could be fun. I could take you up to deck thirty-six. We could visit the dance clubs, the pleasure pods, go to a live sex show—"

Holding up her hand, Elanie said, "I hate that deck. And I already tried the trial version."

"Really?"

"For 0.025 milliseconds."

"Wow," I said. "That long?"

Missing the sarcasm, she made a pinched, repulsed expression, like she'd sucked the slime off that elevator Blurvan's seventh toe. "It was long enough, believe me. It was...messy."

"That's fair," I conceded. "But you should do it anyway. You may find it won't kill you to participate in something other than categorical disdain every once in a while."

"Well, Sunny, as someone once said, life is far too short not to do what you love as often as you can."

While I burst into laughter, Elanie left my pod, flipping her soft, glossy hair off her shoulders as she walked through the door.

ACCESSING the files in my VC while I made my way to the staff room, my headache fading to a dull throb, I perused the dossiers of the special guests expected to board in the upcoming week. A conference of Delphinian magicians had arrived earlier in the morning. Delphinian magicians, while mostly harmless, were occasionally disastrous guests. A drunken magician's finger snap three years ago had resulted in the still unfillable pool on deck sixteen. Every time the crew tried to fill it, the water vanished with an infuriating *fizz-pop* sound. Considering the pool on sixteen had been my favorite, I had a hard time hiding my annoyance with the outer-rim planet's obsession with tricks.

A senator from Tranquis would arrive tomorrow. This was odd. We didn't get many politicos on the ship—something about our reputation as an orgy-in-orbit tended to keep them from booking. And this senator, Sonia Ramesh, planned to stay with her wife and ten-year-old son until they reached Portis for the Known Universal Senate meeting. Which would take more than a month. The *Ignisar* was not built for speed, and if this senator wanted to use the ship simply to get to Portis, there were much more efficient and economical methods of travel available to her. With much less of a risk of destroying her political career when she accidentally ate a piece of warple cake at Sunday brunch, and vids of her dancing naked in the atrium went viral on Vchirp.

<What do you know of the senator?> I commed Elanie.

<No more than you,> she responded. <Why?>

<You don't think it's odd? A senator on holiday with her wife and child on this ship, of all places?>

<I'll admit it is a strange booking. But we have been marketing more to families with our Wholesome Deck Initiative. Perhaps the WDI is working. Hurry up. Chan brought cake.>

<Cake?> This perked me up. <I'll be right there. How's the new L&C?>

There was a moment of silence before Elanie replied, <He is...adequate.>

Detecting the rare hesitation in her response, I said, <Only adequate? Is that all? Chan must be so upset.>

<He's...fine.>

More hesitation. Now she had my attention. <Fine? Elanie, are you blushing? I can *hear* you blushing.>

<Just get in here.>

When I walked into the staff room, I found the rest of the crew huddled at the far end of the big table. I was a breath away from announcing my presence when I realized someone was talking, telling a story. The new L&C, I assumed. He held the crew in the palm of his hand, and even though I couldn't hear what he was telling them over their laughter, they clearly hung on his every word.

I took a step their way, but then the laughter died down long enough for him to say, in the most delicious Venusian accent I thought I'd never hear again, "And that was the last time I ever went drinking with a Gorbie."

The air in my lungs vanished like I'd been sucked out of an airlock. My heart kicked so violently against my ribs it caused me physical pain. I knew that voice. That laughter. Those hands. *Stars save me,* those hands.

Noticing me standing wide-eyed and frozen in the doorway, Chandler, the *Ignisar*'s cruise director, pivoted his hoverchair my way and waved me over. "Oh, good. You're finally here," Chan said. "Come meet Freddie. Freddie, this is Sunastara Nex, our hospitality specialist."

Freddie? Not Joshua, but Freddie? His name was Freddie. He was Freddie, and I was Sunny, and there was no way this was happening. I pinched my arm. Hard. But nothing changed. I was still in the staff room, and he was still real.

As the wall of my fellow crew members parted, revealing his long, lithe frame poured into a fine suit, that wry twist to his lips, that amused sparkle in his eye, I practically whimpered. And I *never* whimpered.

It took a second, maybe two, but then he saw me, noticed me, *remembered* me. While his eyes locked on mine, his fork—and the bite of cake perched on it—fell with a *clink* against his plate. "Phoebe?" he said, unblinking, unmoving, stuck with me in the same time dilation.

While I was rendered so speechless I wasn't sure I'd ever known any words at all, Elanie—fully aware of the alias I used on *Squee*—whipped her head around and commed, <Stars above, Sunny. Must you sleep with everyone in the entire Known Universe?>

I registered Elanie's snark, but she sounded like she was a million kilometers away, on a raft, in the middle of an ocean, all the way across the wormhole. Maybe on Venus.

"Phoebe?" Joshua—or Freddie—repeated while he stared at me with those intense, storm-gray eyes I'd been dreaming about for months. "How?"

"You two know each other?" Chan asked, his gaze shifting between us.

"Yes." Freddie's expression was blank, and his voice—missing the sultry swagger I'd remembered—warbled. "We've met."

This was bad. This was very, very bad.

"Sunny?" Chan's head tilted, his finger flicking out to point at Freddie. "You know our new L&C?"

I couldn't answer. I was too busy swallowing what felt like a gwarf—an Aquilinian fruit resembling a golf ball covered in mildly poisonous spikes. He was a dream, a memory. He was supposed to stay that way. And now he was here. He was a member of my crew. I'd have to see him every day, live with him on this ship, work closely with him. Permanently. *Holy shit.*

"I'm terribly sorry," I said to no one in particular. "If you'll excuse me for a moment."

Spinning on my heel—because while I had no idea what to do, I knew I had to get out of there—I attempted to walk smoothly through the door. But I tripped over the threshold and stumbled out into the hallway instead.

"Sunny, wait. Stop." His honeyed voice had its own gravitational field, slowing me down, pulling me back. Reeling me in.

I took a deep breath and blew it out. *Get a grip, Sunny*. I was a grown woman. This was my ship. And I refused to be stunned into silence on my own ship. It was a shock, seeing him again, but I could do this. I could say words to him. I could converse. I could be normal. When I turned around, however, his smile took me out at the knees.

"Sunny—or is it Sunastara? That's a beautiful name," he said once he reached me. "You work on this ship? You... I can't believe it." He took my hand in his, pulling me into a quiet alcove next to a moon jelly tank. The watery blue light emanating from the tank danced over his cheekbones in graceful ripples. "Sunny, say something. Anything."

You're beautiful. You smell like the best dream I ever had. I want to lick your face. "Hello, Fredrick," I said stiffly.

"Freddie, please call me Freddie."

"Okay, Fred—"

"I thought I'd never see you again," he said in a rush. "I haven't been able to stop thinking about you since that night. I tried to find you on *Squee*, but your profile never reappeared. And now you're here." He released my hand only so he could reach out and cup my cheek, making me wonder how something could feel so good yet so awful at the same time. Like watching a perfect sunset with sand in your eye. "It's impossible," he said. "Isn't this impossible?"

I wanted to tell him that it *was* impossible. That I hadn't stopped thinking about him either. But fear flooded my veins, my bones, my skin. The same cold, paralyzing fear that always gripped me when someone tried to get close or looked at me the way he was looking at me. I had to make it stop. Like my life depended on it. So I backed away from him and said, "Freddie, I—"

His sharp inhale stopped me short. "I didn't even think to ask. Are you already with someone?" He looked devastated, like someone had popped a balloon full of puppies.

"No, I'm not with anyone." *I will never be with anyone. That's the point.*

"Thank the stars." When he tried to take another step closer, I stood straighter.

"But I can't be with you either," I said, each word scraping its way out of me. But at least this much was true. "I don't get involved with my coworkers. Ever."

He didn't miss a beat. "Is that all? Not a problem. I quit." Wheeling around, he shouted back toward the break room, "Sorry, Chan, but I qui—"

"*Shh.*" I threw my hand over his mouth, smiling despite myself. "You can't quit. We need a good L&C, and I've heard you're one of the best." His lips curved against my palm, and I yanked my hand back like I'd been electrocuted.

"You can find someone else," he assured me, unfazed. "It's not a difficult job."

"Right," I said. "It only takes nine years of higher education, an additional five of fieldwork, and two advanced residencies. Languages and customs experts practically grow on trees."

"They do, in fact. I can recommend several." His voice went so soft I could have fallen into it. "I have to be with you, Sunny. I've never felt anything like the connection I felt—I *feel*—when I'm with you. And to meet again, here..." He looked around the deck like he couldn't believe his luck. "It has to mean something."

It was true that when I saw him leaning against that shelf, I wanted nothing more than to run to him, throw myself into his arms, and kiss him until we both nearly died from it. But he had no idea who he was talking to. He knew Phoebe, not Sunny. Phoebe was put together. Phoebe was carefree. Phoebe was light and fun and desirable. Sunny was none of those things. Sunny was a disaster. Sunny still spent her days walking over the thinnest layer of ice, knowing that any extra weight would shatter the surface beneath her feet, and she'd be lost.

Providing a blessed break in the tension, a group of Delphinian wizards—as this particular group of magicians wanted to be called—swept down the hall, their red and black robes swishing against their legs. One of them said, "That's when I realized the incantation, when recited quickly, sounded just like, 'I poured butter on a bear's underbelly,' in Common." And when another replied, "That's random. Remind me again, what is a 'bear'?" I tried not to laugh, but I was treading dangerously close to hysterical, the type of hysterical where everything was funny, whether it was catastrophic or not. So a shrill laugh came out anyway.

When Freddie laughed too, delighted, like hearing my laughter *delighted* him, I gave my head a firm shake and said, "Maybe all it means is that you and I were meant to work together."

He scoffed. "It's more than that."

Somehow, by the grace of the cosmos, calm returned to me by degrees. I hadn't seen this man in months. We probably had nothing in common. He probably liked sardines and hated reality television. "Freddie," I said, trying to sound convincing, "we hardly know each other. Trust me, you don't want to throw this job, this very good job with an excellent crew on a beautiful...*ish*," I clarified, "ship away over one random night months ago. You'll love working here. And you and I? Well, we can be fr—"

He moved so close that his breath brushed over my lips. It smelled like cake. "If you say friends, I'm going to shout *fire*."

I tried to back away, but my ass bumped into the moon jelly tank, startling the little blobs into a slightly less slow-motion whirl away from the glass. Freddie's lips hovered a hairsbreadth from mine, and my weight tipped itself onto my toes to get closer to them—entirely without my permission, I might add.

"Sunny—"

"I can't," I said, placing a hand on his chest, ignoring the warmth of his skin under his shirt to push him away. "I'd like to be fr—you know what I mean," I said with a flapping gesture that I hoped conveyed *please don't actually shout* fire. "I understand if that's not something you want. But I can't give you more." Because I had nothing more to give. All I had was this job, this ship, this little life. And I couldn't lose any of it. Not for all the orgasms in the galaxy. "I'm sorry."

Backing away, some invisible bucket of cold water washing all the heat from his expression, he said, "I see." He slid his hands into his pockets. "Then I'm sorry too." Clarity surfaced in the deep pools of his eyes, along with something like shame, which made me feel awful. He had nothing to be ashamed of. He wasn't the problem here. This was all me. "I shouldn't have come on so strong."

"It's fine," I said, needing the moment to be over, needing some time and space to process...everything. "But we should really get back to the party. You're the guest of honor, after all."

"Of course," he said with a slow nod. "After you." He stepped to the side, and when I made myself walk past him back to the staff room, he watched me go without another word.

"Everything all right out there?" Chan asked around a mouthful of cake as I walked back through the door, Freddie filing in a few steps behind me.

"Right as rain, Chan," Freddie said, his voice reed thin. Then, in a lighter tone, "Would you look at that? I leave for five minutes, and my new crewmates try to finish my cake without me."

Tig, our head of IT, froze, her blue eyes wide and her bite of cake halted halfway to her mouth. "Sorry, Freddie," she said, pushing her plate away and pulling the hood of her sweatshirt over her pink hair, her small, round face disappearing in its shadow.

"I was only joking." He slid her plate back in front of her. "Forgive me, Tig."

I pulled out my chair, my heart still pounding, my palms still sweating, my chest still tight. While I sat, shaken but determined to pretend that everything was normal, Chan, Elanie, Tig, and the twins, Rax and Morgath—hulking, green-skinned ex-Royal military from the smaller planet of the Aquilines who ran our security—gorged themselves on sheet cake with chocolate frosting and *Welcome to the Jungle* scrawled across the top in blue icing.

Eventually, Chan raised his cup in a toast. "Well," he said with a tight, nervy laugh, "it seems our new L&C has already made quite the impression on our little group."

My gaze betrayed me, sliding to Freddie's across the table. When he smiled, meeting my stare, I whipped my head back toward Chan so fast, something in my neck popped.

"Yeah," Rax said, frowning at me in that way he did when he was wondering if someone needed *straightening out*, which in the twins' world usually resulted in a trip to the med bay. When he looked at Freddie, his frown turned downright menacing. "What was that all about?"

"They slept together," Elanie stated like she was reading the weather report.

I choked on nothing while Freddie's eyes tripled in size.

"Elanie," Chan hissed.

"What?" Her shoulder hitched. "It's true. Sunny, tell them."

Since Elanie was a relatively young bionic and still unskilled at societal norms, I gave her a pass. But that didn't mean I wouldn't be talking to her later about why we don't air our coworker's dirty laundry at staff meetings. "Just to keep ship gossip from reaching critical mass," I said to the room. "Freddie and I met on the CAK a few months ago. We had a"—heat seared my cheeks—"nice night. However, that is in the past. We are both professionals and will behave accordingly."

All eyes turned to Freddie as color rushed up his throat, a throat I wished I didn't remember kissing and licking in such vivid detail. "Oh. Um, well. You see," he stammered. "What Sunny says is true. We, uh, did..." He trailed off, straightening his tie, reminding me of his other tie, the one currently coiled under my pillow. "I am a consummate professional, however—"

Morgath snorted. "Y'all got freaky, didn't you?" He grinned, scratching his thick fingers into his unruly mop of green hair.

Elbowing his brother in the ribs, Rax muttered, "Shut up, dingus."

"Anyway," Chan said over the chatter. "Welcome to the team, Freddie. Our last L&C was exemplary, so you'll have some very big shoes to fill. But I'm sure you'll be plenty big enough."

Freddie coughed on his vitoWater.

Chan's gaze flew to mine, surely finding *what the actual fuck*? written in my expression.

"I mean, your *feet*," he amended, wincing at Freddie. "Your *feet* are big, not you. Not to imply that you're small..."

Bright-red patches exploded across Tig's cheeks. Rax and Morgath turned even redder as they tried not to laugh. Freddie stared industriously at his uneaten cake, as if it held all the secrets of the Known Universe. And I prayed to all the stars in all the skies that I would somehow get through this without blowing up my entire life, a life I was barely holding together as it was.

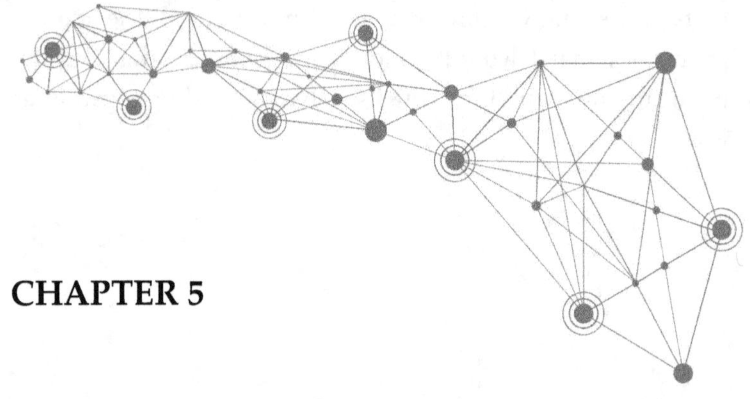

CHAPTER 5

PRETENDING my world wasn't overturned by the sudden appearance of the only man who had ever made me drool was harder than I'd anticipated. And I'd anticipated it to be plenty hard. When I sent the ultra-demanding young Martian celebrity power couple who'd monopolized my every waking moment over the last week on their way back across the wormhole, I should have been ready to pop a bottle of champagne. Instead, I was mildly relieved at best. I was too preoccupied with Freddie's smiles, his gaze catching mine across the staff room table, the eyes I remembered far too clearly staring up at me from between my legs. *Fuck.*

As I meandered back to the elevators, a cleaning drone whirred along the carpet, bumping gently against the wall, and I wondered, *did I recharge my vibrator this morning?*

<Elanie?> I commed, stepping onto the elevator and pushing the button for twelve.

<Yes?> she responded warily.

<What do you think of him?>

<More specific. With you that could mean anyone.>

I raised my eyes to the ceiling. <You really can be a twit. You know that, right?>

<More specific, *please*,> she said, meaning it about as much as I'd meant it when I told those Martian brats I couldn't wait until they stayed with us again. <Is that better?>

<Yes. Thank you,> I commed, exiting the elevator on deck twelve, wanting nothing more than to hide out in my pod for the rest of the day. <And I meant Freddie. What do you think of Freddie?> I placed my hand over my pod's security panel, staggering inside when the door slid open.

<He seems...nice.>

<Nice?> I plopped down on the edge of my bed. <So far, you've called him adequate, fine, and nice. If I didn't know better, I'd think you were downplaying your—>

<He is adequate, fine, and nice,> she commed. <And also... very handsome.>

I laughed, but then I caught my reflection in the mirror. I looked a lot like I felt. Sapped. While I pressed my fingers into my pale cheeks, Elanie commed, <Why do you keep asking me about him?>

Because he's invading my dreams. <No reason,> I lied. <It's just that you and I will be working closely with him. I wanted to make sure you didn't have a bad feeling about him or anything.>

<Uh-huh,> she said slowly, not buying it.

<So, nice, then?>

<Yes, nice,> she repeated.

<And handsome,> I reiterated. <Your words, not mine.>

Shocking me to my core, Elanie let her laughter ring through the comm. <Please be sure to visit Senator Ramesh and her family first thing tomorrow. They'll be expecting you after boarding.>

<Of course. First thing,> I commed, ignoring the icy dread trickling down my spine and resisting the urge to ask Chan to assign someone else to the Ramesh detail. Someone whose

hands didn't shake at the thought of being around a child. <Thank you, darling.>

After clicking off the comm, I stared at my dresser, where my favorite shirt to sleep in—an oversized dark-blue tee with faded glow-in-the-dark constellations as seen from Lathinaes, the mountain town on Tranquis's southern hemisphere where I'd grown up—called to me. I'd run myself ragged over the last week, working eighteen-hour days babysitting the Martians, catering to our other guests, reuniting with the only lover who'd ever given me seven orgasms in one night... A nap seemed necessary.

<Hello, Sunny?>

I jumped up off my bed. *Speak of the seven-orgasm devil.*

<I'm sorry to bother you,> Freddie commed while my heart battered my ribcage. <But do you have a moment?>

It was the first time he'd accessed my VC, and the intimacy of his voice in my mind sent goose bumps flickering across my neck and racing down my arms.

<Hello, Freddie,> I replied, trying to sound normal while I brushed the raised hairs on my arms flat. <What's up?>

<I'm in a bit of a predicament.>

<Already?>

<I know, right? It's probably a record.>

I wasn't smiling. I swear. No matter what my reflection said.

<I'm in the small ballroom on deck five with a very drunk Argosian who says he knows you. He's refusing to leave unless you come talk to him. He is, uh, very large. And he's, well, I think he's dancing? With a serving drone. He's scaring the guests—and me, I'm not too ashamed to admit.>

<Oh boy.> The nap would have to wait. <I'm on my way.>

<Morgath, you busy?> I commed, stepping back onto the elevator and pushing the button for deck five.

His response was swift. <I'm never too busy for my favorite hospitality specialist.>

<It's hopefully nothing,> I said. <But there may be a need for some increased security in the deck five ballroom.>

<Mechs or men?> he asked, straight to the point in the way I always appreciated about both Morgath and his brother.

The elevator dinged, and the doors slid open, emptying me out onto deck five. <Mechs will do. Only one or two.> I always kept my estimates low because with Rax and Morgath, one meant eight and two meant twenty.

<They're on the way. Let me know if you need more.>

<Will do. Thank you.>

I hightailed it down the hallway, convincing myself along the way that the nerves bubbling up in my chest had everything to do with possible Argosian chaos and nothing to do with seeing Freddie again. Then I slowed as I neared the ballroom. While loud, warbling singing—interrupted by ground-trembling hiccups—echoed through the door, I commed Elanie. <Are you there?>

<Where else would I be, Sunny? You're literally in my head.>

Weaving through the guests that had amassed outside the ballroom, I peered inside. Yellow coveralls sleeves slid along the floorboards as the half-naked Argosian—*my* Argosian—spun in circles with...*yep*, that was definitely a serving drone. <Did Freddie comm you regarding the situation on deck five?>

<Negative,> Elanie replied.

<If you're not too busy, I could use your help. Small ballroom, please.>

<I'll be right there,> she said, then clicked off.

Four of Morgath's security mechs—titanium balls a meter in diameter that housed all manner of weaponry, crowd-dispersal tech, and ultra-intimidating voice programming—floated to my location, roving red lights encircling their circumferences like ominous Yuletide decorations. I positioned the mechs on either side of the ballroom doors, more to keep any guests who might decide to play hero out than present a show of force to the Argosian within. But I'd learned over the years that one could never be too careful.

Slinking silently into the ballroom, I spotted Freddie sitting at a table by himself, his chin resting in his hand, his suit jacket folded over his chair back, his tie pulled loose. When he saw me, his face brightened, and I lost my footing.

<You okay?> Freddie commed, standing halfway from his chair.

<Super,> I replied, gesturing for him to sit back down.

<Thank goodness you're here.> He took his seat again. <He's tried to pull me onto the dance floor twice already.>

I hid my grin, sliding along the wall until I reached his table. "What happened?" I asked while he pulled out a chair for me.

Rubbing thoughtfully at his chin, he admitted, "I don't know. He's been in here for about an hour, ten minutes of that spent sobbing in the middle of the dance floor, another ten drinking—and this is not an exaggeration—five bottles of rum, and the rest dancing with that drone he's taken to calling 'Kasa.'"

"*Kasa*!" the Argosian roared, squeezing the serving drone so tightly it *bleep-bleeped* out a warning while a bright-yellow light flared from its central panel.

I winced. "Was that its pressure sensor?"

"Third time it's gone off. I'm worried he'll crush the poor drone to bits."

"Those aren't cheap," I said.

"Precisely." Freddie leaned in close, his lips tilting up. "If he breaks it, who will give him the bill?"

"Not me, thank you very much," I replied, realizing that this wasn't bad. In fact, it felt almost easy, sitting with him while we watched a purple giant sway from side to side with his tiny drone. Easier than I'd thought it would be. Maybe we could become friends. Partners, even. Vertical, fully clothed work partners.

"He asked for you," my work partner told me. "He said you'd know what to do. Do you know him? His name? Whenever I ask, he bellows, 'Not worth night soil!' and starts sobbing again."

I watched the Argosian twirl the drone in circles, the crystal chandeliers above them casting kaleidoscopic shadows around his feet. His face was wet, his shoulders hunched, his steps surprisingly graceful. "I don't know his name. But I do know him. He and I, we. Well…"

"No." Freddie's eyes popped, his jaw hanging open. "And you're still alive?"

I snorted. "Not that. We weren't *worthy* of each other."

"Thank your lucky stars." He shook his head, and I appreciated the lack of judgment in his tone. Then again, we did meet using *Squee*. Maybe he messed around as much as I did. Maybe more. With how spectacular he was, it would make sense. "Never got his name, though?" he asked.

"Never came up. Or if it did, I don't remember. I was drunk. Argosian ripple."

"Oof," he said, sympathizing. "Worst hangover of my life, that stuff. Never again."

We both flinched as the Argosian wailed something in his native tongue. My VC translated: "Our rows were to travel together. Our seeds were to burrow into the soil as one. Now all is *rot*." The last word came out as a growling sob, followed by a tremendous burp.

"That sounds like heartbreak," I said.

Freddie nodded in agreement. "Those were old Argosian

mating words, often recited at the ceremony for hand joining. Obviously, something has gone wrong."

"Hmm," I murmured, pretending my knees weren't shaking. I didn't think the Argosian would hurt me. But I didn't imagine he'd be dancing with a million-credit robot like it was his prom date either. Strange things happened on this ship.

Steeling my nerve, I pushed back from the table, readying myself to go to the enormous, distraught, intoxicated male. But Freddie's fingers wrapped around mine, holding me back, making my skin tingle.

"Do you want me to come with?" he asked.

The Argosian swayed and spun, slumped over now, the full weight of his head resting on the serving drone's tray, pushing the weight limit of its thrusters to the max.

"No need," I replied. "Walk in the park. And Elanie's just arrived. She's all the backup I'll need."

"I will pretend not to feel unmanned by that statement," he said evenly as he let me go, his fingertips sliding away.

<Where do you want me?> Elanie commed.

<Come sit next to Freddie. But look alive. We may need to go hands-on.> Like all Bionics, Elanie was strong enough to incapacitate almost any being in the KU, even the inebriated mountain of muscle waltzing over the ballroom floor.

With a sharp inhale, I stood, looked down at Freddie, and said, "Wish me luck."

His eyes sparkled, crinkling at the corners. "Sunny, I have a feeling you are far too good at what you do to demean it with something as fickle as luck."

My heart stuttered mid-beat, fluttering around like a stunned bird after flying into a window. I wasn't uncomfortable with compliments, but I never sought them out. I got all the external validation I needed from a job well done. His praise, though? How genuine it was, how warm? It tempted me to bask. And when he winked and said, "Now go save our serving drone," my wobbling knees had nothing to do with the Argosian.

Once Elanie arrived at the table, I pulled myself together, focused on the task at hand—I could bask later—and started across the ballroom.

The Argosian's voice resonated, echoing off the metallic surface of the serving tray his head was still slung over. He sang a mournful song now. One that—according to my VC—was about a once lush field that had gone fallow because nobody had taken the time to water it.

Once I reached a spot a few feet from him, I quietly, carefully, cleared my throat.

He stopped singing.

I held my breath.

<Be careful,> Freddie whispered over a shared comm.

Not whispering, Elanie added, <This is the worst idea you've ever had.>

"Hello," I said, ducking my chin, my hands raised, palms facing out, and fingers splayed wide.

The Argosian's head rose to wobble on his neck as his deeply set purple eyes found mine. "At last." His voice rumbled like an avalanche. "You're here."

My shoulders dropped away from my ears. He was distressed, devastated even, but he wasn't murderous. That much was clear.

"I'm sorry it's taken me so long. What happened, darling? What's wrong? How can I help?"

He pointed a finger the size of a small Kuiper worm at a half-empty bottle on the floor. "I saved a bottle for you." Squinting at the bottle, he clarified, "I saved half a bottle for you. Drink with me."

My keen sense of self-preservation—along with my still trembling knees—told me I needed to comply with this demand. Bending down slowly, I wrapped my fingers around the neck of the rum bottle and pulled out the cork with a *thwomp*. The rum was dark and sweet and tasted like vacation. Not that I'd really know, since I never took any.

<Do you really think that's a good idea?>

Sliding my eyes to the side, I replied, <Yes, I do, Elanie. Thank you.> I took another swig, then met the Argosian's blurry stare. "It might take me a while to catch up with you." When I toed the pile of bottles surrounding us, one slipped free, rolling across the floorboards until it clinked to a stop against one of the marble pillars. Extending a hand toward him, I asked, "Care to dance with someone less automated?"

He swallowed, then nodded.

Gingerly, I pried his arms away from the serving drone, and while the traumatized drone careened away wildly like a launched pinball, I stepped into the Argosian's embrace, letting him take the lead. He held me close but gently, like I was precious, delicate. Wrapped inside his thick, solid arms, nestled against his warm chest, I suddenly felt safe and protected, soothed. Whoever this Kasa person was, she was really missing out.

<Elanie, I think we're good here,> I commed. <Could you please take the serving drone to Tig for analysis?>

<I'd be happy to. If I could catch the damn thing.> Running after the drone with her arms outspread, Elanie zigged and zagged as the poor thing whirred and squealed, bobbing and weaving away from her.

"She looks like she is trying to wrangle a bokbok into its den," the Argosian slurred, gurgling a sound that might have been a laugh.

As his big chin rested gently on the top of my head, I took another swig of the rum, catching Freddie's stare from the corner of my eye. <You can leave too. If you have other things to—>

<Not a chance,> he replied before I'd finished my thought.

Peeling my gaze from Freddie, from his loose tie and disheveled hair and amused half smile, I returned my attention to my dance partner. "I don't think I ever got your name."

I braced myself for the yelling Freddie had described, but the big male only grumbled, "Garran."

Argosians tended to have lengthy names they earned over their lifetimes, names that spoke of their greater virtues. So I ventured, "Garran the…?"

"Once," he rumbled, spinning me out in two full circles before reeling me back into his arms, "I was Garran the Brave. Then, Garran the Verdant. Now"—he hung his head—"they may as well call me Garran the Desolate. Better yet, Garran the Barren."

While he snorted miserably at his own joke, I asked, "Well, Garran, would you like to talk about it?"

He pulled away to stare down at me, his violet brows tangling into the most impressive furrow I had ever seen. "You thought I was a good choice, did you not? There was no *worth* between us, but you chose me for your bedmate. You had many other options." His throaty Argosian accent was thick with sorrow.

I took in his golden tattoos, rows of corn that originated at the bridge of his nose, growing taller as they swayed to encircle his bald head. He was magnificent, in a gargantuan sort of way. "I did."

When he spun me around again, the rum clouded my head so much that I kept spinning well after he let me go. But suddenly, his arms dropped to his sides, and he collapsed to sit on the floor. A floorboard cracked.

Glancing at Freddie as Garran sobbed into his hands, I shrugged, unsure how best to handle this turn of events. Freddie's answering shrug was no help at all, even if it was kind of cute.

After one more lengthy pull from the bottle, I pushed the

cork back into place and sat down next to Garran on the floor. "Is this about Kasa?" I asked.

"Kasa grows in my heart, but I do not grow in hers," he said into his hands. "I wanted to plow her fields."

I pinned my lips between my teeth to keep myself from laughing at the innuendo, especially since I was pretty sure it was unintended. Although the winters on Argos were frigid and brutal, they were short. The remaining six hundred and fifty Standard days that made up its calendar year boasted an exceptionally moderate climate, giving Argos the longest growing season of any planet in the Known Universe. As a result, most Argosians made their livings as farmers. Garran, quite literally, wanted to help Kasa plow her fields.

"She doesn't want the same?" I asked.

He nodded, then hiccupped, his massive shoulders jerking toward his ears.

"Do you know why?"

"She says I am too green."

I wasn't familiar with the saying, so I asked Freddie. <Do you know what "too green" means?>

<I believe it means too young. Or, more likely in this case, too inexperienced.>

That's hard to believe. "Is Kasa on the ship?" Perhaps this situation merely required my unparalleled matchmaking skills.

"She arrived from Argos this morning," Garran said. "But I have loved her since we were seedlings."

"Is she with someone else? Or is there someone else she wants?" Many species regularly engaged in polyamory, and since Garran had taken me to bed, maybe Argosians did as well.

When his head whipped up, I fell backward on reflex.

"She says there is not. But if there is," he growled, "I will be very hurt."

I sighed. He really was a gentle farmer. Never judge an Argosian by their muscle mass.

"Well, Garran the Brave, Garran the Verdant." I took his thumb in my hand. "You have asked for the perfect person this evening. I happen to be quite good at this sort of thing. Worlds class, in fact. In order for me to help you, though, I need you to tell me everything you know about Kasa. And don't spare a single detail."

A smile bloomed across his face. "Okay. I will tell you everything."

I sat with him for at least an hour while he told me how he and Kasa met, what sorts of things she liked, what sorts of things she didn't, how her hair reminded him of billowing fields of grain bathed in the violet glow of twilight. Garran, as it turned out, was quite poetic. About halfway through our conversation, I convinced him to let Freddie join us since I'd need help pulling off this matchmaking endeavor.

Warily, Freddie walked across the ballroom and sat cross-legged next to me. When he did, his knee brushed against mine, and I wondered if it was by accident. As we shared the remaining rum and Garran went on and on about Kasa's eyes, I might have stretched, reaching my arms into the sky, using the movement as an excuse to slide over a fraction until that *brush* turned into a *touch*. So much heat built at the place where our bodies made contact that by the time I knew enough about Garran and Kasa to get started, the rum had vanished, the tips of Freddie's ears had turned pink, Garran could hardly hold his eyes open, and I had exercised every ounce of self-preservation I possessed by not sliding even closer, turning that *touch* into a *press*.

Eventually, I sent the security mechs back to Morgath and shot Elanie a <thank you> over my VC. Then Freddie and I—supporting the crushing weight of Garran's arms slung over our shoulders—led the stumbling, lovesick Argosian back to his suite to sleep it off.

"You did well with Garran," Freddie said as we walked side by side back to the deck twelve crew quarters. "Not that I'm surprised."

"Thank you," I replied. I'd definitely bask in that one in my pod later.

"Saved my hide, for certain. I wouldn't have made such a graceful dance partner." His words had thickened after the rum, but they still rolled off his tongue.

"Sometimes a situation needs a more feminine touch," I replied, giving myself a mental slap when I realized I also wouldn't mind rolling off his tongue.

"We make a good team," he said. Then, before I was able to summon any sort of response, his head tilted toward a pod door. "This is me."

His pod was only a few doors down the hall from mine. But no matter what, I would not spend the rest of the night imagining him sleeping mere meters away. "Good night, Freddie." I held out my hand. It felt intolerably awkward.

Ever the gentleman, he took my outstretched hand in his and gave it a firm and professional shake. "Good night, Sunny." When he pressed his palm against his security panel and entered his pod, his door slid closed before I could even peek inside.

Later that night, after I took a (cold) shower, then slid beneath my covers, I reached under my pillow—the secret place where I'd kept Joshua's necktie. It was only supposed to be a reminder. Of his laughter, the hysterical stories he'd told me over dinner. Of his lips on my skin and his fingers grasping my thighs.

But even months later, I still sometimes slept with his tie wrapped around my hand, wondering if I would ever see him again — feel him again — knowing it was probably for the best if I never did. Tonight, sliding my fingertips down the soft gray fabric, the raised bumps from its embroidered detailing tickling my skin, I wrapped his tie around my hand again. Despite my little self-pep talk, I let my thoughts wander to him, just down the hall, actually here, actually real. So close. Closer than I'd ever imagined he'd be. And yet, somehow, farther away than ever.

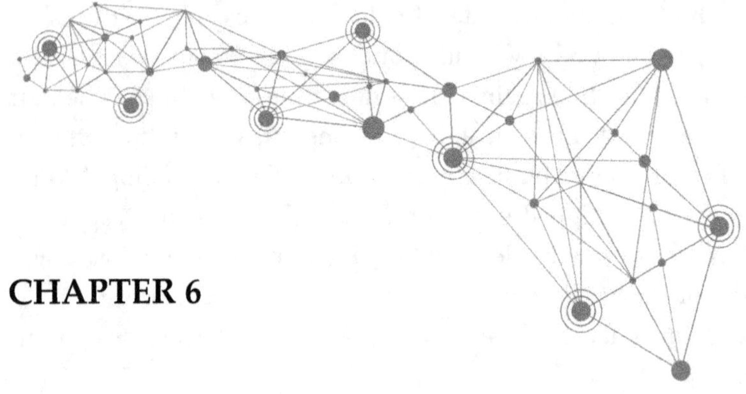

CHAPTER 6

THE SENATOR'S door slid open after a couple of light knocks, revealing a lovely brown-skinned female in a soft white wraparound sweater and ornately detailed green silk pants.

"Hello there." Lena, the senator's wife, had a rich yet delicate voice, like cream poured over ice.

"Good morning. I'm looking for—"

"Sonia," she interrupted, shouting over her shoulder. "It's for you." Turning back to me, Lena waved. "Please, come in."

"Just a moment," came a deep voice from a back room. It was firm, confident, brimming with self-possession, *senatorial.*

"Hi. Have you come to visit my moms?"

Stopping in the middle of the living room, I looked down to find the source of this question. A black-haired and brown-eyed child sat cross-legged on the floor, staring up at me with a quizzical expression. When he hopped to his feet, I wondered if he'd recently hit a growth spurt. He was long and gangly, stretched out like taffy. His fingers worked absently at a small wooden puzzle while his attention roved over me from head to toe. I'd never had a child look at me quite like that before, like I was a riddle to be solved. I won't lie; it was a little unnerving. Or maybe it was just me. Most things about children unnerved me these days.

"Hello, little one," I said stiffly. "I'm here to visit with all of you. My name is Sunastara Ne—"

"Nex," he completed, blinking his long, black eyelashes. "You are the *Ignisar*'s hospitality specialist. My moms have been expecting you." He flipped a wooden peg on the puzzle into place and handed it to me. The puzzle now assumed the shape of a perfect sphere. "It's not an easy one," he said. "But do you wanna try it?"

He wore wide-legged black pants and a pink, long-sleeved T-shirt with a *hang loose* symbol on it. But my eyes, for some reason, drifted to his bare feet. As lanky as he was, he still had the short, pudgy toes of a younger child, and they grasped gently at the looping carpet. I took the puzzle.

"Hmm. I've never seen anything like this before." Spinning the sphere in my hand, I tried to find a place to start.

"Of course you haven't." His smile was wide and toothy. "I made it myself."

"You did?" I smiled too at first. But then a sudden, hollow nausea gripped me. This boy had been given so much time to learn so many things. Not like my boy. Not like Jonathan. His time had been stolen, ripped away. Such a senseless, ridiculous thing. Five years later, and I still couldn't wrap my head around it. Why me? Why my child? Just...why?

Shoving the memory of blond hair and blue eyes and little feet running down the hallway in little shoes out of my mind the way I always did, I gave him his puzzle back. "How long did it take you to make it?"

Mysteriously, he popped two wooden pegs out of the sphere with his nimble fingers, twisting the top half counterclockwise while pulling on the bottom. Another peg sprang free. "This one took me two months. It's the hardest one I've made so far."

"Sai, come eat your breakfast," Lena called from the kitchenette.

The boy wobbled away, his eyes on his puzzle, his bare feet padding across the carpet. I watched him hop up onto a barstool and spin around in one full revolution before taking a huge bite out of a pastry so fragrant it filled the suite with spice.

Striding into the kitchenette, Senator Ramesh tied her raven-black hair up into a tight bun at her nape. Wearing a simple blue dress and black heels, she was short but striking, poised, and intimidating as hells. "Sunastara Nex," she said. "Welcome to our suite."

I extended my hand toward her and bowed my head, as was custom on Tranquis when meeting someone of high esteem. "It's a pleasure to meet you and your family, Senator. And please, call me Sunny."

She shook my hand, bowing her head as well. "And you will call me Sonia."

"Tell her about the tart, Mom," Sai said from his stool.

When Sonia smiled at him, it kicked me in the ribs. I remembered smiling like that. The joy. The pure love. *I have to get out of here.*

"Sai would like to report a burnt tart from the instaWave," Sonia said, suddenly grave. "Apparently, the oven refused to turn off no matter how many buttons he pushed. The fire-suppression system was employed."

"Oh dear," I replied, making myself stay, forcing myself to live in the present moment. "Was there any damage? We will remunerate you for any losses." The thick, white foam used to snuff out fires on the ship was next to impossible to clean from clothing.

Sonia leaned in close. "We believe he asked the oven to cook the tart for thirty seconds instead of three. But he maintains this was not the case. We're not pushing the issue. I think he's embarrassed."

"Of course," I said, coming back to myself by degrees. "Such an easy mistake to make." Then, louder, "We had another insta-Wave malfunction on this ship last week. Nearly burned down an entire pod."

Sai's head whipped my way, his eyes wide, mouth sprung open. "You did?" While he might've been a clever child, his poker face needed some work.

"I'm just glad no one was hurt," I said with all the sincerity I could muster. "Dangerous thing, a malfunctioning oven. How about we only let your mothers operate it from here on out?"

He nodded vigorously, looking relieved.

"How does he know who I am?" I asked Sonia, keeping my voice low.

Walking to her son, she mussed his hair before smoothing it back out. "I receive dossiers on the staff of every ship I travel on. Sai likes to peruse them over my shoulder, and we encourage his curiosity."

"Is that so?" Fear spiked in my chest. What had Sonia found in my dossier? How much did she know about me? About my past?

As if reading my mind, she said, "There is no personal information in the files—just where you're from, how long you've worked aboard the ship, any military or political background. That sort of thing." She planted a soft kiss on Sai's head, then moved to stand at the end of the counter. "But I did see that we're both from Tranquis."

"Yes, ma'am."

"Lathinaes, correct?"

"That's where I grew up. My parents still live there, but I haven't been back in years."

Sonia sighed. "I haven't been to Lathinaes in over a decade. But I love it there. It's so quiet, so green, and the mountains..." She whistled. "Breathtaking. What a wonderful place to grow up."

"It was," I agreed. "Very peaceful. Although not much of a nightlife."

Sonia's laughter was low and breathy. "I imagine not. At my age, however, that's much less of a concern."

I frowned at this. The senator was only a few years older than I was. And I wondered if I'd still crave the escape of dark bars, stiff drinks, and warm bodies if my life had turned out differently, if I was in the senator's shoes, if I was a wife now, a mother still.

"Come sit, Sunny," Lena said, setting a steaming kettle on the counter. "Have some tea."

I hesitated, my gaze landing on the empty stool next to Sai, then floating up to the boy's grinning face.

"Yeah, Sunny," he said. "You can sit next to me." He held up his puzzle, which now resembled an exploding star with twenty or so tiny pegs sticking out from a central core. "I'll show you how it works."

"Thank you for the offer." My voice was shakier than I wanted it to be. It wasn't his fault, but being around him felt like hands wrapping around my arms, my neck, pulling me back, dragging me into a past I would do just about anything—and *had* been doing just about anything—to race away from. "But I'm afraid I'll have to take a rain check on the puzzle, and the tea." Accessing both Sonia's and Lena's Vmails through my VC, I told them, "I've sent you both my direct VC link. Please don't hesitate to contact me if you need anything at all. Any time, day or night."

Sonia nodded. "Thank you, Sunny."

"And I'll take you up on that rain check," Lena promised.

"Me too," Sai called out before taking another bite of his pastry.

I turned to leave, but then he said, "Hey, wait a sec." His sweet voice stuck me in place while he wiped his mouth with his napkin. "You didn't send your link to me. I might need to contact you too. I…" He paused, bit his cheek. "I get bored sometimes."

Smiling at him, trying to make it look kind instead of pained, I said, "My apologies, Sai," and sent him the link. "Better?"

"Yes," he cheered, his fist pumping in the air.

"Now, Sai," Lena said. "Sunny is a busy woman. You are not to contact her unless it's an absolute emergency. Do you understand?"

"I know. I won't bug her. Promise." But at that precise moment, he commed, <I have a ton more puzzles to show you. You know, if you aren't too busy. And please don't tell my moms I commed you.>

I commed back, <I'm never too busy for you. And my lips are sealed.> Walking to their door, I remembered something and turned around. "I hope you're both planning to attend the Fire Ball. It's my favorite event on the ship. Aside from New Year's."

Standing at Lena's side, Sonia slid an arm around her waist. "We've heard all about it and wouldn't miss it."

"Oh." I held up a finger. "There is one thing. If you happen to see anything on a dessert display called *warple cake*, you might want to avoid it."

"Why is that?" Lena asked, blowing on her tea.

"Warple cake is a powerful aphrodisiac. It might lead to some…questionable behavior, if you catch my meaning. And if you see anything with *bliss* as an ingredient, you'd do well to steer clear of that too."

With a knowing smile, Sonia dipped her chin. "Thank you for the warning, Sunny."

But as I stepped out into the hall, I heard Lena whisper, "Maybe we could bring some of the warple cake back to the suite with us after the ball." Then the door slid closed on the senator's quiet laughter.

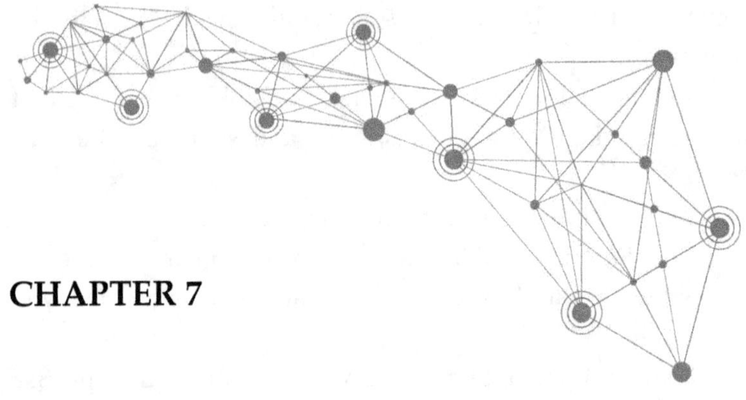

CHAPTER 7

THE WEEKS on the ship passed by with relative ease, aside from how hard I'd had to work not to stare too long or too hard at Freddie. Professional Freddie, all-business Freddie, *never-once-flirting-with-me* Freddie. Which was good, the lack of flirting. It was a good thing that he wasn't interested in me anymore. It was exactly what I'd asked for. What I'd wanted. What I *still* wanted. One hundred percent.

But today, I sensed that relative ease slipping away. Because Chan had brought booze to yet another staff meeting, and when he clinked his glass of champagne with his fork, my *what fresh bullshit will this be?* meter pinged off the charts.

"Let's all raise a toast to our new L&C," he said, holding his glass high. "In the short time Freddie has been with us, he's already prevented Aquilinian on Martian violence, resolved a Ulaperian scone crisis, and averted a cataclysmic misunderstanding by rerouting that Delphinian flash mob to deck sixteen where they wouldn't upset the Gorbies staying on fifteen—since we all know how offended our guests from Gorbulon-7 get by unexpected dancing." Grinning a little too widely, Chan tilted his glass toward Freddie. "We're so happy to have you, and that you are so brilliantly capable because..." His gaze darted around the table, never really landing on anyone while he chewed on his lower lip.

"Chan?" I prompted after several seconds of suspicious silence.

"Oh, right." His Adam's apple bobbed. "Because now is the perfect time to, ah..." He stalled out, then steamrolled through the remainder of his sentence with a single breath and no breaks. "...let you all know that we will be hosting a party of Kravaxians in three weeks' time."

My mouth sprang open. Freddie spluttered on his sip of champagne. Tig pulled the drawstrings of her hood fully closed. And Rax and Morgath burst from their chairs, shouting, "Over our dead bodies!" at the same time.

"I'm sorry." I shook my head. "I must be hallucinating. Did you say *Kravaxians* will be boarding?" I blinked. "On purpose?"

"No," Rax growled. "They will not."

Toggling his hoverchair controls, Chan rocked nervously back and forth. "Isn't it, uh, exciting?" He couldn't hide his grimace as the words left his mouth.

Rax and Morgath bellowed their objections, Elanie mumbled something to herself about "morons," and Freddie frowned, opening and closing his mouth like he almost had a response, like it was on the tip of his tongue but just wouldn't come. Which was not something I remembered him having any issues with *at all.*

I know, I know. This was not an appropriate thought to have at a staff meeting, certainly not in the face of Kravaxian visitation. And yet...

"Everyone, calm down, please." Chan's voice carried over the din of outrage and general bafflement ricocheting off the staff room walls. "Let me explain."

"Oh, there's no need to explain." Morgath's hands splayed flat on the table as he hovered ominously over Chan like a muscle-bound green gargoyle. "You've obviously lost your godsdamned mind. There is a senator on the ship, for fuck's sake."

I met Freddie's stare before we both turned toward Morgath, then toward Chan, then back to each other, both of us so mystified I almost laughed.

The problem with Chan's revelation was that Kravaxians were, not to mince words, terrifying. They were space pirates, murderers, arsonists, chaos breeders, and—if one believed the rumors—raging cannibals. Clever, vicious, brutal, and with no allegiances aside from the all-mighty credit, they were, in my humble opinion, exceptionally bad cruise ship guests.

Freddie cleared his throat and, with some hesitation, suggested, "Perhaps we should give Chandler a chance to explain."

"Explain what?" Rax snapped, flinging his hands into the air. "That we've decided to invite Godzilla into the city?"

Silence descended as all beings at the table stared blankly at Rax.

"What's that?" I asked, having no idea what a *Godzilla* was.

Rax grunted in frustration as Morgath said, "Old Earth movie monster. Giant lizard thing. Destroys buildings, shoots lightning-fire out of its mouth, kills everyone. That sort of deal."

"Ah, well, then." I nodded, acknowledging the similarities. "Accurate."

Looking up from her nails, Elanie said, "Bright side. We won't have to worry about feeding them. Our guests should suffice."

Chan palmed his forehead. "It's not what you think. They won't eat our guests."

Tig trembled. "They'll eat me first, won't they? I'm, like, bite sized."

"Really, *Chan*? Why do you want Tig to get eaten, *Chan*?"

Morgath, still on his feet, punctuated Chan's name like he might as well have been saying *asshole* or *dipshit.*

Poor Chan—who couldn't get a word in edgewise over the irate twins spiking accusations at him in rapid succession—tried to shout above their verbal assault. "Nobody is going to get eaten!"

"I didn't know they made muzzles big enough to fit a Kravaxian," Elanie said under her breath.

"And the captains signed off on this?" Rax asked in utter disbelief.

"They did." Chan leveraged this bit of camaraderie from the captains to wrangle the conversation back in. "And if you'll give me a second, I'll tell you why." He leaned over, fished some brochures out of the side pocket of his chair, and passed them out. "The Kravaxians we will host have been hand selected by LunaCorp as a local task force leading the Bring Labor and Industry to Kravax initiative—or BLIX, as they're calling it."

"BLIX?" Elanie scoffed. "That's the best they could come up with?"

Chan shrugged. "They were going to go with BLIK, which is, objectively, much worse."

"This all sounds like a load of trestal shit to me," Morgath grumbled.

I turned the BLIX brochure over in my hand. On the front, Kravax hovered, a marbled brown and green planet with its two tiny moons glinting in the darkness. And on the back, the New Earther entrepreneur-turned-CEO of LunaCorp, Brock Karlovich, stood on the steps of the LunaCorp HQ building, his hands clasped behind his back, his gaze piercing. I studied Mr. Karlovich, with his smug grin and chiseled jaw and… I looked closer. Was he wearing makeup? Self-tanner? Maybe some blush? He looked far too orange to be real. For any species.

Tig, always one for gathering as much information as possible, took a break from biting her cuticles to ask, "What sort of industry are they hoping to bring to Kravax?"

"Uh," Chan wavered. "I believe they will start with manufacturing, tourism, and...banking?" He said it like a question, like even he couldn't believe it.

"Banking?" Freddie repeated, not believing it either. "With those thieves?"

"Mr. Karlovich feels that Kravax presents an untapped resource. Namely, a species that is"—Chan paused again, seeming to gird his loins to quote—"'very good with money.'"

Freddie laughed out loud at this, followed by Elanie. And then we all erupted into hysterics. Even Chan.

"That's one way to put it," Freddie said with a little giggle that was too delightful to even talk about.

Rax shook his head. "This is absurd."

"I agree that it's not ideal," Chan said. "But the Kravaxians have been training with LunaCorp execs for the last six months. They have evidently earned a holiday with us. We are to show them a"—he drew air quotes—"'good time.'"

We all groaned while Rax and Morgath spat a litany of Aquilinian expletives that would have turned their sweet mother's hair gray. But it didn't matter. We all knew there was no way out of this one.

LunaCorp owned the *Ignisar*, along with most of the ships and asteroids streaking through the KU, as well as several moons, including the one orbiting New Earth. When LunaCorp snapped its fingers, you jumped. But the last time corporate had instructed us to show our special guests—some sportsball team from New Earth they'd been trying to recruit to Mars—a "good time," the hooligans stole an oorthorse from the Cosmic Spectacle stables and hid it in their pods. Where what it didn't ruin with its copious shitting, it ate. And then shat that out too.

Sometimes working for one of the colossal conglomerates

that ran almost everything in the KU felt a lot like being squished under an enormous boot heel. One that was commonly covered in shit.

Apparently recalling those same events, Chan said, "It won't be like last time. For starters, we've tripled the security mechs around the Cosmic Spectacle. Second, I've read all the reports on the Kravaxians, and I will make them available to Freddie directly after this meeting." He turned to Freddie. "If you aren't convinced of their civility after reading the reports, we won't allow them on board."

Freddie's brows floated up. "But..." he started, as if waiting for the inevitable shoe to drop.

Chan sighed. "But we have been *strongly* encouraged to take them."

With a resigned press of his lips, Freddie said, "Of course."

"How many are there?" I asked, wondering what sort of strings I'd need to pull to meet the Kravaxians' unique hospitality needs. Trying to secure, house, and milk a kurot alone would be next to impossible. Kurots were a bit like New Earth cows but bigger and meaner, and Kravaxians bathed only in their fresh milk. Or so I'd heard.

"Four," Chan answered. "Two men, two women."

Giving his head a shake, Rax grumbled, "Four fucking Kravaxians."

Elanie sighed. "There goes the neighborhood."

After Rax gave Morgath a meaningful look, the twins stood from the table. "We'll need time," Rax said. "To work out the security logistics of protecting our guests from the FFKs."

"FFKs?" Tig asked, leaning back in her chair to stare up at the twins.

"Four Fucking Kravaxians," Morgath snarled.

Freddie hid his laughter behind a cough.

"Of course." Chan blew out a breath, probably relieved that the meeting might end without a staff resignation—or a need to put in a work order to fix the big table. "Whatever you need, it's yours."

After Rax and Morgath stalked from the room, Freddie asked, "There's no chance this is all some hysterical initiation prank you're pulling on me, is there?"

With a deep, troubled frown, Chan said, "I'm afraid not."

"HELL OF A FIRST FEW WEEKS," Freddie mused.

We walked side by side down the staff quarters hallway again, like we did at the end of every day now. He always kept his hands in his pockets, his eyes facing forward, his body language friendly and professional. But each night, we moved a bit closer, drawn to each other like we had magnets in our pockets. "At this rate," he said, "I wouldn't be surprised if we wake up tomorrow to find the ship overrun by fungus rats."

"Don't tempt fate." I shuddered. "That almost happened once."

"No." He gasped. "Really?"

I nodded, wishing he'd take his hands out of his pockets just once so my knuckles might accidentally brush against his. "They'd snuck into a guest's bags after they'd visited Gorbulon-7 and had gotten lost in the mold swamps. Must've picked up some rats along the way. It was horrific."

"I can only imagine." When we reached his pod, he turned to face me. "Most disturbing thing I've ever seen—and that was only a baby fungus rat in a cage at the *Foulest Creatures in the KU* exhibit on Venus. The teeth, the growths." He grimaced. "The *smell*."

I laughed, and he asked, "Do you know what they call a group of rats?"

"They're not just called a group?"

When we stopped outside his door, he gave me a wry smile. "No. They're called a mischief."

"Well," I said, smiling back, "if you think Rax and Morgath were upset today, you should have seen them when they had to chase after a mischief of fungus rats running loose around the decks."

We laughed, then stared at each other, and then he closed his eyes. "Oh, Chan just sent me the FFK's file," he said, opening his eyes again, standing a little straighter. "I suppose I'll be spending the rest of the evening reading the reports and brushing up on my Kravaxian nonverbals. Wouldn't want to offend a ruthless space pirate with an accidental thumbs-up."

My eyes popped, my stomach dropping to somewhere around my knees as I realized, quite suddenly, the very real dangers inherent in FFK visitation. "Good idea," I said. "And note taken, no thumb movements. Wait, what would that mean? If I did give them a thumbs-up?"

Taking a step toward me, moving close, he said, "It would indicate that you were *interested* in them."

"Interested?" I repeated as heat flashed across my cheeks.

He backed away again, leaning his shoulder against his door. "That's correct."

"Well," I said, flicking my bangs off my forehead. "I won't be doing that, then. No, sir. And thank you. For the warning."

"Of course." He winked. "It's kind of my job."

"Ha. Right." My voice was all wrong, too loud, too high. *Chirpy*.

"Tell me, Sunny," he said, changing gears. "What should I expect from the upcoming Fire Ball?"

I had to tear my eyes away from his juicy lower lip before replying. "Anything and everything, darling."

He hummed. "That sounds...intimidating."

"Oh, it is. But it's also wonderful, exhilarating. A night without inhibitions."

The way he looked at me, like he wanted to say something, like he wanted to *do* something... I retreated a step, and then another, just to be on the safe side. Which was, to be honest, probably located halfway across the hall.

Taking his own backward step, he said, "I can't wait. Good night, Sunastara."

"Good night, Freddie."

And as much as I tried to deny it, it was useless. I wanted him. Every night, every walk back to our pods, *stars save me*, I wanted him even more. I wanted to kiss him and taste him and feel him again, and he probably knew it. He probably knew how much I wanted that *good night* to turn into a *good morning*. It was there in his eyes. Mischief, just like those damn rats.

Turning on my heel to keep myself from inadvertently grabbing him by the lapels of his suit coat and pulling his mouth to mine, I waved over my shoulder while marching away from his door.

It wasn't against the law, wanting him. It didn't even mean anything. He was attractive. I had eyes. I could want him all I wanted. I'd just have to do it in my pod, in private, alone, with my vibrator.

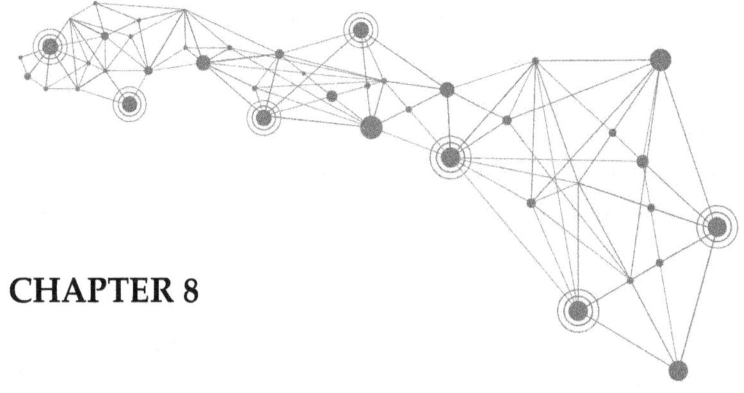

CHAPTER 8

<SUNNY. Fire Ball prep meeting in the staff room in ten minutes. Don't be late.>

<I won't be late,> I commed Elanie back, miffed. <When am I ever late for anything?>

<Where should I begin?> she replied. <Morning meetings, Rax and Morgath's birthday, the Solaris roast, the captains' briefings. I could go on.>

<I was not late to the Solaris roast,> I protested. <I was an hour early.>

<An hour early for what?> Elanie asked. <Being two hours late?>

<No. I left because I was early. Then I came back. And *that's* when I was late. So it doesn't count.>

<You're ridiculous. And you're also late.>

<Whatever,> I grumbled. <I'm almost there.>

But when I walked through the door seven minutes later, I found the staff room empty—aside from Freddie. He sat across the table, staring at me. Had Elanie set us up to meet like this? It seemed unlikely, but the fact that I was here and she was late was a little too ironic. And Elanie didn't do irony.

"Hi, Sunny." His cheeks were flushed, his hair slightly out of place, the top button of his shirt undone, his eyes twinkling. He looked relaxed, deliciously loose. He looked like—

"Why are you staring at me like that?"

"Like what?" I blurted out, even though I knew exactly how I was staring at him. Like he was a snack, and I was hungry.

His lips twitched. "You're staring at me like you know something I don't."

He'd been the perfect gentleman, treating me with kindness and respect, giving me all the space I'd stubbornly demanded. This behavior had only served one purpose: making my pink parts even more inappropriately perky in his presence.

I licked my lips. "Well, it's just..."

"Just what?"

Fire raced up my neck, pooling at the base of my throat. "You look... The way you look right now... You're reminding me—"

"Sunastara Nex." He leaned forward onto his elbows, grinning up at me. "Are you blushing?"

"No," I insisted. "I just raced up here so I wouldn't be late. So I'm...hot."

He snorted at me, sitting back in his chair again. "You're hot."

"That's what I said."

"No." He was the one insisting now. "That's what *I* said."

This conversation was spiraling out of control.

"Wait, are you getting hotter?" he asked. "Because your cheeks are even red—"

I groaned. "Fine, it's just... You look like *him* right now, okay?"

His head tilted. "Him?"

"Oh, for star's sake. Joshua. You look like Joshua."

He frowned, glancing down at his shirt. "I do?"

"Yes." Waving my hand in the air over him, I said, "Messy hair, loose shirt, loose tie." I scowled—because he was doing everything he could not to laugh, and it wasn't enough. "This is how you looked when you first walked into that bar on the CAK. When we..." I shoved my foot metaphorically into my mouth. "Anyway, it's a whole Joshua thing."

"Well," he said, still laughing but also combing his fingers through his hair, straightening it into place. "I didn't mean to." He hiccupped.

Pursing my lips, I narrowed my eyes. Now things were making sense. "I think I might know what's going on here. Is there any chance that you are currently intoxicated?"

He winced. "Quite, unfortunately. Garran found me this morning, and to make amends for damaging our serving drone, he demanded that I join him for a mimosa brunch on deck nine."

"Demanded?"

He nodded. "Argosians can be very persuasive. And the mimosas were"—*hiccup*—"very bottomless."

"That's a job hazard, for certain. And with the Fire Ball still to come..." I tutted at him. "You, my friend, are going to have a rough day tomorrow."

"Your *friend*," he repeated slowly, deliberately, looking like he'd nibbled on the word and wished he could spit it out. Staring directly into my eyes with a boldness only afforded by a morning spent drinking too much champagne, he said, "Such a small word to describe one of the biggest disappointments of my life."

Within the space of a heartbeat, my breath caught and my mouth went as dry as a Neptune desert.

Freddie blinked, then his face paled, like he'd just realized what he'd said. "Oh shit. Sunny, I'm sorry." He reached for me. "I didn't mean it. I mean, that's not true. I meant it. But I shouldn't have said it. I think I might have gotten drunker than I meant to get. No, that's not right. I hadn't intended to get drunk at all. I'm only drunk on accident. *Stars*, I'm making this worse, aren't I?"

I sat as gracefully as I could for someone whose legs wobbled like flicked springs. His arm was still stretched across the table, his hand open and waiting for me, and I couldn't stop myself from taking it. When his fingers closed around mine, so soft and warm, I knew I'd made a mistake.

I was drawn to him; there was no denying it. But giving in to that pull, letting myself fall into bed with him, possibly into more, would be like willingly venting myself into space: exhilarating at first, painful later, and ultimately disastrous.

Taking a shaky breath, I pulled my hand from his. "It's fine."

"It is not fine." His fingers curled in toward his palm before he placed his hands in his lap. "I was out of line."

"No, you weren't," I said.

"Yes, I was," he insisted.

"No, you weren't."

"Yes—"

Tig wandered into the room, saving us from going back and forth another round. She didn't notice us, her attention focused on the techPad in her hands, her pink hair poking out from under her hood.

"Afternoon, Tig," Freddie said.

She jumped, almost dropping her pad but recovering quickly. "Oh. To you too. Um"—she pulled back her hood, taking the seat to my right—"to both of you."

"Thank you, darling," I replied while my heart sagged against my ribs, either relieved that my conversation with Freddie was over, or miserable about it. Maybe both. "Are you ready for tonight?"

Tig nodded. "It shouldn't be too bad this year. Only some fancy lighting, mist generators, sound effects. And, of course, the pyro." Tig managed all the special effects for the ship's various events.

"Any concerns about the magic show?" I asked. Apparently the Delphinian wizards planned to "wow the ship" with their tricks during the Fire Ball.

"Right," Freddie said, straightening his tie. "I heard about what that other group did to the pool on deck sixteen. I wonder what they'll accidentally mess with this year."

"I think it'll be okay," Tig replied with some confidence. "They seem to know what they're doing.

"There's no unexpected group dancing during the show, though, right?" Freddie asked. "There's a large group of Gorbies vacationing on the ship who want to come to the ball, and I'd prefer not to upset them. They're already right on the edge with how dry it is in their rooms. The humidifiers are on the fritz, and apparently it's a 'nightmare situation' for their hair."

On a planet as humid as Gorbulon-7, big, frizzy hair was as much of a status symbol as bountiful crops on Argos or the number of bathrooms in a Martian billionaire's mansion.

Tig shook her head. "No dancing. But there will be animals. Hopefully nobody has any objections to that."

"Animals?" Freddie and I said at the same time, equally concerned.

"Well, just one," Tig clarified. "A goat named Dave. But he's very well trained."

"How in the worlds did they get a goat on board?" I asked. "I've had no luck at all trying to get a kurot for the FFKs approved for interplanetary travel, and they have a goat?"

Tig's grin was mischievous as she twirled her fingers in the air and whispered, "It's magic."

"No shit? Any chance they could"—I mimicked her finger twirl—"*magic* me a kurot?"

Freddie snorted.

I was only half joking, but Tig shrugged and said, "I can ask. Oh, and speaking of the pool on sixteen. One of the wizards fixed it for us. She said it was a fairly simple spell. Any child could do it."

"What?" I scoffed. "We've had, like, twenty Delphinians try to reverse that spell. They all said it was impossible."

Tig shrugged again. "Like I said, these wizards seem to know what they're doing."

That was music to my ears. Before that drunk Delphinian's spell had made it unfillable, I'd gone to the pool on deck sixteen nearly every day. It was the smallest pool on the ship, almost private since only a few guests had known it existed. I used to love swimming laps before bed, or floating on my back and watching the stars slide by through the pool's flexGlass ceiling. "That is fantastic news."

Tig grinned. "I knew you'd be happy to hear it."

Just then, someone barked a howling laugh in the hallway.

"What was that?" I asked, turning to look through the window.

"It's Chan," Freddie said. "I don't think I've ever heard him laugh like that before."

"Me neither," I muttered, squinting suspiciously at the back of his hoverchair.

"Who's he talking to?" Tig's pink brows pinched together as we all tried to catch a glimpse of the mystery being hidden behind Chan's chair.

Finally, Chan drifted to the side, sliding away to reveal—

"That's her," Tig shouted. "She's the wizard who fixed the pool."

The female chatting with Chan was Delphinian, but instead of the black-and-red robes her fellow wizards had been wearing, she wore a pair of skinny blue jeans, a simple black T-shirt, and strappy black flats. Her heart-shaped face framed a clever smile. Her long black braids were gathered into a ponytail that swayed past her hips. And somehow, impossibly, she started laughing too.

"Is Chan making a female laugh?" I asked. "That is laughter, right? Not tears?"

"Is that odd or something?" Freddie asked.

I spun back around in my chair. "Super odd. Look, Chan is the warmest and most genuine being I have ever met. But he has absolutely no game."

"It's so bad," Tig agreed. "He's, like, a chemistry black hole."

"He can't be *that* bad." Freddie frowned. "Can he?"

"He's catastrophic," I said. "A few years ago, I informed him that some females liked being complimented on their shoes. And the very next female he took on a date filed a report with LunaCorp HR accusing him of being a 'creepy foot fetishist.'"

Tilting his head to peek past us through the glass, Freddie said, "I don't know. Looks like he's holding his own to me."

I turned back to the window just as Chan said something else to the Delphinian that, *stars above*, made her laugh again. She flipped the few braids that had escaped her ponytail back off her shoulder in a move that was unmistakable *I am into you* body language for every species that had hair.

"Remarkable," I whispered, staring in pure amazement until Rax and Morgath stomped down the hall, grumbling past Chan and the Delphinian.

"What's everyone staring at?" Rax grunted while he took one of the chairs next to Freddie. Morgath thudded down onto the other so that the twins flanked him like intimidating bookends.

"We're staring at Chan," Tig said. "Because he's out there, somehow not blowing it with that Delphinian."

"For real?" Morgath asked skeptically.

"Yes," I whispered, watching Chan wave an exuberant goodbye to the Delphinian before cruising toward the staff room. "But don't say a word. This is a monumental achievement for Chan, and I don't want to embarrass him."

Everyone nodded. But it didn't matter. Because not two

seconds after Chan entered the staff room, Elanie strode in behind him, staring over her shoulder at the Delphinian who'd already made her way back down the hall. "Who's that?" Elanie asked at full volume. "She was laughing, Chan. *Laughing*. Did you actually make a female laugh?"

"Never mind," I muttered as Chan stammered a stream-of-consciousness explanation about the Fire Ball and logistics and magic shows and how everything was "completely professional." The poor man's entire head had turned as red as Martian sand, but when he started in on the difficulties of organizing appropriate living arrangements for Dave the goat, I decided to step in.

"What are our assignments for the evening?" I asked, pushing my voice louder than the muffled snorts around the table.

Composing himself, even though he was still red-faced, Chan gave us our duties for the Fire Ball. Elanie would manage the Delphinians—and Dave the goat. Freddie and I would be stationed on the floor to keep the peace. Rax and Morgath would work security at the doors. And Tig—not a huge fan of crowds—would run the music, lighting, and effects from the master control booth above the main deck ballroom.

After the meeting adjourned, I gave myself three side assignments for the ball: 1. Learn everything I could about the Delphinian Chan had been speaking with. 2. Make sure the night didn't end before Garran spun Kasa around the dance floor as flawlessly as he'd spun our serving drone. And 3. Avoid staring at Freddie all night like all I wanted to do was sleep in his suit jacket, preferably while he still wore it.

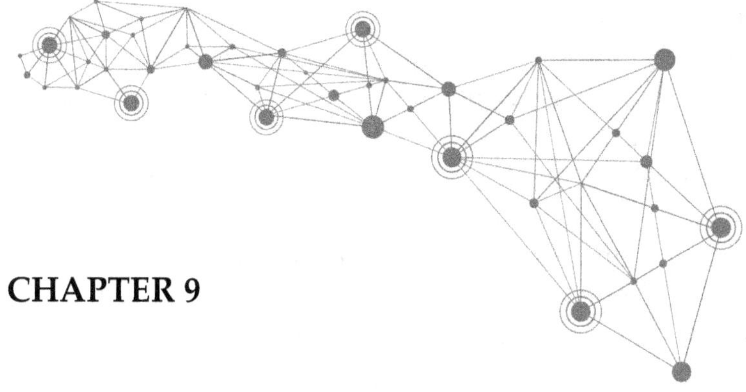

CHAPTER 9

"I FORGOT TO TELL YOU," Elanie said, walking in step beside me back to our pods. "Raphael is on his way. He'll arrive in an hour."

Stumbling over a bit of nothing on the carpet, I said, "What?"

"You know, Raphael. Tall, dark, dreamy." She made a show of studying her nails. "Your semi-annual 'fuck buddy.' He'll be here for the Fire Ball."

"Elanie," I said, almost too stunned to reply. *Almost*. "I have never referred to anyone as a 'fuck buddy' in my entire life. And are you serious? How? How is he coming? I haven't seen him on the itinerary." My blood ran cold, which was absolutely upside down. Under normal circumstances, the news that Raphe would be on the ship would cause the exact opposite effect.

"He didn't want me to list him. I told him he was being ridiculous, but he said he wanted to surprise you."

"That's...sweet," I managed. I was surprised, all right. My right foot falling off would have surprised me less. Raphe was coming. He'd be here tonight. And instead of racing to my pod to decide which dress would make my tits shine or how I could steal twenty minutes alone with him before the ball, I was thinking about Freddie, my mind stubbornly tracing over his crooked nose, toying with the soft strands of his hair.

Raphe was gorgeous, easy, uncomplicated. A sure thing. And as a private lawyer to one of the largest and wealthiest of the Aquilinian Royal families, he was also extremely busy and could never stay on the ship longer than a day or two. I was under no illusions as to how much of his precious time he was spending on me tonight. Normally, this was a massive turn-on. But nothing about my life was normal right now.

Sighing, Elanie said, "Sure. Sweet. Whatever you say."

"What's that supposed to mean?" I braced my hands on my hips.

"Honestly, Sunny," she said. "I do my best to stay out of your love life. The way you choose partners is too much like throwing darts at a board blindfolded. It's dangerous for any bystanders and occasionally leaves holes in the wall. No offense."

That stung a bit. "What exactly is the point you're trying to make here, Elanie?"

"I don't know." She shrugged. "All these lovers. All these random encounters. It all seems so…futile."

That stung a lot. "Futile, is it?" I snapped. "Do you know what's futile? Refusing to install a recommended upgrade. *That's* futile."

"No need to get personal," Elanie said, flinching like she'd flicked a trestal on its beak and was offended when it decided to peck her back. "I'm only stating the facts."

When we reached my pod, I bowed to her. "Thank you for letting me know about Raphael." Straightening, I slapped my hand on the security panel, then winked. "Gives me plenty of time to think about my life choices while I sharpen my darts."

After a scalding shower and a few moments standing under the quikDri, I sat on the edge of my bed, twirling a longer strand of my hair around my finger. I'd accessed the ship's manifest a few minutes ago to see that Raphe had already boarded. He always stayed on deck twenty-three, toward the bow of the ship—about as far from staff quarters as possible. He did this for me, for privacy. He was very thoughtful when it came to clandestine hookups.

And *ooh*, he was staying in the Afterglow suite. It was one of our most luxurious accommodations, boasting a fully automated bar, a jetted tub so wide you could swim in it, and a null-Grav pod—which might be interesting—and with the portside wall made entirely of flexGlass, the views from the suite were phenomenal.

All things considered, I knew I should be more excited than I was. I knew I should be throwing something on and running to the Afterglow suite before I had to report for duty. I knew I shouldn't feel this conflicted. I needed to *stop* feeling this conflicted. There was nothing to feel conflicted about. Nothing had changed.

I sat up straighter, inspiration striking. Maybe Raphael's visit was a good thing. Maybe the best way to reestablish my professional boundaries with Freddie was to reestablish my personal relationship with Raphe.

Standing from the bed, I walked to my closet, and—without even thinking—grabbed my favorite little black dress, pulled it on, and smoothed it over my hips. After spending an extra ten minutes on my makeup, I made my way to the Fire Ball.

The main deck ballroom was an inferno. Serving drones drifted through the air with trays so full of fiery cocktails they looked like they carried torches from table to table. Digital flames engulfed the room's eight marble columns, crackling and popping as they climbed the pillars to lick at the rafters. Fire danced across the floor in some marvel of interactive lighting that submerged the entire room in a blazing river. Whenever a guest walked across the floor, the flames parted and reformed or slid up their legs to wrap around their thighs. It was stunning, enthralling. In the five years I'd known her, I'd never been so proud of Tig.

Suspended from the rafters, sixteen iridescent-skinned, long-limbed Ulaperian acrobats spun from metal rings or dangled from wide swaths of silk. They wore black contacts over their round, pearlescent eyes, which—while well suited for the darkness of their outer-rim planet—were far too sensitive for the lighting in the room. But the effect turned them into writhing, erotic fire demons.

I gasped as one of the acrobats released her silks, falling in a death drop all the way to the floor before catching herself with a foot hooked around the shimmering fabric. The trick drew everything from shocked screams to dog whistles to wild applause from the guests standing at the bar or seated at their tables.

The Fire Ball was a celebration specific to the *Ignisar*. Occurring between several planets' major holidays and festivals —the Tranquis Yuletide, the Solstice of New Earth and Mars, Ulaperia's Great Conjunction, and Blurvos's Goo Fest—the Fire Ball exploited all of them, providing an excuse for the guests to eat too much, get shit-faced, and participate in nonstop debauchery until sunrise sim. Tonight, nothing was off-limits, nothing was taboo, hedonism ruled, and I had to remain a sober voyeur until they kicked everyone out.

I spied Elanie ducking behind the red velvet curtain at the far end of the ballroom, presumably to keep an eye on the wizards and their goat while they prepared for their magic show. I wanted to apologize for our argument, but after a few steps in her direction, Freddie waltzed into view, and I hit an invisible flexGlass wall.

He hadn't noticed me yet, so I let myself notice him. He was devastating in a fitted black suit, crisp white shirt, slim black tie. His hair was impeccably styled. It mesmerized me, the way he moved fluidly through the ballroom, winding around tables and guests like a stream around its banks. He bent down to swipe an errant cocktail napkin from the floor, tucked it into his back pocket, then said, "Oop!" while spinning on his heel to snatch a saltshaker from a server before they accidentally placed it on a Blurvan's table. Touching the server's shoulder, he told them something—judging by their horrified expression, it was likely what salt does to a Blurvan's gelatinous lower half.

"Sunny." Lena Ramesh's voice yanked my attention. "Come say hello." She waved me over to the table where she, Sonia, and Sai sat sipping steaming bright-red beverages in tall glasses shaped like flames.

I was surprised they'd decided to bring the boy. But the Fire Ball didn't typically go fully off the rails until well after sunset sim. So why not?

As I crossed the room toward their table, I stepped to the side just in time to keep Tig from bowling me over as she beelined back to the control booth with her hood up and her head down.

"Careful, Tig."

Yanking down her hood, she said, "Sorry, Sunny. But I'm trying to get"—she pulled at her collar, her slightly bloodshot eyes darting around the room—"the *fuck* out of here."

With a small laugh, I took Tig by her shoulders and squeezed. "The party is miraculous. The effects are amazing. Your best work yet. Tomorrow, I'm taking you for a spa day to celebrate. And a massage," I said when Tig's shoulders tensed. "I feel like I'm squeezing a bolt of lightning."

"That's exactly how I feel," she said with a nervy warble. "But I don't really like spas. Or massages."

"Hmm," I considered. "I know. How about tea at the bistro on deck thirty? You, me, views of the cosmos?" I waggled my brows. "And pastries?"

Her eyes lit up. "That sounds perfect."

"Then it's a date," I said, kissing her cheek before she skirted around the crowd, heading back to the safety of her control room.

Resuming my path through fire toward the Ramesh's table, I scanned the expansive ballroom. I doubted Raphe would have arrived this early—he was likely sitting at the desk in his suite, poring over legal documents, his broad shoulders filling out his tailored shirt, his brows pressed together in concentration, a pen between his teeth, a hot cup of coffee steaming beside him. But he'd surprised me before. Like when he arrived today unannounced, for example.

I did want to see him. I was sure of it. Being with Raphael was like being with a world leader. He was strong, decisive, skilled. He knew what he wanted, was exceptionally easy to please, and was always quick to compliment. In short, he was a hospitality specialist's wet dream. So, *yes*, I was excited to see him. Extremely excited. Because we made sense. Raphael and I made sense.

Who the hells needs seven orgasms in one night anyway?

"Hey, Sunny. This is so cool! Isn't this so cool?" Sai's high-pitched voice rang across the ballroom as I approached his table. Leaning over in his chair, he swiped his fingers through the digital flames that danced around his feet.

"It's amazing, isn't it?" I said, waving my hand to encompass the room. "One of my best friends made all of this."

"Really?" Sai's eyes ratcheted wide. "Can I meet them? I need to know how they did this. I have a million questions. Two million."

"Of course you can meet her, Sai. I'll set it up."

The boy's smile stretched from one ear to the other. "Awesome! Thanks, Sunny," he said before he returned to playing with the fire.

Patting the seat beside her, Sonia met my stare and said, "Take a load off."

I nodded my thanks and took the chair, partly because my feet had started to ache, but mainly because when the senator said jump, I had a feeling everyone within a light-year of her laced up their sneakers. "Are you enjoying yourselves?" I asked, and when Sonia ducked her chin, I leaned in close to tell her, "This ball tends to get a bit rowdy as the night goes on. You might consider—"

Waving me off, Sonia said, "We are only staying for dinner and the show."

"And a piece of that—what was it called?" Lena asked with a twinkle in her eye. "Warple cake?"

Angling my head toward the back of the room, I said, "I spotted some on the table in the corner. But promise me you'll wait until you're back in your suite before you eat any."

Sonia leaned in close and said, "Of course." Then she stopped my heart mid-beat with "I heard a rumor that LunaCorp is bringing Kravaxians onto the ship before we reach Portis."

Trying and failing to keep my shock in check, I stammered, "W-where did you hear that?"

"I have my sources. Is this true?"

It wasn't necessarily classified information, but I was well aware of the fact that I should neither confirm nor deny the rumor of FFK visitation. If word got out too soon, there could be panic, chaos, a security nightmare that would make fungus rat–era Rax and Morgath seem like characters from a children's story.

"I'm not really sure if—"

"Do not lie to me, Sunastara." The senator's voice had gone cold, as had the blood in my veins. The woman was intimidation incarnate.

Realizing I was not getting out of this situation without admitting something, I weighed my options. I could lie, but the senator would know it and only become more suspicious. If I told the truth... Oh, who was I kidding? She already knew the truth. This was a test of allegiance, if nothing else.

My only true allegiance was to this ship and my crew, but I highly doubted the senator would want to start a riot on the ship her family was currently staying on by spreading gossip. So, with some hesitation, I admitted, "Only four. But they're... special Kravaxians."

The senator raised a brow while Lena distracted Sai by asking him how he thought the Ulaperian silk dancers learned their tricks.

"They'll be here purely on LunaCorp business," I added. "And they have been thoroughly vetted."

"Thoroughly," Sonia repeated, leaning back in her chair, her tone suggesting that they might as well have attempted to thoroughly vet a Kuiper worm. "I see."

"You don't approve," I surmised.

"Of Kravaxians cohabitating in an enclosed space with civilians? No, Sunny. I do not approve."

When something terrible happened, I knew more than most how tempting it was to search for a reason, for a pattern in the chaos, for some sort of magical meaning to justify the unending wrongness of things. I'd tried for years until I finally learned the truth. There were no reasons. There was no meaning. And there were no coincidences. Coincidences like a prominent KU senator being on my ship at the same time as corporate-sanctioned space pirates.

"Why are you on the *Ignisar*?" I asked, cutting to the chase perhaps a bit too sharply. But I had to know. "We don't typically have politicos, let alone their families, traveling with us. At least not publicly. And Portis is far away for a simple—"

"That is a question for another time." Clearing her throat, Sonia returned her attention to her drink, and I knew the conversation was over.

"How late does the Fire Ball usually last?" Sai asked, breaking the meter-thick tension that had slammed down around the table.

Giving him a smile, I said, "Believe it or not, Sai, this room will still be buzzing at sunrise sim."

His mouth popped open. "The entire night?"

"Not for you, young man," Lena said, ruffling his hair.

Sai frowned, clearly not happy with his curfew, then he sipped his drink from a swirling straw.

Clasping her hands on the table with an abrupt *thump*—a move that no doubt served her well in senate meetings—Sonia said, "Thank you for stopping by, Sunny. But I'm sure you have work to get back to."

Not missing the dismissal, and, *yes*, having plenty of work to get back to, I stood from my chair, smoothed my dress back into place, and said, "Of course. I hope you'll all have a wonderful evening."

"You as well," Sonia said, not bothering to look up at me.

It chafed a little. I understood the senator's concerns about the Kravaxians. I shared them. But it wasn't like the FFK visitation had been my idea. I was only doing my job.

I was about to spin on my heel and walk away when Lena snatched my hand, pulled me close, and said, "Don't mind Sonia. She gets like this when she's worried."

I tried to give Lena a polite nod, but when she added, "You look gorgeous tonight. That is such a perfect little black dress. Where'd you get it?" the floor vanished beneath my feet.

I hadn't realized, but, *stars save me*, I was wearing the dress. *The* dress. The same dress I'd worn on the CAK the night I'd first met him. The same dress he'd peeled off my body inch by inch, covering each bit of my exposed skin with his hands and lips and tongue. The same dress I'd worn when I'd been Phoebe and he'd been Joshua.

"Sunny?" Concern laced Lena's expression. "You've gone white as a sheet. Are you all right?"

What was wrong with me? How could I have worn this dress? How could I not have noticed? Had he noticed? No. No, he wouldn't have. He was a man, after all. They rarely remembered things like what dress a woman wore. It was fine. Everything was fine.

"I'm fine," I said with a brittle, forced laugh. *I just have to go change before my life implodes.* "Only a few bites of the warple cake," I warned, backing away from the table. "Too much, and the effects can be very..." Turning around carefully, I scanned the ballroom, trying to spot him without being obvious, without him noticing me, without my thoughtless outfit choice being too "...consequential."

It was too late. He saw me. He wasn't more than twenty feet away, sitting at a table of Argosians, staring at me. And judging by his expression, his wide eyes, his parted lips, the hand rising to his chest, he knew. He remembered.

My heart tripped over itself. Because the way he looked at me, the sheer intensity? Did he think the dress meant something? Did *I* think the dress meant something? Was it all random bad luck? Or was it some unconscious corner of my mind insinuating itself into my personal life against my will?

Shit. Shit, shit, shit.

He stood from his table. I stepped away from mine. Then he tilted his head toward a hallway leading from the main ballroom and started walking.

I didn't know what to do. I was paralyzed, my breath burning my throat, fire searing my chest, scorching my lungs. At least my panic was staying true to theme.

But once he disappeared from sight, a funny thing happened. My feet moved, carrying me toward him, to where he waited for me at the end of the dark, quiet hallway, leaning back against the wall, his face angled up to the ceiling.

"Freddie," I said, surprised my voice still worked. "I can explain."

Wheeling around, he strode toward me in bold, breath-stealing strides and didn't stop until he was so close I felt him everywhere. "You're wearing the dress. *Her* dress," he said in a harsh, almost pained whisper. "Sunny, why are you wearing her dress? Are you trying to torture me?" His mouth hovered inches from mine, his hand landing on the wall beside my head. "Because it's working." He licked his lips. "I am tortured."

His other hand hit the wall beside my hip, his hair brushing my forehead, and my heart thundered so hard and fast against my ribs I was sure he saw it through my dress, maybe even heard it. Maybe the entire room heard it. I was panting, light-headed, confused, and I didn't care. I didn't care about the ball or the dress or the voice in my head screaming at me to push him away. I didn't care.

He invaded my senses, enveloping me until he was all I could see or feel or breathe. My knees buckled, and I couldn't fight it anymore. I had never wanted another being the way I wanted him. Like I really was on fire, and he was the only drop of water in the entire star system. I wanted to touch him, hold him, kiss him so desperately it was an ache in my bones. I wanted his lips on mine, his hands on my body. I wanted to wake up with the sweet taste of him still on my tongue, the smell of him on my skin, the memory of him inside me. But as his head angled, his lips lining up with mine, so close I felt their softness in some magic stronger than anything the wizards could produce, reality crashed into me.

I shouldn't do this. I *couldn't* do this. The job was one thing, but there was so much more. He was not some one-night stand anymore. He was in my life, all day, every day. If I gave in to this wanting, he would eventually want things from me in return. Things I couldn't give him. He wasn't casual. He wasn't no-strings-attached material. He was the kind of man who'd want to be as close as possible, and he'd end up resenting me because I'd only ever push him away. He deserved better. He deserved better than a broken woman who only knew how to run the second shit got real. Because that's what I did. I ran. I hid. It was what I was good at. It was what I needed to do now. Maybe I was being a coward, but I'd had enough pain in my life already.

With Herculean effort, I pulled my hands—which had somehow found their way to his hips—back to my sides. Then I pressed my palm against his chest and pushed.

"Sunny?" He looked down at my hand. "Don't—"

"I didn't mean to wear this dress," I admitted. "It was a mistake. I…I didn't realize."

"A mistake?" he repeated, breathless.

"I'm going back to my pod to change. Right now. I didn't mean it."

"Please." His hand slid over mine where it still pressed into his chest. "Please don't push me away."

But couldn't he see? Didn't he know? That was all I'd ever do.

He touched his forehead to mine, his breath warm on my lips. "Why can't we try? I wish we could try. I know you think it will be hard or scary or jeopardize our jobs. But I don't think it would. I think it could work. Please, Sunny. You're all I want."

I had to leave, to run. Otherwise, he would try to kiss me again, and if he did, I wasn't sure I'd have the strength to stop him a second time. I had to shut this down. I had to make him see how terrible I'd be for him. I had to stop all this wanting, because wanting something, no matter how badly, was never enough. It never worked.

While my stomach sank like a stone and my throat closed like a fist, I said the only thing that would make him stop, make him leave. "Freddie, a man is here to see me. A man I have a history with. I'll"—I fought through an excruciating swallow—"be with him tonight."

After that, there was nothing left but an empty, unforgiving cold as he stepped back, pulling the warmth of his body away from mine. With an unreadable expression, he slid his hands into his pockets, closed his eyes, and said, "I understand."

Dropping my hand from his chest, and with a horrible tremor in my voice, I said, "I'm so sorry." Then, like the coward I was, I ran.

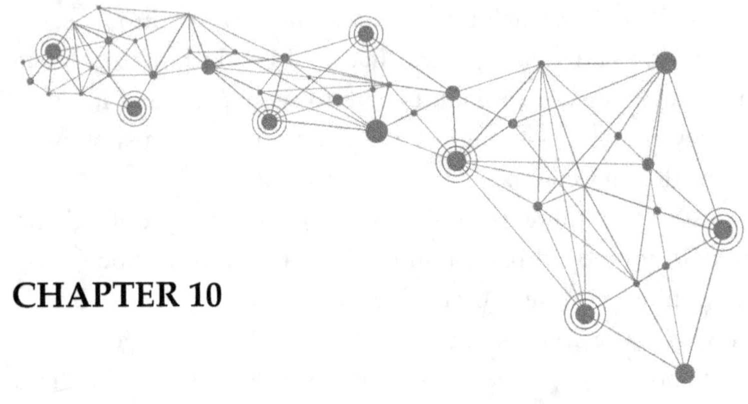

CHAPTER 10

AFTER STRIPPING off what used to be my favorite little black dress, I flung it into a dark corner of my closet where it could sit and think about what it had done. Yanking a random not-grounded dress off a hanger, I pulled it on, turned around, and slammed my palm into my door sensor so hard I left a dent.

With each step back toward the ballroom, a cold emptiness enveloped me. But at least the panic trying to burn me up from the inside out when I'd been in that hallway with him, with his eyes staring into mine, his arms bracketing my body, his heart in his hands while I callously swatted it away, had faded.

Turning the final corner, I took a breath, shook out my shoulders, and fluffed my hair. It hurt, a deep, piercing ache. But there was also some relief, knowing I'd saved him from—

<Where are you?>

<Good gods, Elanie,> I hissed, trying not to have a heart attack for the third time tonight. <You have *got* to stop yelling at me when you comm. I swear, I'm going to change your permissions to invite-only.>

<Where are you?> she repeated, ignoring the threat. <Where have you been?>

<I had to change.>

<You had to... Why?>

<Don't ask. I'm almost back. Did you need something?>

<Yes. Two things. One, Raphael has arrived. And two, so has your Argosian.>

<Garran?> My life might be in ragged, perpetual shambles, but at least I had my work. <How is he?>

<I don't know,> Elanie replied flatly. <Huge? Purple?>

<Be serious.> Walking into the ballroom, I had to zag to avoid stepping on a passed out Vorpol's foot. Apparently, the party was already in full swing.

<He's, well, he's smiling. A lot. He won't stop. It's fairly terrifying, if I'm being honest.>

<Yikes. I'm on my way.> Before clicking off the comm, I asked, <How does Raphael look?>

<Handsome, I suppose. He's been waiting for you. Freddie told him you were dealing with a wardrobe malfunction.>

My eyes flared. <Freddie spoke to Raphael?> That couldn't have gone over well.

<Yes. Why? Was he not allowed?>

With a deep sigh, I commed, <As always, Elanie, you are a bright light shining into the darkness of my weary soul.>

<I am detecting sarcasm in your tone.>

<Well done, darling. It was pretty thick.>

I clicked off the comm, and the lights began to dim. *Showtime.* As the bass thumped and the crowd grew quiet, I scanned the room, searching for Garran. He stood near the bar, holding what looked like a gigantic fishbowl full of some flaming blue drink. He was still smiling from ear to ear, looking like a toothy, deranged psychopath. Elanie was right; it was fairly terrifying.

"Hello, Sunastara," Garran said when I reached him, his smile still pasted into place, the stretch of his cheeks looking painful.

"Garran," I said calmly. "Remember when I told you that females like a male who smiles?" I'd given him this advice in the ballroom on deck five. Evidently, I should have been more specific.

His smile blossomed wider as a bartender drone zoomed around the counter behind him. "It is good, right?"

Materializing from a cloud of artificial smoke, Freddie stepped up beside me, and every single hair along my neck shot for the ceiling.

He placed a hand on Garran's shoulder. "Everything in moderation, my friend."

Garran's smile faltered. "Is it too much?"

Freddie laughed. It was a small laugh, but it seemed genuine. In fact, he seemed fine. Perfectly fine. And that was good. That was *great*. Why shouldn't he be fine? Why shouldn't everyone be just completely fine? I was fine. The weird pressure in my chest was probably indigestion.

"That is good. My face hurts." After massaging his fingertips into his cheeks, Garran took a massive sip of his bowl-drink.

"Which one is Kasa?" I asked, repositioning the strap of the red dress I'd thrown on because it was at the front of my closet, even though it had never fit right.

Garran pointed out a petite—*for an Argosian*—female at the same table of Argosians Freddie had been visiting with earlier. She was striking. And Garran wasn't wrong; her violet hair did resemble twilight.

"She's here on holiday with her mother," Freddie said, nodding toward a much larger female to Kasa's left, who sat with her arms crossed and a surly expression stamped on her face.

"Her mother hates me," Garran grumbled.

Trying my hardest to ignore Perfectly Fine Freddie beside me, I reached up to take a hold of Garran's arms. "All right. Here is what you're going to do tonight. You are going to be polite. You are going to be clearheaded. You will *not* get drunk—"

"What?" His frown was almost as ridiculous as his smile had been, his lower lip sticking out a full inch. "Really?"

"Really."

"But Sunny"—he held up his bowl—"have you ever tried one of these? They are delicious."

"I'm certain they are," I said. "And after the ball, you can drink them to your heart's content. I'll even have some sent to your suite. But as long as you're in the same room as Kasa, you will remain sober. Eye on the prize, big guy."

"Fine," he agreed glumly.

"You will be polite and kind," I continued. "But you'll keep your distance. You will not ask Kasa to dance tonight. Instead, after the magic show, you'll ask *me* to dance with you."

"I will?" His big, bushy brows crashed into each other.

"Yes." I gave him a tight, decisive nod. "Kasa needs to see what she's missing. So you and I will put on our own show for her, and for her mother. And then, before the night descends into complete chaos, you will bid them good night, leave the ball, and get as inebriated as you desire alone in your suite."

A corner of Freddie's mouth tipped up, and I pretended that it didn't send shivers racing down my arms. "Devious plan," he said. "I like it."

"It sounds wrong," Garran insisted. "Would it not be better if I showed them how much fun I can be? I can be very fun."

"*No*," Freddie and I said at the same time.

"Garran, you want to be with Kasa, right?" I asked. "Not only for tonight, but forever?"

With his eyes glazing over while he stared at Kasa from across the room, he put a hand on his chest and said, "With all my hearts."

"Then you need to trust me. I know what I'm doing. If she doesn't come looking for you tomorrow, I'll eat my hat."

With a ground-shaking grumble, Garran set his fishbowl back on the bar and said, "I will trust you. But why would you eat your hat? I did not think beings from Tranquis ate clothing."

"It's only an expression," I replied, giving his arm a little pat.

The matter sorted—at least for the time being—I turned toward the stage. As the curtains drew back and spotlights flared on the Delphinian wizards readying to stun us with their tricks, I spotted Raphael sitting alone by the front of the stage, sipping a martini, as handsome as ever.

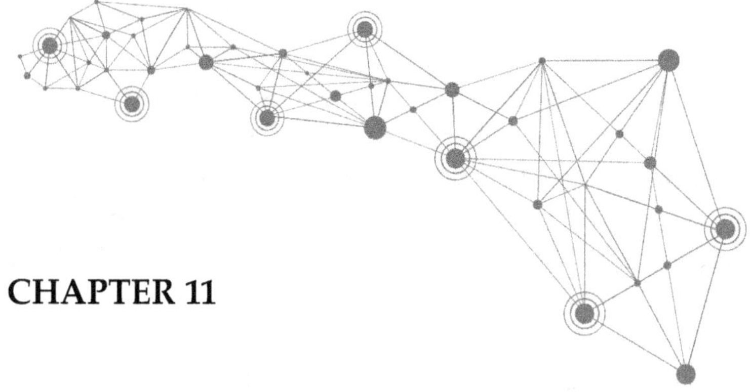

CHAPTER 11

"WHAT SHAPES OUR LIVES?" bellowed a lanky wizard in flowing robes who stood beneath a glowing spotlight, his arms sweeping over his head as yellow and orange flames erupted from his fingertips. "What inspires our destinies? What fills our dreams and fuels our passions?" His voice thundered through the sound system as he roared, "Magic!" to a wild onrush of applause.

Deafening techno music surged through the ballroom in driving, *oontz*ing beats that vibrated through my chest while twenty more wizards took the stage. I sensed a sharp tension radiating off Freddie's shoulders when the wizards began chanting incantations in time with the music.

<It's all right,> I commed him. <Tig promised, no dancing.>

He scanned the ballroom, wincing when his gaze landed on the bank of tables where that large party of frizzy-haired Gorbies sat. Three Gorbies stood from their seats, posturing with two of their four hands on their heads—which, on Gorbulon-7, was an indicator of outrage. Something like *you dare to flatten my hair!*

<Tig is wrong,> he commed back. <They're going to dance.

It feels like they're going to dance. Please don't dance. Please don't dance.>

Squashing my smile between my lips, I commed Tig. <No dancing, right? Freddie's about to rush the stage.>

<No dancing,> she replied. <Tell Freddie I've got his back.>

<Tig? How do they do it?> I asked as two wizards rose above the stage with fire shooting from their bare feet like rocket boosters.

<Do what?>

<The magic, you cheeky little pixie. Are you helping? Is it tech?>

<Sunny, have you ever considered that it might be real?>

<Of course not.> I scoffed. <Wait, are you serious?>

<Did you think I kept that pool on sixteen cursed all by myself? With effects? Why would I do that?>

<I don't know. I always figured they'd put sand guppies in the filters or something.>

<We replaced all the filters, the drains, everything. Not a sand guppy in sight. It's magic. Deal with it.> And with that, Tig clicked off the comm.

Leaning in close enough that Freddie's linen scent surrounded me, rudely taking advantage of the relationship between breathing and inadvertently smelling things, I said, "I'm going up front."

"Be careful," Garran shouted, making my ears whine. "I do not like magic. It is not natural." As if on cue, a dragon made of fire leapt from one of the wizard's hands, growing to the size of an Imperion gunship as it roared above the crowd. Garran's eyes slammed shut while he uttered some guttural Argosian oath, making the sign of the Tilth—his planet's three-pointed constellation thought to be the giver and taker of abundance—on his forehead.

After squeezing Garran's arm, I gave Freddie a tight and awkward smile, receiving a tight and awkward nod in return.

Then, taking a deep breath once I was out of Freddie's scent-range, I skimmed along the wall to move closer to the stage, and to Raphael. On my way, I spotted Chan staring up at the magic show with wide eyes and an even wider grin.

With her braids lashing through the air around her, Chan's mystery Delphinian summoned a ten feet tall ring of fire stage left while another wizard conjured an oorthorse made of light to leap through it. Before the oorthorse's hooves touched the ground, the animal exploded into thousands of tiny embers that flitted away toward the ceiling, winking out one by one.

Sneaking up beside Chan's hoverchair, I leaned in close. "She's lovely."

His head whipped toward me. "Sunny," he shouted over the music. "You scared the shit out of me."

I tilted my chin toward the stage. "Who is she?"

With a wistful glance at the Delphinian, he muttered, "Someone I don't stand a chance with."

If I was a genie, those would be the words that would summon me from my lamp. "Is that so?"

He nodded miserably.

Stooping to take his chin in my hand, guiding his attention to me for a moment, I winked and said, "We'll just have to see about that."

There was an unmistakable, if fledgling, gleam of hope in his eyes. "We will?"

"Chan," I said. "If it's what you want, I promise to do everything in my power to get you laid."

He snorted, his cheeks flaring redder than the fire rippling below his hoverchair.

After I kissed him on one of those blushing cheeks, I walked in long, determined strides toward Raphael's table.

<Sunastara Nex. As I live and breathe.> Raphe's deep voice sliding into my VC felt like sliding into a warm bath. This was exactly what I needed. A night of no-strings-attached fun. A

night to remind me of who I was, what I was good at. A night to move forward, even if I was really only standing in place. Semantics. *Whatever*.

His wry smile fell. <You don't look surprised to see me.>

Settling into the seat beside him, I explained into his ear, "Elanie."

"Hmm. She's usually better at keeping secrets."

Without warning, I burrowed my face into his neck and breathed him in. I probably seemed deranged, judging by his "uh, Sunny?" response. But this was important. It was important for me to remember that Raphael always smelled good too, like citrus and sandalwood, like comfort and familiarity. And he looked phenomenal: smooth black skin, dimples bracketing a neatly trimmed goatee, sharp brown eyes.

"I love that dress," he said, his lips brushing against my ear.

The sensation was nice. When by all rights it should have been exhilarating, erotic even, it was...nice. "I'm glad you came, Raphe. I'm sorry I have to work so late."

Leaning away, he commed, <Save me a dance? It's all I want.>

It was so *not* all he wanted, but he'd always been good at taking my cues, sensing my moods. <As soon as I'm finished making a lovesick Argosian appear irresistible, I'm all yours.>

He chuckled. <You do have the most fascinating job.>

After a quick brush of my lips over his cheek, I pushed my chair back, stood, then froze as a spotlight flooded our table. Raphe shot me a concerned glance, and I grimaced, realizing all too late that we were about to be part of the magic show.

<Tig,> I commed while the wizards gathered at the front of the stage, gesturing wildly at our table, uttering some indecipherable incantation that sounded nothing like *bears* or *butter*. <What is about to happen to us?>

<Oh no.> Tig's giggle trilled between my ears. <I should have told you not to sit there.>

<What? Why?>

"What is going on?" Raphe asked, his shoulders coiling and his body tensed like he might burst from his chair. Grabbing his hand, I held him in place.

<It's not that bad,> Tig commed. <It's just the—>

Before she finished her sentence, Dave the goat materialized out of thin air on top of our table, and I let out a little scream. Furiously flicking his tail, the goat met Raphe's wide-eyed stare, leaned forward until their noses touched, and bleated.

Shying away, Raphael cried, "What in hells is that?"

<Raphe,> I commed, trying my hardest not to laugh, but the whole thing was so absurd. <Meet Dave the goat.>

As quickly as he'd arrived, Dave blinked out of existence again. Only to reappear on another table, then behind the bar, then on some unsuspecting Blurvan's tail. The entire ballroom burst into squeals and laughter while the wizards deployed poor Dave as their grand magical finale, whisking him through the crowd.

Calmer now that he understood the gag, Raphe grinned, cheered the goat on, and said, "This is ridiculous."

It *was* ridiculous. So ridiculous I'd almost gained a new appreciation for the showmanship of Delphinian magicians.

As the wizards exited the stage, the applause died down. Dave the goat continued to wander around the ballroom like the most irritable party favor. And I left Raphael at his table with instructions to a nearby serving drone to re-up his martini.

Walking back to the bar, I looked up in time to catch Sai waving goodbye. I waved back as his moms led him from the ballroom—the senator holding his hand, Lena carrying a plate with a worryingly large piece of warple cake atop it, all of them smiling and laughing, the portrait of a happy, healthy family. My arm dropped to my side, my smile fading, my chest burning. My heart aching.

What was happening to me? I didn't do this. I didn't let my heart ache in public. Hardly even in private. I didn't look back like this. I didn't live in the past. I didn't dwell. Because life was hard. Terrible things happened every day. There was no fairness. I was not special. And I was not going to spend another second of this night feeling sorry for myself. Or, more to the point, feeling anything at all.

I spun on my heel but stopped short with a gasp, narrowly avoiding running face-first into Freddie's chest.

"That show was outstanding," he said brightly, pointing at Dave, who was busy licking an Aquilinian's dessert plate clean on a nearby table. "That goat bit was..." When he turned back to face me, all the brightness in him dimmed. "Sunny, are you all right? You look—"

"I'm fine," I snapped more than I'd meant to. But why was he asking me if I was all right? After what I'd done to him in the hallway, why did he want to talk to me at all? "I'm heading up to chat with Tig."

Giving me a thin, polite smile, he said, "And I'm off to congratulate the wizards."

Who was this man? How was anyone so unflappable? He should've been upset with me. Angry, bitter, anything. But he wasn't. He was entirely, perfectly, infuriatingly fine. And it was such utter bullshit!

When he turned away, my arm shot out before my brain could hold it back, my fingers grasping his forearm.

"Sunny?" He frowned down at my hand. "Did you need some—"

"Why did you ask me if I was all right?" I blurted out, ignoring the electric spark where my fingers wrapped around his tensing muscles. "After what I did, what I said to you, why do you care? Why aren't you pissed at me? Why don't you hate me? I mean"—I scoffed, fairly hysterical—"are *you* all right?"

Faster than I ever had before—possibly a worlds record—I

slammed my mouth shut. Because in the next blink, whatever wall of detached civility he'd built around himself came crashing down. His expression transformed, hardened, his eyes shadowed, as he slid his arm out of my grip.

Pulling my hand back, I held it against my chest, curled it over my pounding heart. I waited for him to say something, anything. But he only stared at me, his jaw clenched, his chest rising and falling with every silent breath. Until, with a dark growl, he bit out, "Am. I. All. Right?"

While the lights came up and softer, atmospheric Delphinian synthwave replaced the booming bass of the magic show techno, he took a single step back, shoved his hands into his pockets, and let me have it.

"Let's see, Sunny. Let's see if I'm 'all right.' Hours ago, I tried to kiss the woman I am out of my mind about in a public hallway because I thought she was trying to tell me something she wasn't. I stood there, begging her to give me a chance, *again*, even though I knew better. Even though I knew"—his eyes closed long enough that it couldn't be called a blink—"I *knew* she didn't want me."

When I opened my mouth—planning to tell him...what? That he was wrong? That I did want him? A hundred other things I shouldn't say because whether they were true or not, they wouldn't be fair?—he said, "And now I have to stand by and pretend that everything is normal, just perfectly *fine,* while knowing she's about to spend the night with another man. A man she *does* want. And to top off my shittiest day in recent memory, I can't even get drunk over it because I'm on the clock."

Forfeiting any distance he'd put between us, he stepped close enough that the flecks of blue in his gray eyes shone under the lights, his voice barely raised over a whisper. "I know I have no claim on this woman whatsoever, and she is free to be with whoever she chooses. But the fact that she isn't choosing to be with me tonight might actually be killing me. So to answer your question, Sunastara, no. No, I am very much *not all right*."

His words were an assault. Quick, darting jabs aimed at my chest. And I decided—clasping my hands behind my back to suppress the temptation to slap him, or possibly grab his face and disappear into his mouth—that his anger was wildly unfair. Only a moment ago, I'd been sinking into an endless pit of despair. But now I was abruptly, intensely, refreshingly enraged. "Now you listen here, Fredrick. I never once said—"

With a raised hand and an exasperated "pffft," he shut me down, turned around, and walked away.

The nerve.

"Hey! Stop!" I ran after him, grasping his forearm a second time, again ignoring the spark, the muscles. "You don't get to just *pffft* and walk away."

Wheeling around with fire in his eyes, he ground out, "Yes, I do."

"No, you don't."

"*Yes*, I do," he insisted. And when I opened my mouth to disagree again—because I'd be damned if he got the last word—his shoulders fell, all the fight leaving his body in a ragged breath. "*Christ*, Sunny. What do you want from me?"

In the silence that followed that question, I only stared at him. What *did* I want from him? I didn't know. He confused me, confounded me, made the ground beneath my feet slant sideways. I couldn't stand it.

"You asked me to back off," he eventually said. "So that's what I'm doing. But you don't get to dictate *how* I do it. You don't get to tell me you don't want to be with me, or to even try to be with me, then expect me to react exactly how you want me to. It's not fair."

As if gravity had instantly quadrupled, my mouth hinged

open, my jaw dropping. "I didn't... I haven't..." I sputtered out, my anger ebbing a fraction. Was he right? Was I being unfair?

"You want your space," he said, his voice strained. "And I really am trying to give it to you." His features softened as he reached for me, sliding the loose strap of my dress back up my shoulder. "I'm just doing a terrible job of it."

This time when he turned away, I let him go, watching on in a dazed, bewildered—and somehow also blisteringly aroused—silence as he paused on his way backstage to lean down and scratch Dave the goat between his horns.

Crossing my arms over my chest in an attempt to hold back the emotions warring beneath my ribs—anger, desire, confusion, annoyance, *did I say desire*?—I stomped across the ballroom like a petulant teenager. It was possible, I realized, that Freddie had a point. Maybe I was being unfair. I knew I wasn't perfect; you couldn't toss a rock on this ship without hitting one of my insecurities. And I'd accepted the blame for wearing that dress. I should have been more careful. But I had been crystal clear with him since his first day on this ship. It wasn't my fault he was upset with my choice to keep our relationship professional.

He was mad now, but his anger wouldn't last. Eventually, I had no doubt, he'd realize the atomic bomb he'd avoided by not being with me, and he'd be grateful.

Taking a deep but not very cleansing breath, yanking my dress strap up again because the fucking thing refused to stay put, I forged ahead through the crowd. I still had an Argosian love match to make, and nothing—not wizards or fire dragons or confoundingly gorgeous coworkers—was going to get in my way.

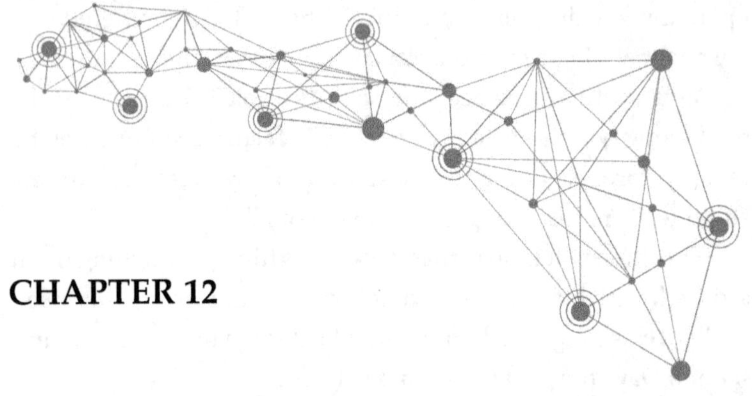

CHAPTER 12

GARRAN KNELT in front of Dave, feeding him happles—a Ulaperian fruit that tasted like New Earth apples but were shaped like smiling mouths, hence the name—from the hors d'oeuvres table and whispering to him in Argosian that he was a "very fine goat."

Clearing my throat, drawing his attention from his new barnyard friend, I said, "Hello, darling. Are you ready?"

Garran's purple eyes met mine, and when I tilted my head toward the dance floor, he stood, wiping his hands on his coveralls. "Are you sure about this?"

"Positive," I said. I might be an absolute disaster about some things, but this wasn't one of them. "I'll be out there, close enough to Kasa's table that she'll see me, but not so close that I'll seem obvious. As soon as the next slow song starts, come find me and ask me to dance."

He hefted his shoulders. "If you say so."

"Trust me, Garran. I'm a professional."

After giving me a slow, uncertain nod, he gazed down at Dave. "I enjoy this goat," he said, his lips tilting into a sideways grin. "I have many goats back on Argos. Their milk makes fine soap." When he turned toward Kasa's table, his tone softened. "I made soap for her once—jasmine and honeysuckle."

I sighed. *Must everyone on this ship be a hopeless romantic?* "You've got this, big guy. Just do as I say and follow my lead"—I gave him a wink—"and you'll be lathering her up in no time."

While his cheeks turned a dusky maroon, I left him with the goat and made another pass by Raphael's table. While Raphe ran his fingertips up my arm, I reminded my flailing mind that all I wanted tonight, or any night, was the simple pleasure of a wonderful time with a willing being and not a single string attached. Which, by the way, was all Freddie was supposed to be in the first place.

On my way back to the dance floor, I spied Captain Declan and Co-Captain Isla Jones making their appearance, strolling arm in arm through the fire. Isla was breathtaking, her dark-brown skin glowing against a stunning red satin gown, her hair down in tight spiral curls that bounced gently off her shoulders. She waved, and I waved back as Declan pivoted her toward the bar. Normally, I'd have followed them or asked them to come sit with Raphael and me when they were finished getting their drinks. But instead of doing any of that, I found myself in the middle of the ballroom ten minutes later, with Garran's arms slung low around my waist and his big, warm hands swaying me side to side.

It had been awkward at first, slow dancing with a being twice my size. But after the third song, I didn't even have to pretend I was having a nice time anymore. And while our performance wasn't necessarily genuine, when he spun me around in a circle, then dipped me nearly to the floor, the laughter that bubbled out of me was one hundred percent authentic. And maybe that was the touch that sealed the deal. Because before my laughter had fully faded, strong fingers tapped on my shoulder.

"Kasa," Garran said while his grip on my waist loosened, letting me slide free of his arms.

"Dance." The word was more demand than request. Kasa gave me an impressively withering side-eye as she edged me out. "Now."

While triumph surged through me—and also terror, because I'm pretty sure Kasa growled—I stood on my tiptoes, gave Garran a quick kiss on his cheek, and whispered, "One dance, then you leave," before getting the hells out of Kasa's way.

Garran pulled Kasa into his arms, and with a ghost of a smile, because at least one thing had gone right tonight, I made my way backstage to see if Elanie needed any help with cleanup.

Popping my head behind the curtain, I found Elanie sitting next to Chan and—*would you look at that*—that Delphinian female he'd been making heart eyes over. This was usually the point where I'd rub my hands together and start scheming all the ways I could get them together, but my hands were frozen at my sides, useless. Because across from Chan, with his suit coat open, his tie loose, and the top button of his shirt undone, sat Freddie. I stepped into view, and the smile that had been lighting up his face died like fire in a rainstorm when he noticed me.

"Sunny," Chan shouted, waving me over. "How are you?"

"Super," I lied. "I think this might be the best Fire Ball we've had since I came aboard."

"I saw Raphael out there. Nice of him to come, wasn't it?" Chan waggled his eyebrows, and I fought the urge to palm my forehead.

"I'm Sunny," I said instead, introducing myself to the Delphinian. "You were wonderful up there. And you have my undying gratitude for fixing my favorite pool."

While Chan found something fascinating to look at on his

hoverchair control panel, the Delphinian said, "I'm Makenna. Thank you. And it was nothing."

"Not according to every other magician from your planet who's tried," I said, taking the empty chair next to her. Turning her way, crossing my legs, doing everything possible to avoid looking in Freddie's general direction, I told her, "The show was phenomenal."

She beamed. "We've been preparing for ages. Really came together tonight, though." When she pulled her braids back off her shoulders, revealing her long, graceful neck, I didn't miss the way Chan sat forward in his hoverchair. I also didn't miss the way Makenna responded, her attention drifting toward him, her hands clasping in her lap, her lips tilting, hinting at a smile.

<Well done, Chan,> I commed. <I don't know how you've managed it, but she is absolutely feeling you.>

<No,> he commed back, toying with his control panel again. <She's just being nice.>

<She's just undressing you in her mind.>

<What?> His head snapped up. <She is? How do you know?
>

<It's as obvious as the stars. Keep doing whatever you're doing. Because it's working.>

Clicking off the comm, I rose from my chair and said, "Well, I'd better get back out there." Elanie seemed to have everything under control—and I seemed to have stumbled into a private party I felt somehow uninvited to. While I said my goodbyes—and despite my very best efforts not to let it happen—some invisible force grasped my head and turned it toward Freddie. Our gazes locked for an electric instant before his dropped like a stone to his shoes. The moment was over before it had even started, but the intensity of it crackled over my skin. And then the loss of it rolled over me like a wave, dousing everything in its path.

<What's wrong with you?> Elanie commed. <Why do you look like someone just died? Did someone just die?>

I loved her, but she really needed to learn a lesson about when to mind her own business. <I got my period,> I said, trying not to laugh at the utter horror contorting her features. <Heavy flow. Terrible cramps.>

After comming, <Hormones are horrifying,> with a body-wide shudder, she left me alone while I snuck out from behind the curtain with as little fanfare as possible. I didn't dare a single glance at Freddie even though I could feel him staring at me, like a hand on my lower back, fingers grazing across my neck. While a shiver tried to race down my spine, I strode with purpose across the ballroom and took the seat Raphe slid out beside him.

"Are you finally mine?" he asked, brushing his knuckles over my cheek.

"Yes," I replied, leaning into him, ignoring the restless ache in my heart, the magnetic pull tugging me behind the stage, back to where Freddie sat between a gap in the curtains, running a hand through his hair, laughing at something someone must have said, happier now that I was gone. "I'm all yours."

ALTHOUGH I COLLECTED hang-ups the way Morgath collected comic books, uncertainty had never been one of them. When faced with a dilemma, I followed my instincts, made my choice, put my head down, and never looked back. Tonight, however—after the Fire Ball unraveled into warple cake and ambrosia cocktail–infused mayhem, and we had to shut it down—there it was, slinking over my skin like mist off a mountain. Uncertainty. And I did not care for it one bit.

As Raphael led me from the ballroom, I glanced over my

shoulder, spying the crew making use of the dregs from the bar, the music, and the now empty dance floor to have their own party. Chan tilted his hoverchair from side to side with Tig in hysterics riding on his lap. Rax and Morgath stomped around in whatever bizarre moves passed for dancing in the ranks of the Aquilinian military. And Freddie laughed, his necktie looped around his head, Elanie holding the ends in her hand as she led him around the dance floor like a little lost puppy. A puppy I hadn't had the courage to say good night to.

"Sunny." Raphael winced. "You're squeezing my hand."

"Oh, sorry," I said. I hadn't noticed I'd been gripping him so tightly. The same way Freddie hadn't noticed me leaving.

Exiting the ballroom, uncertainty hanging heavily over my shoulders, I followed behind Raphael. Each step was slow, labored. Like trudging through the marshy depths of a Gorbulon-7 bog while it tried to suck you under. In the elevator up to the Afterglow suite, the sinking sensation intensified.

Raphael and I stood far enough away to fit at least two Blurvans between us. And as the decks ticked by, I couldn't stop thinking about a different elevator. A different man. When I stood as close to him as physics would allow. So close our hips touched, our shoulders. When his thumb brushed so softly over mine that I felt the ghost of it even now. When my body had needed his, ached for it. When I thought I might have screamed if he didn't—

"The captains are looking well," Raphe said, yanking me out of one elevator and into another. "I still can't fathom what brought them to the *Ignisar*. Did you know they were both New Earth Space Administration astronauts before they jumped to the private sector?"

I gave him a stilted nod. "Mm-hmm."

"Combined, those two have more space-walk time under their belts than any other New Earthers who've ever stepped foot into the big black. That they've settled for life as captain and co-captain of this ship is—"

"A bit of a head scratcher," I admitted.

Small talk. I was forcing Raphael—a brilliant, gorgeous, and entirely too-busy-to-make-small-talk man—to make small talk. *What is* wrong *with me?*

While panic rushed in, while my palms *and* my armpits started to sweat, the answer popped into my head. There was nothing wrong with me. I was fine. Totally fine. It had just been far too long since I'd gotten laid. That was all. Once I did, everything would make sense again. Everything would click back into place.

Edging close to Raphael, I skated my hands under the lapel of his suit coat. While his pecs tensed under my fingertips, I said, "It is good to see you, Raphe." *There. That was normal.*

With a glint in his eye, he purred, "It will be good to do something other than only see you." But then he closed the remaining distance between us, lowering his lips to mine, hovering only a breath away. And, *okay*, there was definitely something wrong with me, because I flinched, leaned back, contemplated faking a sneeze just to get out of kissing him. And I would have, one hundred percent, if the elevator doors hadn't chosen that moment to slide open.

"After you," Raphe said smoothly, waving me through.

Maybe he hadn't noticed the way I'd frozen up. Maybe I could swerve my weird mental block into some sort of kinky role play. The shy, inexperienced ingénue...or whatever.

The walk to the Afterglow suite took a planet's full rotation around its sun amount of time. Raphael followed a few steps behind me, but when I reached his door, he caught up, pressing the hard length of his body into mine.

Reaching his hand around me to place his thumb on the suite's security panel, he touched his lips to the back of my neck and said, "I've missed you, Sunastara."

When the door slid open, I practically did a dive roll away from him, racing to the bar like it was a raft bobbing in shark-infested waters.

"Sunny?" he asked, walking into his suite at a perfectly normal speed. "Is everything all right?"

"Oh, yeah." I gave him a dismissive wrist flick before pulling the cork from a bottle of dark Portisan rum some benevolent god had stocked his bar with. "Just thirsty."

"Okay." His brows slid together while I brought the bottle to my lips and started chugging. "Do you want a glass?"

Wiping my mouth with the back of my hand, I said, "I'm good."

He loosened his tie, undid his cuff links. "Give me a moment?"

Yes, absolutely, take all the moments. "Of course," I said before downing another swig.

While he disappeared into his bathroom, I spun around, sank onto one of the couches facing the flexGlass wall, buried my head in my hands, and groaned, "Fuck."

I didn't know what to do. I didn't know why—*am I getting sick? PMSing? Exhausted beyond all rational thought?*—but for some unknowable reason, I couldn't be with him. I just couldn't.

"Raphe?" I rose to my feet, head cocked, brow furrowed, when he returned from the bathroom. I'd been expecting him to come out swinging, gorgeous in a robe, maybe only his boxers. Definitely not in exercise shorts, tennis shoes, and a sporty hooded sweatshirt. "What are you wearing?" Maybe he wanted to role play too? Sexy athletic trainer meets sedentary party girl?

Pointing his chin toward the couch, he said, "Have a seat, Sunny."

He knew. *Stars save me*, he knew. I didn't know what he

knew, but he knew enough. Dropping onto his couch again, I shut my eyes and slammed my hands over my face.

"No." Sitting beside me, he pulled my hands down, one at a time. "Don't do that."

I kept my eyes shut, hiding. From him or from myself, I wasn't sure. "I'm so sorry, Raphe."

His hand slid over my cheek. "Open your eyes. Talk to me. Tell me what's going on."

I cracked one eye open, then the other, but I had no idea where to begin.

After I stared at him for a moment, failing to find my words, he asked, "How long have we been doing this, you and I?"

"Since I started working here." *Since tragedy shook my life to its core, and I ran away to this ship to hide from it all.* "Almost five years."

"Five years." He sighed, his lips pressing into a resigned smile. "Not a bad run. But I knew, eventually, it would come to an end."

"Nothing is ending. I'm just—"

Brushing my bangs back from my forehead, he said, "But maybe it should. End, that is. Maybe it's time to let go of whatever has been holding you back."

"What are you talking about?" I sat up, my heart lurching painfully into my throat. "Nothing's holding me back. I'm just tired. It was a long night. That's all."

He shook his head, rueful. "I always hoped I might be the one you'd choose, but that man—what was his name? Freddie?"

"Freddie?" I asked, looking at him like he'd made up the word.

"Yes," he said with a small, patient laugh.

"What about Freddie? There's nothing... We aren't... We're not together. At all."

"Are you sure?" he asked, a sleek brow raised. "Because he looked at you so many times tonight, I stopped keeping track."

I blinked, something light and bubbly fluttering in my stomach. "He did?"

"And you," he said slowly, like he was begging me to disagree, "couldn't take your eyes off him either."

Slumping back against the cushions, I relented, too exhausted to deny it. Plus, he was a lawyer. He'd see through me anyway. "I have been a miserable date."

He clicked his tongue. "Not my finest hour, I'll admit. I wanted to have you at least one more time before you left me."

Turning toward him, I took his hoodie in both hands and pulled, still trying to convince myself that none of this was happening. I was still Sunny, and he was still Raphe, and we still made sense together when nothing else did. "It's not too late," I said, even though we both knew it was.

Air rushed from his nose. "Sleeping with a woman while she's thinking of someone else isn't really my thing."

"Fuck," I groaned again. "Why is this happening to me?"

Taking my hands in his, he squeezed gently and said, "It happens to us all, eventually. If we're lucky."

"No." I shook my head in fierce denial. "It's not that. It's only an infatuation. It'll pass."

"In the five years I've known you," he said, cutting through my bullshit like a surgeon with a laser scalpel, "I have never, not once, seen you this affected by another being. I won't pretend to know the circumstances of your relationship with Freddie—"

Mind-blowing one-night stand that has left me in an utterly unraveled heap ever since.

"—but something like this doesn't come along every day, Sunny. It's fleeting and precious, and it should never, ever be ignored. Whether you want to be with him or not, for whatever reason, you should talk to him. Really talk to him. Because he feels something for you, I can tell. And if you feel something for him, you owe it to yourself, and to him, to tell him. At the very least, even if nothing comes of it, he'll know that he isn't losing his mind."

He was right. I'd been so unfair to Freddie, and to Raphe. But not without reason. "What if I can't? What if I'm too"—I summoned every ounce of courage I had in my entire body to utter the word—"scared?"

He cupped my face between his hands, brushed his thumbs over my cheeks, and gazed into my eyes. "You do what we all do when it's required of us. Be brave."

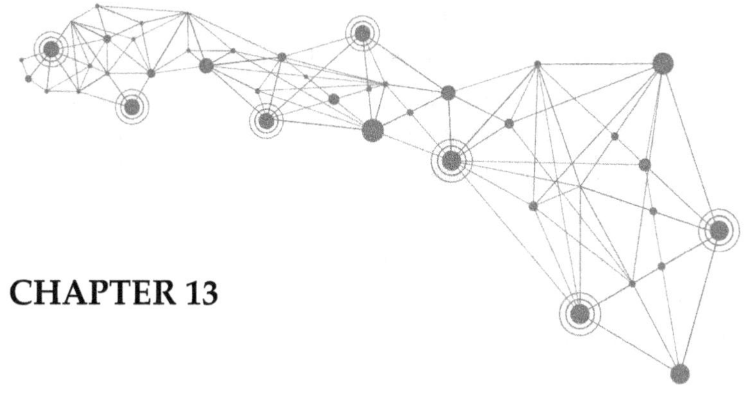

CHAPTER 13

After another hour in which Raphe helped me figure my life out, I left his suite, hugging him for a solid minute before he went to the gym to "work off some steam." Staggering numbly into the staff elevator, I pushed the button for deck twelve and swayed on my feet while the doors closed. It was late. Well, technically, it was early. I should be a good girl and go to my pod, get some sleep. But as the doors slid open, a strange and bitter clarity clawed its way to the surface.

Because I should be sleeping soundly in Raphe's arms, completely spent after a spectacular night. The fact that I wasn't, that I couldn't, was an issue that needed to be sorted out. Immediately.

Stomping down the hall, propelled by a renewed sense of purpose, I reached his suite, clenched my jaw so tightly something squeaked, and knocked three times on his door. It wasn't like I knew exactly what I was about to say to him; there was nothing poetic in the words bouncing around my head. But I had a general idea, a gist, a few salient points.

When he opened his door, however, wearing rumpled flannel pajamas with tiny bow ties all over them and a sleep mask pushed up onto his forehead, spiking his bangs, I violently shoved down what felt like the beginnings of a laugh.

"What are you doing here?" he asked, looking as surly as a being could look while wearing flannel bow tie jammies. "Let me guess. You haven't wounded me enough already tonight, so now you've come to gloat?"

"Excuse me?" I gasped. "No, I did not come to *gloat*. As a matter of fact, I have nothing to *gloat* about, thanks to you." Elbowing past him, I barged into his pod.

"Oh, well. Yes. Please. Come right on in, why don't you." He mashed his security panel, and his door slid closed. "I wasn't doing anything important like, I don't know, sleeping. And... wait. What did you say?" The sting slipped from his voice. "What do you mean you have nothing to gloat about?"

Wheeling on him, I flung out my arms in a frustrated arc. "What I mean is that despite my best efforts, nothing happened with Raphael tonight."

Freddie, wisely, didn't say a word.

"That's right. We were alone, in his room, two consenting adults. And I couldn't do it."

Sitting down on the edge of his bed, he said, "That's... interesting."

"Interesting?" I repeated, glaring down at him. "You think it's interesting that I couldn't sleep with a man I've been sleeping with—with much enjoyment—for the last five years?"

His shoulders inched toward his ears. "I mean..."

My eyes narrowed.

"What, uh..." He scratched his head. "What happened? Why couldn't you, um, do it?"

He looked so absurd in his pajamas, with his bangs pushed up by his sleep mask. Nobody could have a conversation like this. "I can't even take you seriously right now," I said, pointing to the mask. "Can you please take that ridiculous thing off?"

Wincing, he said, "Sorry." Then he slipped off the mask and

folded it neatly on his lap. While he ran a hand through his hair, I tried not to study the way his bangs slid back into place, the way the muscles of his forearm flexed, the way his veins traveled over his wrist like lines on a map. Either I didn't try hard enough, or—and more worryingly—when it came to Freddie, it didn't matter how hard I tried. I couldn't stop looking at him. I couldn't stop finding reasons to be closer to him. I couldn't stop wanting him. I couldn't stop.

What I was about to tell him was dangerous. And probably stupid. But sometimes, despite one's best efforts, the only thing left to do was the stupid thing. "What happened was," I began, clearing the tremor from my voice, "every time I looked at Raphael, every time he touched me, every time he merely breathed beside me, all I could think about, all I could see, all I could *feel*...was you. And, well, he didn't find that very appealing. Neither did I, for that matter."

His eyes were comically wide. "Sunny, I—"

I raised my hand. "I don't know what any of this means, Freddie. I wish I did, believe me. But one thing I do know is that I will not be an enjoyable person to be around if I can no longer have sex."

He laughed. The man actually laughed.

"You think this is funny?" I scowled. "This is humorous to you?"

For a moment, he had the decency to look ashamed. Until he burst into laughter again.

"Freddie!"

"I'm so sorry," he said, not looking sorry at all. "I realize this is a difficult time for you. But Sunny, you just told me you've been thinking about me. And considering how much time I spend thinking about you"—a smile tilted his lips—"you can't blame me if I'm a little happy right now."

Ignoring every rational thought still pretending it had any sway over me—and even though it felt like flying into the event horizon of a black hole—I took a step toward him. "I don't know what to do here, Freddie." I took another step. "But I'm thinking, maybe..." This next step brought me up to his knees, which he politely spread apart for me. After a small breath and one final step, I settled into the space between his legs. Maybe it was reckless, what I was about to suggest. But in that moment, in my sleep-deprived brain and orgasm-deprived body, it was the only thing that made sense. "If I can't have sex with anyone else," I said while his eyes found mine, his hands sliding up my thighs. "Maybe I can at least have sex with you."

He stared up at me, and aside from my thundering heart, an eternity of silence stretched out between us. In that silence, his fingers squeezed my thighs gently, sending a surge of electric heat through my chest, spiraling in my core, sparking into each one of my toes. His warm hands moved up my body, over my hips, his fingertips grazing my sides, and I moaned at the need rushing through me. But then, suddenly, he wrapped his arms around my waist, yanked me close, turned his cheek to rest against my belly, and said, so softly, so sweetly, "No."

What?

"No?" I repeated. "Did you just say no?"

"Yes."

"Wait." I stiffened in his arms. "Yes, you said no? Or no, you said yes?"

"I said no." He shook his head against my stomach. "No sex."

The sound that burst out of me was one I'd never made before, like a cat with laryngitis coughing up a hairball. "Are you kidding me?" I pushed against his shoulders, trying to break away, but he held me tight. "Let me go!"

"Wait," he pleaded. "Sunny, please. Let me explain."

"Explain what? That I'm being denied by two men tonight? Of all the preposterous horseshit."

His laughter rumbled against my belly.

I squirmed in his grip. "Stop laughing. This isn't funny."

"Stop fighting, and I'll stop laughing."

With an exasperated grunt, I tried for one last escape, met his resistance, and gave up. "Fine." I let my arms hang limp at my sides. "Get on with your explanation, then."

He turned his head, propping his chin on my stomach, and gazed up into my eyes. "Sunny," he said, while butterflies swarmed in my belly. "I can't have meaningless sex with you."

"Why not? We've done it before. And I believe we both found the experience"—my core gave a little flicker at the sense memory of his lips on my skin—"adequate."

"I can't have meaningless sex with you, because when it comes to you, I want more. I want to be more than a hookup. More than just another night. You can't sleep with other beings right now because of me. And I can't sleep with you, if that's all it is. I may have some self-destructive tendencies, and believe me, your offer is tempting me more than you'll ever know. But" —his arms loosened around me—"if anything ever happens between us again, I want it to mean something."

Despite my newfound freedom, I didn't back away, too busy cracking open, right down the center. I wanted it to mean something too, being with him. In another world, maybe it could. But in this one, it was impossible. "Freddie, I can't be what you want right now. I'm not—"

"I know, Sunny." He leaned back, settling his hands on the bed behind him. "I know there's something other than our jobs keeping you from wanting to be in a relationship. I won't ask you what that thing is, but I've been thinking about this. A lot, to be honest. And since you're here, since you haven't walked out on me yet, I might as well shoot my shot." His chest heaved through a fortifying breath. "I have a proposal for you."

"A proposal?"

He nodded once. "Yes."

I considered that for a moment, accidentally spending most

of that moment staring into his eyes, which pulled on me the way a planet pulled on its moons. Yanking myself free, I straightened to my full, unimpressive height and said, "All right. I will hear your proposal."

Slowly, his gaze sank, landing somewhere below my breasts. "I know you aren't looking for anything serious," he said, his voice soft and measured. "But I don't think I can stay away from you anymore. So what if there was a way we could be together, more than just sex, but less than a relationship. Not as Sunny and Freddie, but"—he paused for another breath—"as *them*."

"Them?" I asked, not following. "Them who?"

"Them. Phoebe and Joshua."

"Phoebe and Joshua?" I repeated, still not quite getting it.

His brow furrowed. "I know it sounds mad, but bear with me. Freddie and Sunny work together on this ship. They are professional, friendly, and in no way involved with each other. But maybe, after the workday ends, Freddie and Sunny could become Joshua and Phoebe, vacationing singles who've made an undeniable connection once and now want to feel each other out. See where things might lead."

I probably needed to say something, but nothing coherent came to me. This proposal... Either he'd gone completely sideways, or he was the most brilliantly seductive male in the entire KU.

"I thought I could be patient," he went on, despite my silence. "I thought I'd be able to stand by and wait until I charmed you so thoroughly you'd have no other choice but to give me a chance. But if tonight taught me anything, it's that there is not enough patience in the entire galaxy for me to withstand the idea of you being with someone else. Unless, perhaps, that someone else is me. Or another version of me, anyway."

There was a good chance I'd gone completely sideways too, because I started to imagine how it might go. A late-night movie at the Rialto, a walk along the promenade on deck twenty-eight, a dip in the pool on sixteen, a stolen kiss overlooking the atrium. It might be romantic. It might be fun, and I loved fun. A hidden romance, hidden lives, hidden pasts. It might not be real, but the real world was a place I'd been hiding from for years. It might be nice to have someone join me in the make-believe.

"Say something," he whispered, his breath warm on my belly. "Anything."

Sliding my fingers under his chin, I angled his face up to mine. "You must know how unhinged this sounds."

"I don't have a single hinge left," he admitted with a reserved grin. "But I think this could work, Sunny. Please, say yes."

Carefully, I ran my fingers through his hair. I didn't know if fingers had the capacity to feel relief, but considering how long mine had ached to touch his soft, thick strands, they practically sighed.

"Sunny still thinks it's"—*terrifying, risky, destined to end in heartache*—"absurd." I huffed a laugh as my brain, apparently pushed over the edge of some bottomless cliff, plummeted into the void. "But Phoebe thinks it's one of the best ideas she's ever heard."

Wordlessly, but with a deep, easy sigh, he pulled me in, holding me as close as he'd held me before. Only this time, the thought of trying to get away never crossed my mind.

Leaning over him, I buried my nose in his hair, breathing in his linen scent, and something else, vanilla and lavender. Once again, mouth-wateringly edible. And then, with our plan firmly in place and any lingering uncertainty scampering back into whatever dismal cave it had emerged from, I hiked up my dress, climbed into his lap, and started unbuttoning the top button of his ridiculous jammies.

"Sunny." His fingers closed around my hips.

"It's Phoebe now," I said, slipping another button free. "Remember?"

Reaching for me, he stilled my hands. "Stop."

"Stop?" I frowned. "Why?"

"I, um..." Color rushed into his cheeks. "*Joshua*, I mean, would like a chance...to—"

"Yes?" I encouraged, high on need, short on patience.

He took a deep, steadying breath. "He would like a chance to...*woo* Phoebe."

While my eyelids grew heavy with desire, or maybe exhaustion—it was impossible to tell at this point—I brushed my thumb over his lower lip, and said, "That ship has sailed. No wooing required, promise."

Grasping my hand to kiss the tip of my thumb with an achingly sweet tenderness that melted my skin, he said, "Joshua disagrees." Abruptly, he stood from the bed, taking me with him, and set me on my feet. "Therefore, respectfully, I will need to ask you to leave."

The disappointment tumbling through me must have been noticeable, based on the way he raised his hands and said, "I don't think you'll have any regrets. Not to toot his own horn, but Joshua is pretty good at wooing."

I scoffed. "Did you just say, 'toot his horn'? Are you actually eighty? And how highly skilled?"

While his smile skewed into an impossibly charming smirk I felt suddenly compelled to kiss right off his face, he said, "You'll just have to wait to find out."

Had I ever wanted another being as badly as I wanted him right now? I had, I realized. Him, months ago in that elevator, tasting those chocolate-covered cherries on his tongue. He thought I needed to wait. I thought I'd waited long enough. Time to play hardball.

Pushing up to my tiptoes, I brought my mouth close enough to his that we shared the same breath. "How long?"

His resolved wavered, teetering like a glass about to fall and shatter. "Not long," he ground out, staring at my lips, his hands sliding up my arms.

If I was a betting woman, I'd put everything I owned or ever would own on winning this kiss. Let me point to his darkening eyes, his fingers closing around my arms, his tongue slipping out to wet his lips. I had it. It was mine. Take a bow.

But a second before our lips met, he stepped back, spun me around, and ushered me briskly toward the door. "But tonight," he said, all business, no play, "Joshua needs his beauty rest. He has sonnets to compose. Or dirty limericks at the very least."

I wanted to object, tried to, but he had me out in the hallway in a blink, waving with a tight "good night," before he retreated back into his pod and slid his door shut.

My head swimming, heart pounding, mouth smiling so wide it hurt a little, I stood outside his door, waiting. I couldn't seem to leave. I didn't want to leave. I was *not going to leave*. Not without something. I only had to knock once, and his door slid open.

"Yes?"

Of course my brain would choose this precise moment to succumb to the turmoil of the day and blank out. "Um, well," I said, stalling. "Oh, how do you think they did that trick? The one with the goat?"

He stepped toward me, just close enough to slide the strap of my dress back up my shoulder and not an inch closer. But when he did, I angled my head away from his fingers, elongating the slope of my neck. *Phoebe knows a thing or two about wooing too, Joshua.*

With an audible swallow, he lowered his hand and said, "No clue. Let's ask them later. Good night, or good day, I suppose," he stammered before backpedaling into his pod and closing his door again.

Damn. Bet lost. No kiss.

Carrying a mountain of sexual frustration but a helium-light heart, I turned and started walking toward my pod. I wasn't two steps away, however, when his door whooshed open again, and he emerged, muttering "fuck it" before grabbing my wrist, pulling me back inside, taking me into his arms, and kissing me.

His mouth was hot and greedy, and I moaned into it, grasping at him with frantic fingers, pulling him closer, craving as much of him as he would give me. The kiss was hungry, ravenous as his arms wrapped around me, as he lifted me off the floor, one of my shoes slipping off my foot to tip onto its side on his carpet. He slipped his tongue into my mouth, and somehow, through the demanding, blistering heat of the kiss, it was soft, gentle as it caressed mine.

I shuddered in his arms, burned, nearly combusted. Then, mercifully, like the sky right after the sun sank below the horizon, the fiery red surge of the kiss cooled to soft streams of violet, blue, pink. His hand rose to cradle my head, his fingers firmly supporting its weight, and everything slowed as he deepened the kiss, pulling me down with him, setting my feet back on the ground.

I was sure that, by now, I'd experienced every known variety of kiss, but I was wrong. This kiss was a novel species, an unidentified element, an uncharted star I would place my finger over in the night sky and proclaim, *this one here, this is mine.*

When we parted, our chests heaving, our foreheads touching, he said, "Sorry. I couldn't help myself."

Nestling into the space between his neck and shoulder, I rested my cheek on the soft, adorably bow-tied fabric of his pajamas. While he held me, he breathed in a slow, hypnotic rhythm that pulled my eyelids lower and lower with every exhale.

"You should go to bed before you fall asleep here in my

arms," he said, his lips brushing the shell of my ear. "Do you want me to carry you there?"

Still not entirely trusting myself or him or our *arrangement*, I shook my head, slipped my foot back into my shoe, and let him walk me to his door.

When I somehow made it to my pod without falling asleep on the way, I stripped off my dress, bra, and panties, then crawled onto my bed and collapsed. Before unconsciousness claimed me, however, I slid my hand under my pillow, finding the coil of Joshua's necktie. Pulling the tie out of its hiding place, I unraveled it and looped it around my neck, falling asleep wearing his tie, a smile, and nothing else.

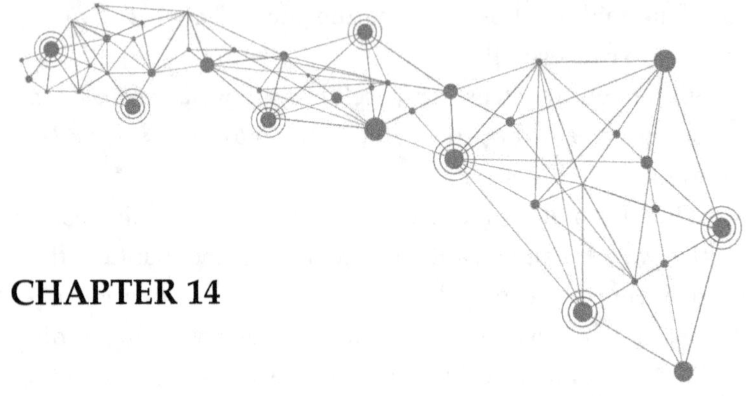

CHAPTER 14

AFTER SNATCHING a scant three hours of sleep, I walked, bleary-eyed and fuzzy-headed, to the bistro on deck thirty for my date with Tig—that I would have absolutely slept through if Elanie hadn't commed me to <*get up*!> thirty minutes ago.

Designed to resemble those found along the Old Earth rue de la Paix in Paris, the bistro was quaint and quiet, with black-and-cream-checkered floor tiles and wrought-iron tables covered with crisp, white tablecloths.

"Sunny," Tig called out, half-obscured by a tiered tray of sliced baguettes, brioche, and delicate pastries. She sat beside a window that overlooked a weather-controlled biogarden bursting with violets, lilies, and magnolias, and ringed by cherry trees in perpetual full bloom. "I was worried you might not come."

"I'm not late, am I?" I asked, stooping to kiss her cheek.

"No, but I was still worried. I'm always worried, I guess," she said with a brittle laugh.

"Darling, the effects last night were spectacular. And I wouldn't miss celebrating your success with you for anything in all the worlds." Despite my genuine enthusiasm, when I sat heavily in my chair, I did it wishing it was my bed. "Did you sleep?" I asked, scanning the bistro for a serving drone, needing caffeine more than oxygen.

"Yeah," Tig said, slathering a flaky croissant in honeyed butter. "For a few hours, anyway. But I'm wrecked."

Moaning in gratitude as a serving drone set a kettle of steaming water, fragrant teas, and two cups of espresso with tiny cherry blossoms worked into the foam on our table, I reached for a cup.

"You can have mine too." Tig nodded toward the espresso. "Caffeine makes me jittery."

Corralling both cups of espresso in front of me, I downed one in two gulps. Then I plucked a macaron from the tray and took a bite. It was crispy and sweet, filled with a buttercream that tasted like figs and almonds. "Stars, Tig. This is the most delicious thing I've ever had in my mouth." The statement was, I realized, utterly false. But I always did my best to—*not think about that kiss, about his soft lips and softer tongue*—behave myself around Tig. Innuendo tended to make her break out in hives.

"I know, right?" Tig said, pouring hot water over a sachet of bright-green tea leaves, the sharp tang of ginger and lemongrass rising into the air. But when she brought the cup of tea to her lips, I didn't miss the tremor in her hand. It was possible she was only tired, but she seemed more distracted than usual, her eyes darting around the bistro, her other hand clenching the napkin next to her plate.

"Is everything all right?" I asked while selecting a cream puff from the tray. "Is there something on your mind?" I popped the entire puff into my mouth, my soul briefly departing my body from its warm, soft perfection.

"I'm not sure." Her lips twisted, her brows inching together. "Maybe. Maybe not."

"That sounds like a *yes* to me."

Glancing around again, she lowered her voice. "Could be nothing. It's probably nothing."

"Good grief, Tig. You're as white as a sheet. What happened?"

"Okay," she said in a whisper, leaning halfway over the table. "But you can't tell anyone."

I swiped a finger across my heart. "Go on."

"Last night, I was running an unscheduled security sweep on the ship's data streams prior to the ball. Just a precautionary measure considering the amount of computing power all the effects required. Anyway, I found something...odd."

"Odd?" Now I was intrigued. "How odd?"

Leaning even closer, she said, "Over the last couple of weeks, someone off-ship has been accessing our manifests, as well as our guests' itineraries."

"Could it be corporate?" I asked. "They do that sometimes, don't they? The eye in the sky making sure we're toeing the line and all that?"

"That's the thing. It isn't necessarily out of the norm for LunaCorp to access our manifests, although it doesn't happen regularly. What's odd is that while these recent breaches do have LunaCorp credentials, they're all expired, and the origins are all wrong."

"How so?"

She shrugged. "They're not from Luna or the CAK or New Earth or Mars or any location that a legitimate LunaCorp access would conceivably come from."

Tig's concern must have been contagious, because a sudden need to look over my own shoulder gripped me. "Where are they coming from?"

"For the life of me, I can't tell." She ruffled the pink strands of her hair. "The origins are untraceable, and if I were to do any deeper digging, I'd quickly become...conspicuous. If you catch my drift."

That, I understood. If a being wanted to keep their job, the last place they'd ever want to be was on LunaCorp's radar. "Have you spoken about this with Chan? Or Rax and Morgath? The captains?"

"No. Not yet. I need more information first. That's why I don't want you to tell anyone. Honestly, like I said, it's probably nothing. Just an aberration." She took a tiny bite of her pastry, then set it back down on her plate.

"An aberration," I repeated, icy fingers brushing across the nape of my neck. And while we found other things to talk about, neither of us ate much more after that.

I left the bistro worried, but the exhaustion pouring lead into my feet quickly gained supremacy in my list of immediate concerns. I needed sleep, otherwise I'd have to visit the med bay and beg Dr. Semson for stims just to make it through the rest of the day.

After my door slid open, I staggered into my pod, gazed at my bed like it was an oasis in the middle of a Neptune desert, and made a solemn vow to worry in full as soon as I woke up. But when I took a step, something in the middle of my floor tried to trip me.

"What the?" I said, looking down. It was a box. A gift box, to be exact. And the card tucked into its red satin ribbon had a single, eye-opening word scrawled across the front: *Phoebe.*

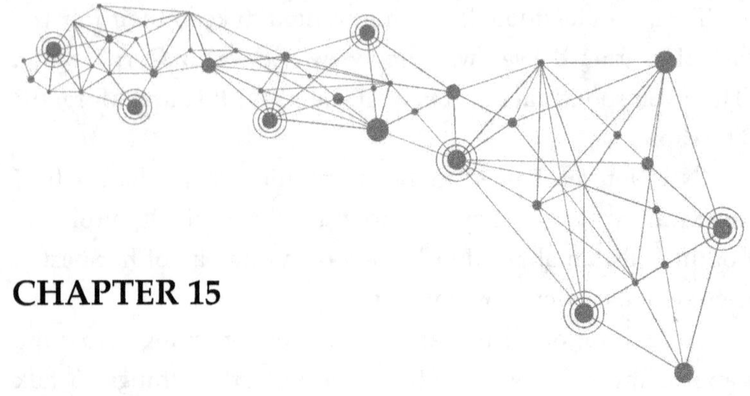

CHAPTER 15

SITTING ON MY BED, I turned the card over and stared at the opening line, tracing a finger over its slightly slanted letters.

> *My dearest Phoebe,*
>
> *A little bird told me you had to wake up early this morning. On the off chance that you have time to nap later today, I hope these might help you sleep. Tonight, if you're feeling up to it, is there any chance you'd like to meet up with me? Dinner and drinks? My treat.*
>
> *Respectfully yours,*
> *Joshua*
>
> *P.S. I can still feel your lips on mine. Still taste them, even sweeter than I remembered, like honey. Please say yes.*

After pressing the card to my chest for a moment—for

reasons I couldn't quite explain—I set it down beside me, pulled the red ribbon free, and raised the lid on the box. Inside, covered in a thin layer of white tissue paper, I found a soft, thick pair of cream-colored Venusian wool socks and a sleep mask identical to the one he'd been wearing when I'd stormed into his pod in a hot swell of indignation. Holding the mask to my nose, I breathed in the same vanilla and lavender scent I'd noticed on him then. Maybe it was the sweetness of the aroma, or the sweetness of the gift, but I suddenly had a very hard time remembering why I'd been so upset with him to begin with.

Stripping out of my clothes, I rolled on the socks, put on my favorite nightshirt, inhaled the sleep mask one more time, and crawled into bed. Opening the *Squee* app in my VC, I found Joshua's profile and clicked *chat*.

> Phoebe: This might be the most thoughtful present I have ever received.

I awaited his reply for one minute, two, my patience fraying around the edges. I'd almost given up when a message from *Squee* popped into my vision: **Joshua is requesting a video chat. Do you accept?**

After scrambling to find the techPad on my bedside table so frantically I chipped a nail, I assumed my most convincing *I'm just lounging on my bed, not at all losing my shit over a pair of socks* pose and clicked on the incoming *Squee* call. "Hello, darling," I said after he appeared on my screen.

"You like them?" he asked. His face was dark, barely lit.

"Where are you? I can hardly see you."

His grin was impish. "I'm hiding in a utility closet. I've been reading in the library."

"This ship has a library?"

He chuckled. "It's not much bigger than this closet. But it does. And I never thought I'd know something about this ship that you didn't."

I took that one on the chin. "What were you reading?"

"Oh, nothing much. Poetry, mostly."

"Poetry?" Why did this make me bite my lip? "Anything notable?"

His gaze sank to my mouth, lingering there, and I felt it like a live wire wrapping around my heart. "There was this one verse. It's from a poem by a Portisan empath named Lurian, about sleep, ironically."

"Read it to me?"

"Okay. Let me find it again." He glanced down at the book in his hand, his techPad bobbling while he flipped through the pages, showing me his chin, his throat, his chest covered by a crisp white button-down. Repositioning the techPad, he swept his bangs back off his forehead and recited,

"I feel the change in your breath
a whisper after the storm
and in your dreams we float on our backs
while I vow to love you forever
under these stars that formed us
so long ago"

"Hmm." I sighed, sinking back onto my pillow. "That's lovely."

"It is." He set the book down, bringing his techPad closer. "You look beautiful," he said, his eyes glittering in the darkness. "But a bit tired."

I laughed, appreciating his diplomacy. "I'm sure I look more than a bit tired. But now that I have this"—raising my hand, I dangled his sleep mask from my fingers—"I think I might finally get some sleep."

He cleared his throat. "Did you get the socks too?"

"I did."

"Are you...wearing them?" he asked, his pupils dilating.

"I am."

"Can I see?"

Standing from my bed, I propped my techPad on my dresser, then moved far enough away that my body filled the frame. I teased the hem of my shirt, raising it just enough to reveal the top of the socks. They were so long they reached above my knees.

"Good lord." He bit his knuckle. "That is the single sexiest thing I have ever seen in my entire life."

I snorted, looking down at my fuzzy, wool-covered legs. "You are a strange man." I raised my shirt a bit higher. "But I think I have something you might find even sexier."

"Wait. What are you doing?" he said in a flustered rush.

"What do you think I'm doing?"

"Sun—Phoebe, I mean. Don't. You shouldn't. *I* shouldn't."

"You want me to stop?" I teased, sliding my shirt up an inch higher, and then another. "What are you afraid of, Joshua? It's not like anyone can see you, all alone in your little closet."

He pressed his lips together, stifling a moan. "Yes, but 'The *Ignisar*'s new L&C Gets Caught Masturbating in Closet' is not a headline I ever want to see."

"Really?" I said as my shirt reached the tops of my thighs, so close to revealing the soft curls and smooth skin between my legs. "Sounds like a stimulating read to me."

His eyes slammed shut. "If I am ever fortunate enough to see you naked again, it will not be on my damned techPad. You need to get some sleep. And I need to go to my pod to take another cold shower."

"Another?"

With his eyes still closed, he admitted, "Yes." When he cracked a lid, finding me back on my bed, all covered up like a good girl, he asked, "Dinner tonight?"

Maybe it was the fatigue. Maybe it was the poem. Maybe it was just...him. But I didn't hesitate to answer, "Yes."

"Good." He ran a hand through his hair, like he was trying to make himself presentable again, even though I'd hardly begun to take him apart. "I'll pick you up."

Before he clicked off the call, I said, "Wait. Should I wear these socks?"

His sexually frustrated groan was the last sound I heard before I passed out cold.

A WALL-SHAKING *BANG, bang, bang* wrenched me from a blissfully deep and dreamless sleep. Pushing my sleep mask off and tossing it onto the pillow beside me, I rolled off my bed. "I'm coming," I tried to call out, my voice a scratchy croak as the fist banged again. "Please stop trying to break my door."

"Oh, sorry," someone boomed through the battered panel.

I knew that boom. Stumbling across my pod, I hit the door sensor, shielding my eyes from the light pouring in from the hallway as it slid open, revealing— "Garran?" I said, squinting up at him. "How did you know where to find me?"

"Your pink-haired friend told me which pod was yours. Before she ran away." He grimaced. "I think I frightened her."

As my eyes adjusted, I looked him over. He was so tall he'd have to duck if he wanted to come inside. So broad he'd have to step through the door sideways. "Well, I suppose you can be a touch intimidating."

When he looked me over, head to toe, he grinned. "Oh, those socks are very fine. Very warm. They would get you through a full winter on Argos."

"Thank you," I said, my cheeks heating for some absurd reason. "They were a gift. What can I do for—"

"A fine gift," he interrupted, his grin spreading like a sunrise. "Very thoughtful."

I had to bite my damn lips between my teeth not to grin myself. "I suppose it was. Do you want to come in?"

"No." He peered past me into my pod. "I would not fit. Can we talk out here? It will not take long."

"Of course. How can I help?"

For such a large male, Garran did sheepish modesty better than anyone I had ever met. "Kasa has asked if I would like to go dancing with her, alone, this weekend."

"Dancing? That's wonderful."

"I do enjoy dancing," he said with a nod. "But I have never been on a date. With a female. On purpose. I do not know what to do."

There was no point in trying not to grin anymore, so I patted his gigantic arm and said, "Not to worry, big guy. I've got you."

AFTER A BRIEF but insightful chat with Garran about his dating concerns, I got dressed, then commed Freddie. <I am awake. It is>—I accessed the time—<seventeen hundred. And I just had the most fascinating conversation with our favorite Argosian.>

He responded almost instantly. <Good afternoon. About?>

The professional response was a relief. I liked knowing we could keep things separate—work and play, business and pleasure. Clear lines drawn in molten lava. <Kasa has asked him on a date this weekend.>

<Good man.> Laughter rang through his voice. <He's feeling unsure of himself, I gather. If he came to find you.>

<That is correct. I could use your help. Care for a late night this weekend?>

After a brief moment, <A late night working, you mean.>

I took my own moment. An evening spent hiding behind the scenes, turning Garran into Argos's most eligible bachelor, could be fun. It could be romantic. But it was also clearly work. <Yes, that's right. Working.>

<Then I am at your disposal.>

<But do me a favor?> I commed, detecting the hint of disappointment in his tone.

<Anything.>

<Please let Joshua know that Phoebe is looking forward to seeing him for dinner tonight.>

His low laughter rumbled over the comm, the vibrations sinking straight into my core. <As soon as he stops fantasizing about how soft Phoebe's lips are, I will.>

I HAD JUST STEPPED out of a scalding shower when a comm from Chan came through.

<Sorry to bother you on your day off, Sunny. But something's come up.>

His tone was dire, tinged with apology, which only meant one thing. While I swiped my hand through the steam on my mirror, Phoebe watched date night with Joshua slip like sand through her fingers. <Hello, Chan. How can I help?>

<Senator Ramesh has been called in for an emergency meeting of the KU senate, and her wife has gone off-ship briefly due to a family emergency.>

A cold sweat broke out Pavlovian-like across my forehead, my face going from shower-blushed pink to a waxy pale in the mirror. <Leaving Sai alone,> I commed, silently pleading with the universe that he wouldn't ask me to—

<Can you watch him? You're the only crew member available who's even slightly qualified to babysit a child.>

I inhaled sharply, my cold sweat freezing to ice in my veins. Because what was he talking about? How would he have any idea what kind of experience I'd had with children? Did he know something?

<You did such a stellar job watching over those Martian movie star brats last month,> he explained, settling my heart rate a few beats per minute. <A ten-year-old boy should be a walk in the park by comparison.>

Leaning forward, resting my elbows on the sink, I tried to catch my breath. He didn't know anything. Of course he didn't. Because I'd never told him anything. I'd never told anyone anything. <I'm not very good with children,> I lied.

<Please, Sunny. I'd ask Elanie, but she watched him the other day, and, evidently, it didn't go well. Sai told his moms that she sat on the couch and scowled at him the entire time. Except for when they tried to play Galactic Ship Builders and she stole all the pieces, built an F1 hypercraft, and made Sai pretend to be her pit crew for two hours while she became 'the first bionic to win the Worlds Championship.'>

A snort slipped through my dread. <That's Elanie for you.>

<Senator Ramesh should be back before midnight,> Chan went on. <I'd watch Sai myself, but I have a meeting with the captains in an hour.>

Maybe it would be okay. Maybe I was ready to spend some time with a child again. Maybe, it might even be fun. *Be brave, Sunny. Be brave.* <Of course, Chan. What time do I need to be there?>

<Would right now work?>

<You bet.>

So much for date night.

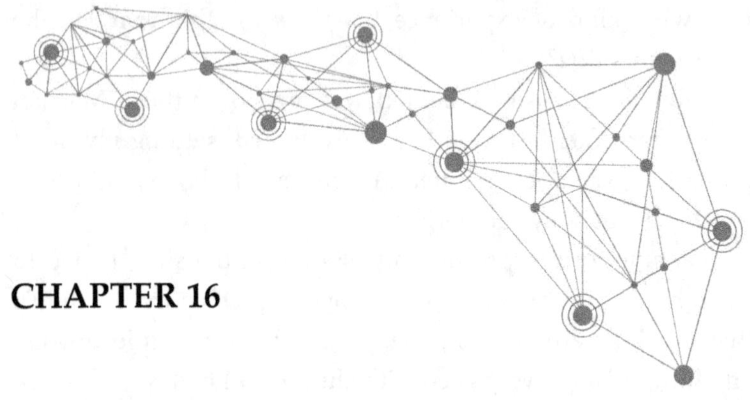

CHAPTER 16

When I commed Freddie that Phoebe was no longer available for dinner, he was surprisingly understanding. On second thought, it wasn't surprising at all. Because of course he understood. Of course he wouldn't have read my silent, telepathic cues to somehow save me from this situation by being demanding or upset or any number of things he would never be. It was hopeless, I realized while standing outside the Ramesh suite. I wasn't getting out of this.

I puffed out my cheeks, raised my hand, and watched the door slide open before I'd had a chance to knock.

"Hi, Sunny," Sai said, waving up at me. He wore faded jeans and an oversized yellow hoodie, his feet still bare. "Chan told me you'd be coming, so I've been watching the Vcams, waiting for you."

"And here I am." I bowed deeply. "At your service."

His smile when I stood up straight was all teeth. "Come in. Have you had dinner?"

"Not yet. You?"

Bouncing into his kitchenette, he pulled a dish out of the fridge. "No, but my mom made me some palak paneer before she left. It's *so* good. Want some?"

The dish he set on the counter smelled incredible. "I don't think I've had that before."

"Really? It's my favorite. But"—his lips pulled to the side, his eyes hiding under his thick lashes—"ever since the incident with the tart, my moms won't let me use the instaWave."

"Ah, well," I said. "That's simple enough."

After successfully warming the dish without any fire suppression required, I sat with Sai at the counter. The food was spicy, creamy, and absolutely delicious. It paired surprisingly well with the gigantic glass of lemonade he'd poured into a bright-blue tumbler and set in front of me.

"Stars, Sai. This is amazing."

"Right? I knew you'd love it."

"Tell me, what is this?" I raised my spoon, which held a small white square of something buttery and delectable.

Studying the object with a deeply furrowed brow, he said, "I think it's cheese. But I'm not sure."

I popped the probably-cheese into my mouth. "Well, it's phenomenal. And this"—I raised my glass—"is the best lemonade in the entire KU."

He beamed. "I made that. I made the lemonade."

Pride radiated from him like starlight. His expression, his smile, his unbridled joy, I'd seen it before, so many times it was stamped onto my mind like a footprint. And yet, somehow, I'd forgotten it. How could I have forgotten that? How could I have forgotten one single thing about Jonathan? *Stars save me*, what else had I forgotten? What else was hiding from my mind and my heart, only waiting to resurface when the universe randomly chose to remind me?

I set down my spoon, my hands suddenly trembling, my throat spasming. I closed my eyes, but no matter how hard I tried, I couldn't catch my breath, couldn't slow my racing heart.

"Are you okay?" Sai asked. "Is it the lemonade? Is it too sweet? My moms always say I make it too sweet. But I can't help it. I just like it better that way. I'm sorry if you don't like it. I can get you something else. NearMilk? VitoWater?"

This was a mistake. I shouldn't have agreed to watch him. I knew it would be too much. My mouth went dry and my fingers tingled as white light crowded the edges of my vision. Next came the dizziness, the nausea, the buzzing sensation vibrating behind my forehead, into my chest, my legs.

"I'm fine, Sai," I managed, sliding off my stool. "I just ate too quickly. Please excuse me. I'll only be a minute."

Not wanting to scare him, I did everything I could to walk calmly to the bathroom. Closing the door, I flipped down the toilet seat cover, sat, and bent forward, squeezing my head between my knees. "You're all right. You're all right. You're all right," I whispered, chanting it, trying to make it true. But I was not all right. I would never be all right. Maybe if I could breathe, if I could get to one of the ship's sensory rooms and drown everything else out. Maybe if I could at least cry, just once, even a single tear—

<How's the babysitting going?>

His voice in my head sent me reeling. I rocked back, grasping the edges of the toilet, clinging to the sensation of the cool porcelain underneath my numb fingertips.

<Freddie. Please. I need help.>

<What is it? What's wrong?> he asked, suddenly stern, serious as death. <Is it the boy? I'm on my way.>

<Wait. Stop. It's not Sai. It's only me. I...I'm having a panic attack. It's bad. I can't breathe.>

<Ah. I see.> He hummed over the comm. <All right. Where are you now?> His voice was quiet and slow, serene. It settled over my mind like a heavy blanket. <Do you want me to come? >

<I'm hiding in the bathroom. And no, you don't need to come. But...don't leave me, okay? Don't click off yet. Talk to me. Just talk to me, please.>

<I'm not going anywhere, Sunny. I'll talk to you all night long if it's what you need.>

<I won't need all night.> At least I hoped I wouldn't. <Just a few minutes, and it'll settle.>

<Well then, let's see.> There was a brief silence. <Here's something. Have I ever told you about the sea lion population on Venus?>

<No. I don't think so,> I replied, coaxing small sips of air into my lungs. A moment passed, and then another. Too much silence. <Freddie, are you still with me?> I asked, my panic spiking.

<Sorry. I'm here. I'm with you. I just had to take care of something. Where was I?>

<Sea lions.>

<Right. When LunaCorp terraformed Venus, the sea lion introduction program went a bit round the bend after their natural predators—namely sharks and whales—didn't fare as well in the harsh early climate on the planet. As a result, the sea lions thrived.>

<That's interesting,> I managed, struggling to focus on his centering voice rather than my heart's insistence on bruising my ribs.

<When the first settlers arrived from Old Earth Europe,> Freddie continued, <they had no idea what to do with the literal millions of sea lions crowding the coastlines. Some they ate, others they made furs from, but they quickly realized that there was something strange about the Venusian sea lion.>

Carefully pushing myself upright, the dizziness and tingling ebbing a fraction, I commed, <What was different about them?>

<I am so glad you asked,> he said brightly, and impossibly, my lips curled up at the corners. <While the sea lions of Old Earth were not necessarily violent toward humans, they were far from friendly. The sea lions on Venus, however, were quite

fond of the settlers. They'd come up onto the shore for pats on their noses, ride the ocean waves for applause and treats, and roll over in the sand for belly scratches. It wasn't long before the settlers stopped killing them and started taking them home as pets instead.>

Air puffed through my lips. Not quite a laugh, but getting there. <Is any of this true?>

<Of course it's true,> he commed in feigned shock. <You see, in the initial cloning and breeding program, something incredible happened.>

<Incredible?> I asked doubtfully.

<Yes. Do you want to know what it was?>

Leaning to the side, pressing my cheek into the cool tile wall, coaching myself through a slow, deep breath, I commed, <Tell me.>

<Well, somehow—and nobody has ever figured out when it happened, or who's to blame, or where it started—>

<Tell me,> I insisted, my impossible smile giving way to inconceivable laughter.

<Don't interrupt me, and I will.>

<Okay, okay.>

<Somehow,> he continued as the vise around my chest slid free, <although, like I said, nobody knows how. But somehow, golden retriever DNA ended up mixing with the sea lion supply.>

Laughing freely now, I shook my head. <This is such a load of sea lion shit.>

His soft chuckle caressed my mind. <Aye, you've found me out. But did it work? Do you feel better?>

As my panic faded—a whisper after the storm, just like in that poem he'd read me—I commed, <I do. Thank you. Oh no!> I bolted to my feet, slamming a hand against the wall for balance. <Sai. I left him alone out there.>

<Well, no. Actually, you didn't. I know you said not to come,

but I figured he might be scared. So I came anyway. Forgive me. And what is this amazing food?>

Groaning, I buried my face in my hands. <It's called palak paneer. I'm so embarrassed.>

<Don't be. I told Sai that sometimes females just need some alone time in the bathroom. To which he rolled his eyes and replied, 'I know. I have two moms.' We'll be out here whenever you're ready to join us.>

<Thank you, Freddie.>

<Anytime, Sunny.>

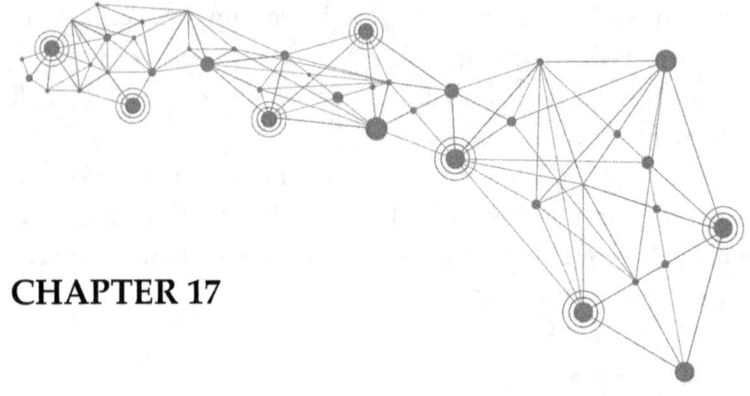

CHAPTER 17

SINCE I COULDN'T STAY in the bathroom forever, I splashed water on my face, patted it dry, and did my best to push all thoughts of Jonathan back into that deep, secret place in my mind where they usually lived, always there, never far, but far enough that I could at least function.

I was shaken, visibly so, as I stared at myself in the mirror, at the ashen face that stared back at me. But as Freddie and Sai's laughter filtered down the hall, I pinched color back into my cheeks, finger-combed my hair, and opened the door. When I stepped out into the hallway, Freddie turned the corner, meeting me halfway.

"Are you okay?" he asked, his head tilting with concern.

"I'm fine." I forced a smile. "Really."

His hand rose, his knuckles brushing over my cheek. "Glad to hear it."

We both knew I wasn't fine. But he didn't ask, he didn't press, and I really wanted to kiss him for it.

"Are you two done making out or what?" Sai shouted, standing at the end of the hallway with his eyes closed, apparently reading my mind.

I gaped at him. "What do you know about 'making out'?"

As I followed behind Freddie into the kitchenette, Sai hopped back up onto his stool and said, "They're always doing it in my moms' shows. You know, like this." When he raised his arms as if he held someone between them and stuck out his tongue, wiggling his head around and making a *muah* sound, Freddie and I burst into laughter.

"You're right, Sai," Freddie said, turning around to rummage through a cupboard. "Sunny and I were absolutely hugging the air and sticking our tongues out at each other. Thank goodness you missed it."

Sai grimaced. "Gross."

While his laughter faded, Freddie set three items on the counter—flour, nearButter, sugar—and said, "Tell me, Sai. Where do your moms stand on cookies?"

Turned out—according to Sai—Sonia and Lena were "huge fans" of cookies. And Freddie, in an entirely unsurprising turn of events, had a secret family recipe ready to go.

After we stuffed our bellies with warm, gooey sugar cookies, Sai ran himself a bath, and I helped Freddie clean up. As I dried the last dish, I turned to tell him he could leave, that I was okay now, thanks to him. But Sai padded back into the living room. Dressed in light blue pajamas decorated with purple smiley faces, holding a children's book with an astronaut gorilla on the cover, he smiled at Freddie and said, "Will you read to me?"

I never knew how, what magic they used, but children always had an innate sense of who was the best storyteller in the room.

After Freddie said, "Okay, but fair warning, I go extra hard on my voices," and followed Sai to his bedroom, I sat down on the couch, rubbed at the sudden warmth spreading through my chest, and picked up the remote.

Even though every show ever created was available in full-sensory virtual reality through everyone's VC, we still supplied all of our guest suites with televisions. Sometimes, especially when I was tired, I found it nice to disconnect from my neural implant and watch an actual screen.

After locating reruns of my favorite show, I kept the sound muted, listening in while Freddie read to Sai about the adventures of a deep-space pilot named Captain Zorba and his gorilla second mate Bartholomew. The story was charming, and Freddie hadn't been lying. His voices were next level, especially the goofy drawl he used for the gorilla. It made Sai guffaw in that way children did when they were lost to it, when the laughter came from the bottom of their bellies.

Once the story was finished, I heard Freddie close the book. But instead of leaving, he asked Sai to tell him about his day, if anything happened that he might remember forever. Sai mentioned several options: his visit to the Cosmic Spectacle oorthorse stables, the sugar cookies, Freddie reading to him. Freddie asked him about the Cosmic Spectacle since he hadn't seen it yet. And Sai's voice was so soft and sweet when he talked about the enormous horses, how some were white, some black, some golden. He went on about all the tricks they could do, how brave their riders were, his words interrupted more than once by long, slow, sleepy yawns—

"Sunny, you've fallen asleep."

"I did?" Raising my head from the couch pillow, I blinked, clearing my blurry vision until Freddie's face swam into view. "Did Sai do the same?"

Kneeling in front of me, he said, "Out like a light." Then he looked over his shoulder at the television. "What are we watching? Ooh, reality TV. My favorite."

"You like reality TV?" I asked.

He turned back to me with a gleam in his eye. "I do. Especially this one." He pointed his thumb at the screen. "*Kuiper Worm Chasers* is epic. So dangerous, so daring, so stupid."

He couldn't have known this, but if I had a love language, it was reality TV. *The Real Housewives of Imperion*, *Keeping Up with the Royals*, *Kuiper Worm Chasers*. I loved them all. He might as well have just sucked my earlobe into his mouth. "You know," I said, reaching out to brush his bangs back off his forehead, "technically, this is still our day off."

"That's a good point." A small but mischievous grin tugged at his lips. "We aren't really working right now."

"And Phoebe and Joshua were supposed to have a date tonight," I added helpfully.

"Maybe"—the heat in his gaze transformed his careful expression into something else, something risky—"it's not too late."

Scooting forward, making room for him, I patted the couch. "Watch TV with me?"

Wasting no time, he crawled in behind me, his warm body curling around mine, his arm resting gently over my waist. I'd never fit together with a partner this way, my hips nestling into the hollow of his, my back sinking into the firm support of his chest, our knees notched together like interlocking puzzle pieces.

We stayed that way for a while, coiled into each other, watching grown beings willingly risk their lives to hunt three-hundred-meter-long carnivorous invertebrates in the Kuiper belt for not nearly enough credits. But as a young Ulaperian narrowly escaped a worm's multi-rowed teeth when his ship's reactor went on the fritz, I noticed the fingers that had been resting quietly against my belly had slipped under the hem of my shirt.

With the softest touch, his fingertips brushed over my skin, lightly skimming along my hip, across my belly, back again. With each slow line he drew across my body, his fingers rose, only a little, barely enough for me to be entirely certain he was doing it on purpose. Until they reached the border of my ribs—and kept going.

I sank my teeth into my lower lip as his fingers traveled upward in shallow, dipping switchbacks, his hand now hidden entirely under my shirt. My heart pounded and my core thrummed, my nipples pulling so tight they chafed deliciously against the lace of my bra.

His touch was meandering, painfully unhurried, as his fingers ghosted over the undersides of my breasts. He had to be teasing me, torturing me with a promise of pleasure that was so close I could taste it, but still so far I was a breath away from begging him for it. But through the haze of desire thickening around me, I wondered if maybe his slow progress was his way of asking for permission, giving me plenty of time to stop him if I wanted to. It was sweet, but ridiculous. I wouldn't have told him to stop to find water if I was on fire.

He was so silent behind me. Not a breath, not a sigh. Not a single movement aside from his hand, his fingertips sliding over lace, still not where I needed them. The unanswered craving was agony, each sweep of his fingers sending hot, flickering pulses between my legs. But as much as I wanted to grab his hand and guide it to where I wanted it, where I was desperate for it, I refused to give in. Even if this wasn't teasing. Even if he really was seeking my permission, we'd come too far now for me to just give it to him. On this, I would stand firm. I would not break. I would try very hard not to break.

His thumb slipped over the side of my breast, close enough to brush my nipple but still refusing to. And, *fuck*, I was going to break.

As luck would have it, we broke at the same time. While I moaned, grinding my hips back against him, he cursed into my ear, pulling my bra down, freeing my swollen, aching breasts.

I rolled toward him as he cupped my breast, finally finding my nipple, rolling the stiff peak between his thumb and finger. Snaking my hand around his neck, I pulled his mouth down to mine while his hand traveled to my other breast.

He kissed me fiercely, silently, sweeping his tongue across my lips. When he pinched my other nipple and I moaned into his mouth, his hand slid out of my shirt, moving south.

"Shh," he warned when I gasped. But what did he expect when he slipped his hand into my pants? When he pushed my panties to the side? When he sank a finger inside me?

"Stars," he ground out. "You're so wet."

Pulling him into another kiss, I burrowed my hands into his hair while he withdrew his finger, sliding it up to apply a firm, warm pressure over my clit. My breath vanished, my mind abruptly emptied of all previous thought. And then his finger started to move. Brisk, flawless circles. Six, seven, eight was all it took, and I was shuddering under him, burying my harsh, groaning breaths into his neck as release barreled through me, light and heat soaring from my toes into my belly, spreading out until a primal, pulsating pleasure wrapped itself around me. Until I levitated off the senator's couch. As the waves of sensation loosened their grip on me, I raised my head, meeting his stare, watching as he brought the finger that had been inside me to his lips and sucked it into his mouth.

"Joshua," I said in a breathless, mindless whisper.

He was rock hard now, pressed firmly against my thigh. Taking his face with one hand, kissing him again, I reached between our bodies, desperate to touch him. But he stopped me.

"What's wrong?" I asked.

Gently, he brought my hand to his lips and pressed a kiss into my palm. "That was just for you. Besides, I don't want to be here when the senator gets home."

"Senator? What senator?"

His laughter brushed over my skin. "I should go."

"She'll know you were here. Sai will tell her."

Sitting up, he pulled my legs into his lap. After slipping my shoes off one at a time, he upped the pleasure ante by rubbing my feet. "I know," he said while I melted back into the couch. "But it's one thing to bake cookies and read bedtime stories. It's another thing entirely to have mutual orgasms with the babysitter in the living room."

When he put it that way... "Can Phoebe visit your pod later? After the senator gets back."

Releasing my feet, he pushed himself up to his, tried to smooth his shirt over his obvious erection, and replied, "Joshua would like that."

I reached for him, pulling him back down, kissing him one last time—while I might have also palmed him through his pants. He groaned into my mouth, and I devoured the sound. When I let him go, he stared down at me, swiped his thumb over his lower lip, and said, "Yes, Phoebe should *definitely* visit Joshua later."

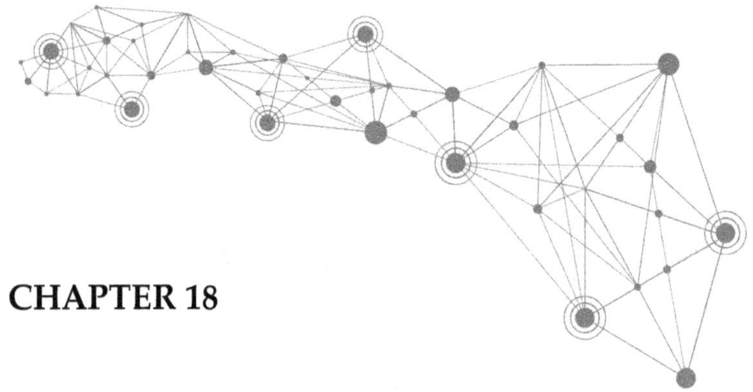

CHAPTER 18

BUZZING, smiling, and supremely satisfied, because he'd been right—Joshua *was* quite good at wooing—I'd barely drifted off to sleep when the *whoosh* of a door sliding open had me bolting upright.

The senator released a bone-weary sigh as she entered her suite, slipping out of her heels, kicking them off next to the door. After reaching back to unzip the top few inches of her skirt's zipper, she pulled a pin from her hair, running her fingers through her raven-black waves until they settled over her shoulders.

"Welcome home, Senator. How was your meeting?" My voice sounded wrong: tight, awkward, *guilty*.

With a sharp inhale, she clasped her hand over her heart. "*Gods above*, Sunny. You startled me."

"I'm sorry. Long day?"

"An understatement." She dropped her hand. "How was Sai?"

"An absolute angel," I replied, trying my level best to sound normal, look normal, *be* normal. "Perfectly behaved."

Sonia huffed a knowing laugh, sitting on the chair across

from me. "He's always on his best behavior for anyone who isn't one of his mothers."

"Especially once Freddie came over to make cookies for him," I admitted in a rush, wanting it all out on the table. Well, not *all* of it, exactly. "Sai assured us you wouldn't mind."

Her attention homed in on me. "Freddie came?"

Not yet, I thought with a lopsided smile—that Sonia snatched right off my face when she raised a pointed, knowing brow at me. "I called him in for reinforcements," I explained, cursing the heat rushing up my throat. "Sai wanted cookies, and I…can't bake." *I can't bake?* That was the best I could do?

Sonia's slow nod up and down said *bullshit*. "I see."

Not knowing what else to do with them as she stared me down, I folded my hands in my lap.

"You know," she said, leaning forward. "I do like that Freddie. He's smart. Capable. And rather handsome. Don't you think?"

It was definitely time to leave. Sonia was as skilled as a Portisan when it came to reading minds. "I should go," I said instead of answering. "Let you get some sleep."

But before I stood from the couch of shame, Sonia said, "Stay, Sunny. For a moment."

Settling back against the cushions, folding my hands back in my lap because…why not, I said, "Of course."

"I know your time is precious. But there's something I'd like to say to you."

I nodded as gravity reasserted itself, the memories of those weightless moments on the couch pulled down to some more appropriate level of consciousness.

"You'd asked me at the Fire Ball why I was traveling on this ship," Sonia said, a resigned expression moving across her face. "As much as possible, I try to keep my professional and personal lives separate. But I would not be where I am today if I didn't have a keen sense of when to ask for help."

"Do you need my help?" I asked, gravity doubling.

Running two fingers up and down the bridge of her nose, she said, "I fear—no, I'm quite certain that my family is in danger. Tell me, Sunny. Have you heard of Proposition 2126?"

I shook my head, my attention snagging on two words: family and danger.

"What I am about to tell you is highly classified information. Can I trust you to keep this between us?"

I wanted to tell her yes, but it was impossible. "It depends," I said. "One of my duties is to keep everyone aboard this ship safe. If what you're about to tell me compromises my ability to do that in any way—"

She waved me off. "You're right. Of course. I shouldn't have asked."

My mind rewound to the bistro, to what Tig had told me. If the senator's family was in enough danger that she was about to share highly classified information with me, I needed to tell her what Tig had found. "Senator, our IT specialist found something distressing the other day. Someone off-ship has been hacking our system to access our guests' itineraries."

So quickly I almost missed it, her eyes flared with something like alarm. "That's troubling."

"These security breaches started around the time you and your family came aboard. Do you think this has anything to do with your proposition?"

Curling her fingers around the armrests of her chair, she said, "Perhaps."

It wasn't much, but it was all I needed to hear. "I would like to help you, but I need to know what's going on. And I need to be able to share that information with my crew."

After a tense moment, a muscle in her jaw flickered, and she sighed. "Very well. I have committed myself to introducing a"—she paused briefly—"*controversial* proposition at the upcoming KU joint sessions meeting on Portis. Certain information regarding the proposition has been leaked, although I'm not certain how. Nevertheless, my comings and goings have been a source of much interest of late, and my security officers —who are also guests aboard the *Ignisar*, although you won't uncover who they are unless they want you to—devised this plan to travel to Portis on this very crowded, very public ship in efforts to dissuade any attacks on me or my family before we reached the meeting."

I sat up straight. "Is my ship in danger, Senator?"

"We do not believe so," Sonia said, leaning back in her chair. "The negative press of anything happening on the *Ignisar* would make the risks too great."

This was an odd statement. Who, aside from LunaCorp themselves, would care about the negative press of something happening aboard one of LunaCorp's ships? I wanted to ask what the proposition entailed, but the thumping of little feet down the hall put an end to our conversation.

"Hi, Mom," Sai said, rubbing his eyes. "What are you two talking about? You woke me up."

Sonia rose to her feet and walked to her son, picking him up and swaying him from side to side. "Sorry, bubs," she said, kissing his cheek. "I've missed you. Did you have a good time with Sunny and Freddie?"

Sai squeezed his arms around her neck. "We made cookies."

Sonia laughed and set Sai down, then turned back to face me, all business again. "I'm certain you'll need to discuss what I've told you with Chan, and I realize that it was unfair of me to ask you not to. All I can do is request your entire crew's discretion in this matter."

"Of course," I said, getting to my feet. Straightening my top, I said good night, then watched Sonia lead Sai back to his room before seeing myself out. And heading directly to Freddie's pod.

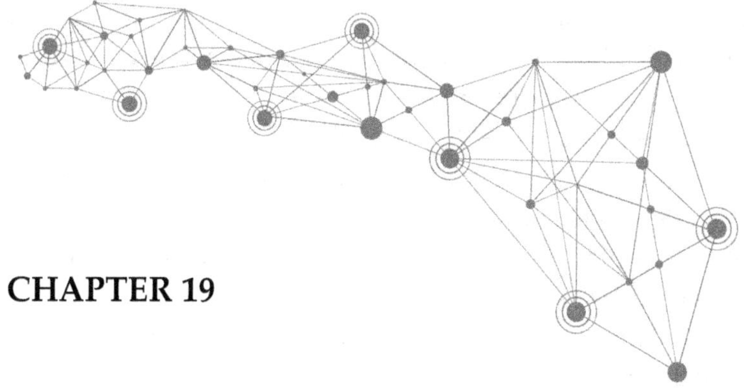

CHAPTER 19

He opened his door after one knock, wearing a soft white T-shirt and an even softer pair of gray sweatpants. He must have showered, because his hair was damp, and his linen scent rushed out to greet me. Maybe it was his soap, or his shampoo, or just some pheromone his body produced, but all I wanted was to get him all dirty again.

"The senator made it home safely?" he asked, backing away from the door to let me inside.

"She did. I told her about the cookies. And she told me that her family might be in danger."

He coughed into his fist. "What?"

As succinctly as possible, I told him about Tig's findings and the senator's concerns.

"That's troubling," he stated, sitting on the edge of his bed.

"That's exactly what Sonia said," I replied. And we spent a silent moment thinking, processing, while I also might have fantasized about tracing the vein that traveled across his left wrist and up toward his elbow. But then something caught my eye.

I turned, walking to his wall, where he'd programmed an array of digpics. Scenes of Venus, mostly. One pic was of him as a child, maybe a few years younger than Sai. He stood between two people I assumed were his parents on a black sand beach, waves crashing against the rocks behind them.

"Those are my parents," he said while I studied the pic.

He seemed so carefree in the moving image, so happy while his parents gazed down at him, a soft breeze rustling his mother's loose blond curls. She was beautiful. No surprise there, considering how handsome he was.

Walking across his pod, I stopped at the table under his digital window. It was covered by a half-completed puzzle of some vivid, multicolored nebula, an empty coffee mug, and a small stack of leather-bound books—more poetry.

When I looked back at him, he was on his feet again, staring at me with a patient, dare I say, amused expression.

"What are you doing?" he asked.

"Oh, just checking out your pod. It's nice. Although, bring a stranger here, and I'm not sure they'd be able to tell if this pod belonged to you or to your grandfather."

With a soft laugh, he glanced down at his bare feet.

I picked up one of his poetry books, leafing through the delicate pages. "Has anyone ever told you that you are very old-fashioned?"

He slid his hands into his pockets, still watching his feet. And there was something about a man who typically wore fine suits dressing down, looking so casual in sweatpants, so comfortable. I honestly couldn't decide which version of him was more enticing. *Why not both?*

"It's not such a bad thing, is it?" he asked. "Being old-fashioned?"

I almost laughed. Only someone so old-fashioned would be insecure about something so indescribably sexy. Moving toward him, stopping a few paces away, I said, "No. It's not a bad thing." And then I was lost in his clear blue-gray eyes, drawn to his lush, pink mouth, remembering the press of his lips on my mine, the slide of his finger inside me. "I think Phoebe still has some unfinished business with Joshua."

"You do?" He swallowed, his throat bobbing. "You don't think we should talk more about the senator and...*stuff*?" His voice cracked on the word as I stepped closer to him. "Alert the crew?"

Deliberately, I licked my lips, rolled them together, then shook my head. "They're all asleep. We can tell them in the morning."

With every step I took toward him, he moved one step away, retreating until his back ran into his door, until I stood directly in front of him, until he had nowhere left to go.

My gaze dipped from his eyes to his lips, his throat, to the spot where his pulse leapt above his collarbone, down the broadness of his chest, lower. My fingers followed suit as I traced his pecs through his shirt, his abs. As I stroked the growing hardness of him over soft pants.

His eyelids fluttered closed, his mouth opening in a silent gasp. "This isn't necessary," he strained to say. "Joshua's not expecting any—"

"Shh." I brushed a kiss over his lips, sinking to my knees, hooking my fingers into his waistband. "Phoebe insists."

When I pulled, he sprang free, his sweatpants dropping to the floor in a puddle around his feet. I nuzzled him, pressing soft kisses onto his stomach, over the slope of his hip, inhaling him deeply. It must have been pheromones, because he smelled even more amazing down here, like fresh wash drying in a summer breeze.

He muttered something unintelligible as I took him in my hand, and then into my mouth, running my tongue over his soft skin, smooth as silk. I kept my pace unhurried, steady, methodical, as I savored him, memorizing the shape of him, learning what made his breath catch, noticing the moan I pulled from somewhere deep in his throat when I swirled my tongue over his tip.

True to form, he was a gentleman even now. He didn't grab my hair or push into me or give me suggestions or orders like some lovers did. Instead, he became a statue against his door, his arms pinned at his sides, his hands clenched into fists, quiet as a mouse aside from that little moan and the occasional breathy praise he offered up to the ceiling, although I assumed it was meant for me.

He was perfect, always perfect. *Too* perfect. It must wear on him, the pressure he put on himself to maintain his impeccable manners, his even temper, his kind and considerate demeanor. I wondered, on my knees before him, holding him quite literally in the palm of my hand, if I could pierce his perfect politeness here in the safety of his pod and give him permission to be, at least for a few moments, a little rude.

Slowing my pace, I lightened my touch. And after another whisper-quiet but decidedly frustrated moan, I smiled around him. Then I slowed even more.

"Please," he begged, his voice strained, his fists balled so tightly his knuckles turned white. "Please."

Even now, even with my teasing, he still asked so sweetly. So politely. So I pulled off him, and as he looked down at me with a pained, confused expression, I dragged my tongue over his slit.

He groaned, his hooded gaze meeting mine, dipping to my lips, finding my devilish grin. I slid my fingers up the inside of his leg, his knee, higher. When I reached the apex of his thighs, I stilled my hand, not yet touching him, and hovered my mouth directly over the head of his cock, huffing out a warm, wet breath.

"Please," he pleaded again, not moving, not reaching for me, so restrained, so well-mannered.

Sliding my hand a bit higher so that my palm grazed him, I said, "Let go for me. It's okay. I want you to. I can take it."

His eyes fell closed as I finally made contact, cupping him, massaging him. When I took him into my mouth again, moving faster this time, his back arched, his head thudding against his door, and a thrill shot through me. Grasping his hips, I moaned around him, pulled him into me, hollowing my cheeks, taking him as deeply as I could. And then, as if unable to bear it one second longer, he let go, and I claimed my victory.

His hands unclenched, his fingers diving into my hair, and with an exquisitely grunted "fuck," and still as politely as anyone ever had, he thrust into me once, twice, and came entirely undone.

When I looked up again after working him all the way through his orgasm, I almost opened the photo app in my VC so I could snap a pic of him leaning against his door, breathing hard, releasing his hold on my head to cradle my face gently, reverently. Because I never wanted to forget him like this, so beautifully disheveled.

"That was... I've never... How did you...?"

Placing a sticky kiss on his hip, I pulled his pants carefully back up and over him and led him to his bed. "I'd say years of practice, but I'm not sure that's what you want to hear right now."

With a breathy laugh, he said, "Practice makes perfect, I suppose," while collapsing onto the edge of his bed. And then, as if coming to his senses, he looked up at me, his brows pinching together above his wide, concerned eyes. "I'm sorry. I'm so sorry if—"

Leaning down, I kissed him deeply before he could utter another word. "No apologies. I loved every second." A corner of my mouth ticked up. "Especially that last little bit."

He took my hand to pull me down beside him. I let him, resting my head on his shoulder. The mirror above his dresser reflected a picture of a dazed but happy man and a contented woman I didn't quite recognize.

His eyes finding mine in our reflection, he said, "We look good together."

It was a simple statement, almost benign compared to other professions he'd already made to me. And he wasn't wrong either; we did look good together. In another life, maybe we would have lived happily ever after. But not this one. In this life, we were Phoebe and Joshua. In this life, we were only having fun. In this life, none of this was real.

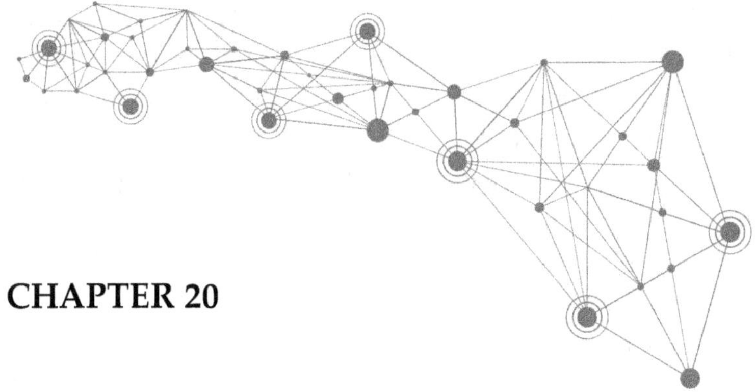

CHAPTER 20

"You mean to tell me the senator has her own security detail staying on this ship, pretending to be guests?" Rax barked, skipping over the objectively more important details of the briefing Tig and I provided to land on this concern. "And we knew nothing about this until now?"

"Yes. That is exactly what we mean," I said, holding up my hands. "Don't murder the messengers."

Sharing Rax's outrage, Morgath chimed in with "That she doesn't trust us to at least know who her SOs are is an insult of the highest order." Darting his gaze between each member of the crew, he slammed his green fist down on the table. "It is an insult to everyone in this room!"

"I'll admit it is unusual," Chan said, his hand running uneasily over his close-cropped hair, betraying his composed tone. "But given her situation surrounding whatever this proposition is, as well as the fact that someone is hacking into our system to monitor her family's comings and goings, I can understand why she wants to keep her security undercover."

Tig had informed the crew that while several of the guests had their itineraries accessed by the hacker, the senator's had been accessed by far the most often.

"Well, I can," Rax snapped. "She should have warned us before coming aboard, given us time to prepare. Or to decide whether we wanted to let her on the ship at all. Now we're caught with our pants down."

My eyes flared, heat flooding my chest, leaping into my throat at the memory of finely muscled thighs dusted with soft hair, sweatpants falling to the floor. When I chanced a glance at Freddie, I found him dutifully studying an imperfection in the table, but his cheeks were flaming. Apparently, we had some work to do on the *secret* part of the whole secret relationship thing.

"So, what do we do?" Tig asked, pulling at the strings of her hoodie. "I could try harder to uncover the source of the breaches, but I might get caught."

"That seems like a bad idea," Elanie said. Bionic skin was truly a marvel, because with how often and how deeply Elanie scowled, she should really have at least one wrinkle by now. "I'm not sure how much we want to implicate ourselves in whatever the senator is wrapped up in."

Chan nodded, Rax and Morgath grunted their agreement, and I began to simmer. "Excuse me," I said, my annoyance bubbling over into hot indignation. "But if somebody is bypassing our security to obtain protected information on our guests, I believe we have an obligation to do everything within our power to keep those guests safe as long as they are aboard this ship."

Freddie raised his head. "I agree with Sunny," he said, nodding in a show of support. "Any threat against any one of our guests is a threat against everyone on the ship. Knowing what we know, what can we do to minimize our risk?"

"I think I can trace the breaches without being detected." Tig bit her cheek. "But it will take time, lots of time. And I'll need some backup."

Whistling a weird, two-note song, Chan said, "Funny you

should mention that, Tig. Turns out"—his laughter was forced—"some relief is on the way."

One by one, we turned our heads to stare at him, and he avoided our questioning glares by picking at one of his hover-chair's armrests.

"What 'relief'?" I asked, breaking the charged silence. "Who is coming?" Besides the FFKs, there were no special guests or LunaCorp tech visits on the docket. And Chan wasn't possibly implying that some deep-space pirate could assist Tig in high-tech espionage. Right?

"Funny story," he blurted out. "I mean, it's wild, really. You won't believe it—"

"Spit it out, Chandler," Rax growled between his clenched teeth.

Repositioning himself in his chair, shifting his weight from one hip to the other, Chan said, "Well, while they're here, Luna-Corp wants us to...uh...train the FFKs in—"

Rax and Morgath surged to their feet, the explosion of green outrage pushing me and everyone else back from the table.

"If the next words out of your mouth have anything to do with giving Kravaxians access to our IT, you can consider our employment aboard this vessel terminated," Morgath said with a calm fury. Rax—not so calm and far more furious—grasped the edge of the table so tightly, I was worried he might break off a chunk of it and hurl it at somebody. Even considering the news, the twins seemed more highly strung than usual. It had been a while since I'd checked in with them. I should schedule them a day at the spa. Maybe an afternoon in the pleasure pods—

"Rax! Morgath!" Tig shouted, snapping my attention. I didn't think I'd heard her raise her voice once in the entire time we'd served on the ship together. Pride filled my chest when she added, "Calm down!"

Their matching grumbles resonated through the room, but the twins took their seats again.

"If LunaCorp wants me to work with a Kravaxian or two," Tig said, "I can do that without compromising our intel."

"Our intel has already been compromised, though, hasn't it?" Elanie asked, at least trying to come off less judgmental than she probably was. "With these breaches?"

Tig's shoulders curled inward, her earlier confidence deflating. "That's different."

"I know this situation is extreme," I said, trying to rein the meeting back in. "But Chan is still the boss. We need to at least hear what he has to say."

With a resigned sigh, Chan said, "Thank you, Sunny. But nobody is going to like what I have to say next, not even me. All I can ask is that you remember we are all in this together, and"—he looked directly at the twins—"if you break anything in this room, it's coming out of your paychecks."

While Morgath shrugged, Rax turned his palms up on the table as if to say *don't care*.

Soldiering on, Chan said, "LunaCorp is using this holiday for the FF"—he stopped himself, his jaw flickering—"for the *Kravaxians* as an opportunity to provide them with some on-the-job training. One will be assigned to IT with Tig. One will spend the week with me. And the remaining two are to shadow"—not only was his swallow audible, but it looked like it hurt—"security."

After several seconds of stunned silence, Rax and Morgath burst into laughter. Doubled over with his head on the table, Morgath wheezed like a serving drone on its last thruster. Rax, red-faced, clapped his brother's back, releasing a lengthy post-laugh "hoo" at the ceiling.

Elanie rolled her eyes. "Are you two finished? I don't want to spend the rest of my life at this meeting."

"And the captains are still in agreement with this plan?" Freddie asked, his arms crossed thoughtfully over his chest.

Chan nodded. "They are. They've had briefings on the situation from Brock Karlovich himself, and they both feel confident that the Kravaxians present no danger to this ship."

In possession of his faculties again, Rax growled, "I don't give a flying fuck what the CEO of LunaCorp says. We are not training Kravaxians. It's not happening."

Impressively undeterred, Chan fired back. "It is indeed happening. And you and your brother will behave yourselves, do your jobs, and give the Kravaxians a fair shake before you write them off. Or you will find another ship to work on and another director to put up with your tantrums. So, you know, good luck with that."

While Rax and Morgath at least had the good sense to look contrite, Chan, riding on momentum, ended the meeting in no uncertain terms. "When the Kravaxians arrive, we will be polite and accommodating. And we will not create a Known Universal incident by showing them mistrust and hostile aggression when they have done nothing to earn it. Is that clear?"

"That was intense," Freddie said as we huddled near the moon jelly tank.

When I replied, "*That* was Chan at his finest," it earned me a knee-buckling smile, all tilted lips and crinkled eyes. His tie was a bit crooked, and for the life of me, even though Elanie and Tig were standing right next to us, I couldn't shake the desire to straighten it for him.

"As stimulating as this morning has been," Elanie said, following my gaze to Freddie's smile, then to his tie, then rolling her eyes. "I really do have work to do." Before any of us had a chance to say goodbye, she turned on her heel and disappeared down the hall.

Staring after her, his lips pursed, Freddie said, "She is a very unique bionic. Like a breath of fresh air that occasionally, for reasons unknown, slaps you hard across the face."

I laughed out loud. "That is the best description of Elanie I have ever heard."

Tig stopped chewing on her fingernails long enough to nod her agreement, but then she said, "I should go too. I've got a hacker to expose."

Squeezing Tig's elbow, I said, "Be careful."

"I'll try," she replied before walking off toward her office.

"What are your plans today?" Freddie asked. We were alone now, and when he turned to face me, the blue and purple light from the moon jelly tank rippled over his cheek. Just like it had during his welcome party. It was strange, I thought, how long ago that day seemed. But he was staring at me now, waiting, so I said, "I think I'm on damage control."

"What damage?"

"Aquilinian twin damage," I clarified. "I should probably do whatever it takes today to keep Rax and Morgath from interrogating random guests in order to find out who the senator's SOs are. And then I need to prepare for Garran and Kasa's date later this week."

"That's right." His eyes twinkled. "Still want my help?"

"Yes. Please. I could definitely use your charm with my attempts to play Cyrano. And if you're not too busy, I could probably use your help with the twins...today...too—What?" I said, distracted by his grin, even more crooked than his tie.

"Did you just call me charming?"

Giving into temptation—something I was concerned might become a habit around him—I reached out for his tie, straightened the knot, and said, "Don't let it go to your head."

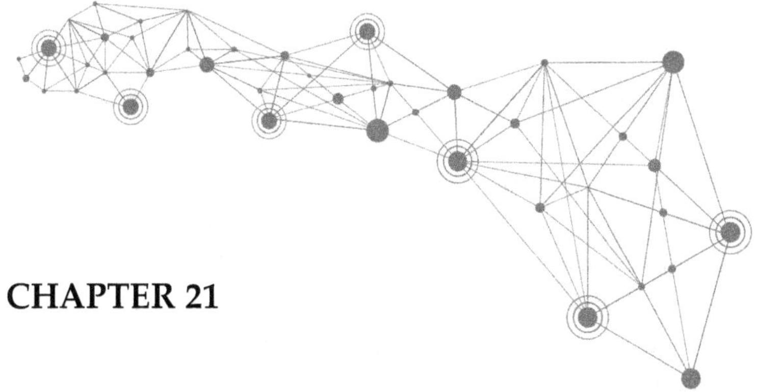

CHAPTER 21

THE THIRD BAR FREDDIE, the twins, and I stumbled into—after sipping martinis while watching Old Earth twentieth-century flappers dance at the jazz club on deck five, then sampling the objectively bizarre but surprisingly delicious cocktails at the Blurvan tavern on eighteen—was one of my favorites on the ship. It was a dimly lit Venusian pub with dark wood tables and chairs surrounded by rich leather booths, one of which we piled into while a fiddler serenaded us from a small stage in the corner.

It had taken far too many drinks, but the twins were finally loose and laughing. And no longer eyeing every other guest with deep—and honestly kind of menacing—suspicion. Mission accomplished, even if my sobriety was collateral damage.

Sitting across from me, Freddie ran two fingers over the reddish-brown leather of our booth. "I like this place. It reminds me of home."

I nodded, my head swimming, while Morgath dropped his forehead onto my shoulder and confessed, "I think I'm drunk."

Rax snorted, muttered, "Lightweight," then hiccupped.

Nestling my cheek into Morgath's green hair, I said, "Never

admit to being drunk, darling. We deny it until our faces are deep in the toilet."

"What in the worlds is going on here?" said a terribly sober voice.

"Chandler!" Freddie almost shouted, scrambling to straighten his hair, his tie, trying his level best to appear sober while I considered hiding under the table. "Sunny and I were only trying to set the twins' minds at ease regarding the FFKs and that other business with"—he looked around, then mouthed dramatically—"*the senator.*" While Chan raised a brow, Freddie explained, "We thought, you know, whiskey ought to do the trick."

"Did it?" Chan asked. Even his hoverchair seemed dubious, humming reprovingly at us as the fiddler finished one song and started in on another.

"Yep," I chirped, then asked, "What are you doing here?" shifting the focus away from our drunkenness and aiming it toward the fact that Chan rarely went out to any of the bars on the ship. Certainly never by himself.

Running a hand over his head, he said, "There was an incident at the bowling alley on deck nine. A Vorpol was 'accidentally'"—he drew quotes in the air—"tripped by a Gorbie during his hopping approach to the line. And in the ensuing scuffle, a bowling ball found its way first through one of the light fixtures, then halfway through the floor on its way back down."

That wasn't good. Aside from stepping on their foot, tripping a Vorpol was as disrespectful as getting a Gorbie's hair wet. Wars had been started for less.

"Did you say the ball *found its way*?" Freddie asked, his head tilting, his lips fixed in a pensive pout.

Chan sighed. "Unfortunately. Who threw the ball was a mystery I couldn't solve. And in the name of keeping interspecies peace, I abandoned the investigation in favor of providing unlimited free bowling for both parties. After that mess, with no help from any of you, by the way, I wanted a drink."

"Alone?" I asked, my suspicion mounting, my cupid senses tingling. "You're at a bar by yourself?"

"Well, not exactly," he replied. His chin ducked. His ears turned pink. *Gotcha.*

Scooting to the edge of my seat, I peered around our booth, trying—and failing—to be inconspicuous. Failing even harder when I spotted Makenna at a two-top table in the corner of the bar and gasped, "*Chan*. Are you on a date?"

"Chandler," Morgath said knowingly, extending his fist for a bump. "My man."

"Keep your voices down," Chan hissed, pushing Morgath's fist out of the way. "It's not a date. It's a friendly get-together. That's all."

"Doesn't look like it's only a friendly get-together to me," Freddie said, angling his head to sneak a peek at Makenna. "She's staring at you. She's also smiling at you. She's stare-smiling. Smile-staring? Smaring?" He snorted. "I made up a word."

"Bravo, Chan," I cheered, beaming with unrestrained pride. "But why are you here talking to us when you should be over there telling Makenna that her skin is more luminous than the glow of Ulaperia's moons over the Senasar Sea?"

"Sunny." His eyes flared. "Could... Can I steal that?"

"Take it and run," I said. My words were thick and slow, but I didn't care anymore. I was too busy propping my elbow on the edge of my table, watching Chan cruise back to Makenna, trying to read their lips. Which, in my current state, was surprisingly difficult.

"Shit." Rax shook his head. "I think I'm drunk too. Come on, Morg. We gotta go."

"So soon?" I asked, then bit back a squeak when Freddie dove beneath the table to pick up the napkin he'd dropped—and so he could run his fingers up the back of my leg.

"Sorry, Sunny." Sliding out of the booth, Rax nodded toward his brother and said, "Let's go, dingus. We're hitting the training room at zero five hundred."

"Seriously?" Morgath tripped over his own feet when he tried to stand. "We can't take one day off?"

Shoving Morgath toward the door, Rax scoffed. "Asks the king of skipping leg day."

"Bye, Morgath. Bye, Rax," Freddie shouted after them once he popped back up into his seat. With an elated grin, he said, "I think they're starting to like me."

"Well, of course they are, darling. Who wouldn't like you?" The change in the air was sudden, like a drop in barometric pressure, a realization that it was only me, only him, only a table separating us. We stared at each other, the space between us charged and sparking. "Should we go?"

He nodded, and we climbed out of our booth. I made it down the hall, past the atrium, all the way to the elevator banks before I slid my hand into his, squeezing, brushing my thumb over his skin, the same way he'd done to mine once upon a time. But as soon as the elevator doors slid open, I yanked him inside, pushed him to the back of the car, and said, "Hello, Joshua."

With a needy growl, he slid his hand up my back to cup my neck, wrapping his other arm around my waist, pulling me close, kissing me deeply. The way his lips fit so perfectly over mine, the soft glide of his tongue, the liquid press of our bodies, it was hard to tell where I ended and he began. Until the elevator dinged, pulling us apart, and I asked, "Walk me home?"

With a quick nod, he followed me out into the hallway, and after checking that the coast was clear, we practically sprinted to my pod. Which, in retrospect, probably wasn't the best idea. Because by the time we arrived, my head was spinning, and not in a good way. But it would be fine. I'd rally. I'd make it work.

Slamming my hand over the security lock before yanking him inside, I kissed his neck, his mouth, loosening his tie. And he let me, his hands closing over my hips, but something was off. He was hesitant, holding back.

"What's the matter?" I asked between his lips while I slid his tie free and tossed it to the side. "Don't you want me?"

Grabbing my ass in both hands, he urged me close, the hardness of him answering my question. "More than anything, but I'm not sure it's the right time."

"No time like the present," I said.

"That's...true," he stammered when I took his earlobe between my teeth. "But I think you might be a bit drunk."

"What?" I pulled back. "Do you have any idea how much alcohol this liver can process? I am a professional."

"I have no doubt." Assessing me with a furrowed brow, he said, "But it's not your liver I'm worried about."

Closing an eye to keep him from separating into two, I said, "What do you mean?"

"Well,"—he brushed my hair from my forehead—"you're not normally this green."

Those were evidently magic words, because once he'd uttered them, nausea roiled through me. Grasping my belly, I stumbled to my bathroom, dropped to my knees, and leaned over the toilet in the nick of time.

Somewhere behind me, he turned on the water.

"Maybe I am drunk," I admitted while he took a knee beside me on the tile.

"Happens to the best of us," he said softy, running his hand up and down my back in long, soothing strokes.

I heaved again, amazed there was anything left inside me. When I was done, he flushed the toilet and handed me a damp washcloth.

"This is so embarrassing," I said, hiding my face behind the washcloth.

"You should be proud." He tucked my hair behind my ear. "I've seen volcanic eruptions that were less productive."

I laughed, then groaned as he helped me to my feet.

"Drink this," he said, pressing a glass of cold water into my hand.

I did as ordered, and when he handed me two anti-nox tabs, I took those too.

He led me to my bed, unzipping my dress, kneeling so I could lean on his shoulder while I stepped out of it while he slipped my shoes from my feet one at a time. Then he stood, draped my dress on my dresser, and reached around me to unclasp my bra.

"Hmm," I murmured, taking one of his hands and placing it over my breast. "That's more like it."

He huffed a laugh, but while he used his free hand to reach inside my dresser drawer for something for me to wear, he humored me, his thumb rolling over my nipple, pressing down, almost making me forget how dizzy I was. Until I closed my eyes and the room spun.

"Arms up," he instructed.

I complied, wobbling on my feet while he slipped my constellation nightshirt over my head. He'd picked that one specifically, like he'd known it was my favorite.

"Now," he said, turning me around and giving my ass a surprisingly firm swat, "into bed with you."

When my eyes cracked open, it was late, past midnight. My head pounded and my throat burned. I vowed never to go drinking with Rax and Morgath again. But despite it all, I smiled.

<Are you awake?> I commed him.

<Are you alive?> he commed back.

<Barely, but yes. Thanks to you. You are very chivalrous, although part of me wishes you weren't.>

After a moment, he said, <I have regrets.>

I laughed. <Did I wake you?>

<No. Couldn't sleep. I've just been working on my puzzle.>

Pulling my covers up to my grinning lips, I asked, <Are you a real person?>

<Aye. I've got the parents to prove it and everything.>

<They looked lovely in your digpics.>

<Thank you. They are lovely.>

I rolled onto my belly, immediately regretting the motion as the dull throbbing behind my temples sharpened. <What are their names?>

<Madelyn and Ethan.>

<Your mother is beautiful.>

<That she is. What are...your parents' names?>

He'd hesitated, sounded nervous. And I realized it might have been the first personal question he'd ever asked me. Because he was being careful with me, cautious, respecting my barriers even though he didn't know why they were there. Which had the effect of making the walls surrounding me softer, thinner, becoming so transparent I could almost see what life might be like on the other side.

<Charity and Cosmo.> It felt heavy, saying their names, thinking of them. Because I loved them, but I'd hardly spoken to them since the accident. The accident whose anniversary loomed. The walls hardened, closing in again.

Until he said, <Well, that explains a lot.>

<Hey.> I rolled onto my back again, grinning up at the ceiling. <What's that supposed to mean?>

His laughter was a warm breath between my ears. <Just that Sunastara is a...*unique* name.>

<Ah, yes. Charity and Cosmo are card-carrying starbies—I think you call them 'hippies' on your side of the wormhole.>

<Does it mean something? Your name?>

Reaching blindly for the cup of water he'd left by my bed, I took a tentative sip. <Not really. My mother wanted to name me Sun, my father Star. They compromised.>

<I love your name. It's beautiful.> After a pause, he said, <*You* are beautiful.>

After an even lengthier pause—one in which the soft brush of his words tried to prickle my skin and curl my toes—my smile fell, and I sighed.

He was Freddie right now, not Joshua. I was Sunny, not Phoebe. And Freddie and Sunny shouldn't do this sort of thing. They shouldn't have late-night VC conversations while lying in bed, no matter how good they felt. No matter how many more questions I wanted to ask him, how much of his life I wanted to know. Because he'd want to know more of my life too, and I'd end up pulling back or shutting down. Or worse, lying to him. Not wanting to do any of those things, I commed, <I should get some more sleep.>

<Should you drink some water first?>

<Already have. Luckily, someone left me a full glass on my nightstand.>

<Whoever did that must be very thoughtful.>

<Extremely.> Maybe the most thoughtful being I had ever met.

In the ensuing silence, I wondered if he'd clicked off. But then he said, <You take care of everyone aboard this ship. You deserve to be taken care of too. Thank you for letting me. Have sweet dreams, Sunastara Nex.>

My heart fluttered against my ribs, delicate and light like butterfly wings. How did he always say these things I didn't even know I needed to hear? It was unfair. It was lovely. It was tempting. It was time to click off. <You too, Freddie... Wait, what's your last name?>

<It's Caruthers.>

<Really?>

<Unfortunately.>

<Fredrick Caruthers?> I snorted. <*Stars*, even your name is old-fashioned.>

<Now you know why I had little choice in how I turned out. Nobody's asking Freddie Caruthers to the hip hangouts, are they?>

<Certainly not if he called them 'hip hangouts.'>

<Ouch,> he commed with laughter in his voice.

<Well, good night, Fredrick Caruthers. Is that like the third or fourth? That has to be a family name, right? Handed down from your great-great-great-grandfather?>

<Haha. You're very funny.>

<You didn't answer the question.>

<The third,> he admitted. <I am Fredrick Caruthers the Third.>

<Amazing,> I said, adding, <Freddie?> before he clicked off.

<Yes?>

I wanted to thank him for helping me, for being kind, for being...him. But as much as I wanted to be, I wasn't brave. <Have fun with your puzzle.>

I couldn't see his wry grin, but I knew it was there when he said, <I always do.>

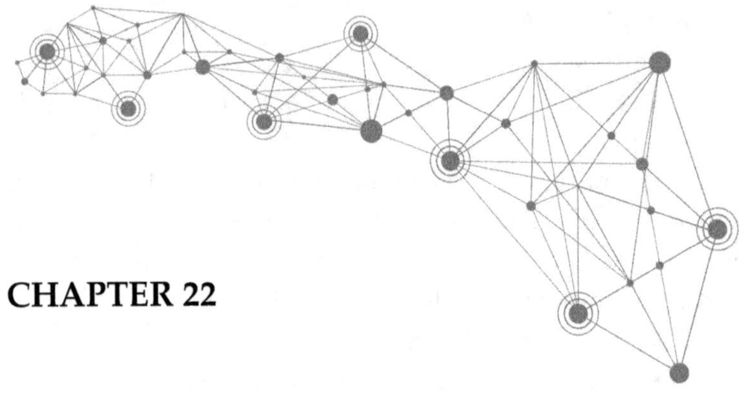

CHAPTER 22

"WHAT DO you have in store for Garran and Kasa tomorrow night?" Freddie asked as we walked together from the breakfast buffet on deck seven back to the staff room for morning meeting.

I felt like a new woman after sleeping straight through the rest of the night. Waking up to a well-dressed Freddie at my door with a cup of coffee in one hand and two more anti-nox tabs in the other didn't hurt either.

"He's taking Kasa to dinner, then they're going to the masquerave in the small ballroom on deck five. So I'm thinking stealth. We could pretend to be working the party, listen in through his VC, provide pointers."

"Or," he interjected, and I raised a brow. "Just hear me out. It's a costume party, correct? Why don't we dress up, pretend to attend the masquerave ourselves?"

I slowed to a stop. "Have you ever even been to a rave?"

"No." He shrugged. "But they've always sounded fun. Flashing lights, loud music, hot." His brows waggled. "Sweaty."

Smashing my grin into a tight line, I said, "I'll think about it. But it's still work." I pointed a finger into his chest. "Only work."

He raised his hands, innocent as a schoolboy. "Of course it's only work. What else could it be?" And there was a twinkle in his eye when he said, "What a dirty mind you have, Sunastara" under his breath.

MORNING MEETING WENT AS WELL as expected. Rax and Morgath —both looking as haggard as I felt—reported that they'd tripled the security mechs assigned to Sonia and her family, as well as installed an outrageous number of Vcams not only around her suite but all around the ship. How they got the credits approved for the enhanced security was beyond me, and with their current state of general grumpiness, I wasn't about to ask.

Tig still hadn't found the source of the breaches, but she'd narrowed her suspected targets down to Ulaperia, Vorp, or Gorbulon-7. So at least she only had to search on this side of the wormhole now, even if that search still included three entire planets.

Only two weeks remained before the ship reached Portis and the senator disembarked, one of which would be spent entertaining Kravaxians. It would be a miracle if we made it through without incident.

Elanie hadn't attended the meeting, which was odd. She hadn't answered any of my comms either. So when her voice popped into my head right as Freddie and I were about to part ways for the day, I grabbed his hand and held him still.

<Sunny? Where are you?> Elanie's distress clanged between my ears.

<Outside the staff room. Why? Where the devils are you?>

<Deck thirty-six. Something's wrong up here. Something is seriously, *seriously* wrong.>

"What is it?" Freddie asked with a frown.

"I'm not sure. Elanie says something's happening up on thirty-six."

<I need more information,> I commed. <What exactly is wrong?>

<Everyone is... They're all... *Why?*> She made a gagging noise. <Just get up here, please.>

I clicked off. "Well, whatever it is, it's enough to make Elanie gag. I guess I'm going up to deck thirty-six. Care to join me?"

Squeezing my fingers, he said, "If whatever's going on up there is bad enough to gross out a bionic, you bet your ass I'm coming."

As soon as the elevator dinged, it rolled through the doors, shoving me back—a thick, raw tension like a planet-sized harp string seconds away from springing free from.

"What in hells is that?" I shook my head, trying to clear out the warm, silky fog sinking over me.

Before Freddie could answer, Elanie raced down the hall, sliding between us to take our place in the elevator. Pale, almost green, she looked from Freddie to me, then said, "I quit," while the doors slid closed.

"She can't quit," I said, frowning at the elevator. "Can she?"

Freddie only shrugged, then he asked, "Is it hot up here?" When he squeezed the back of his neck, that round vein popped across his wrist. "I feel hot."

"It might be a little"—I swallowed, overcome by a need to not only trace that vein, but to lick it too—"hot."

Music floated through the air, enthralling, atmospheric, impossibly dreamy as we walked down the hall, passing lingerie shops, strip clubs, the entrance to the live sex show on this extremely racy deck. All empty. "Where is everyone?" I asked.

Instead of answering, Freddie bent down to pick something up from the floor, pulling my attention to his gorgeous butt. *Stars*, it was spectacular. So round and firm. While I considered what it might feel like to bite it, he turned toward me, his lips as red as cherries, his eyes dark and smoldering. A pink thong dangled from his finger. "I think someone's lost their underwear." Dropping the thong back to the floor, he blinked. "Something's happening to me. I feel"—he tugged on his collar—"strange."

Tearing my eyes from his throat, his chin, his lips, I looked past him down the hallway. He was right. Because he was always right. He was right and delicious, and I needed to kiss every single inch of his entire body—

"Sunny?"

Rolling my neck, I said, "Me too. I mean, I'm strange too." I undid the top button of my blouse. "And my clothes feel too tight."

"Speaking of clothes." Freddie pointed at the light fixtures along the wall, the paintings and digpics serving as hooks for discarded shirts, pants, bras, and underwear, even a pair of Argosian coveralls. "What in the worlds is going on up here?"

Barely hearing my voice over the blood drumming in my ears, I said, "I don't know. But stay close to me." And he did, closing the distance between us, the heat from his body warming my already scalding skin.

Each step forward felt like fighting the tide, an undertow of need and desire swirling around me, pulling me back toward him.

"Sunny. This is... I'm not..." His voice came out strained, hoarse, stirring the tiny hairs on my neck.

"I know," I told him. "I know. Just keep walking." But when we reached the end of the hallway where it opened into the galleria, I gasped. "Good gods."

Tangled on the floor, sprawled over chairs and couches,

half-submerged in the fountain, hundreds of guests writhed in a naked, moaning, multi-species free-for-all.

Freddie's hands curled around my arms, and I vanished into the sensation, nothing else in the worlds existing but the indentation of his fingertips on my skin. Until he said, "What the fuck are they doing?" and I burst suddenly into manic, giddy laughter. He did too. And as we stood there, watching, laughing, I thought, *oh no*.

Somehow, the hysteria broke through the incessant onrush of mindless, endless wanting long enough for a single coherent thought to override my short-circuiting brain. I knew what this was. I'd felt this way before. Wanted like this. *Needed* like this.

Scanning the galleria, I hissed a curse. This was bad. This was really, really bad. "It's the pleasure pods," I said, pointing to the bank of kidney-shaped capsules along a far wall. They were all open, all active, with bright-red light spilling from each one like wine from a glass. "They're malfunctioning." I fanned my neck as a bead of sweat seared a path down my spine. "All of them."

"That's not good." Freddie yanked his tie loose. "We need to tell somebody, right?"

"Yes, definitely. We should tell someone because—" Because what? Because *something*, I was sure. But my thoughts kept slipping, floating away from me like startled moon jellies. I closed my eyes, overwhelmed by the scene before me, by the hormones pumping through my bloodstream, the pleasure pods hacking my hypothalamus, pushing my pleasure centers into overdrive.

"Are you okay?" Freddie asked, his chest pressing up against my back, his breath skimming over my neck.

"I don't think so," I said on a rushed exhale. And when he touched me again, his fingertips ghosting up my arms, my head lolled back to rest against his shoulder.

The tip of his nose slid along the curve of my neck, and I

reached back, grasping his hip, scrabbling for purchase as the universe tilted, swirled, sanity dancing away from me, all but vanishing as he dropped his lips to my ear and whispered, "Phoebe."

Spinning around in his arms, I wrapped my fingers around his tie and yanked his lips to mine. I thought the kiss would give me some relief from the deep, driving desire animating my arms and my fingers and my lips. But I couldn't kiss him enough. Couldn't be kissed enough. There was no enough.

He pulled away, that same unrelenting not-enoughness blazing in his eyes. In the space he'd put between us, I stared up at him, pleading, begging him for something. For anything. Maybe for everything. And then he offered it to me, pointing his chin over my shoulder, his chest heaving, his pupils blown. "I think there's a utility closet—"

"Gods, yes." Pulling him by the tie still clutched between my fingers, I accessed the security lock for the closet in my VC, and we barreled through the door.

I grabbed at his coat, his shirt, his tie, tearing them off in a blur of soft fabric and expensive tailoring. When he pushed me up against a shelf, I laughed. Then I moaned when his teeth sank into my shoulder, the bite just shy of painful.

Dropping to his knees, he nosed under my blouse to kiss my belly while his deft fingers undid my button, unzipped my zipper, pulled my pants down over my hips. My panties joined the rest of our clothes in a heap in the corner.

I let him ease my legs apart, his hands gliding from my ankles to my calves as his lips skimmed along the ultra-sensitive skin of my inner thigh. When his mouth reached my swollen, pulsing, neurochemically aroused core, he only had to slide his tongue over me once, and I tumbled, gasping as waves of pleasure crashed over me again and again, refusing to let me come up for air.

"I'm sorry," he said against my thigh. "I didn't want it to be like this. I wanted to be patient. I wanted to wait until it was right. But, *stars save me*, I need—"

Grabbing a fistful of his hair, I pulled on him until his eyes met mine. "If you're not inside me in five seconds—"

It only took him three.

Standing, unzipping his pants, stroking his rigid length while I hooked my thigh over his hip, he drove into me, and I drowned in mindless, scorching, neuro-hacked bliss. A sea of sensation surged and receded, ecstasy thrumming through every cell in my body in time with his hips. It was magnificent. *He* was magnificent. It was so much more, so much deeper, so much fuller and sweeter and thicker and harder than anything I'd ever experienced before. I never wanted it to end. And after my third orgasm and his second, in a brief moment of lucidity, I realized that it might never end. And that would be bad. *Probably*.

"Our guests," I slurred, my head hanging over his shoulder, my brain struggling to function. "We need help."

"Who?" He pulled back, his eyes heavy lidded, his lips wet and parted. "Who could help?"

Right. If anyone else came up here, they'd suffer this same fate. Well, maybe not this exact fate. This fate belonged to us, only us, until the end of time. Taking his face between my hands, I kissed him, brushing my tongue over his, feeling him swell again inside me. My legs trembled, and I clung to him as he pulled out, moved us to the floor, hauling me into his lap. Lowering myself onto him again, I ran my hands through his hair, each strand uniquely silky as it slid through my fingers. "Were we talking about something?"

"Help," he said, drawing a single finger down the center of my spine. "We need to get help."

"Elanie. She hasn't upgraded yet. She's immune. She was able to"—I groaned as he grasped my hips, sliding me up and down his shaft—"walk away."

"Can you comm her?" he asked, slowing his pace, giving me a chance to try.

Even so, accessing my VC was like sifting through wet sand. <Elanie,> I commed. <Help. It's the pleasure pods. You're our only hope.>

<Are you kidding me?> she snapped back. <Why can't you fix it? I can't come back up there.>

<Too...hard.> I would have laughed at the phrasing if he hadn't swiped his tongue up my throat. <Please hurry.>

<Ugh, fine. Give me five minutes.>

I would have given her forever, longer than forever, to the point when time no longer existed and we were nothing but stardust. But our guests, they needed us. <Thank you, Elanie. Thank you.>

It wasn't quite like a switch flipping, the moment she deactivated the pods. It was softer, slower. It was the quiet calm after the storm, waves receding into the ocean. It was waking up from the most wonderful dream, wishing you could fall asleep again so it wouldn't end.

Sitting in his lap with his hands cradling my ass and sweat dripping between my breasts, I wheezed, "Holy hells."

With a breathy laugh, his shoulders shaking under my palms, he leaned back, looking me over. "Are you all right?" His eyes were glossy, his cheeks flushed, his hair sticking to his forehead in sweaty little strands.

"I'm not sure I'll be able to walk tomorrow," I said, smiling at his red cheeks and his messy hair and his dazed, sated expression. "But I'm fine." That was a lie. In truth, I was so much better than fine that the word itself was a dull, gray speck in a technicolor universe.

Blinking away the last wild remnants of lust from his eyes, he asked, "How long have we been in here?"

I accessed the time. "Ninety-seven minutes."

"That long?"

Brushing his damp hair back from his forehead, I asked, "Have you ever been in a pleasure pod before?"

"No. They've always intimidated me," he said. "For good reason, apparently."

I traced his crooked smile with the pad of my thumb. "You don't experience time when you're in a pod. Or hunger or thirst. Or if your hair is on fire, for that matter. The only thing you experience is the pleasure."

With the word hovering between us, we seemed to realize at the same time that he was still inside me. Sliding his hands over my hips, he started to raise me up, and I squeezed my legs around him. "Wait," I said. "Not yet."

Relaxing, slinging his arms low around my waist, he said, "Okay."

After what we'd just done—and how many times we'd done it—some might call it ridiculous, the nerves tightening my throat. We'd just shared ninety-seven minutes of intense, carnal, worlds-shattering ecstasy. I was still breathless from it, my bones heavy, muscles loose, skin as warm as an afternoon lying under real sunlight. But it wasn't enough. I still wanted him, more than I should, more than *Sunny* should. But even though the pods no longer drove me near to madness, the push was still there, the buzz, the hunger. Later, when I wondered what had gotten into me, I could blame it on that.

"Stay with me," I whispered into his ear.

He was silent, his chest rising and falling like the tide. And I closed my eyes, bracing for the sting of rejection. But there was no sting, only his fingers sliding up my sides, his hand cupping my breast and bringing my nipple to his lips, sucking it into his mouth. I moaned when his tongue swirled over my stiff peak, in pleasure, in relief. Maybe both.

He spun me around, laying me down, pulling a towel over from one of the shelves to slide under my head. I was sore, my muscles aching, but it didn't matter. The sight of him propped above me, gazing down at me, his lips curving into a soft, unguarded smile…nothing else mattered.

"How did this happen?" I asked him, running my fingertip over the crooked line of his nose. "Did you break it?"

"Aye." His voice was quiet, soothing as he notched himself at my entrance. "I was twelve. A boy in my class had chased a girl during recess. She hadn't liked it, so I'd told him to stop. He broke my nose, I kicked him in the shin, and that was that."

"Did he leave her alone?" I asked, cupping his cheek while he slid into me again.

His smile grew as he started to move his hips. "He did."

"Did she thank you?"

"Aye, Molly McDay. My first kiss."

Snaking my fingers around his neck, I said, "Lucky lass." Then I pulled his mouth to mine, losing myself in him while he lost himself in me. This time, of our own free wills.

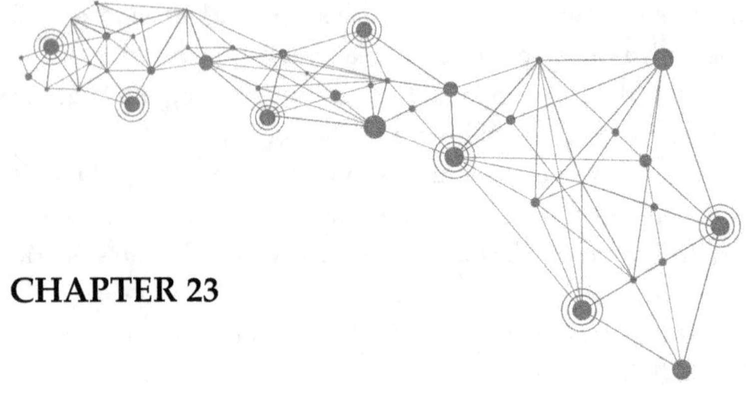

CHAPTER 23

THE FALLOUT from what would go down in history on the ship as Podgate was minimal, with the general consensus of all beings involved including some form of *that was the best night of my life*. Not necessarily surprising, considering the typical state of affairs on deck thirty-six. The final rule on the pod malfunction—excessive overuse—didn't surprise me either. All the same, more stringent safety measures were being installed on all pleasure pods throughout the ship today.

Also a casualty of excessive overuse, I'd woken up brutally sore and completely worked, like I'd run a marathon—or had gotten fucked through one. At least Freddie wasn't faring much better. He'd commed me to check in, admitting he hadn't been able to get out of bed until the three anti-nox tabs he'd taken kicked in.

Despite the pain—and the bouts of staring off into space whenever the sense memory of being taken so many times, in so many ways, and for so long, invaded my brain—I still had a job to do. Today, that job entailed first having breakfast with Sonia, Sai, and Lena in their pod, where we'd discussed their lingering security concerns while I'd tried and failed to solve Sai's newest puzzle. And now, because somehow this was my life, I was on my way to pick up the gigantic, hairy, and indescribably stinky Kravaxian bovine I'd miraculously secured before FFK day.

As I approached airlock A-6, the sharp, musty odor seeping into the hallway was enough to put a Gorbie off their lunch—and Gorbies thought fermented bog slugs were a delicacy. Burying my nose in the crook of my elbow, I pressed my thumb onto the techPad to sign the shipping receipt before gingerly accepting the kurot's lead rope from the relieved-looking postal droid.

There were times in a being's life when the realization that they were in way over their head felt as tangible as the ground beneath their feet. Walking out of the docking bay, pretending I had an ounce of control over a two-ton ungulate with a rope half the size of my wrist, was without question one of those times. Especially when she kept shying sideways at every guest that walked by, every digpic on the wall, every time the air conditioners cycled on.

"Need help with that?"

Wheeling around halfway to the Cosmic Spectacle stables, I spotted Makenna walking toward me.

"Yes. Yes, I do," I said, and I would have fallen to my knees if it wouldn't have put my head at the beast's mouth. "Do you know anything about kurots? She keeps trying to eat my hair. And stars above, she smells."

"Well, no," Makenna said with a low, throaty laugh. "Not really. But I have been taking care of Dave for the last week, so..." She shrugged. "Heading to the stables?"

"Stars willing," I replied.

"She's cute," Makenna said, taking the lead from me. "Shaggy. But *yeesh*." Her nose scrunched. "She does stink. Like cheese left out in the sun."

"I'm not sure I'll ever get the scent out of my clothes." I

sniffed my sleeve, trying not to gag. "And don't let her near your hair."

Pulling her braids over her shoulder, Makenna said, "Thanks for the warning."

With each step that drew us closer to the stables, the temptation to ask her about how things were going with Chan bubbled up inside me. But considering that every single effort I had ever made to meddle in Chan's love life had failed miserably, I held my tongue. Or I tried to.

"How long will you be staying with us, Makenna?"

Pulling a braid the kurot had somehow managed to get in its mouth free, she muttered, "Gross," while shaking a string of drool from her hand. "We're here until we dock in Portis."

"That long?" *Interesting*. "You'll be here for New Year's, then."

"I will. Does the *Ignisar* celebrate?"

I scoffed. "If you thought the Fire Ball was something..."

"Better than the Fire Ball?" Her brows rose. "Is that possible?"

With a small laugh—and a huge inward smirk—I said, "I'm glad you're staying. It was nice seeing you and Chan out together the other night. He's always working. It takes something, or someone, extraordinary to get him to take a break. I certainly never manage to do it." *Oops*, that was definitely meddling.

Slowing, turning her head toward me, she said, "Can I ask you something, Sunny?"

"Of course."

"Why hasn't Chan...? Why does he still...? Why won't he...?" She stalled out, her expression turning plaintive.

"Why is he still paralyzed?"

While her lips made a tight line, she nodded.

Modern medicine could repair the damage to Chan's spine. But—as he'd confided in me a few years ago while we'd watched sunrise sim over an empty bottle of Venusian bourbon —his injury was important to him.

"Has he told you how he got hurt?"

"No," she said. "I've never asked."

"He'd been a lieutenant in the Asteroid Belt Wars for over a decade," I said. "Until there was an ambush on the asteroid he was ordered to secure for LunaCorp. The fallout was catastrophic. Only he and a handful of his soldiers survived. I asked him once why he kept his injury. He told me that the soldiers he'd lost could no longer breathe or laugh or love or have children or grandchildren, and he could no longer walk. I think he feels that keeping his injury is a small price to pay so that he never forgets their sacrifice."

"*Saints*," Makenna said. "I guess I understand why he would feel that way. But still, does he honestly think they'd want that from him? Doesn't he want to move on?"

My brows knit together, my shoulders hitching at her tone. I was sure that Chan knew his battalion wouldn't have wanted him to carry the weight of their loss forever. I was also sure that it didn't matter. Because Chan wasn't ready to put that weight down yet. Maybe he never would be. Maybe it was unfair, even cruel, to expect a being to simply move on because a certain amount of time had passed. Because maybe the sun would burn out before that certain amount was even close to enough. Maybe some weights couldn't be put down, as impossible to shed as one's own skin. Maybe—

The kurot blew a heart-stopping snort at a passing cleaning drone, her bushy legs jumping wide, her big, black nostrils flaring, red-brown eyes wide and rolling.

"Hush," Makenna said, soothing the beast while I slammed my hand over my thundering heart.

Eventually deciding that the tiny cleaning drone wasn't a mortal threat, the kurot shook herself out from nose to tail, flinging a thick string of slobber across the portrait of Brock Karlovich on the wall beside us.

"We'd better get her locked up before she sees a compactor droid and passes out from shock," I said, forcing a laugh, forcing my memories down, back into the dark where they belonged. Where they were safe.

After leading the kurot into the stables, Makenna handed its lead rope over to a stable hand I'd never seen before. He was a young, rangy human with a beak of a nose who accepted the rope like it was a rotten fish.

"What the hell is this thing?" he asked, his accent placing him squarely from New Earth, New York. "Looks like a cow on steroids and, *ugh*, smells like shit."

"It's a kurot," I told him. "And it will need to be milked twice a day."

"What?" His revulsion intensified when the cow on steroids sneezed in his face.

"By hand," I added, and because I didn't feel like ruining this kid's day even more, I chose not to say *for Kravaxian bathwater*.

While Makenna and I walked out of the stables, I squeezed her hand. "Thank you for your help, darling. You are a lifesaver."

"Anytime," she insisted, waving me off with a quick flick of her wrist. But color rose into her cheeks.

Never able to resist capitalizing on a blush, I tilted my head. "Chan was right," I said, studying her. "You do have the most magnificent eyes. And he described them perfectly, like liquid amber poured into a bright-blue sea."

"He...said that?" she asked, her lovely eyes flaring.

I smiled, nodded, and crossed my fingers behind my back that my meddling might actually work this time.

"Do I look okay?" Garran asked. Taking a night off from his customary yellow coveralls, he was devastating in a fitted black suit and a silver mask with a sun on one side and two intersecting half-moons on the other. Behind the mask, a healthy smudge of black eyeliner made his eyes glow a deep, electric purple.

"Stunning." I kissed my fingers and flung them into the air. "Absolute perfection. Are you ready?"

Rubbing a hand over his freshly shaved chin, he said, "I think so. We have been speaking over our VCs at night, Kasa and I. After her mother goes to sleep."

"Ooh, do tell," I encouraged.

His cheeks turned a deep burgundy. Two for two with the blushing today. I gave myself a mental high five.

"She is funny. And we both love the same flowers. When we get back to Argos, I will plant an entire field of tulips on my farm, in a rainbow pattern, just for her. And she is proud." His eyes softened behind his mask. "She is like you—proud, competent. I like that in a partner."

Now it was my turn to blush. "Garran, I'm not sure you'll need my help at all tonight. I think you've got this."

"No," he said, panicked. "I need you. Please. This is too important. I will mess it up."

"Fair enough," I said, raising my hands. "Your wish is my command."

After a beat, he asked, "Is Freddie coming?"

"I'm on my way to pick him up." I spread my arms out wide. "How do I look?" When I'd opened my closet this evening, I'd dug it out, hoping it wouldn't be too wrinkled. It felt risky, sliding back into my favorite little black dress, this time on purpose. But some risks were worth taking.

"Beautiful," he said. "You look beautiful. Freddie will be pleased."

I coughed. "What? I'm not wearing it for Fred—"

Garran's booming laughter rattled the walls. "You are trying to lie. But you are not good at it."

"I beg your pardon. I am an excellent liar."

"I do not think so." He ducked his chin, lowered his voice. "Can I tell you something?"

When a being as large and earnest as Garran asked a question like that, the only possible response was "of course."

"You and Freddie are drawn to each other. It's as obvious as poppies in the snow. And yet you try to hide it. Deny it. Try, *poorly*, to lie about it. Why?"

My mouth swung open.

He stepped closer, covering my entire shoulder with his big hand. "I have upset you. You look like an infant after dunking day."

Closing my mouth, I shook my head.

"I did not mean to make you uncomfortable. But you and Freddie," he continued, his eyes going soft, "there is *worth* between you. Most beings do not know this, but on Argos, *worth* has more than one meaning. It can mean the way two bodies fit together. But on a deeper level, it means the way two hearts fit together, two lives. You may not see it yet, but you and Freddie, you fit. You have *worth*." He smirked. "And not only in the obvious way."

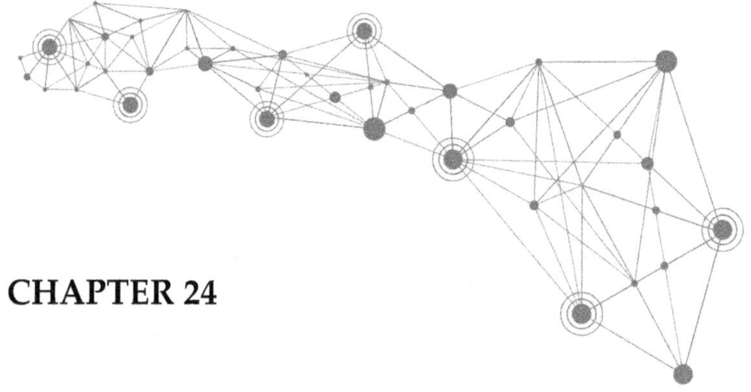

CHAPTER 24

"BLOODY HELL," Freddie gasped after his door slid open.

Raising my black cat mask from my eyes, still a little shaken from my conversation with Garran, I purred, "Well, hello to you too."

As his gaze traveled down my body and back up again, leaving a trail of sparks in its wake, he took a breath and said, slowly, carefully, "You're wearing the dress. *The* dress. Do you know that you're wearing the dress? I mean"—he cleared his throat, sliding his hands into his pockets—"this time, tonight, did you...mean to wear it?"

I nodded, my breath catching in my throat as he took a step toward me, the fire in his eyes close to singeing *the* dress straight off my body. "Are you sure you want to work tonight?" he asked. "The ship is passing the Spiral star cluster. We could go to the observatory."

"Is that a pretty one?" I asked, feeling him move into my space, heating it up like morning shifting into afternoon.

He leaned in close, his lips brushing over my ear as he whispered, "Gorgeous."

"Garran would never forgive us," I protested weakly, my

conviction teetering, my hands fisting at my sides when he pressed a kiss onto my neck. "Besides, after yesterday—"

"Mm-hmm." His voice was a seductive rumble, his breath a soft caress on my skin. "I remember yesterday. I can still *feel* yesterday."

"Stop," I gasped when his fingertips slid over my hip.

"Stop what?"

"Stop *Joshua*ing me." Summoning all the willpower I possessed in my entire body, I placed my hand on his firm chest and pushed him back a step. "We need to focus. We've got a job to do, and it doesn't involve making out like teenagers in this hallway."

He feigned a silent gasp. "Making out? I was only suggesting we spend the night looking at some stars. *Ahem*, eyes up here, sweetheart."

My gaze snapped up from his pants. "Stars above. I'm sorry. I don't know what's gotten into me."

"I do," he said with a raised brow and flawless timing.

I snorted, almost a guffaw. This was terrible. "Can we go now? Please?"

"One moment." He disappeared into his pod, returning with his mask in hand. He looked good tonight. Dark-gray suit, black shoes, black tie, hair expertly coiffed. He was very well put together, and all I wanted to do was take him apart. But not tonight. Tonight, we were working.

Falling into an easy, comfortable silence, we made our way to the Argosian restaurant on deck fourteen where Garran had planned to take Kasa.

"Uh-oh," Freddie said, pointing his chin at the pair. They sat on opposite sides of a square table, not speaking, barely making eye contact. "That's not good."

As we slid into a booth at the far end of the restaurant, I frowned. "Agreed. Let's patch in."

<Garran,> I commed. <Don't be obvious. Don't look—>

Despite my warning, the big man's head whipped around while he knocked over the saltshaker, spilling his glass of water when he tried to right it. Unimpressed, Kasa scowled at him.

<You startled me,> he commed back, wiping his suit pants down with a napkin. <But thank the Tilth you are here. I am floundering. We have already talked about the weather three times. And the weather is always the same on this ship.>

Having joined in on the comm, Freddie muffled his laughter with a hand over his mouth.

<Tell me what to say,> Garran pleaded.

My brow ticked up. "This sounds like a job for you, Mr. Charming."

Interlacing his fingers to crack his knuckles, Freddie gave me a wink and said, "I do love a challenge."

While I wondered if *I* was the challenge he was referring to, Freddie said over the comm, <Kasa looks lovely, Garran. Have you told her that?>

Through our shared channel, we heard Garran say, "Kasa, you look beautiful tonight."

<That's good. You could also add something specific. Something that applies only to her.> Looking directly at me, Freddie said, <Something like, I love what you've done with your hair.>

Reaching up, I brushed my fingers over the small black clasp holding my bangs back. <Yes, Garran,> I commed, staring back at Freddie. <That's very good advice.>

There wasn't much to Kasa's hairdo, a simple braid pulled tight and trailing down her back. But her smile after Garran's compliment was luminous.

<Have you asked her about her day?> Freddie commed.

Garran's shoulders deflated. <No. What is wrong with me? I am terrible at this.>

<We all have to start somewhere,> Freddie said. <But when you do ask her, really listen. Give her your undivided attention. Don't just think about what you want to say next.>

<That will not be a problem,> Garran grumbled. <I do not *have* anything to say next.>

<Then let her do the talking for a while,> Freddie said. <Try not to contradict or interrupt her. Say yes more than no. And don't be afraid of a little silence. Be genuine, be kind, be curious. You've got this.>

I couldn't have torn my eyes from Freddie's even if berserkers chose that exact moment to raid the ship. "That was fine advice," I told him, my voice quiet, my heartbeat loud. "It was wonderful, really."

His foot slid forward until his calf rested warmly against mine. And with a wry tilt to his lips and a sparkle in his eye, he said, "Sunastara, tell me about your day."

If we'd been alone, if the restaurant had been empty, if we hadn't been working, I might have joined him on his side of the booth. I might have taken his face between my hands. I might have kissed him, just a press of my lips against his. I might have wanted more, sliding into his lap, kissing his upper lip, his lower lip, slipping my tongue between them—

"Sunny?" he asked. "Are you still with me?"

"Yes," I said, my gaze locked on his lips, tracing the path of their upward curve. "One hundred percent."

DINNER WENT OFF WITHOUT A HITCH. With Freddie's expert guidance, the conversation between Garran and Kasa flowed like the Tranquisian auroras. As an unexpected but not unpleasant side effect, Freddie and I had time to talk. As coworkers, as friends, as something I couldn't—or wouldn't—define. Even if I didn't know exactly what we were doing, I knew that it was nice.

It *was* nice, his warm laughter across the table while I recounted my stint as a kurot wrangler. Also nice, the way my cheeks got smile-sore when he told me about how he'd publicly berated a Mercurian teenager after catching him terrorizing some poor Ulaperians by shining flashlights into their highly sensitive eyes. It was all so comfortable, so sweet, so nice. And a small, hesitant voice inside me wondered if I could have him like this, to tell stories to and laugh with and feel nice with, and not only in secret. It wondered, while I inched my hand across the table, maybe to intertwine my fingers with his, if I was ready for something real.

<We are leaving,> Garran commed, and I pulled my hand back into my lap. <To the masquerave. Will you come?>

<Of course,> I replied while Freddie stared at the spot on the table where my hand had been. <We are all yours tonight.>

I SLID my mask into place, following behind Freddie into the rave. After passing through a cloud of generated mist at the door, we were suddenly surrounded by swirling lights and swallowed by a sea of bodies covered in phosphorescent glow paint as, wall to wall, beings danced with their heads thrown back, tails tilted up, frizzy hair bouncing and long arms swaying to the driving beats of the trance music.

Ravers scattered while Garran growled his way onto the dance floor. When Kasa yanked him close, taking his ass in both hands and squeezing, I commed, <Bravo, big guy,> and laughed when he replied, <I am so happy right now.>

Clicking off the comm, I staked a claim to a table along the wall and scanned the crowd for Freddie. He'd split off to the bar to stand in an absurdly long line. Spotting him walking back toward me twenty minutes later, I frowned at his crooked black mask, the uncharacteristic stumble in his step.

"Here you go," he shouted, passing me some sparkling

martini-type beverage, red bubbles rising from its stem. He raised his into the air, half-empty. "They are delicious!"

I focused on his mussed hair, his lopsided grin, his tree-like sway. Then I looked down at my drink, at the tiny red pill dissolving rapidly at the bottom. "Oh no."

"Not *oh no*," he said with a wobbly shake of his head. "Oh *yes*."

When he tried to take another sip, I stood, taking his drink from his hand and looking inside. If there had been a tiny red pill in the bottom of his glass, it wasn't there anymore. "Do you remember what this drink was called?"

"Hmm." His lips twisted. "I think it was called follow your... something."

"Bliss?" I guessed.

Freddie snapped his fingers. "That's it."

I groaned. That little red pill in my glass, the one that *had* been in his, was a party drug called Bliss. Apparently, they were serving fast-acting and extremely potent designer euphoria enhancers at the bar tonight. "I think you just took drugs."

"Drugs?" His smile was practically incandescent. "I've never taken drugs before."

I had to bite back my own smile when he tried to straighten his mask, leaving it even more crooked. "Oh, darling. You'll be face-first in the punchbowl in half an hour."

"I will?" He stepped toward me, brushing his fingertips down my arm. "But everything feels so good."

"I'm sure it does," I said, trying my hardest not to laugh. I failed when he dropped his head back, swaying in time with the kaleidoscopic fractal lights swirling into one another above us.

"I can *feel* the music," he said to the ceiling. "It's moving through me. It's part of me."

I was going to murder catering services in the morning.

His eyes found mine, slender blue-gray rings orbiting pitch-black pupils. "Drink yours. You need to feel this with me. It's phenomenal."

Not that I was averse to such things, but after ingesting a mind-altering drug he'd never taken before, he was going to need a babysitter. "Not tonight."

He pouted, and it was so cute I almost changed my mind. Under more appropriate circumstances, taking Bliss with him might have been lovely. But I didn't think he'd want this, to be altered like this when it hadn't been his decision. To be out of control like this in public, where the guests might see him, where he might look unprofessional.

<Garran?> I commed. <How's it going?>

<Good. But Kasa says she wants to leave soon. What do I do?>

<That's wonderful, big guy,> Freddie chimed in brightly. <Do you want to know what I think you should do? I think you should take her back to your pod, run a steamy shower, and—>

I muted Freddie from the conversation.

<What has gotten into him?> Garran asked.

About twenty credits' worth of Bliss. <I think he's coming down with a cold. I need to take him home.> What I needed to do was get him back to his pod before he started licking everyone in the ballroom.

<You are leaving?> There was a hint of panic in Garran's voice.

<I think we'd better,> I said while Freddie reached into the air, playing with shapes that didn't exist. <Listen, you are crushing it. Have fun, be safe, and no matter what, make sure she comes first.>

When I clicked off the comm and looked at Freddie again, I snorted. He was gone, his gaze swooping around the room, his mouth hanging open in utter awe.

"It's all so beautiful," he whispered, placing a hand over his heart. "So achingly beautiful. I love every single one of these beings. I feel like I know them, like I've always known them. Ever since I was a tiny baby. Maybe even before, when I was only stardust, I knew them. And I loved them."

All right. Time to shut this down. Holding my hand up in front of his face, I asked, "Do you see this?"

"Yes," he said. "It's magnificent."

I kept my hand raised, letting him run his fingers over the lines of my palm, up and down the peaks and valleys of my fingers. I remembered enjoying this sort of thing when I'd been in his condition.

Sliding his fingers between mine, he drew me to him. "Dance with me, Sunny."

My heart stuttered.

Sunny.

In all the times we'd been close like this, touching like this, he'd never once used my real name. Because we didn't do that. Because that was the line we'd drawn. So why was I melting at the hushed sound of it now? Why did I want him to say it again while we were close like this, so I could feel it through my chest pressed against his?

Reaching up, I straightened his mask, then I placed my hand on his shoulder. One dance would be okay, I told myself while his hand slid into the hollow of my back, while my body molded to his. One dance before I helped him back to his pod. One dance in the darkness, hiding behind our masks. One dance to imagine what my life might be like if I was able to be his, to meet up with him after work in our pods, to let him sway me side to side, holding me close while we talked about our days, our friends, our families. While we planned our nights, our futures, the way normal, healthy beings probably did. The way I might have done with someone like him before the accident changed me, made me into who I was now, broke me. One dance to imagine myself whole, all my shattered pieces put back together again, held in place by warm hands and strong arms. Just one dance.

As if reading my mind, he urged me even closer and said, "I wish we could always be like this. You take my breath away, Sunny. I think we were meant to meet. At the CAK. On this ship. There is a gravity between us." He lowered his forehead to mine. "Can you feel it?"

The thing was, I *could* feel it, the irresistible force drawing me toward him. And in that moment, I realized how powerless I was to fight it. Because against every single one of my better judgments, against every ounce of self-preservation that remained in my body, when he leaned in, his head slowly tilting, I closed my eyes and held my breath, and I let him kiss me. Not only that, but in this very public place, surrounded by guests and coworkers and irresponsible bartenders, I kissed him back, slipping my fingers into his hair, sighing as his arms wrapped tightly around my waist.

And, *oh,* this was bliss. Kissing him like this, enveloped by his arms, no pharmaceutical enhancement was required. This was bliss. And maybe it was time I stopped fighting the gravity pulling us together. With the anniversary of Jonathan's death only days away, maybe it was time to try, to take a chance, to let myself have the kind of life I knew my son would have wanted me to have.

But not tonight.

Tonight I needed to get him to bed before he started taking off his clothes.

Breaking the kiss, backing out of his arms, I spun him around, aimed him toward the door, and said, "Okay, Romeo. It's time to go."

It was like walking behind a child in a candy store as I ushered him from the ballroom to his pod. Everything was "fascinating" or "glorious." That light fixture, this doorway, even the carpet. The carpet on deck twelve was evidently the most amazing thing since the invention of faster-than-light drives.

When we finally reached his pod, I took his hand and pressed it to his security panel, which he spent another thirty seconds marveling at.

"How are these even made?" he asked. "Who? Who is able to make these?" His voice dropped to a reverent whisper as he ran his fingertip over the panel. "Geniuses, that's who."

"To bed with you," I instructed, finding a glass on his dresser and filling it with water from his sink.

"No." His headshake was vigorous. "No bed. Shower. Let's take a shower. Take a shower with me. Please? Please, please, please?"

His pleading would have been much more persuasive if he hadn't already crawled onto his bed and started fluffing one of his pillows. "It's so fluffy. How have I never noticed how fluffy my pillows are?"

Walking around his bed to place the back of my hand over his forehead, I said, "You're hot."

"You're the one who's hot," he replied, reaching for my waist, gazing dreamily up at me. "And gorgeous. And beautiful. And why does my mouth feel like I've been chewing on sand?"

"Here." I handed him the glass of water while he smacked his lips. "This will help."

"Yes. Yes, you're right. You're so smart." After releasing me to spin the glass of water in his hand for a moment, he guzzled it down.

I walked to his sink to fill the glass a second time, and when I turned back around, I squeezed it close to my chest. He'd already passed out, sprawled on his bed with his face smooshed into one of his fluffy pillows. With a contented sigh, I set the water down on his nightstand. Then I slipped off his shoes, his socks, his jacket, and while I undid his tie, he mumbled something into his pillow.

"What's that, darling?"

"I love you," he said softly, hugging his pillow tightly, his little pinky with its bitten-off tip pressing into the foam. "I love you so much."

I knelt beside his bed, because that's what a being did when their knees gave out, when their lungs stopped expanding, when their heart stopped beating.

With trembling fingers, I traced the arch of his eyebrow, the crooked line of his nose, the bow and curve of his full lips. I'd done this to him once before, when he'd fallen asleep during our night together on the CAK. I'd wanted to commit him to memory then, to make him real for as long as possible before we left each other forever. And now, against astounding odds, he was here. I didn't need to remember him. I didn't need to make him real. He was real. He was real and he was here and he loved me. Impossibly, he loved me.

And what was that deep ache in my chest? What was deep, contented sweetness wrapping itself around me, making my eyes sting? Was that love? Did I love him too?

The answer was right there, the words hovering on the tip of my tongue. I only had to say them. He wouldn't know. He wouldn't remember. I could say them now, believe them now, *mean* them now, and I'd still be safe in the morning. It could be like practice. A chance to see what might crack inside me if I did say them, or maybe what wouldn't. Because what if I told him, and I was still whole afterward? What if, because of him, I was healing?

Gathering whatever courage I had left, my heart pounding, my pulse thrumming in my ears, my breathing shallow and ragged, I opened my mouth and—

“Serena,” he whispered into the darkness. “Serena, I love you.”

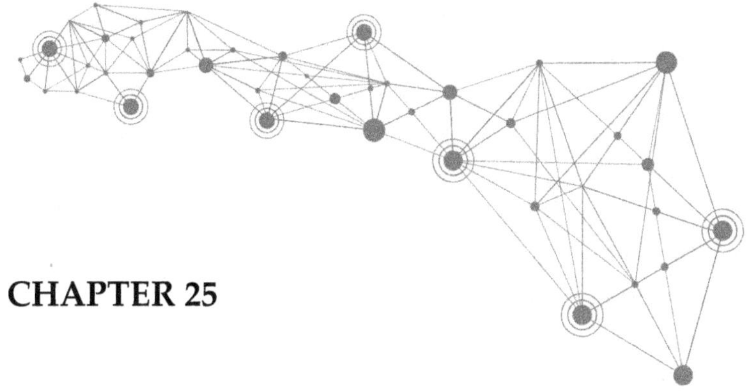

CHAPTER 25

In the space between where I knelt frozen in place on his carpet to where Freddie slept peacefully in his bed, the universe expanded, stretched, pushing itself outward until it might as well have been a light-year separating us. He hadn't been thinking about me. He hadn't been talking about me. He didn't love me.

He'd asked me once if I'd had someone else, but I'd never thought to ask him the same thing. And since that day, all I'd done was push him away, keeping him firmly at arm's length, forcing him to pretend to be someone else entirely just to get close to me. Who did that? What kind of being did that to someone they claimed to care about?

Of course he'd found another lover. Or maybe he'd had one all along. We weren't exclusive. We weren't in love with each other. We weren't even real. None of this was real. How could I have been so stupid?

My eyes stung and my nose burned. The sensation was so foreign to me—the prickling pain, the mist clouding my vision—that I didn't recognize it at first. But when I wiped the single tear slipping down my cheek away, something worse than pain slammed into me, worse than disappointment or misery or even heartbreak. It was disgust. Staring at the wetness on my fingers, I was disgusted with myself.

Because I didn't cry. I'd wanted to, desperately, but I never did. Not once in the last five years. When Jonathan was taken from me, when I'd gotten the call that he was gone, at his service, I hadn't been able to shed a single tear for him. There were so many nights I didn't sleep, sitting up in my bed, trying to make the tears come, knowing that if they did, maybe I'd feel less guilty, less numb, less empty. But they never came. Never. And now, this was how it happened? This was what I cried over? Not my son, but a man?

Fury ignited inside me, sudden and tremendous. It wasn't Freddie or my son or even the cold, uncaring universe that had taken him from me that made my hands clench into fists, made my fists press into my eyes. It was me. I was the one who'd let myself believe I could move on, make a new life, be happy again. I was the one who'd let myself get so vulnerable. I was the one who'd let this thing between us go too far. I was the one who'd forgotten the truth. The truth that Chan knew. That any being who'd suffered so much loss knew. There was no moving on.

I had to get out of here. I couldn't do this anymore, stare at his sleepy smile, his arms holding his pillow close, his heart full of love for someone who wasn't me.

Pushing myself to my feet, I staggered to his door and stumbled numbly back to my pod. Once I was safely inside, I stripped down and contemplated throwing my little black dress into the flash incinerator because it was obviously cursed. Then I stood under a shower so scalding my skin was red and tender when I emerged twenty minutes later, still not feeling clean.

I knew I wouldn't sleep. I knew I was in shock. I knew that even though I was numb now, the pain would find me in the morning. So I sat cross-legged in the middle of my bed, flipped on my TV, and stared at the screen until my eyes burned.

<SUNNY, what happened to me last night? I don't remember anything.>

Even though my alarm had trilled through my VC twenty minutes ago, I hadn't moved from my spot in the middle of my bed. I'd been waiting for him, knowing he'd comm me when he woke up. But I still wasn't prepared for the way his voice grabbed the jagged pieces of my shattered heart and squeezed until they pierced one another.

<Bliss is what happened.> This came out harsher than I'd intended. I'd been aiming for nonchalant but landed on *and you told me that you loved another woman in your sleep* by accident. <Our drinks were spiked.>

<Spiked? *Christ*. Are you okay?>

<I'm fine. I didn't drink mine.>

After a moment, he said, <You sound upset. Did something happen? Did I do something? Was I embarrassing?>

My jaw clenched. <Nothing happened. You were fine.> I swallowed down the lump rising viciously up my throat. <You had fun.>

<Sunny,> he said, suddenly deadly serious. <Something's wrong. Talk to me.>

My heart battered my ribs until they felt bruised, my mouth going dry, my fingers tingling, panic surging inside my chest. <Who is Serena?>

<Serena?> Shock snapped through his voice, but there was a darkness in it too. Something I'd never heard from him before. I thought it was anger. <How do you know about Serena?>

Stars, I shouldn't have asked. Because it didn't matter who Serena was. Because there was no conceivable reality in which I'd be able to sit and listen while he told me about this other being he had feelings for. I couldn't hear it. Refused to hear it.

He couldn't tell me how he loved someone else. Because I was in love with him.

Somehow, despite our deal, despite how careful I'd tried to be, despite everything, I'd fallen in love with him. Not like. Not infatuation—even though, if I was being honest, there was a bit of that too. But love. Foolish, terrible, inevitable love. I already knew it was, but I couldn't hear it from him that my love was a mistake.

<Never mind,> I commed. <It doesn't matter. Listen, Freddie—>

He responded quickly with <Sunny, wait. Let me explain,> and a fresh wave of pain rolled over me at the desperation in the words.

<No. It's too late.> Grinding the heel of my palm into my sternum, trying to make it hurt as much on the outside as it did beneath my ribs, I said, <Last night, I realized that this is all moving a bit too fast for me.>

There was only silence on his end of the comm.

<It's not your fault,> I said. <It's not anyone's fault. I just need some time. Some space. I need things to slow down.>

When he uttered a single, agonized <Why?> another tear slipped down my cheek.

<Things have gotten carried away between us,> I managed, somehow keeping my voice steady while I swiped the tear away. <And we—*I*—need a break.>

<Please, Sunny.> His voice broke. <Don't do this. Give me a chance. I love y—>

I clicked off the comm, my eyes drying, my shoulders sinking, my chest cold and empty and caving in on itself. It was awful. Everything hurt. But it was done.

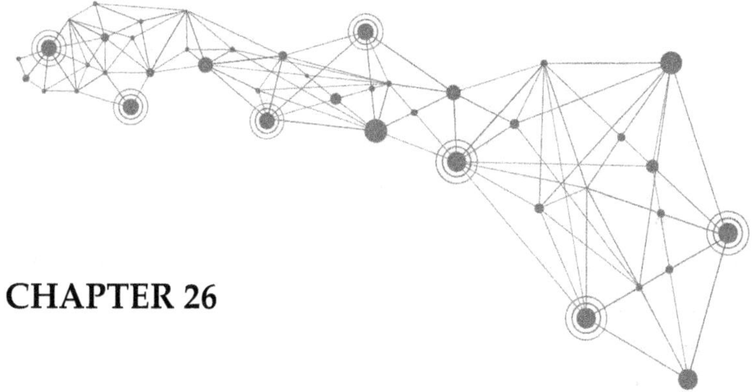

CHAPTER 26

Avoiding Freddie would be difficult, but not impossible. We had a staff meeting first thing, and then I'd spend the rest of the day preparing for the arrival of the FFKs. I could easily keep myself busy staging the Kravaxians' rooms and stocking their refrigerators and minibars with their requested snacks and beverages—gelatinized trestal eggs, dried gwarfs, crater eel jerky, and, *oddly*, fruit punch.

I knew I couldn't stay away from him forever, but I couldn't bear to speak to him or have anything explained to me or be forced to explain anything back. Not for the next few days.

<You're late,> Elanie snapped into my VC. <Again.>

<On my way,> I replied, chipper, trying to sound like I wasn't a walking, talking bruised heart. <How is it in there?>

<It is aggressively uncomfortable,> she replied. <I don't think Tig has slept in two days. Rax and Morgath keep growling. Chan can't stop looking around like he expects the room to explode. And Freddie is an absolute disaster. Did something happen to him last night?>

<I...couldn't say.>

The comm went silent for a few seconds—millennia for a

bionic—and then she said an understated, and far too understanding, <I see.>

When I walked into the staff room, my plan was to smile genially at everyone around the table, take a seat, zone out during the meeting, and be the first one out the door. But then I saw him. Only someone born without a heart could have smiled. And the sharp ache piercing my chest was proof enough of mine.

He sat hunched forward, his face pale, his eyes sunken and rimmed in red.

<Sunny,> he commed, sounding as tortured as he looked, as tortured as I felt. <Can we talk? Please?>

It wasn't fair. His sunken eyes, his pleading gaze. I shouldn't have to feel sorry for him. I'd asked for space. I needed time. I had things to do, important things. I was at work.

<Of course,> I replied evenly while taking my seat, the one closest to the door, keeping my eyes on my hands in my lap.

<After the meeting?> he asked.

Chan, *bless him*, saved me from having to answer. "Good morning, everyone," he said brightly. "Today is FFK day. I trust you all know your responsibilities?"

"Keeping trained killers from destroying our ship," Rax muttered.

"Check," Morgath replied, flicking a checkmark into the air with his finger.

The twins were armed to the teeth with nonlethals: flash grenades, chuck-cuffs, short-range jammers, paresis darts, sonic cannons. And some sort of massive laser gun thing I'd never seen before sat on the table in front of them. I didn't even want to know what that was.

"Good morning." The deep, commanding voice behind me snapped me out of my misery-haze, pulling me and everyone else at the table up to our full attention.

"Captain, Co-Captain," Chan said, raising his hoverchair a few inches. "How wonderful to see you both this morning."

"Excuse our intrusion," Declan said. "We won't take more than a moment of your time." He didn't wait for a response. "As you know, LunaCorp is sending Kravaxians to holiday with us today, and to train with some of you."

Rax's grumble earned a scathing *are you kidding me right now?* glare from Chan.

"We want you to know how important this visitation is for this ship, as well," Declan continued, his tone level but his meaning as clear as flexGlass, "as for our employer. I have no doubt we will all treat our friends from Kravax with the professionalism and hospitality we are known throughout the KU for." He looked directly at Rax and Morgath, and to their credit, they nodded, showing the captains the respect we all felt for them.

"We know there may be some reservations about this visit," Isla added. "And we all have our own preconceived notions about Kravaxians. But Declan and I can assure you, there is nothing to worry about. These are not barbaric deep-space raiders. These are bright, dedicated beings who only want to move their planet into the thirty-first century. Thank you for all your hard work getting ready for this visit. I heard we were even able to secure a kurot." With a smile, she winked at me. Likely noticing my current state of level-ten disaster, her brows pulled together when she said, "Prime work."

And with that, the captains left as quickly as they'd arrived. But not before Isla gave me another concerned glance on her way out the door. Even though the nerves in the room seemed to settle in their wake, I was crawling out of my skin to be anywhere else.

<Please don't look at me,> I commed Elanie. <But I need your help,>

<What can I do?> she asked, and if I hadn't already been

desperate to bolt, the sympathy in Elanie's voice would have done the trick.

<I don't want to talk about it. So please don't ask. But I need you to find me directly after the meeting to tell me there's an emergency situation at the main deck buffet that requires my immediate attention.>

<The buffet? Do you really think he'll believe that?>

It was a relief, the snark I knew and loved.

<I don't particularly care what he believes.>

<Listen, Sunny. I know this isn't my specialty—or something I know anything about at all—but if you ever do want to talk about it, I'm here.>

Rubbing my palm into my sternum again, wondering if I should see Dr. Semson because this amount of chest pain couldn't be good, I commed, <Thank you, Elanie. But I'll be fine.>

When Chan called an end to the meeting, I stood, turned, and tried my hardest not to race for the door.

"Wait," Freddie said, hot on my heels. "Sunny, wait."

Because I couldn't just run away, I slowed, stopped, turned around. Staring at my shoes, I said, "Hello, Freddie."

"I need to explain," he said. "This morning. You caught me off guard. But I can—"

I raised my eyes, and then I raised my hand to cut him off. Because if he thought *he'd* been caught off guard—

"Sunny." Elanie appeared at my side. "There's an emergency situation at the main deck buffet that requires your immediate attention," she said, repeating my request verbatim and without inflection, just like the half robot she was. I should have asked for Tig's help instead.

Freddie's shoulders sank. "An emergency," he said, defeat in his voice, in his expression, knowing it was a lie, knowing I'd asked Elanie to save me from having to talk to him.

Daring to meet his eyes, I said, "I'm sorry, Freddie. I have to go."

He reached for me, but when I took a step back, his hand fell to his side. "Can we talk later? Please, Sunny. Give me a chance."

I nearly caved right there, nearly buckled under the weight of his sincerity. "Let's get through the Kravaxians," I said, because then I'd be through the anniversary too. Then I wouldn't be so weak. "Then we can talk."

He nodded, looking resigned but also relieved. "All right. I'm here. I'll be here."

Giving him a tight smile, I walked to the elevators. Stepping inside, I pressed a random button, because I didn't even know where I was going. I only knew I couldn't be here. Just before the doors closed, I watched Elanie say something to Freddie, placing her hand on his arm while he shook his head, his chin dropping to his chest.

<Sunny,> Tig commed. <Have a minute?>

Since leaving Freddie in the hallway, I'd been hiding out in the Kravaxian's rooms, programming their walls to display surprisingly beautiful digpics of their planet. Rather than the barren wasteland I'd pictured, Kravax was lush and mountainous. It reminded me a little of Tranquis. Which reminded me of Jonathan. Which reminded me of everything.

<Of course, Tig,> I commed back, hearing the exhausted strain in my own voice. <What can I do for you?>

<Well, I've found out some stuff.> If I sounded exhausted, she sounded completely wrecked.

<Darling, when was the last time you slept?>

Skirting the question, she commed, <Remember the senator's Proposition 2126?>

<I do.>

<I haven't been able to stop thinking about it. Like, why would the senator mention it if it was no big deal? Why bring it up at all? So I did some research.>

<Find anything helpful?> I asked, programming another pic.

<No. Nothing. By all accounts, it's a fairly benign proposition requesting increased Imperion funding for deep-space exploration—practically identical to a bill that passed without issue ten years ago.>

<Hmm,> I murmured. <Hardly something that would inspire hacking into a LunaCorp database and threatening a woman and her family.>

<Exactly,> Tig agreed. <It doesn't make any sense. But it does make me wonder even more why the senator mentioned it. I need more information. Do you think you could talk to her about it?>

I nodded, even though she couldn't see me. <I will. As soon as I can. Thank you, Tig. Did you find anything more about who the hackers might be?>

<No. The signal keeps bouncing. It's maddening.>

After selecting the last digpic, I sighed at the wall. <Take a break, love. Get some sleep before your trainee arrives.>

She groaned over the comm. <I really hope they don't expect me to talk too much. You know how awkward I am with new people. Can you imagine how awkward I'm gonna be with a Kravaxian?>

<If it's any consolation, I think we're all going to be a bit awkward. But it's only for a week. It'll be over in a blink.>

<The longest blink in the history of the cosmos,> she grumbled before clicking off the comm.

Plopping down onto the bed, I rubbed my tired eyes. With Freddie, the Kravaxians, and the anniversary looming, it was...a lot. And for a moment, sitting there, I let myself feel it—the disappointment, the pain, the sorrow. At first, it was tolerable, a manageable ache. But then, like it always did, the pain swelled, expanded, and soon, I had to bite my cheek against the crushing weight of it. Against the certainty of how easily it could hold me down and never release me if I let it.

So I didn't let it. Because I was good at keeping it out. Keeping everything out. Keeping myself safe. I'd made a mistake letting Freddie sneak in. It wasn't his fault. Maybe it wasn't even my fault. Either way, it wouldn't happen again.

With my mind made up, I got to my feet, inhaled sharply, and blew the air out through my lips. Only one thing would keep me going, keep my head above water, keep the pain at bay. The same thing that had kept me afloat for the last five years. Straightening my shirt, pinching my cheeks, and smoothing my bangs across my forehead, I got back to work.

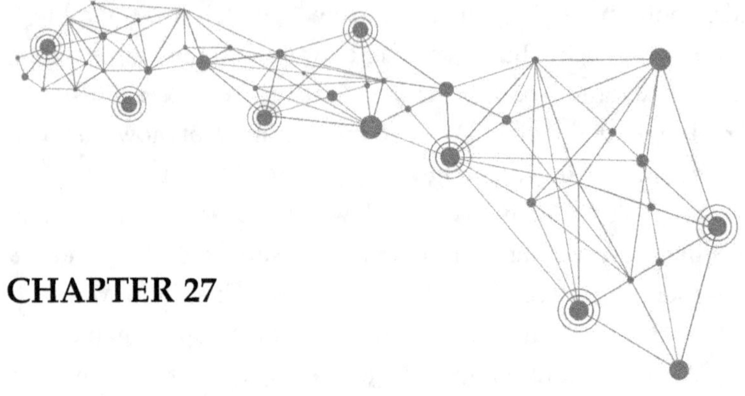

CHAPTER 27

WAITING outside the airlock with Freddie and Chan, watching the FFKs' shuttle dock with the ship, I shifted from foot to foot, tapping my fingernails on my belt. This would go one of two ways. Either LunaCorp was right, and this would be an uneventful week spent training a few new employees. Or the ship was about to be raided.

Once the airlock finished cycling and the doors slid open, Chan, dressed in his finest suit, pulled his hoverchair forward. "Welcome aboard," he said while the FFKs stepped over the threshold.

They were tall, all with deep-brown eyes, moon-pale skin, and jet-black hair. I wasn't exactly sure what I'd expected, but the reality was strangely disappointing. There were no necklaces made of noses. No finger-bone earrings. There wasn't even a single menacing tattoo. Instead, the two males looked sharp in well-tailored suits, and the two females stunned in black skirts and crisp white blouses. The younger of the females wore a pair of fabulous shoes, red heels with thin straps that wrapped twice around her ankles. If I'd thought in a million years that I'd be dying to know where a Kravaxian had bought her shoes...

"Hello," I said, giving them a small nod, not extending my hand because—according to the sensitivity training Freddie had provided to the crew last week—Kravaxians only shook another being's hand when agreeing to a fight to the death. Although he did add that this might have been inaccurate since so little was known about Kravaxian customs, I wasn't taking any chances. "I am Sunastara, your hospitality specialist."

One of the males stepped forward, the tallest and oldest—mid-forties in standard years, if I had to guess. He had a heavy brow, a jawline chiseled from marble, and the broad chest of someone who spent a great deal of time lifting heavy things. "I am Tano," he said, waving his hand toward the female standing next to him, her chin jutting out proudly, her arms held stiffly at her sides. "This is my partner, Marisia." He nodded toward the younger male to his right who had a wry twist to his mouth and friendly—*for a Kravaxian*—eyes. "My associate, Axel." Last, Tano introduced the female wearing the phenomenal shoes. She was younger than the rest, maybe Tig's age, with fine, birdlike features and a hesitant smile. "And this is Reya."

"It is wonderful to meet you all," I said. "Welcome to the *Ignisar*."

I'd be lying if I said I wasn't surprised when it was Reya who replied.

"Thank you." Her voice was quiet but unwavering. "It's wonderful to meet all of you as well."

When I shifted my gaze from Reya back to Tano, a sudden chill skittered across my neck. Despite his bland expression, there was an intimidating sharpness about him. Also, he looked strangely familiar. Something about his eyes, his cheekbones.

When he squinted back at me, suspicious, I gave him my best approximation of an unconcerned smile. Freddie took a moment to introduce himself then, his hands remaining in his pockets. Which reminded me of the night I'd found him in his pod, in his gray sweatpants, his hands sliding into his pockets like they were now—

I closed my eyes, forcing my heart to remember, to hear the name again. *Serena, Serena, Serena.*

"Let me show you to your suites," I said, needing to be anywhere but standing this close to Freddie. And while the FFKs gathered their bags, I leaned over to whisper into Chan's ear. "You should cruise by Makenna's pod while you're wearing that fantastic suit."

"Ooh. Good idea," he whispered back.

When I straightened again, I sensed Freddie standing beside me, closer, that gravity between us pulling me toward him. It was so much harder than I'd thought it would be, not speaking to him, not having his friendship, his support, let alone anything else. Let alone his hands or his lips or his body moving over mine.

Stars above, he made me weak. When, right now, more than ever, I needed to be strong.

Gathering myself together, I said, "Please, follow me," to the FFKs. Then I marched straight out of the docking bay without looking back.

AFTER I SHOWED Tano and Marisia to their shared suite, I led Axel, and then Reya, to their private rooms.

"This is very nice," Reya said, running her fingers over her bed linens. "Thank you, Sunastara."

"Please, call me Sunny. And you are more than welcome. I'm glad you find the room adequate."

"It's more than adequate," she said, wide-eyed. "I have never seen such a beautiful room, let alone slept in one. I was raised on a ship, although one much smaller than this. It feels good to be back off planet." Her silky, sable hair—just brushing her chin on one side and hanging to her collarbone on the other—slid forward as she examined the stitchwork on her comforter.

"Who are you training with during your stay?" I asked, my fingers crossed behind my back.

"IT, I believe. Someone named Tig?"

My smile was instantaneous. Of all the FFKs, Reya would have been my pick to work with Tig. She was young, talkative, and not at all intimidating. If Tano had been assigned to IT, I might have rioted on Tig's behalf. "That's wonderful," I said. "Tig is one of my dearest friends, and she is excellent at her job. I'm certain you will learn a lot from her."

Reya toyed with the comforter, her gaze rising to meet mine. "Sunny, I know how much of a risk it is for you to have us here. I know of my planet's reputation. And I appreciate you—all of you—so much. All I want is to make our planet safer, stronger, with more legitimate opportunities for young people like me."

I wasn't knowledgeable enough in the ways of Known Universal commerce to deduce what LunaCorp's long game was with Kravax, but one thing I did know was that I believed her. This was what she thought was best for her planet. And if I could believe Reya, maybe I could believe the rest of them too.

"Take some time to get yourself situated," I said, taking a backward step toward the door. "Dinner is in two hours with the rest of the crew. The refrigerator and minibar are stocked, and there is fresh kurot milk next to your bathtub."

"Fresh what?" Reya snorted, then she laughed, hard.

I frowned. "Is that funny?"

"I'm so sorry," she said with a hand over her mouth, still laughing between her fingers. "But only my ancestors bathed in the milk of kurots. That tradition has not been practiced in centuries. Where in the worlds did you find fresh kurot milk?"

My mouth could not have opened wider if the kurot

currently stinking up the Cosmic Spectacle stables had just stomped on my foot. "You have got to be kidding me."

When Reya dissolved into laughter again, I laughed a little too.

"I had the thing shipped all the way from the CAK," I admitted. "And they only had one because of LunaCorp's new interplanetary petting zoo in their Central Park. It was pure luck that she happened to be female."

"Orion's eye," Reya exclaimed. "I'm so sorry to put you through all that trouble. But, if I'm being honest, Tano is very old-fashioned and still holds to many outdated customs and beliefs"—she didn't roll her eyes, but I could tell that she wanted to—"and superstitions. He might enjoy bathing in kurot's milk."

Giving her a little bow, I said, "Then it has all been worth it."

When I left Reya's room, I walked away far less worried about the FFKs than I'd been before their arrival. But now I had two hours until dinner with little to do. I should go to my pod. I should catch up on sleep while I could. But being alone right now seemed dangerous.

<Elanie,> I commed. <Are you busy?>

<Very,> she replied. <Why?>

Shit. <Never mind. See you for dinner.>

Alone it was. I could handle it. I could somehow avoid curling up in my bed and spending the next two hours thinking about—

<An opening in my schedule just presented itself,> Elanie commed cryptically. <What did you need?>

Normally, I would press her on this, make sure she wasn't making things harder for herself just to help me—which bionics were known to do. But today, I was desperate. <Drinks? I'll pay.>

<I only drink vitoWater. It's free.>

<I know,> I commed, laughing miserably at myself. <It was a kind of a joke.>

<That was a joke? Aren't those supposed to be funny?>

I groaned. Until she said, <Where would you like to meet?>

One very dirty martini later, the tightness that had bound my chest all day finally inched loose. I'd needed to talk to someone about Freddie, and Elanie cared just enough to listen, but not enough to offer advice, and she would never tell another soul if I asked her not to.

"You love him?" She asked this with a genuine curiosity, like she wanted to know in what possible equation variable A and variable B would combine to produce the solution of two beings falling in love.

I nodded, plopping the olive from my second martini into my mouth. "Unfortunately."

"What does it feel like? Being in love?"

"Right now," I said. "It's a bit like an icepick through the heart."

"What?" she blurted out, incredulous. "Why in the worlds would anyone want to feel like they were being stabbed in the heart?"

I was being sarcastic, but Elanie was not. So I answered her question as honestly as I could. "The problem with love, darling, is that it doesn't feel this way all the time. It always hurts, at least a little. But only because it's so precious. You don't want anything bad to happen to it. Because when you're in love, you get to experience feelings that are so much bigger than that little hurt."

She leaned in so close I was a little worried she'd fall off her barstool. "What kind of feelings?"

"Excitement, for one," I said. "The way your heart thumps

and your breath catches when you see each other. It's intoxicating. And then there's the comfort of knowing you've found another soul in the universe who sees you, really sees you—that to them, you matter." I took her hand, a bit surprised that she let me. "It is important to feel like we matter, Elanie. Also the joy. It is a joyous thing, being in love. Being loved in return. And when it's true, it should be cherished."

"But it isn't true love with Freddie? It isn't comforting or exciting or joyous?"

Releasing her hand, I downed the rest of my martini, then forced myself to say a heart-wrenchingly dishonest "no."

LETTING myself get tipsy before a work function with special guests was something I would typically never do. Thankfully, the Kravaxians weren't opposed to alcohol. After the main course, we were all a bit soused. All except for Rax and Morgath, standing stalwart by the door, their arms crossed, their scowls menacing. And Elanie, who would rather shave her head and eat her own hair than lose an ounce of control over herself in public.

Tig and Reya seemed to be getting along at least, talking all through dinner with bright smiles. Tano and Marisia had spent most of the night in silence, occasionally joining Chan and Freddie in whatever they were talking about. I didn't know. I couldn't look in Freddie's direction without reality shouldering its way into my buzz. So I spent my time chatting with Axel.

"How long have you worked on this ship?" he asked, swirling the Ulaperian red in his glass.

Not wanting to subject myself to the worst hangover of my thirties after no sleep in more than twenty-four hours and two martinis on an empty stomach, I took a sip of my vitoWater and said, "Going on five years."

"What did you do before?"

I didn't mean to glance to the side. I didn't mean to lock gazes with Freddie for a breathless moment. I didn't know he'd already been looking at me. "I worked on another LunaCorp ship," I said, suddenly too warm. "One across the wormhole that traveled between New Earth and Mercury. How about you?" I raised my glass to my lips. "What did you do before LunaCorp snatched you up for BLIX?"

"Deep-space piracy, of course," he said with a wink.

I choked on my water.

When Axel touched my shoulder, I heard Freddie cough across the table. "I'm only joking," he explained with a low chuckle. "Customs. I worked in customs."

"I see," I said, clearing my throat. "So you allowed all the pirated goods to come into your planet legally, then."

His low chuckle matured into a genuine laugh. "That sounds about right."

As I talked with Axel, I felt Freddie watching me still. Occasionally, unable to help myself, I watched him too, finding his lips pressed flat, his jaw clenched, his knuckles turning white around the glass of whiskey in his hand whenever I laughed at something Axel said. All of it made me feel unfairly awful. As messed up as I was, I didn't want to hurt Freddie. I didn't want him to think I might be interested in another being. Because that would be a truly terrible thing to do to someone a person supposedly cared about.

When dinner came to an end, I walked the Kravaxians back to their suites. Axel's suite was located farthest down the hall, so by the time we reached his door, we were alone.

"Thank you." He grinned down at me. "You've all been very kind to us."

"My pleasure," I said with a small nod that left me dizzy. A profound exhaustion swirled around me like mist. Through the bleary fatigue, I sent him the link to my VC. "If you need anything at all, don't hesitate to contact me."

He stared at me long enough, meaningfully enough, that I wondered if he would make a pass. I also wondered how I'd gone so quickly from being a woman who would have been thrilled when a handsome new guest showed interest in me, found me desirable, offered me an easy night or two of escape in the palm of their hand, to one who simply...wasn't. I suppose I needed a new hobby. When my subconscious suggested puzzles, I gave it the finger.

In the end, thankfully, Axel didn't make a pass. He only nodded back and said, "Good night, Sunny."

THE NEXT FEW days passed by in a blur. Security on the senator and her family remained a top priority, but the crew had relaxed considerably now that we knew the Kravaxians hadn't come to scuttle the ship and vent everyone aboard her into space. Even Rax and Morgath had behaved themselves while training Axel and Tano in LunaCorp security protocols. Chan and his mentee, Marisia, got on as well as could be expected, considering the woman never spoke, as far as I could tell—and considering Chan kept running off to have lunch or afternoon tea with Makenna.

And Tig and Reya, well, I'd never seen Tig so excited about spending time with another being. As for me, scheming endless possible *whoops, this innocent picnic under the willows in the atrium is actually a date*–type scenarios for them was a surprisingly effective distraction.

Speaking of which, Freddie had given me all the space I'd asked for. He hadn't commed or tried to contact me on *Squee* or tried to speak to me at all unless it was something work related, and even then, he'd been efficient, all business. Hurt still hung behind his eyes, though. It hurt me too, like pressing on a bruise. But he'd respected my request, like he always had and probably always would. And every day that passed, a voice—quiet at first, but growing louder—spoke up inside me: *Maybe, just maybe, you've got it all wrong.*

I needed to talk to him. I owed it to both of us. But not today. Because today, I woke up with the weight of a planet slamming into my chest, pushing me back down into my bed. Smothering me.

Today was the anniversary.

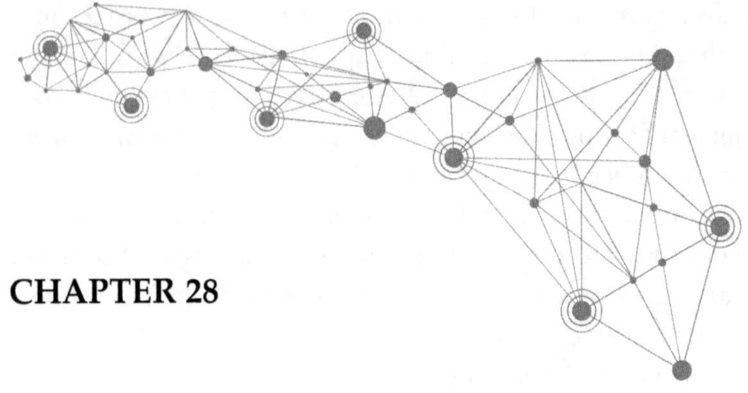

CHAPTER 28

It always snuck up on me. Every year, I knew it was coming. Every year, I counted down the days, tried to prepare myself. Every year, I thought I'd be able to move through it with more ease and grace than the one before. And every year, I was wrong.

It never got easier—the grief, the devastation. It was always right there, waiting for me, as strong as ever.

I'd struggled through morning meeting like a ghostfly through honey. Freddie's concerned stare across the staff room table alone made me dig my fingernails into my palms so hard one of them left a half-moon indentation in my skin. After the meeting, I'd asked Chan for the rest of the day off, and he hadn't hesitated to give it to me, looking at me like I might break into pieces right in front of him. Which was exactly how I felt.

I should have been able to manage this better. I should have been compartmentalizing and developing coping strategies and accepting my loss—all the things the therapist I never had the courage to see would have taught me how to do. But the list of all the things I should have done stretched out farther than I could see. *I should have been there. I should have made sure he was safe. I should have been a better mother. If I had been, maybe he'd still be here.*

But he wasn't here. He was gone. So like I did every year on this day, I disappeared, hiding in one of the ship's sensory rooms, huddled under the domed ceiling, sitting on the floor I'd instructed the room's climate controls to make feel hard and cold.

This was the only way I could get through it, bombarding myself with so much sensory input, there was no room left for anything else. Once I was completely overwhelmed by the wind and the thunder and the crashing waves all around me that I was numb, then I could remember him. Then I could look at the pictures and watch the vids I only let myself watch on this day. Then I could miss him without it ruining me.

I accessed the room's controls again through my VC, turning up the wind until it drowned everything else out. Everything. Even the opening and closing of the sensory room's door.

When a hand slid over my shoulder, I yelped.

"It's okay," Freddie said against my ear. "It's only me." His hand slid away from my shoulder as he sat down behind me. "I didn't mean to scare you," he said while I dimmed the audio. "I knocked, but it was so loud."

"What are you doing here?" My voice was a rasp. "How did you know I was here?"

I felt more than heard his sigh. "Elanie."

Turning around so we faced each other, both of us sitting cross-legged on the floor, I asked, "How? Nobody knows I come in here. How did she..." My shoulders sank as I closed my eyes. Elanie knew. She'd hidden it, but of course she knew. She knew everything.

"I'm not sure," Freddie said. "She only said that today would be hard for you. That every year on this day, it's hard, and you come in here. But Sunny, you look..." He scanned my face, deep grooves creasing his brow, bracketing his mouth, like it was agony for him to just look at me. "You're hurting. And at the meeting this morning, you seemed so...lost."

"Did Elanie tell you why?" With the question, I braced myself for the wave of panic certain to crash over me, that he might know my secret, that Elanie might have told him. "Did she say why today would be hard for me?"

He shook his head. "When I asked, she said she didn't know." He reached out, his fingers wrapping gently around my clenched fist. "You don't have to tell me, Sunny. You don't have to say a single word to me if you don't want to. And I know there's something going on between us right now, but can I sit with you? I can be quiet. I can just be here. So you're not alone."

Whatever I'd been feeling toward him, whatever confusion or frustration or hurt I'd been holding inside over the last few days, was so entirely dwarfed by my heartache now that it might as well have been a single particle of dust floating in the vastness of the universe. I wanted to tell him. I wanted to let him in. I was so tired of being alone. I needed someone else to carry this grief with me. So I tried. I really did. But my mouth only opened and closed, nothing coming out but worthless wisps of air. I had no idea what to say, where to start.

"*Stars*, Sunny," he said, his eyes turning glassy. "Do you need me to leave? I shouldn't have come. I'm so sorry. I can go."

"No," I said, the panic I'd been waiting for arriving in full, sudden force. "Don't leave." But as hard as I tried, I still couldn't say it. I couldn't say the words. But maybe I didn't have to. Maybe there was another way. "Can I send you something?"

"Of course," he said. "Anything. Anything you need."

Closing my eyes, I sent him the stream of pics and vids of Jonathan I'd been watching. When I opened my eyes again, his were distant, his gaze unfocused, his lips pressing together as a tear tracked down his cheek. As I watched his heart break right in front of me.

After a long moment, he asked, "Is this...? Is he—"

<My son,> I commed, because it was easier that way. <His name was Jonathan. He was five years old, and he was the love of my life.> Swiftly, like a river rising over its banks, the words burst out of me. "I was going to have a busy week planning the New Year's celebration on my old ship, and my parents had offered to watch him. So I put him on a shuttle back to Tranquis. It was a Class-Two Euphonia."

Freddie cursed under his breath.

"As you probably know, the Class-Twos were all scrapped after several accidents due to a faulty reactor. Unfortunately"—I swallowed hard—"we were one of those several. They promised me it happened quickly, that he didn't feel any pain. But he was all alone. I should have been with him. I shouldn't have sent him at all. I should have known I was putting him in danger. I should have sensed it, felt it somehow. That was five years ago today. And soon, he'll have been gone longer than he was ever here."

Taking a deep, trembling breath, Freddie said, "He was beautiful."

I tried to smile. "He was. And funny. He was really, really funny."

Running his thumbs over my knuckles, Freddie gently worked my fists open. "I am so, so sorry."

"Me too," I said with the most useless shrug.

We sat for a while that way, holding hands, not speaking. Until I admitted, "This is why I can't be with you. Why you shouldn't want to be with me. I am a broken woman, Freddie. I don't think I'll ever get over this. I'll never get better. I'll never move on. I'm scared all the time. I'm scared of getting too close. I'm scared of losing someone else. I'm scared of my memories, but I'm also scared of forgetting. I'm just...so scared."

So softly I had to strain to hear him, he said, "I had a wife."

My head whipped up. "What?"

"I was married," he said, his gaze still pinned on our clasped hands. "We were high school sweethearts. I loved her. So much."

The floor beneath me vanished. My mouth went dry, my throat spasming, and I gulped empty air. "Freddie."

"Massive pulmonary embolism," he continued. "The worst three words I know, in any language. One minute, she was fine, and the next, she was gone. Just like that, in my arms." He blinked, another tear slipping free. "Her name was—"

"Serena," I finished for him, my chest caving in on itself, coring me out.

Looking up at me again, his jaw clenching, he nodded. "I'm sorry I didn't tell you about her. And when you said her name, when you asked who she was, I should have reacted better. But it was so unexpected, how much I still missed her, how badly hearing her name—"

"Hurt," I said, because he didn't need to explain. I understood, felt the pain of it in my own bones.

"I lost Serena over ten years ago, but sometimes it still feels like it was yesterday. And on the anniversary of that day, I don't get out of bed, even now."

I hadn't thought it was possible for my heartbreak to claw itself even deeper into me. But that was the thing about grief: there was no bottom.

"I'm not telling you about Serena for sympathy or to diminish your loss," he told me, squeezing my hands. "I just wanted you to know, that's all. I wanted you to know that you're not alone. And that you are not the only broken person here."

It was such a heartfelt sentiment. But it was also so wrong. Because he had no idea, and he deserved one. He deserved to know how messed up I really was. So I wiped a tear away from his cheek, rubbed the wetness between my finger and thumb, and told him the truth.

"I have never cried for him, for Jonathan," I said, knowing it would be the end of whatever remained between us. "Not when my parents called to tell me he was gone, not during the funeral, not even after, when I told my parents I couldn't see them again, that it was too hard to be around family, around them. Who does that? What kind of mother doesn't cry for her dead child?"

He said nothing. Because what was there to say? He only sat there for a long while, his eyes wet while mine remained dry. I waited for him to leave. To get up, say goodbye, and leave me for good.

But he didn't leave. Instead, with his voice carrying over the muffled roar of crashing waves still rolling through the room, he asked, "Have you ever been to Neptune?"

I shook my head.

"Have you heard about its terraforming? Its people?"

"Only a little." Neptune's inhabitants rarely left their planet. There were rumors about the type of people who lived there—nomadic, fierce, dangerous.

"The terraforming on Neptune didn't take as it should have. Now the planet is mostly desert, sand as far as the eye can see. Water is the most precious commodity. Not a drop is wasted." With a level stare, he took my hands more firmly in his. "As a result, for the people of Neptune, crying is strictly forbidden."

Another dry swallow burned in my throat. "I didn't know that."

"In such harsh climates, the mortality rate is astronomical. Especially infants, children. An entire planet of parents and grandparents burdened not only with surviving on one of the most inhospitable planets in my solar system, but also forbidden to fully mourn their losses."

Nausea twisted my stomach. An entire planet of beings locked in grief. Like I was locked in grief. It was inconceivable.

But then Freddie said, "Unless it rains."

"It doesn't rain on Neptune, though, does it?" I asked.

"It does. Once or twice a year. But when it rains, and only when it rains, the people of Neptune are free to go outside, sit underneath the downpour, and weep over those they've lost. They call it the Sorrowing."

"I can't do that, though," I said, having a hard time finding my breath, the room closing in all around me. "It never rains on the *Ignisar*."

"It's true," he agreed. "It never rains on the *Ignisar*. But that doesn't mean it can't."

A drop of water splashed onto my wrist. I stared at the trail it made over my skin when another drop fell, and then another. He must have accessed the room's weather controls.

"What are you doing?"

A raindrop landed on his nose. "Letting it rain."

Scant drops became a sprinkling, a pattering on the floor, in my hair. And then the skies opened up. The rain fell, warm but insistent. It seeped into my eyes, my mouth, drenching me until I felt suffocated by it. "Stop," I begged, pleading with him while I struggled to breathe.

<You can stop this any time you want,> he commed softly. <The controls aren't locked.> After another gentle squeeze, the rain plastering his hair to his forehead, dripping off his lashes, he released my hands. <Or you can let it rain, Sunny. You can mourn your loss. You can have your Sorrowing. It's safe now. You're safe.>

I gasped, and water flooded my mouth. I spat it out, but my mouth filled again. The rain was driving, merciless. I shook. I trembled. I gnashed my teeth, wanting to scream, wanting to run, wanting to hit something, anything. But even though a frantic panic raged inside me, stronger than the storm, stronger than anything I'd felt since the accident, I didn't access the controls. I didn't make it stop.

And I wasn't sure when I started to cry. But with the rain streaming down my face as if in solidarity, giving me permission, mixing with my tears, concealing them, I collapsed, folding to rest my head on the cold, wet ground as vicious sobs racked my body.

Freddie's hands were on me, pulling me into his lap. His arms encircled me, holding me together as I dissolved, as the rain washed my tears from my face before they had a chance to drop from my eyes. Brushing his fingers over my hair, he rocked me from side to side. And I clung to him while everything poured out of me. Five years of stored-up grief, of unshed tears.

"I've got you," he said. "I've got you, sweetheart. It's all right. It's all right."

Even through the unrelenting sobs, I felt him there with me. I felt how much I'd missed him—his lips, his touch, the warmth of his body, and how safe he made me feel. It felt like coming home.

After some time, the violence of my tears giving way to something less demanding, I turned my face to his. I cupped his cheek, feeling the wetness that was either from the rain or his own tears, maybe both. And then I kissed him while the storm faded gently away.

"I'm sorry," I said against his lips. "I should have told you, talked to you. I should have been better."

He pulled away, looking at me with a ferocity that stole my breath. "Don't say that. Never say that. You couldn't be better if you tried."

Five years without more than a single tear, and now they wouldn't stop. When I kissed him again, my tears slipped between our lips, salty and cool. Until he broke the kiss to take my face between his hands. "Wait. Who are we right now?" His eyes searched mine, desperate for an answer. "Who am I kissing? I need to know."

More tears swelled, obscuring my vision. Because I knew what he was asking. *Am I kissing Phoebe or Sunny? Is this real or only more make-believe?*

Blinking my tears free so I could meet his gaze clearly, my voice breaking, shattering, I confessed. "I love you, Freddie—you and only you. I love you like I never thought I could love anyone again. And I think I have for a long while now."

We were still soaked, but we were in his pod, on his bed, our clothes in a wet heap on the floor. He'd settled between my legs, kissing me, telling me he loved me, that he was sorry, that I was beautiful.

When he pushed into me, our hearts beating next to each other, our breaths soft and even, all I could do was kiss him back. And while we moved together, slow and careful, I realized that I had never made love to another being before. Not like this, not when it wasn't for pleasure or power or fun, but only to let that other person inside me completely, holding nothing back, leaving no single dark corner of myself hidden from them.

With my gaze fixed on his while his hands cradled my head and mine cupped his face, I felt held, safe, loved. On this, the anniversary of the single worst day of my life, I felt loved. It was enough to make me start crying all over again.

But he was there, kissing my tears away one by one, making love to me until there was no sadness left.

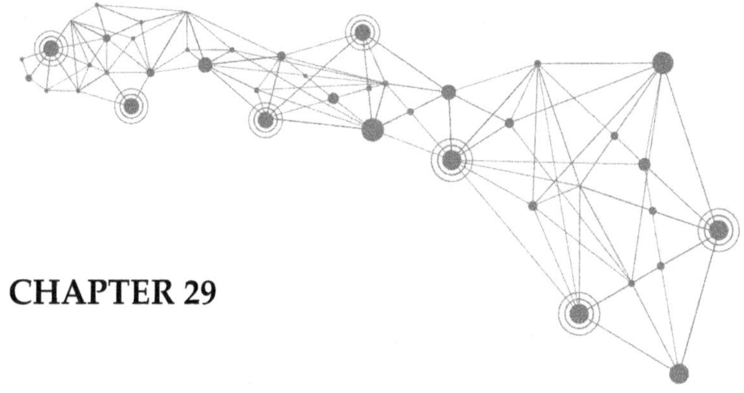

CHAPTER 29

I WOKE SLOWLY, fading in and out of consciousness as the muted golden light of sunrise sim trickled into Freddie's pod. I was nestled against him, the small spoon, where I'd slept the entire night through. Trying not to wake him, I rolled over. A smile spread across my face while I watched him sleep, his lips slightly parted, his long lashes feathering out over his cheeks. Because it was there and firm and warm, I kissed his bare chest, and then I did it again, and again, until he began to stir. "Good morning," I whispered against his skin once his arm tightened around me, his lips pressing a kiss into my hair.

"Good morning," he said sleepily, his eyes still closed while he pulled me over on top of him.

I sat up to straddle him, then I urged him up with me until his chest met mine, until I was cradled in his lap. He opened his eyes and ran his hand up my back. I thought back to when we'd been this way before, this close. Podgate.

Even then, I thought, even when the flood of hormones had driven me out of my mind, a part of me knew that I loved him. I think I'd loved him when we'd stared at our reflection in his mirror. I'd loved him when I watched him bake cookies for Sai. I'd loved him in his bow tie pajamas, when he read poetry to me, when he supported me and waited for me and understood me in ways I didn't understand myself. Maybe even when he walked into that bar on the CAK with mischief and promise dancing in his eyes. Maybe I'd loved him even then.

Running my fingertips along the line of his jaw, I asked, "Did you sleep well?"

He leaned in, kissing my neck, his body still so warm and soft from sleep. "Yes. You?"

"I did. Thank you. I love you."

His laughter brushed over my shoulder. "I love you too."

What was it about saying those words when I truly meant them? And hearing them when they were truly meant? It was addictive. I nearly said them again when his techPad alarm chirped.

"Ugh," he groaned, his hands sliding down to cup my ass. "I forgot to turn it off."

"I'll get it." Leaning over to open the drawer of his nightstand, I fished around for his techPad. But when I sat up again, I brought something else back with me. There was a shoe in his nightstand. *My* shoe. The black pump I'd lost in the hotel hallway during our first night together. The one he'd taken when I'd taken his tie.

"You," I said, staring at the shoe like it was some glowing, priceless artifact, "keep this in your nightstand?"

"I do," he replied, kissing my neck again, my shoulder. "But not all the time. Sometimes I sleep with it cradled in my arms. It's my prized possession."

Placing the shoe back on his nightstand, I laughed at him, and at myself. "I sleep with your tie under my pillow, sometimes wrapped around my hand. Or my neck."

"Sunny." His head rose, his full, pink lips aligning with mine. "I would pay every single credit in my account to see that." And then he kissed me, deep and slow, his fingers pressing into my hips, mine sliding into his hair. He broke the kiss, color tinting his cheeks when he said, "There's something else in that drawer for you. I've, um, been saving it."

"Really? Is it a present?"

"Kind of," he said, his lips twisting adorably.

Grinning at him, I pushed him back down to the bed, leaning over to reach into his drawer again. "Where is it?"

With his hands running up and down my thighs, he said, "Under the techPad. It's a—"

"Digcard?" I sat back up, bringing the card with me. "This one?"

"I went to the hotel gift shop right after I left your room that night," he said, "and I bought this card. I just never thought I'd get the chance to give it to you."

"You've been saving this for all these months?"

He nodded, a corner of his mouth pressing into a shy smile.

"Is this something you do after all of your *Squee* hookups?" I asked, trying to play off the way the card trembled in my fingers, the lump rising in my throat, the pressure stinging my eyes.

"Believe it or not," he said, "you were my first, only, and hopefully last one-night stand."

"What?" *Who only had a single one-night stand? And he'd been so good at it.* "You must be joking."

He laughed. "I mean, I'd opened *Squee* before, scrolled through suggested matches. But it wasn't until I saw your profile that I changed my status to *available*. And even then," he said, not laughing anymore, "I knew right away that one night with you would never be enough."

My heart swelled, so full of love for him I thought it might burst. I wanted to tell him, make him understand how he'd made me feel. But the words wouldn't come.

"It's okay," he said, squeezing my hand that still held the card. "Read it."

Tearing my gaze from his, I swiped my finger through the

digital photo of the CAK's Central Park, through the hedge maze in the shape of Brock Karlovich's face, and I read.

Dear Phoebe,

Have you ever had a chance encounter that changed you, that upturned your every notion of why we exist on these spinning rocks so irrevocably that you knew, after meeting this other being, you would never be the same?

I have.

I'm going to tell you a secret. I stood outside the restaurant last night and watched you before I went inside. You were smiling, talking to the bartender, laughing. Seeing you for the first time altered me, like a star forming. For the first time in years, I felt alive. I was also indescribably nervous. You were so beautiful, so stunning. And I didn't want to do or say anything wrong, anything that might keep me from being able to kiss you, at least once.

I don't know if I will ever see you again. If our paths will ever cross. But wherever you are, I want to thank you for mending a fracture in my heart I'd feared was beyond repair. And I want you to know that when I look up into whatever night sky might spread out above me, I will never find anything as spectacular as you.

Yours always,

Freddie (this is my real name, by the way)

Tears, fat and hot, seared twin paths down my cheeks. "You wrote this? For me?"

Sitting up again, taking the digcard from my hands and setting it back on his nightstand, he said, "It's true, Sunny. Every single word. There was something missing from my life, and for a man who loves puzzles, it was a tough one to solve. But it was you. You were the missing piece. And now"—he pressed my palm flat over his chest, right over his heart—"I'm whole."

While he blurred through my tears, his heart beating under my fingers, I said, "I don't deserve you."

Taking my face between his hands, wiping my tears away with a gentle swipe of his thumbs, he held still while I reached for him, while I slid down onto him, and said, "Yes, you do."

"SUNNY, YOU LOOK"—THE senator scanned me from head to toe, her head tilting, her eyes sparkling with amusement—"different. You look..."

"I believe *well-served* is the descriptor you're searching for, honey," Lena said from her spot on their couch—yes, *that* couch.

I coughed, beating my fist against my chest.

"Are you all right?" Lena asked, fighting a smile.

"Fine." I coughed again. "Just...choking on your words."

With an abrupt, barking laugh, Sonia waved me into their suite. "What brings you to see us this morning?"

While attempting to compose myself, I said, "I have a question for you. If you aren't too busy."

"Is that Sunny?" Bursting from his room, Sai thundered down the hall, racing up to me and throwing his arms around my waist.

Although the instinct to pull back and run away still tugged at me, I pushed against it. Bending down, I picked him up, squeezing him as his feet dangled below my knees. "Good morning, Sai. Did you just wake up?"

He nodded while I set him back down. Then his head swayed to the side as his big brown eyes narrowed. "You look different today," he said, sounding exactly like his mom. "You're all...moist."

"Moist?" I blurted out while Sonia snorted and Lena buried her laughing face in her hands, her shoulders shaking.

With a blush exploding over his cheeks, Sai shook his head. "No, not moist. Shiny, maybe? No, that's not it either. It's...glowing!" he crowed at last. "That's it. You are glowing." Leaning in close, he asked, "Were you and Freddie making out again?"

"Sai, mind your manners," Sonia said, her voice low as she crooked a finger at him, summoning him to the counter for breakfast. After she served him a plate of crispy crepes folded into triangles and served with a jam that smelled like coconut, she kissed him on the head. Then she followed me out of their suite and into the hall.

"What is it you wanted to ask me?" she said over the *whump-whump* whirring of one of the security mechs stationed outside their door as it floated closer.

Side-eyeing the heavily armored orb, I said, "I think you know that Tig has been working tirelessly to find whoever might be hacking our system. Although she's had little luck on that front, she has done some research on your Proposition 2126."

Sonia's jaw set like it was cast in stone. "And what information did she find?"

"Not much," I said. "That's why I'm here. I understand that this is a sensitive topic, and I'm sympathetic to your need to keep certain things private. But you mentioned the proposition briefly the night I watched Sai. We were interrupted then." I lowered my voice as several Delphinian wizards wandered by, their customary flowing robes replaced by striped velour tracksuits, of all things. "But I need to know, is the proposition why you're being targeted?"

Crossing her arms tightly over her chest, she said, "I'm sure Tig has informed you of the mundane nature of the proposition."

"She said its aim is to increase funding for deep-space

exploration—similar to a bill that passed a decade ago without issue."

"That's correct," Sonia said. She sounded as calm as the atrium before sunrise sim, but her left eye twitched. "So, to answer your question. No. I don't think the proposition is why we're being targeted."

I could spot a lie as well as a Vorpol could spot a mismatched-shoe sale. And the senator was clearly lying. I'd opened my mouth to press her on it when she derailed me completely by stepping in close and whispering, "Now, tell me what is going on between you and Freddie."

"What?" I stumbled back a step, more shocked by the question than I would have been had the ship suddenly turned inside out. "N-nothing is going on. He's...a friend. What?"

"You know," Sonia said, keeping her voice low, "I know how to keep a secret." She winked. "I'm a senator. It's pretty much all we do."

I opened my mouth, came up short, closed it again, and dropped my chin in defeat. "Is it that obvious?"

"Glaringly."

Laughing at myself, I raised my head again. "I guess I'm caught."

"I think what you are is in love," Sonia stated, as if this fact was as certain as all the stars in the KU eventually burning out. "And thank the gods for it. We were so worried about you."

I shouldn't have stopped by their suite before heading to the sensory room yesterday. I must have looked terrible. An acute awareness of how many people aboard this ship have been worried about me for years, never asking me about it, never demanding I tell them what was wrong, crashed into me with the force of a collapsing star. I didn't want to worry my friends anymore. I didn't want to keep hiding. "Yesterday was a difficult day for me. My son," I said, clearing the sudden thickness from my throat, wondering if the words I was about to say would get easier or harder the more I said them. "I lost him five years ago, and yesterday was the anniversary."

"Sunny," she gasped, her hand rising to her chest like she was trying to shield her own heart. "I'm so, so sorry."

"Thank you," I managed, blinking back the sting in my eyes. I really didn't want to cry in front of this serious, important, professional woman. "He would be about Sai's age. If he were still here, that is."

Without warning, her eyes filled with tears. She took me by my shoulders and pulled me close, crushing me in a tight embrace. "I'm sorry," she said again with a tremor in her voice, and I couldn't stop my own tears from falling no matter how hard I tried. "I didn't know. I wish I'd known. I might have—"

"It's all right," I said. "Nobody knew." The way it felt to be wrapped inside her embrace, sharing tears with another mother, it was different from what I'd imagined. It wasn't fear or pity or despair. It was love, only love. And as if the anchor that had been weighing my heart down tugged on the rope one final time before it snapped free, I realized there was something I needed to do.

Pulling away, wiping the tears from my eyes, I said, "If you'll excuse me, Senator. I need to make a call."

"SUNASTARA?" My mother's voice was a rushed breath, her bright-blue eyes already glistening on my techPad screen. "Is that really you?"

"Hi, Mom," I said, holding my pad close, wanting to hug it to my chest. "I've missed you. I'm sorry it's been so long. How's Dad?"

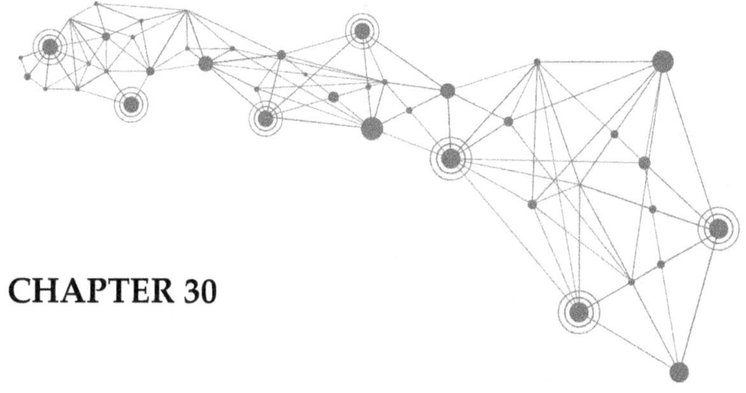

CHAPTER 30

TANO, Axel, and Marisia sat stiffly on one side of the staff room table. Since their arrival, they'd been nothing but pleasant and professional—Tano had even come to visit the Cosmic Spectacle stables yesterday while I'd met with that New Earth stable hand to arrange the kurot's transport back to the CAK, wanting to thank me personally for the kurot milk, telling me it was "the finest cleaning I've ever had."

I'd made sure to appear delighted that he'd enjoyed the antiquated custom I'd unknowingly revived, but deep down, I couldn't shake that nagging feeling that I'd met him before. I also couldn't shake the feeling that—with his slippery smile and heavy-lidded eyes—he'd been checking me out, as well as all the Spectacle's female staff. He'd even tried to flirt with the head oorthorse trainer, a tall and exacting female from Neptune who was so intimidating, I hadn't said more than a handful of words to her since she'd come onto the ship six months ago. Maybe I never would, now that I knew how hard life was on her planet, how strong she must have been, how resilient.

Trying not to stare at Tano across the table, or at Marisia—whose expression since she'd stepped foot on this ship had only wavered between aggressively annoyed and unbearably bored—I leaned over, listening in while Tig and Reya chatted about the tech effects Tig had planned for New Years.

"How are you two getting along?" I asked them, my smile as pure as freshly fallen snow. "Is Tig telling you all her secrets?"

Tig laughed. "Pretty much. Not that I have that many."

When Tig smiled, Reya blushed. Of the two, I would have pegged Tig for the more easily flustered. But she seemed somehow more confident with Reya around. Maybe it was good for her not to be so isolated in her office all day. Or—fingers and toes crossed—maybe they were making more of a connection than just teacher and pupil. Not that the dynamic couldn't be a lot of fun.

"Have you two exchanged contact information?" I asked. "Reya may have questions for you once this holiday is over."

Reya's blush deepened as Tig said, "No. We haven't." She turned to look at Reya. "But maybe we should. If you want to. Do you...want to?"

Reya smiled at Tig, Tig smiled at Reya, and fireworks exploded beneath my sternum.

<What exactly are you doing over there?> Freddie commed.

Shooting him an innocent glance across the table, I replied, <Nothing. Why?>

<You look like you're scheming. Are you scheming?>

<No. I do not scheme.>

<You do too. You're making Reya blush.>

<I am not,> I insisted. <Tig did that.>

<Ah, I see how it is. By the way, have I told you how beautiful you look today? You're stunning, sweetheart. Delicious. All I can think about is the softness of your thighs brushing my cheeks, how tender the skin between your legs feels against my lips, how warm and wet. And how, when I lick you there, you taste like—>

<Fine.> Crossing my legs, squeezing tight, I commed,

<You've made your point. It's not nice to make someone blush during a work meeting.>

He chuckled over the comm.

<I'll behave. But when this meeting is over, please come to my pod as quickly as possible.> It had been over twelve hours since we'd been horizontal. An inexcusable length of time.

While he stared down at his clasped hands on the table, looking politely uninterested for anyone else who might be watching, his lips twitched. <Roger that.>

"Finally," Elanie grumbled when Chan arrived.

While he cruised to his spot at the head of the table, I frowned. Something was up. I couldn't put my finger on the change, but Chan hadn't been himself lately. He'd been intensely focused and staunchly professional, and he hadn't made a single wrong move since the FFKs boarded. He was either angling for a promotion, getting ready to quit and looking for a glowing recommendation, or—and what I considered most likely—he was worried.

<Chan's stressed about something,> I commed Freddie.

<The Kravaxians?> he commed back.

I didn't think so. The FFKs had been pleasant enough, and they were set to disembark in a few days. If they were going to cause any trouble, wouldn't they have done it already? <Maybe. Or maybe it's something else.> Sitting back in my chair, watching Chan adjust his hoverchair to table height, my heart sank. <Maybe it's some*one* else.>

<A certain Delphinian wizard?>

I nodded. I'd been so wrapped up in my own life that I hadn't considered the possibility that Chan might have developed genuine feelings for Makenna. And when the ship reached Portis next week, Makenna would leave with the other wizards, with Sonia and Lena and Sai, and Chan would be alone again.

"Welcome, everyone," Chan said, his voice clear but tired.

"I've called this meeting to present our special guests with their certificates of completion for this week of training with us. I realize we still have a couple of days left, but with New Year's on the horizon, this may be the only time we aren't all too busy to meet. So without further ado..." He leaned over, reaching into one of his hoverchair's pockets. And this time, nobody flinched, nobody tensed, nobody rose from their seats or reached for their chuck-cuffs or flash grenades.

Pulling out four digital certificates, Chan said, "Everyone, please join me in congratulating our trainees."

While the Kravaxians accepted their certificates, everyone applauded—even if Rax's and Morgath's hands came together in more of a golf clap. But then Tano stood from the table, and I huffed a laugh when Rax's fingers dropped to his paresis darts. Some things never changed.

"We wanted to thank you all as well," Tano said, either unaware of Rax's attempt at intimidation or unconcerned, "for your kindness and hospitality." He motioned to Axel, who placed what looked like seven shards of glass onto the table, each one a few inches long, slightly curved, with tips sharpened to a fine point.

"These are known on Kravax as Orion's Teeth," Tano explained, picking up a tooth, twirling it back and forth so it caught the light. "They are the first teeth of the sikka and only found by swimming to the bottom of the Rustiun Sea and digging them from the sand."

"What is a sikka?" I asked, taking my tooth from the table. It was light as air but felt strong as steel.

"Sikka are carnivorous eels that rule the seas on Kravax," Axel answered. "They are highly poisonous, deadly if eaten. But they are also cunning, merciless, and resilient—all traits highly prized by our people."

"When you possess Orion's Tooth," Tano said, "it is believed the spirits of our planet will pass these traits on to you."

When I hovered my finger over the tooth's tip, Axel warned, "Careful, Sunny. They're sharp."

"Thank you." I placed the tooth gingerly back on the table. "It's beautiful."

"You are welcome," Tano replied, his brown eyes sparkling, his gaze lingering on mine a second longer than necessary. Marisia, noticing the eye contact, squinted at me before glaring at him. "While we are looking forward to your New Year's celebration," Tano went on, oblivious to the fireballs shooting from Marisia's eyes, "we are not looking forward to leaving this ship."

Beside me, Reya's chin dropped, and I watched Tig squeeze her hand under the table, giving her a devastatingly sad smile. They would miss each other. It would be difficult for Tig to stay in touch with someone on Kravax since their tech was so primitive. But why couldn't we offer Reya a position on the ship? Tig could use the help. Maybe they'd work together all day, spending their afternoons sharing tea and pastries at the bistro. What started as an innocent friendship might grow into—

<If you are going to sit there with that dreamy, devious look in your eyes,> Freddie commed, <I will not be held responsible for the aftermath when I take you right here on this table.>

I coughed so hard and for so long that I had to wave off half the table when they stood—or raised their hoverchair—asking if I was all right, offering me water.

<That was highly inappropriate,> I scolded over the comm.

<I'll show you inappropriate.>

<*Fredrick.*>

He pushed his chair back.

<What are you doing?> I commed frantically, blood shooting up my throat and into my cheeks. There was no way in hells he'd been serious about the whole table thing. Was there?

"My apologies," he told the room. "But I have a meeting with the Gorbulon-7 contingent on deck twenty in five minutes." Picking his Orion's Tooth up from the table, he said, "Thank you. It has been a pleasure having you all on board," to the FFKs. Then to me, privately, <I'll be in your pod. Naked. Hurry.>

After he left, Chan started talking about something, New Year's, maybe. Maybe Vorp's current position in orbit around their sun. Who could say? I could only hear Freddie's voice in my mind, see his stormy eyes blazing across the table, feel the echo of his lips on my skin. When the meeting adjourned an absolute eternity later, I tried to rush to my pod, but cold fingers wrapped around my wrist, stopping me in my tracks.

"Axel," I said after spinning toward him. I tried to keep my tone light, but his timing was terrible. "What can I do for you?"

The smile he gave me was all charm. "Will you be at the New Year's party?"

Was this the pass he'd been about to make when we'd stood outside his door? "I will, of course. I'll be working the floor."

His thumb ran over the inside of my wrist, his voice sinking low. "That's good. I enjoy spending time with you."

Tano giving me looks. Axel rubbing my wrist. Something was off. Either way, I needed to nip this in the bud. "Axel, I enjoy spending time with you as well. But...I'm not available anymore. I'm with someone."

"You're what?" Elanie cried, materializing as if the wizards had conjured her out of thin air.

"What's Sunny doing?" Chan asked, cruising up next to Elanie.

Tig and Reya joined our growing group, and all I needed now was Rax and Morgath shouldering in beside me to turn this whole situation into my absolute worst nightmare.

Raising an amused brow, Axel said, "Sunny was just telling me that she's with someone."

Puffing out my cheeks, I muttered, "Thank you, Axel."

"Is it Freddie? Are you and Freddie together?" Tig's voice rose with every word. "Really? *Really* really?"

"I guess the trestal egg is out of the nest," I said with a brittle laugh. "But yes. Freddie and I are a thing. Can we please not make a big deal out of this?"

Chan, apparently afflicted by a temporary bout of deafness, fist-bumped the air and hooted like a deranged mountain owl.

<Where are you?> Freddie commed.

<Oh, just telling everyone on deck twelve, and two Kravaxians, that you and I are involved. Because this is how my day is going.>

<Are you all right? Do you need me to come back?>

I looked at my friends—and the Kravaxians—finding nothing but happy faces. Well, maybe entertained was a better way to describe the crooked tilt of Axel's lips.

<I'm fine. And no, you stay put. I'll be right there.>

Eventually, everyone went their separate ways, but I reached out for Elanie's elbow before she escaped. "Darling, do you have a moment? I'd like to say something to you."

"Is it brief?" she snapped, true to form.

"It is," I replied. "I don't want to make you uncomfortable, but I know Freddie and I have one being to thank for bringing us together."

Her brows slid together. "Good for you."

Releasing her elbow, I said, "You've been there for me for years—a steady, supportive presence. A true friend. You've also been there for Freddie while I've been dealing with my...life. And I know you told him to come find me in the sensory room."

"I have no idea what you're talking about." Her voice was stern, but her brown eyes misted.

I stepped closer, lowering my voice. "Elanie, do you know? Do you know why that day is always so hard for me?"

After a moment, she nodded, only once.

"How? I've never told anyone."

The expression on her face was one I'd never seen on her before, not her customary annoyance or exasperation or even pity. I thought it might be a young bionic's attempt at compassion. "You did. Two years ago. You were drunk, and I knew you wouldn't remember it in the morning. But you told me."

I dropped my head. "You're right, I don't remember. *Stars*, I shouldn't have burdened you like that. I'm sorry."

Taking my hand, she said, "You have nothing to apologize for. And yes, you should have."

"Thank you, Elanie." My eyes filled with tears. Because I was apparently a crier now. "You are a wonderful being and a true friend. I love you."

She blinked, and a tear trailed down her cheek. Then, as if coming to her senses, she pulled her hand from mine so she could swat the tear away. "I have to go," she said. "I have a lot of work to do. But," she paused, clenched her jaw, then said in a reluctant rush, "I love you too," before spinning away and disappearing down the hall.

THIRTY MINUTES LATER, after Freddie's head emerged from between my legs and I remembered how to speak, I rolled him over, climbed on top of him, and told him about Elanie.

"She told you she loves you?" he asked, his fingers curling around my thighs.

I raised my hips enough to guide him into me before sinking back down with a satisfied sigh. "She did. It was a big moment for both of us."

He stared up at me with unfiltered hope in his eyes. "No more secrets?"

Leaning forward, and just before my lips met his, I promised, "No more secrets."

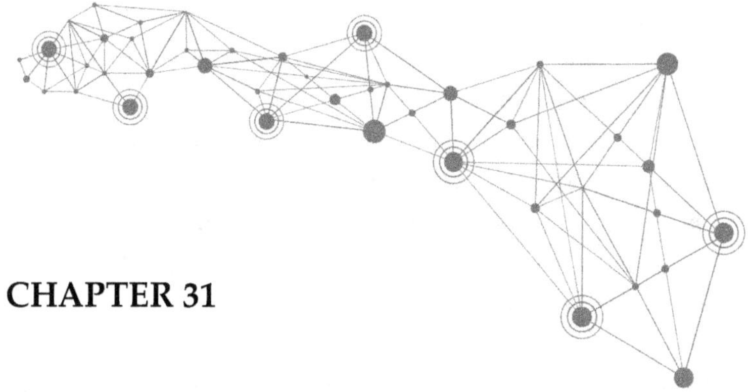

CHAPTER 31

Flowing swaths of white and silver digital gossamer adorned the main deck ballroom, cascading from the rafters to brush against the floor. Tiny bubbles of golden light shimmered over the soft fabric, rising toward the ceiling like the entire room had been dropped into the bottom of a champagne glass. It was pure elegance. Which, let's be real, for this ship, was miraculous.

"Hello, gorgeous," Freddie said, coming up behind me, his breath tickling my ear.

I turned to face him.

"That outfit." His hungry gaze devoured me, sliding down the crimson silk of my jumpsuit, past the matching velvet cuffs encircling my ankles, all the way to my intricately jeweled heels that sparkled in the golden light of the digital effects. "Spectacular."

"You don't look half-bad yourself."

"What, this old thing?" He waved a hand over his immaculate three-piece suit.

Sliding my hands up his chest, I pinched the folded corner of his red pocket square. "It matches my outfit. Which"—I raised a brow—"you haven't seen until now."

He smiled at my bemused expression. "Pure luck."

"Let me guess. You have a collection of pocket squares in your *Perfect Venusian Gentleman* kit. Which you keep nestled between your guide to flawlessly messy hair and whatever magical concoction always makes your breath smell minty."

"Naturally," he said, staring at my tits. "Hmm, I like what you've done here." Carefully, he raised the spindle of my Orion's Tooth from where it dangled between my breasts.

"I thought it would make a nice necklace."

When he pressed the tooth back into place, his finger followed the line of it all the way down to its tip, coming dangerously close to disappearing down my top.

"See you after the party?" I asked, staring down at his finger, wishing we were alone so he could trace a path all the way down my body. We'd both work the floor tonight, but I'd been assigned specifically to the Kravaxians. Which meant I wouldn't see much of him until after the ball dropped.

"Count on it," he said, dropping his hand to his side and kissing my cheek.

I let him go first, mainly so I could admire his butt as he strolled toward the bar, where Garran and Kasa were ordering drinks.

"Sunny," said a low, smooth voice behind me. "What are you staring at?"

I spun around to find the ship's handsome, blue-skinned Portisan physician grinning at me. "Dr. Semson," I said, clearing the guilty I-was-staring-at-Freddie's-ass warble from my throat. "You got the night off?"

He sighed deeply. "Not quite. I'm on call. Crossing my fingers that everyone behaves themselves tonight."

I gave him a dubious look. He sighed even more deeply. And we both laughed.

"Well, it's good to see you out of the med bay," I said. "You work too much."

His silver brows crowded into a concerned furrow. "I don't think I'm the only one."

"Empaths," I muttered, shaking my head. "Don't look at me like that, Doctor. I'm fine."

While his unease gave way to something softer, lighter, he murmured, "Hmm. I think you're right." Pointing his chin at Freddie across the room, he said, "He makes you happy. Wait," he reconsidered, his eyes narrowing, his focus sharpening. "He does more than that. He gives you the space to feel whatever you need to feel. Happy, but also sad." His gaze slid to meet mine. "That can be hard to find in a partner. Oh, crud. Sunny, are you okay?"

Tears had swelled to hover over the brim of my lids. "Yep," I said, refusing to blink, refusing to cry at a party.

"I'm sorry." His blue lips pressed together apologetically. "I was way out of line. It's just, well, it's wonderful. Seeing you like this."

I knew what he meant. He'd been my physician for years. He'd read my past medical history. He was an empath. He knew what no one else did, and yet he'd never said a word, never asked me a single question about Jonathan. Because empaths also knew when a being wasn't ready to speak. "Thank you, Sem," I said, my eyes dry enough now to risk a blink. "You're right. It is wonderful." I looked over at Freddie, watched him place a hand on Garran's forearm. "He's patient and understanding, and he's a good listener. He's helping me...work through some things."

"Sometimes that's all we need," Sem said with a firm nod—an appreciative period on the end of this conversation. "I'm going to try to enjoy myself for as long as I can before at least one of these beings needs IV sobering fluids."

Kissing his cheek, I wished him a long night out of the med bay, then I turned to scan the room. I searched for them, but I didn't see Sonia or Lena. I thought they'd come tonight, but although we celebrated New Year's aboard the *Ignisar* on this date, it was only because all LunaCorp ships followed the Standard year calendar. The actual date of the New Year varied wildly from planet to planet, and on Tranquis, it wasn't for another several months. Perhaps they'd decided to sit this party out.

As I made my way toward the Kravaxian's table, Freddie commed, <Did you know they were leaving tonight?>

<Who?> I replied.

<Garran and Kasa. Their shuttle departs after midnight.>

I stalled out, my heart giving a little hiccup. <They weren't supposed to disembark for another week.>

<I know,> Freddie said. <But Kasa's mother has developed a cough, and Kasa wants to get her back home. Garran has decided to join them.>

<Please don't let them leave without giving me a chance to say goodbye.> Seeing guests off after their stay was a normal part of my life. But Garran was different. Garran, I would miss.

<I won't. And have fun with the FFKs. But I've got my eye on Axel.> Muttering over the comm, he added, <Thinks he can hit on you without anyone noticing...>

<Fredrick Caruthers, are you jealous?>

<Yes.> His laughter brushed between my ears, stirring the hairs on the back of my neck. <Intensely.>

ASIDE FROM REYA—WHO'D spent the entire evening in the control booth with Tig—the Kravaxians all sat at their table, watching the party unfold while they nursed their drinks.

<Enjoying yourself?> Elanie commed.

<Decidedly not. What are you doing?>

<Helping Freddie manage a table of inebriated Blurvans and watching you stare off into space.>

I glanced around the room until I spotted Freddie sitting at the Blurvans' table, his arm slung around a young male's shoulders as they swayed side to side, the Blurvan's gelatinous belly wobbling with laughter.

<*Stars.* What are they doing? Are they>—I squinted—<singing?>

Standing next to the table with her arms crossed over her chest, Elanie commed, <If you could call it that. It's apparently some Blurvan drinking song that goes on and on. They won't let Freddie leave.>

Just to Elanie's side, I noticed a bionic with bright-blue eyes and jet-black hair sitting at a table of other young males and staring brazenly at her ass.

<Don't look now, Elanie. But you are being checked out.>

<What? What does that mean?>

<It means,> I commed, <that someone here is interested in you. Romantically.>

<What?> she commed again, her shoulders hitching toward her ears, her head ducking low like she was trying to hide inside her dress. <Who? Why?>

<A handsome bionic behind you, and because you are exceptional.>

As discreetly as she had ever been, she looked back, pretending to scratch her chin on her shoulder.

<Nicely done,> I commed. <Very subtle.>

<He's cute. I guess,> she admitted.

<Very,> I agreed. <You should go say hello.>

<Why would I do that?>

I snorted, pretending to cough when the Kravaxians turned toward the sound.

<Crew party after the room clears out?> I asked.

<Obviously,> she replied, scratching her chin so she could look at the handsome, blue-eyed bionic one more time.

I COULDN'T SPEAK. I could barely breathe. Beside me, Freddie's face reddened to some shade I could only describe as disastrous, and I wondered if either of us would make it out of this alive.

When the ball had dropped at midnight, and Marisia, Tano, and Axel had retreated unceremoniously to their suites, I'd raced to meet up with Freddie so I could say a reluctant farewell to my favorite Argosian. An Argosian who was currently squeezing us half to death.

Tapping on the purple pectoral my face was currently pressed against, I wheezed, "Garran, put us down. Please."

"I am just so happy," he cried, squeezing me even more tightly in his right arm, crushing Freddie in his left, lifting us both a solid foot off the floor before finally letting us go.

"Thank you," I managed, rubbing at my chest as sweet, blessed air made its way back into my lungs.

"You are together," Garran said, all smiles as he looked from me to Freddie and back again. "You are *worthy* of each other. You fit." The words were simple, but from him, they meant the worlds.

"Are you sure you have to leave so soon?" Freddie asked, rolling his shoulders, stretching his neck from side to side. "We have an excellent physician aboard this ship for Kasa's mother. Dr. Semson is second to none."

Garran nodded, his tattooed head gleaming in the glow from the overhead lights. "I am sure he is very good. But Kasa and I have plans"—stealing a glance at the airlock where Kasa carried her mother's bags toward the docking port, he lowered his voice—"for making things official."

"Official?" I squealed. "Really?"

"Shh." He put a finger to his lips. "Her mother does not know yet. She still does not like me."

His face returning to its normal shade of handsome, Freddie said, "No worries, big guy. She'll come around."

"Do you think?"

"Of course she will," I said. "Because you're Garran the Brave. Garran the Verdant. You're Garran"—I sniffled—"our friend."

While I nestled into Freddie's side, he wrapped his arm around my shoulders and told Garran, "This ship simply won't be the same without you."

"You two should come visit Argos." Glancing down at his enormous feet, Garran suggested, "Maybe when Kasa and I are joined."

Even though my chest still ached from the first time, I threw myself into his arms again and said, "Just try to keep us away."

"Is it always this hard?" Freddie asked while we watched Garran and Kasa's shuttle push back from the airlock. "Saying goodbye to the guests?"

"No." I ran a knuckle under my eye. "Garran was one in a million. Like a special piece of hay in a haystack."

Freddie's head swiveled toward me, his lips flattening. "Where did you hear that expression?"

I shrugged. "Some New Earth American guest, I think. Why?"

"Well, if I may, I'm not sure you're using it correctly. That particular saying is actually 'like a needle in a haystack.'"

Frowning back at him, I said, "That doesn't make any sense. Why would there be a needle in a stack of hay?"

"Hmm," he murmured, considering. "I've never thought about it that way. Why *would* there be a needle in a haystack?"

I slid my arm around his waist. "Don't ask me."

"Baffling nature of the expression aside," he went on while

the lights from Garran's shuttle flared then vanished as it jumped away from the ship, "it's used to point out how difficult it would be to find a certain thing or person. As hard as finding a single needle hidden in a haystack. For your purpose, to borrow another New Earth colloquialism, you might say something along the lines of 'they broke the mold when they made him.'"

I didn't get to see him playing his role of Languages and Customs expert very often, let alone benefit from it. His kind, patient competence was, unsurprisingly, a major turn-on.

"That's exactly what I meant," I said, wrapping my fingers around his tie and tugging him into a kiss.

After a lengthy make-out session that may have gotten a little bit sloppy, Freddie and I walked back toward the party, but I split off to the bathroom because I really had to pee. I'd just started pulling my jumpsuit back up when Tig's voice invaded my mind.

<It's not what we thought,> she commed, frantic. <I read it more closely. I missed it before. I can't believe I missed it.>

<Slow down, darling,> I commed back, hauling my straps over my shoulders. <Missed what?>

<The senator's proposition. It's in the fine print. The funding requested is for deep-space exploration, but only for companies with fewer than twenty-thousand employees. And there's an attached provision to close tax loopholes and more tightly regulate corporate monopolies. Sunny, if this passes, it's an extremely expensive slap in LunaCorp's face.>

<Why would Sonia want this to pass?> Dread shot down my spine. <Nobody in their right mind would go up against LunaCorp like this.>

<It's not just her,> Tig said. <Five other senators helped

draft this proposition. Their aim was to support smaller businesses, increase competition, and provide more diverse opportunities for their planets—with a special focus on asteroid mining.>

I hissed a curse. LunaCorp had cornered the market on asteroid mining since the Asteroid Belt Wars. It was the key to their wealth and continued chokehold on nearly every industry in existence. With the proposition, the senator had just made herself, her family, and now my ship, targets for the largest and most ruthless corporate monopoly in the entire KU.

<And it's all over the KU news. One of those senators' wives and two of their children have gone missing.>

<What do you mean 'missing'?> My feet moved before I had a chance to question them, propelling me from the bathroom, toward the elevators, my hand slamming over the *up* button.

<Missing. Like, gone. And the security breaches,> Tig continued at a breakneck pace while I jumped into the elevator, making it climb. <I finally found them. They didn't come from Vorp or Gorbulon-7. They came from Kravax, Sunny. Kravax!>

<Where is she?> I commed, bursting out of the elevator and racing toward the Ramesh suite. <Where is Sonia?>

<She wasn't at the party?>

Rounding the corner, I slid to a stop at the sight of the twins' security mechs—now disabled heaps of metal on the floor outside of their suite. "Oh gods," I rasped, sprinting to their door, banging frantically, bruising my hand. Nobody answered.

<Rax! Morgath!> I shouted over a shared comm. <Override the security lock on the senator's suite.>

<What's happening?> Rax demanded as the lock disengaged.

The door slid open, and the ground dropped out beneath me. A bomb had gone off in their suite. Tables overturned, glass shattered on the floor, the couch tipped onto its side.

Seeming to rise above my own body, I watched someone who looked just like me run to Sai's bedroom. His bed was empty, his closet empty, his bathroom empty. "Sai," I called out, spinning in a circle, checking under his bead. "Are you here? Are you hiding? It's me." My voice cracked. "It's Sunny."

He wasn't here.

White light crowded my vision, a sob wrenching itself from my chest as I staggered to the back bedroom, whispering, "No. No, no, no. Please no," with every step. Their door was open. Their light was on.

Stars save us.

<Code white! Code white!> I bellowed over the comm, kneeling beside their bed where Sonia and Lena lay sprawled on their backs, their eyes closed, mouths open, not moving. <Disable all airlocks. Lock all docking bays. The senator and her wife are down. The boy is missing. It's the FFKs!>

<I fucking knew it,> Morgath growled.

<Not now, Morgath,> I snapped while pressing my fingertips over the pulse point in Sonia's wrist.

<Is the senator alive?> Rax asked.

A steady heartbeat thrummed underneath my fingers. <Yes.> Reaching across the bed, I felt for Lena's pulse. <Her wife as well. But they're out. Drugged?> Pulling back the blanket covering them as carefully as I could, uncovering the red-tipped darts sticking out of Sonia's right thigh and Lena's left hip, I ground out, <Paresis darts.>

<Get the fuck out of there,> Rax barked. <I'm on my way.>

<Opening the all-crew emergency comm,> Tig said on a separate channel.

<Sitrep,> Captain Jones ordered, his commanding voice rumbling between my ears.

Once Rax arrived, I ran from the senator's suite, listening to Tig and Morgath bring the captains, as well as the rest of the crew, up to speed.

<Where are the Kravaxians?> Freddie asked, his smooth, calm voice in my head making me stumble on my way back to the elevators.

<They all left their suites about fifteen minutes ago,> Tig said. <All...but Reya.>

<Is she with you?> I asked, reaching the elevator bank, pushing the *down* button, waiting.

<She left a few minutes ago. She said she had to use the bathroom. You don't think she's with them, do you?>

<Maybe not,> I commed, my throat cinching tight as a knot as I pushed the button three more times. <But we can't take any chances. You need to lock the door. Morgath, go get Tig. Don't send mechs. They're disabling them. Hurry.>

<On it,> he growled.

Captain Jones took control, barking out orders over the all-crew comm, but on a private line, Tig's ID blinked.

<I can see them on the monitors, Sunny,> she commed in a pained whisper as I stepped into the elevator, my finger hovering over the button for the main deck. <Airlock B-4. They have the boy. And...Reya is with them. Why is she with them? Why is she doing this?>

Slamming my hand over the button for the docking bay instead, I commed, <Morgath is headed your way. Don't worry.>

<Don't let the twins kill her,> Tig pleaded. <She's a good being. I know she's a good being. She has to be a good—>

I clicked off the comm before I accidentally admitted that if Reya had a hand in harming Sai in any way, I'd kill her myself.

Rejoining the all-crew comm while the elevator doors slid open again, I shouted, <Disable airlock B-4! They have the senator's son!>

<Do not engage,> Captain Jones boomed. <Sunny, do you copy? Do not engage. Help is on the way.>

But when I heard Sai's panicked voice echo down the

hallway to the B-gate airlocks, Garran himself couldn't have kept me away.

<I can't disable B-4,> Tig cried. <It's been disconnected from our mainframe and password protected with a suicide sequence. If I try to disable it manually, it'll blow. All other airlocks and docking ports are on lockdown.>

<Enable exterior mechs,> Captain Jones ordered.

<No!> I bellowed. <They have the boy. Do not fire on them.>

<What are you doing, Sunny?> It was Freddie. He'd found me on a private comm. <Where are you going?>

<I'm sorry. I can't let them take him. I can't.>

<Sweetheart, stop. Please. You're unarmed.> His next words, uttered in a broken, desperate plea, were a sledgehammer to my chest. <Please don't leave me too.>

I didn't want to leave him. I had no idea what was about to happen. I might never see him again, speak to him again, hold him again. The thought was unbearable. But I'd lived with the unbearable for years. And if I could save another mother, or mothers, from ever having to live with it too, I'd go to the ends of the Known Universe to do it. Even though my heart was breaking, I had a chance, a chance I hadn't been given five years ago. I only hoped he would understand. <I love you. I love you so much, Freddie. And I'm so sorry, but I can't lose another boy.> I clicked off the comm, wiped my tears away, and sprinted for airlock B-4.

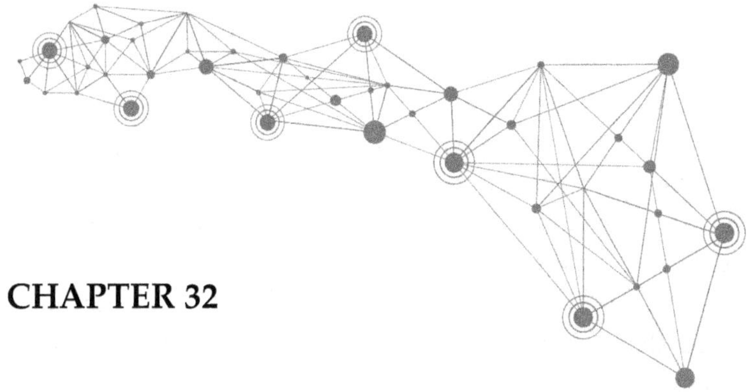

CHAPTER 32

<Sai? Can you hear me?> I whipped around the last turn toward the airlock so fast my ankle rolled, ducking into a vestibule when the shrill whine of blaster fire erupted down the hallway.

<Sunny?> Sai's voice came through strong in my mind. <Where are you?>

<I'm close. What's happening?>

<That Kravaxian female came into our suite—the older one. I tried to fight. I kicked her and bit her. But she was too strong. She dragged me from my suite by my hair. Why didn't my moms hear me?> His voice warbled. <I screamed so loud. I broke glass on the floor. Why didn't they come? Why didn't they stop her?>

<Oh, darling. They would have, but that female did something to them to make them sleep. But they're okay. They'll be okay. They'll be coming to help soon.>

<It's too late,> he commed, fear riding through each word. <Mom's SOs are here now, but there's nothing they can do. The Kravaxians are about to put me onto a shuttle. I'm scared, Sunny.>

A man's thickly accented voice shouted down the hall. "Give

us the kid, and we'll let you leave." I knew that accent, that voice. It was the New Earther stable hand from the Cosmic Spectacle.

"Put down your weapons. There is no way you're getting off this ship unless you release the child." The next voice was even more familiar. So familiar that I found myself creeping closer to the airlock in time to hear a booming *thwump* while Makenna and the stable hand flew through the air, the New Earther's blaster shooting in a wide arc that burned a hole in the ceiling, straight through to the deck above us. They landed hard against the wall, suspended there in some sort of sticky, black webbing.

Makenna was one of Sonia's security officers. For so many reasons, I hissed, "Shit. Shit, shit, shit."

<They're going to take me. I don't know where we're going.>

<Be brave, Sai. Be brave like Captain Zorba and Bartholomew from your books. Can you do that?>

"In the shuttle. Now," Tano commanded while—in an act of pure, blind absurdity—I held my breath, raised my hands into the air, and skirted past the wall where Makenna and the stable hand struggled against their webbing.

"Sunny," Makenna slurred against the sticky black strands covering her mouth. "Don't."

The airlock I stepped into was smaller than my pod, and I found myself face-to-face with four heavily armed Kravaxians and one terrified ten-year-old.

"Sunny," Axel said, his wide-eyed shock giving way to his signature amused expression—although this time there was an edge to it—as he holstered his web-shooter. "What are you doing here?"

"I heard you were leaving," I said, lowering my hands, attempting to give them a smile. "And I never let my guests leave the ship without a personal send-off."

Completely unamused, Tano raised his web-shooter and aimed it directly at my chest.

"No need for that, darling," I said, resisting every life-preserving urge that screamed at me to run. "I'm unarmed and harbor no secret military training whatsoever. I'm as threatening as a cleaning drone. Cross my heart."

"What do you want?" Marisia demanded.

"Well"—my laughter was one note shy of shrill—"it can get pretty boring on this ship. And why take only one hostage when you could have two?" I knew attempting to get them to take me instead of Sai would have been pointless; they needed the senator's son for leverage. The best I could do was make sure he wasn't alone—and hope that the rumors of Kravaxian cannibalism were baseless.

"She's got a point," Axel said with a roguish grin.

I let myself take a breath. I'd only had a second or two to come up with this plan, and it pretty much hinged on Axel's tendency to flirt.

"Fine," Tano bit out. "We'll take her too. But we must leave now." Grabbing Sai by his cuffed wrists, he hauled him into the shuttle.

Axel reached out for my arm.

"I'll come willingly," I said. My voice was inexplicably calm, considering the river of panic rushing through me. They might harm me. They might kill me. It didn't matter. I wouldn't leave Sai. "But I do get jumpsick, FYI."

Shaking his head, he secured a set of mag-cuffs around my wrists. "I thought you were smart," he said low into my ear, nudging me forward into the shuttle. "This is not a smart move."

"What are you doing?" Sai asked me after Axel deposited me in the jump seat beside him. "Have you lost your mind?"

"Probably," I replied. My hands trembled as Axel secured a second set of mag-cuffs around my ankles, connecting both sets with some sort of elastic cable that gave me only enough rein to scratch my nose.

"My moms?" Sai's eyes were huge. "They're okay? You promise?"

Squinting up at Axel while he rose to nearly his full height, having to duck a little in the small shuttle, I asked, "Will his moms be all right?"

He looked at the boy and said, somewhat sympathetically, "They'll be fine after an hour or two. Just a little tired."

"See, your moms will be fine." I arched a brow sharply at Axel, daring him to disagree. "And you will be fine too."

"Doesn't feel like it," Sai muttered as Axel joined Tano and Marisia in the cockpit to initiate undocking.

While Tano steered the shuttle away from the ship, Marisia snapped her fingers at Reya and barked, "Disconnect them."

Reya nodded, standing from her seat to place a thin metal band around my head. "This won't hurt," she said, her eyes swollen and bloodshot, her fingers shaking. "I promise."

"What are these?" Sai asked while Reya fitted another band around his head.

"Short-range EMPs," she explained in a whisper. "They'll frag your VC. That's all."

My VC. <Freddie,> I commed while I still could. <I'm with Sai. We're unharmed. They're shorting our VCs.>

<Sunny, you're being followed by Captain Jones and Morgath in cloaked ships. Don't let the FFKs jump—>

And with a pop and crackle, Freddie's voice vanished. The loss of input from my neural implant thrust me into an abrupt, disorienting silence. Until the shuttle's faster-than-light drive whirred, spooling up for a jump. *Don't let them jump*? How in the worlds did he expect me to keep that from happening?

Leaning in close to remove the EMP band from around my head, Reya whispered, "You shouldn't have come. But they won't harm you or the boy. They aren't like that."

I scoffed. "They—*you*—are kidnapping us, Reya. Forgive me if I don't share your optimism."

"I know this looks bad," she said, emotion thick in her voice. "But we aren't bad people."

"Reya!" Tano barked. "To your seat."

"Stay quiet and do whatever Tano says." She looked at Sai, then back at me. "I'm sorry."

Once she'd buckled herself back into her seat, I turned toward Sai and asked, "Any chance you know how to stall an FTL jump?"

"Are you serious?"

"Of course I'm serious."

"I'm ten years old," he said, incredulous. "So, no."

The shuttle shook as two warning shots from the *Ignisar*'s exterior defense mechs soared over our nose. Tano cursed in Kravaxian. I couldn't decipher it without my VC, but I thought I'd heard something about Orion's balls. "How long until the drive is ready?" he snapped.

"Fifteen seconds," Marisia responded with an ominous, unshakable calm despite the onslaught of super-heated metal.

"That long?" Reya's fists clenched in her lap, her knuckles turning white.

Turning to look at her, Tano said, "Worry not, young one. They will not shoot us. Not with the boy here."

"Tano, stand down." Captain Jones's voice thundered through the shuttle comms. "You are surrounded. Return your captives, and we will be lenient. You have my word."

Tano's only response was a short-lived flex of his jaw as the onboard AI started a five second countdown. The captain didn't shoot at us again, and when the countdown hit *one*, I placed my cuffed hands over Sai's and squeezed. The FTL drive engaged, and there was a gut churning instant of suspended gravity. Then we jumped away from the *Ignisar*, disappearing into the black void of open space.

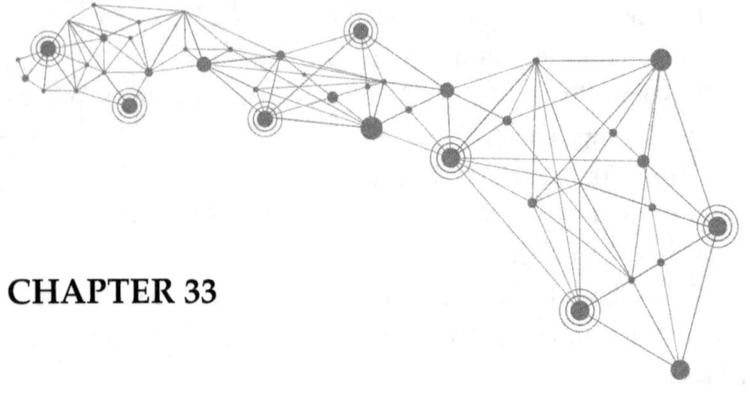

CHAPTER 33

"WELCOME TO KRAVAX," Axel said, waving a hand toward the cockpit windows.

I tried to focus on the dark-green planet rotating off the shuttle's starboard side, but my vision swam, and my temples throbbed. I loathed jumping. Hated it. Would you enjoy being flattened to the width of a single strand of hair, then rebounded so violently to normal size that every single one of your cells heaved? I didn't think so.

Despite the nausea, the cold sweat beading on my brow, I found the strength to say, "Huh," while measuring the unimpressive size of the planet between my thumb and first finger. "It's smaller than I expected."

"Oh, I assure you, Sunny," Axel replied with an arrogant smirk. "It's *quite* large."

I rolled my eyes.

Sai shook his head.

And when Tano growled back at Axel, looking—*dare I say*—jealous? Marisia slammed an overhead storage bin closed so hard something cracked, then strapped herself furiously into her seat to prepare for entry into Kravax's atmosphere.

After a rough landing that made my teeth clatter, Reya led

Sai while Marisia more or less dragged me out of the shuttle. The gravity on Kravax was heavy, at least twice what we simulated on the *Ignisar*, and Sai and I stumbled through a grueling hike through a dense forest to a small clearing bordered by a towering cliff. And in that small clearing, carved into that towering cliff, they led us into...a cave. An actual cave. I sighed. Some planets just couldn't help but live up to their stereotypes.

"Sit," Marisia ordered after shoving me inside the dank, dark, inhospitable space that wasn't much bigger than the shuttle that had brought us here. The ground was hard and cold where Sai and I huddled together, shivering until Tano lit a fire.

"You'll be here for a while," he said, scowling at me in the firelight. "So get comfortable."

"If I may," I interjected, lowering my voice. "I'm assuming this is a hostage for ransom arrangement and not some *we're hungry and you look appetizing* situation?"

It was almost funny, watching someone as intimidating as he was grumble with such long-suffering annoyance. "Despite what you offworlders believe, we are not cannibals. Behave, and you will make it back to your ship unharmed." He stood, wiped his hands on his camouflage pants, and left us to warm ourselves by the fire—Sai in his pajamas, me in my silk jumpsuit, both of us bound in mag-cuffs.

Once we were alone, I looked Sai over. "Are you all right?"

"I think so. Or, no, obviously," he clarified, holding up his cuffed wrists. "But you know what I mean. Are you all right?"

"I'm better than if I'd decided to wear a dress to the party, so there's that at least." I scanned the cave, looking for anything I could use as a weapon. Then abandoned the search when I remembered I wouldn't have the first idea what to do with a weapon, even if I found one. I wasn't a fighter. I was only good at one thing. And if we stood any chance of getting off this planet in one piece, I needed to play to my strengths.

“What do you think they want with us?” Sai asked.

Pressing my shoulder against his, trying to give him some warmth, I said, “I’m not sure. My best guess is it has something to do with your mother. I think they’re using us to get something from her. And once they get whatever that is, they’ll let us go.”

“Will whatever they want hurt my moms?” Sai asked, his chin wobbling even though he was clearly trying to fight it.

“No, Sai,” I told him, hoping I sounded more confident than I felt. “Nobody is going to get hurt.”

Pushing his bare little toes through the dirt, he said, “You’re lying to me. I can tell. But thanks for trying to make me feel better.”

I would have said more, tried harder to soothe him, but boots crunching across the cave floor pulled our heads up.

“Well, how does it feel to be *our* special guests now?” Axel asked, striding over to the fire, squatting to warm his hands over the flames.

“Your hospitality is unparalleled,” I said flatly. It wasn’t that I didn’t feel scared. It was only that I knew I’d be orders of magnitude more terrified if I hadn’t come, if I was still stuck on the ship wondering where they’d taken Sai, wondering if he was all right. Things, I was certain, his moms were wondering at that precise moment, all thanks to the asshole grinning smugly at me.

Axel scoffed, brushing his thick black bangs off his pale forehead. “Did you know that one of the most difficult things we had to learn in order to convince the worlds that we were a kinder, gentler breed of Kravaxians was sarcasm? Sarcasm is not a valid form of communication on Kravax. We find it pathetic, weak, dishonest. But above all other types of expression, sarcasm sets offworlders most at ease. Why do you think that is?”

“We bore easily?” I suggested.

Keeping his head down, Sai stared at the fire like it was the tether that would keep him from floating off into space. Which may have been accurate. Even with the small fire, it was still too cold in the cave for our climate-controlled sensitivities. Aside from being safe in his arms, at that moment, while my toes throbbed from the cold, I'd never wanted anything so badly as I wanted Freddie's wool socks.

When Tano shouted some guttural Kravaxian something or other outside, Axel grumbled, "What now?" He stood, pointed a finger at us. "Stay put, you two."

"Darling"—I raised my cuffed hands as far as I could—"where would we possibly go?"

Once Axel was out of earshot, Sai asked, "Do you think they jumped with us?"

"Who?"

"Morgath and Rax? Maybe Captain Jones? I'm sure they were out there in cloaked shuttles or something."

I blinked at him. "How did you know that?"

"It makes sense," he said with a shrug. "They wouldn't have just let us go. So they probably followed us, right?"

Squinting at the FFKs through the cavemouth, trying to make out their shapes in the darkness, I said, "Isn't it impossible to follow a ship through a jump if you don't know where it's going?"

"It used to be," he said. And when I turned to face him, his eyes shone. "But there's a new thing that makes it possible. Morgath told me."

"Morgath told you that? When?"

"When we hung out last week."

"You've 'hung out' with Morgath?" I asked, looking at him like he'd just told me he used to have a Kuiper worm as a pet.

"Oh yeah, lots of times. Rax too," he continued while my jaw hinged open. "Anyway, it's this new tracker thing. Like a giant laser gun. Morgath said if you tag a ship with it, you can follow it through an FTL jump, even if you didn't know where it was going."

"How in the stars did you end up talking about faster-than-light travel with one of the heads of security on my ship?"

"He was reading my book with me," Sai explained like it was the most normal thing in the worlds. "Captain Zorba was trying to catch a jewel thief, but he jumped and got away. And Morgath said that if he'd used that new tracker gun, he could've followed the thief through the jump. It was the coolest."

"Morgath...*read* to you?"

"Yeah, when he boosted the security around our suite. He took a break to have some lunch. I was reading. He joined me. Is that weird?"

Words failed me, because the image of giant, grumpy Morgath of all beings reading a child's book to an actual child was indeed extremely weird. The only thing weirder would have been if Rax had done it. But if I'd learned anything in my tenure as the hospitality specialist on an infamous pleasure cruise, it was that every single being possessed untold hidden depths. "Sai," I said. "Did Morgath, by chance, tell you if he had one of those trackers?"

"No," he whispered, his shining eyes twinkling with excitement in the firelight. "He showed it to me."

LATER THAT EVENING, Sai and I watched the Kravaxians eat some small rabbit-type animal Marisia had shot with a crossbow and sip from steaming cups of tea made from berries and spruce needles. Reya offered us some of the meat, but Sai—a vegetarian—shook his head. I declined as well, in solidarity. But the tea wasn't too bad.

After dinner, Sai fell asleep with his head on my shoulder,

and I pretended to do the same, closing my eyes and leaning against the wall. But I wasn't sleeping. I was listening.

They spoke in Kravaxian, and after a lifetime spent having my VC translate every known language into Common, words I didn't understand fascinated me. But I didn't need to understand what they were saying to see that Tano, Marisia, and—to a lesser extent—Axel presented a united front, while Reya continually tried to push against them. They weren't arguing, necessarily, but tension mounted in the cave. Eventually, after an hour or two, their conversation faded behind the crackling of the fire, and I'd nearly drifted off to sleep for real, the adrenaline that had propped me up all day giving way to a dense, droning fatigue, when a single word stopped my heart.

Brock.

At first I thought I'd imagined it, some half dream invading reality. But then, there it was again. "Brock," in Axel's clipped voice, followed by a hissed warning from Tano that sounded a lot like *quiet, fool.*

And like one of Freddie's puzzle pieces locking firmly into place, one of Sai's toys shifting from an orb into a star, I realized why Tano had looked so familiar. *Stars above*, it was so obvious now I wanted to scream.

I'd never met him in person, but his broad forehead, wide cheekbones, and chiseled jawline—those I'd seen plenty. Everyone had, considering the vain bastard had them carved into the CAK's Central Park hedge maze. Tano's features weren't identical, but close enough that they had to have been brothers. Cousins at the very least. And even though he'd definitely been wearing makeup in that BLIX brochure to hide his pale face, there was no lingering doubt in my mind that the audacious, outspoken, and duplicitous CEO of LunaCorp, Brock Karlovich, was a Fifth Fucking Kravaxian!

Suddenly, it all made sense. LunaCorp funding initiatives to benefit Kravax. The FFKs learning our systems while "vacationing" with us at the same time as a senator who was about to propose legislation that would penalize corporate monopolies. Sai being abducted to shut Sonia up so that her proposition would never see the light of day. Since nobody would ever think to question who was behind this act—kidnapping for ransom a common enough practice for Kravaxian pirates—LunaCorp and Brock Karlovich would get exactly what they wanted without garnering a single smudge of guilt. *Cunning, merciless, and resilient, indeed.*

This information also gave me an idea of how long Sai and I would have to spend in this cave before the FFKs either released us or killed us. The senate meeting on Portis was in four days. Best-case scenario, if Sonia and her fellow senators withdrew the proposition, the FFKs would release us, and we'd all go about our lives with a fun story to tell our friends. Worst case—and what I now thought was much more likely, since Karlovich was involved—Sai and I would never leave this cave alive.

Even on the off chance that the FFKs did let us go, who would ever believe us when we tried to convince them that a Kravaxian was at LunaCorp's helm? It was absurd. I needed that proposition to pass; the entire KU did. There was no way around it. If we wanted to live, if we wanted to keep LunaCorp from destroying what little free commerce remained amongst the stars, if I ever wanted to see Freddie again, hold him again, look into his eyes and tell him how sorry I was that I left him, how I hoped he understood why I did, how much I loved him, because I hadn't told him enough, not by half, then we needed to escape. And we needed to do it soon.

While my brain's chaotic whirring eventually slowed, I noticed that an ominous silence had descended over the cave. *Shit.* Had the FFKs realized I was awake and listening. Were my muscles too tense? Did an eyelid twitch? Had my breath caught?

Do they know?

It wasn't until the first rattling snore echoed through the cave that I let myself exhale. They weren't on to me. They weren't busy planning my untimely demise, at least not right then. They'd simply fallen asleep.

I cracked my lids, finding Axel snoring on his back, his arms crossed over his chest. Reya huddled in a corner, curled in on herself like a snail, her knees pulled up to her chest. And nestled along the cave wall, Tano slept on his side. Also snoring.

Only Marisia was still up, standing guard at the mouth of the cave. With a stiff set to her shoulders and a jaw clenched so tightly it made *my* teeth hurt, she tapped out an irritated rhythm on her crossbow. All night, she'd seemed annoyed—well, more annoyed than usual. But was her annoyance with us, with the situation, with life in a cave? Or was it with Tano, who, in my professional opinion, appeared to be driving her up the wall? While I wondered if there might be an exploitable crack forming between them, Sai, awake and looking down the top of my jumpsuit, whispered, "What is that?"

Surprised by the turn of events, and not entirely certain how to proceed because *was this some kind of teachable moment*? I explained, "Well, Sai, those are called breasts—"

"Stop. No. Not what I meant. And I know what they're called," he said, only mildly ruffled. "I mean what is *that*? Your necklace?"

Marisia's head swiveled our way, and we waited silently, our eyes half-closed, Sai's head on my shoulder again as we hid behind the crackling flames.

Once she went back to staring resentfully through the cave-mouth, I whispered, "Orion's Tooth," nodding toward my pendant. "It was a gift from these jerks."

"I need that." Sai made a pointed gesture toward his mag-cuffs. "I can *use* that,"

"You can?" I asked.

"Yeah. These are just another puzzle."

"Well, that's good to know. But then what?"

"We run," he mouthed, pointing at the cavemouth. "Obviously."

"We can't just run. We have no idea where to go. We have no food or water. We'll die out there."

Giving me a level stare, he said, "They're going to kill us if we stay here. You know that, right?"

He was too smart. Too damn smart. "Yes." I squeezed his finally warm fingers. "I know."

"But you're right. We need a plan."

Slowly, we both looked out at the sleeping FFKs, our gazes lingering on Reya.

"She's the weak link," Sai said. "You can get her to break. Tomorrow. We'll have to make our move tomorrow."

I frowned down at him. "Don't take this the wrong way, Sai. But you're a teeny bit terrifying."

"I'm a KU senator's son," he explained, nestling against my side again, closing his eyes. "Of course I'm terrifying."

"Is Tig okay?" Reya asked me, her voice a dry rasp. "She didn't get hurt, did she?"

I peered up at her from where I squatted in the dirt, surrounded by a stand of tall conifers with narrow trunks. I'd asked for one of the FFKs to take me to relieve myself, and when Axel offered his services, I requested Reya because of "female stuff." Axel had no issues letting Reya take me after that. Sometimes, it was just too easy.

The hollow, dark circles carved under her eyes made me wonder if she'd slept at all last night. And if not, had she heard my conversation with Sai? It didn't matter. I had her alone. It was now or never.

"I don't know, Reya. The last I heard before you fragged my VC was that Morgath had found her crying on the floor of the control room."

Turning away from me, her shoulders rising toward her ears, she said, "I didn't want this. I never wanted any of this."

After pulling my jumpsuit back up, I took advantage of the moment to look around, trying to figure out where Sai and I might go if we were somehow able to escape from the well-guarded cave in the middle of the frigid night on this foreign and hostile planet.

It was actually beautiful, wherever we were—a small clearing in the middle of a dense pine forest with snow-covered cliffs spreading out into the distance. Since my shoes and Sai's bare feet were hardly appropriate for cliff climbing, our only way out would be through the forest. But we needed a direction. We needed intel.

"Reya," I said, positioning the first chess piece. "What is 'this' anyway? I thought you were different. I thought you wanted change for your people."

Wheeling around, she crossed her arms, digging her fingertips into her skin. "You don't understand. You couldn't possibly. Kravax is not like the rest of the KU. Beliefs here are not modern. We are not evolved. We do what our elders say. Always. We don't have a choice. But"—she paused, her eyes closing—"I really did hope that would change." She opened her eyes again, clearly fighting to hide the emotion welling behind them.

"Did you know all along?" I asked. "Did you know the plan was always to take the boy?"

Her chin dropped to her chest, her black hair flowing forward to curtain her face. "I thought BLIX was real. I was excited about something for the first time in my life. And then, when I met all of you, when I met Tig, I thought maybe, with her, I could finally be"—she shrugged—"myself. Away from this planet, from these beliefs. But no, I didn't know. I swear it. Tano told Axel and me an hour before he made his move."

"And you felt compelled to go along with them because that's just how things are here." I wasn't questioning or judging. I was only validating.

She nodded. "I shouldn't have. I should have pushed back, told Rax or Morgath or you. Maybe if I had"—she paused, and a single tear rolled down her cheek—"I would have stopped it. I should have been stronger, braver. I failed."

I should have been stronger. How many times had I said this same thing to myself?

A bird twittered above our heads, and pine needles crunched under my feet as I stepped toward Reya. Placing a hand over her crossed arms, I said, "Tig will understand."

Her head jerked up, a second tear chasing the first down her cheek. "No, she won't. She will never forgive me."

This was my window. I had to open it. I had to try. "She will," I insisted. "Because she'll know that you are not your people. She'll know that you *are* strong and brave. You are special to her, Reya. And she is special to you. That sort of thing doesn't happen all the time." My heart squeezed out its next few beats, Raphe's words to me, my words to Elanie, Freddie's worried eyes all flashing through my mind. "It's precious."

Glancing around nervously, as if making sure we weren't being overheard, Reya said, "That sort of thing *never* happens on Kravax. That kind of love… It's forbidden."

I risked giving her arm a squeeze. She let me. Time to attempt a gambit. "Listen to me, Reya. The universe is vast and open, and your place in it is not defined by where you were born, what lies you've been told about what is right or wrong, or who you choose to love."

"But how? How can I find my place? I'm here. I'm stuck here."

"I'll tell you how," I said with a fierce determination. "You are going to fight for what you want. You are going to fight for the type of life you want to live, and for who you want to live it with. And you are going to start by helping me get that boy back to his mothers."

Tano waited for us at the cave entrance, his stance wide, his arms stiff at his sides. "Where have you been?"

Reya's head ducked under his intimidating glare.

Mine did not. "You know what they say." I gave him a wink. "Never rush a woman in the bathroom."

Those pale *Brock Karlovich* cheeks of his flushed bright pink. "Get back inside."

"Yes, sir," I said obediently, then, glancing at him under my lashes, I gave him a very obvious, very intentional, *very suggestive* thumbs-up before letting my knuckles brush against his as I stepped past him into the cave.

Looking over my shoulder, catching his gaze dropping to my ass while a crooked, self-satisfied grin spread across his face, I knew that Freddie's warning about the hand gesture being a Kravaxian come-on had been right on the money.

As if on cue, Marisia grunted, scowled at me, then glowered at Tano.

"What are you doing?" Sai asked when I returned to sit by his side, his brows knitted. "Doesn't *thumbs-up* mean sex stuff on Kravax?"

"Sex stuff?" I repeated, shaking my head at him. "How do you know these things?"

"Seriously. What are you doing?"

"My job, darling." My lips quirked at his puzzled expression. "It's simple distraction," I explained. "If Tano is busy thinking about me, and Marisia is busy thinking about him…"

"Then they'll both be less busy thinking about us."

While I nodded down at him, he smiled up at me and said, "Sunny, I think you might be a teeny bit terrifying too."

We passed the day by telling stories, picking at the tart yellow berries Axel had harvested for us, and—in the brief moments when we were alone in the cave—discussing our escape plan. Sai was worried that Reya wouldn't go through with the admittedly thin plan we'd made out in the woods. But while Sai knew puzzles, I knew people. Reya would come through for us. I only hoped she wouldn't get punished because of it.

After sunset, Tano returned to the cave from wherever he'd been all day. Sitting across from Sai and me, he stoked the fire while Marisia, Axel, and Reya left, presumably to hunt for dinner. Poor Sai would be skin and bones if I didn't get him out of there soon. He couldn't live on berries alone.

"So, what's the plan here, Tano?" I asked boldly. In my experience, his type always responded best to directness. "How long are you planning to keep us in this cave?"

His eyes narrowed into slits. "And what makes you think I will tell you anything?"

"No harm in asking. It's not like we can go anywhere or talk to anyone." Leaning toward him, maybe far enough for him to just see down the top of my jumpsuit, I said, "Your secrets are safe with us."

He only grunted. *Charming*.

Overt flirting not doing the trick, I changed tactics. "Is Marisia your wife?"

He grunted again. "I have taken no wife."

"Really?" I asked. "Why not? She seems like she'd make a fine enough wife."

What I could see—and Tano could not—was that Marisia had returned, and now she stood outside the cave with a sizable dead rodent dangling from one hand, her crossbow from the other, and the wrath of a thousand suns blazing in her eyes.

"She would not make *me* a fine wife," he said as the flames picked up, golden light flickering in his eyes. "She has no fire."

His head turned when Marisia made a strangled, disgusted noise, hurled the rodent at him, and stalked back out into the graying twilight.

"Are you sure about that?" I asked. "She seems pretty *fiery* to me."

Grunting for a third time in as many minutes, Tano moved the rodent to the side of the fire, pushed himself to his feet, and grumbled, "Mind your own business. I will go find the boy more berries."

SAI and I sat in silence, watching Tano, Axel, and Reya chew on roasted rodents, and Marisia—refusing to eat—chewing on her resentment instead. While she sent Tano scathing glares, I passed him fleeting, furtive glances under my lashes, popping berries into my mouth, taking my sweet time licking my fingertips clean. Kravax might have cornered the market on violence and intimidation, but they had much to learn about interpersonal relationships. And how easily those relationships could be manipulated to sow dissent among the ranks by someone like me.

After dinner, Sai—who must have been both exhausted and starving, yet hadn't complained once—fell asleep with his head in my lap. Leaning back against the unforgivingly hard rock wall, I pretended to do the same, keeping my eyes mostly closed. I waited for Tano and Marisia to drift off, sleeping on opposite sides of the cave tonight, while I listened for Axel's inevitable snoring after he passed out by the fire. Eventually, only Reya remained conscious, sitting at the entrance of the cave, taking her turn to keep watch. Just like we'd planned.

Not daring to wait much longer, I ran my fingers over Sai's soft hair. When he opened his eyes and turned his head to look up at me, I nodded, took a deep breath, and carefully unclasped my Orion's Tooth necklace. Slipping the tooth into Sai's hand, I mouthed, "Be careful. Don't break it."

Rolling his eyes, he mouthed back, "Yes, Mom."

The pain attempting to pierce my heart at the term, teasing as it was, would have to wait. The only thing that mattered now was making sure we didn't die in the next few minutes.

I didn't know how he did it, but with a press of the tooth's tip, a tiny jiggle, and a firm twist, the cuffs on my wrists, then my ankles, unlinked. After slipping off my heels, I tried to unlink his, but all I managed to do was break the tooth in half, which—while earning me another eyeroll—at least didn't wake the other Kravaxians.

They'd never bothered to cuff Sai's ankles, so even though his hands were still bound, we tiptoed through the cave. Past Axel, still snoring. Between Tano and Marisia, both sleeping with their backs turned to each other, conveniently facing opposite sides of the cave wall.

When we reached Reya's spot as lookout, she placed a finger to her lips, then drew several landmarks and three arrows in the dirt, reminders of the directions she'd told me to run earlier in the day. Directions that would hopefully lead us to a village where we'd be able to find comms. Not viewChips, but hopefully the low-tech, surface-to-orbit radios Reya said were prevalent in the villages in this region of Kravax.

It was a risk, trusting Reya, running through an unfamiliar forest in the dark, hoping the twins or the captain had been able to follow us through the jump and now orbited above us close enough that we'd be able to contact them. But neither of us thought we'd get a better chance than this one. Ushering Sai through the cavemouth, watching him run to the tree line where he'd wait for me, I turned back.

"Come with us," I whispered, extending my hand toward Reya.

She shook her head, whispering back, "I can't." Sorrow lanced through her expression. "Tell Tig I'm sorry. Please."

I nodded, squeezed her shoulder, and watched as she shoved a paresis dart into her thigh. Helping to lower her carefully to the ground, I brushed her hair off her cheek, wishing there had been another way. But it had to look like we'd snuck past her. Like we'd stolen a dart and tricked her. It was the only way we could think of to keep her safe.

I ducked out of the cave, and after a single glance up to the clear night sky, making a silent wish on the stars that they were up there—or maybe that they were down here with us already —I put my head down, and I ran for the trees like my life depended on it.

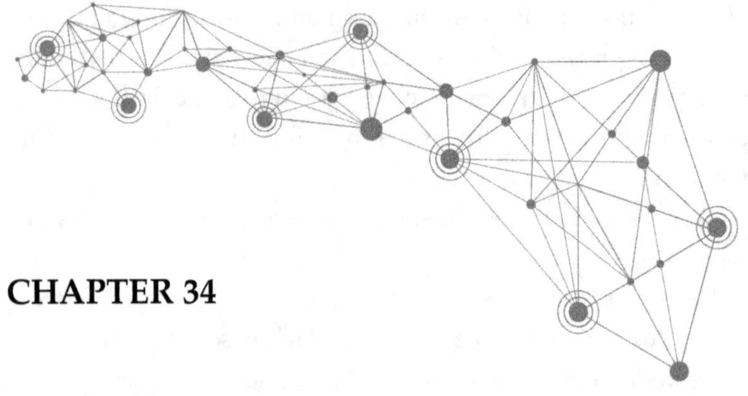

CHAPTER 34

In the dim light of Kravax's two moons, I ran behind Sai, trying to keep up as he weaved around trees and ducked under branches, the silk of my jumpsuit snagging on a never-ending string of pine needles. I had never wheezed so hard in my life, my lungs burning, my eyes watering, my heart thundering. After another five minutes spent wondering if my chance of death by sudden cardiac arrest outweighed my chance of death by Kravaxian, I said, "I think we can slow down—"

An explosion lit the sky, a deafening *boom* shaking the trees, cutting me off.

"What the hell was that?" I cried, spinning around, grabbing Sai by his shoulder, and shoving him behind me. "Is it them? Did they wake up?" I squinted up at the sky, seeing nothing but stars, moons, and then—

"It's not them!" Sai shouted, sprinting out from behind me as a massive flaming dragon burst into the night sky. "Sunny, it's not them!"

"Wait!" I took off after him as he raced back the way we'd come. "Sai, wait."

"It's magic," he called over his shoulder. "It's Makenna. They've found us. Our friends are here!"

Catching up with him, I reached for his bound hands, urging him to slow. "We still…need to…be careful," I said urgently, gasping for air. "We can't just"—I paused, placing my hands on my knees to catch my breath before I passed out—"run out there."

"Yeah, okay." He winced, patting my shoulder. "Are you okay?"

"I'm fine." Standing up straight again, I waved him off. "I've just done more running in the last two days than I've done in my entire life." When he laughed at me, I pointed a finger at him. "Hey, did you know Makenna was one of your mom's SOs?"

He scoffed. "Of course I knew. She's like my aunt." When another dragon made of light roared above our heads, Sai leapt into the air. "The FFKs must be freaking out." His laughter was manic. "I don't think they have magic on Kravax. Or dragons. It's brilliant. This is all *so* Makenna. She's hysterical."

"Wait, Sai," I said as a sudden surge of adrenaline rattled me. "What about Reya? If Makenna is here, Rax and Morgath must be here too. What if they try to hurt Reya? They won't know she helped us."

Grasping one of my hands in his, he yanked me along. "Then we need to move faster. Come on."

He led the way again as we followed the light show back toward the cave, hearing nothing but the snapping of twigs beneath our feet between the occasional deafening explosions of magic. And then, once we were closer, Tano's and Axel's panicked cries.

When we reached the tree line, it was pure chaos. Magical oorthorses, dragons, and even a flaming, stampeding kurot assaulted the silence of the woods. In the clearing, Tano and Axel huddled in their cave, ducking out occasionally to cower in fear at the fire in the sky. I couldn't see Reya, which made sense, since she was likely only now waking up. No Marisia either. Probably hiding in the cave. What was more distressing, when I looked around the clearing, was that there was no sign of Makenna or my crew.

"Where are they?" I turned to Sai. "Do you see them?"

With a brow furrowed in deep concentration, he shook his head.

The biggest magic dragon hovered outside the Kravaxian's cave, flapping its massive wings and slashing at the air with its glowing talons. "Let them go at once!" it roared. "Or perish in eternal hellsfire."

"That's a bit dramatic," I said.

Sai's shoulders shrugged, his lips tilting in amusement. "That's Makenna."

"They are not here," Tano bellowed, white-faced, practically pleading with the dragon towering above him. "They escaped. We do not have them anymore."

Just then, thank the stars, Captain Declan Jones's head popped up from his hiding spot behind a boulder. I pointed him out to Sai, and we slid through the remaining trees until only a few tall pines separated us from the action. Sinking to my knees, I grabbed a small rock from the ground and threw it at the captain. The first rock fell well in front of him, unnoticed. The second rock, however, hit him squarely between the eyes.

He jerked back.

I winced.

Sai snorted. "Nice shot."

The captain rubbed at his forehead then looked at his fingers. When he turned in the direction of my poorly aimed rock, I waved, and relief washed over him.

Sai and I started his way, but the captain raised his hand, his palm facing us in a clear *stay put* gesture.

"Stay here?" Sai asked while I scanned the grounds for Freddie, not finding him—because of course the captain wouldn't bring our Languages and Customs expert on a dangerous recovery mission. Especially since his only useful purpose would be holding me in his arms once it was all over. And even though that seemed indispensably valuable to me, I could see how the captain might disagree.

"It's probably a good idea," I said.

"But I don't want to stay here. I want this to be over. I"—despite his bravery, his steadfast calm in the face of utter bedlam, Sai's little chin wobbled—"want to go home."

"Oh, darling." I pulled him in close, tucking his head under my chin, rocking him from side to side. "Me too. I want to go home too. I—*ungh*."

"Sunny!" he cried, his eyes ballooning as I clawed at the icy fingers twisting viciously in my hair, hauling me to my feet. Yanked back, I screamed, "Help!" and pushed Sai as hard as I could toward the captain, who burst out from behind his boulder to grab him.

"I don't care about the whelp," Marisia hissed into my ear, wrapping her arm around my neck, holding me in a death grip so tight I could barely breathe. "I've never cared. But you tried to turn the head of my mate."

"Oh...give me...a break," I rasped, digging my nails into her arm while she frog-marched me into the clearing.

Cinching her arm around my throat until spots danced in my vision as an otherworldly pressure built from the base of my skull to throb behind my temples, she snarled, "The only thing I will give you is death."

Something sharp wedged itself into my heart then. Something vital roaring to life inside me. I didn't want to die. But more than that, deeper than that, I wanted to live. For the first time since the accident, and maybe because I was facing my mortality head on, or maybe because someone kept showing me all the ways that life could be beautiful again, I wanted to live. I wanted to live and grow and love and get a second chance at all of it. I was going to get that chance. I was going to *live*.

Wheeling me around so we faced the riot in the sky, Marisia roared, "I do not fear your tricks! Come out, offworlders. Show yourselves, or I will kill her."

"Marisia, *no*," Tano bellowed from the cave, cowering in fear. "You must not anger these spirits of fire."

"Ha," she cried, spinning me around, her grip loosening just enough for me to suck in a ragged breath. "No, Tano. You must not anger *me*."

The distraction was apparently all Morgath needed. Because from the corner of my eye, I watched him step out from behind a tree. With a voice as dark as night, an expression so menacing shivers raced up my spine, and a sonic cannon pointed direction at us, he said, "Put Sunny down."

"No...not that," I croaked, trying to shake my head, because while I was relieved to see the nonlethal weapon, I knew—either from Marisia's chokehold or the sensory bombardment of the sonic cannon—that I was about to be knocked unconscious. And I hated being unconscious. "I can fix this," I promised. And when I raised my foot, smashed it down on Marisia's instep, and threw my head back into her face, I thought it might have been enough to convince him to lower the cannon.

It wasn't.

The last thing I remembered before the sonic *boom* robbed me of my hearing, my eyesight, and then my consciousness, was pain searing across the back of my head, the satisfying crack of what I hoped was a broken Kravaxian nose, and Morgath's apologetic wince when he pulled the trigger.

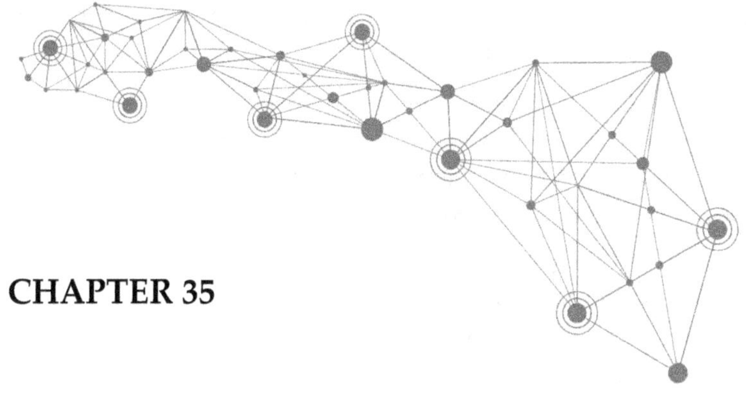

CHAPTER 35

"WAKE UP." Sai's voice was the softest echo, like a whisper in a dream. "Wake up." A whisper growing louder. "Sunny. Wake up!"

"Yep. I'm up," I groaned, forcing my eyes open. "I'm good." I sat up, doubled over, and promptly vomited in the dirt.

"Gross," Sai cried. "You puked."

Wiping the back of my hand over my mouth, I muttered, "Where the hells is Morgath?"

"I don't know," Sai said. "Why?"

"Because I need to kill him."

Captain Jones's chuckle rumbled behind me while he covered Sai with a blanket. Then he draped another over my shoulders. "Morgath is a little busy with the detainees," he said. "But I'll be sure to tell him you're looking for him."

When he dabbed at the small wound on his forehead with his sleeve, I grimaced. "That's not from me, is it?"

"Hell of an arm you've got there, Sunny. But don't worry about me. I wasn't the one taken from my own ship by Kravaxians—"

"Reya," I blurted out, coming to my senses, trying to stand

but only making it halfway before collapsing back onto my ass. "Reya helped us. She didn't—"

"We know," the captain said while offering me a canteen of cold water. "Sai told us. We're holding her with the others for now. But once we get them to Imperion, we will explain her situation to the magistrates."

"You're taking them to Imperion?"

"They kidnapped a senator's son, Sunny. This is a KU governmental matter now."

Stars, he was right. The Kravaxians would be brought to trial. Sai and I would be called to testify. "Captain, there's so much more to this story than a kidnapping for ransom. We are all in grave danger."

Giving Sai a quick, deferential nod, the captain said, "The boy told us everything. Quite the story, but it does explain a lot."

"Sai already told you everything?" I stared up at him, then at Sai. "How long have I been out?"

"Not long." Captain Jones placed a hand on my shoulder. "Only a few minutes."

"I was excited," Sai said with a shrug. "It all just"—he made a *blech* noise—"came out. Kinda like your puke."

"Don't remind me," I groaned, pulling my blanket more tightly around me.

"Sai told us about Karlovich," the captain continued. "He also said you devised the escape plan, played the Kravaxians against each other, and convinced Reya to help you."

"Sai was the mastermind," I insisted, rubbing at the dull headache hammering behind my temples. "Not me."

"I guess we'll call it teamwork," the captain said, winking at Sai. Then he handed me a comm. "Someone would like to speak with you."

While I stared at the comm in my hands, the captain

walked across the clearing to join the twins in securing the FFKs for transport to Imperion.

Sai nestled into my side, and I clicked the talk button. "Hello?"

"Sunny. Sweetheart, you're all right," Freddie said, his voice ruining me, shattering the wall I'd built around myself the second I'd followed Sai onto the Kravaxian's shuttle. "Thank the stars. I was so worried. I was—"

"I'm sorry," I said, tears stinging my eyes, my voice a hoarse, broken mess. "I'm so sorry."

"Don't be sorry. Just be in my arms. Come home. Please come home."

"We're taking her to the shuttle now, Freddie," Rax called out as he walked to stand at my side. "She'll be close enough to smooch in no time."

"Ew," Sai groaned. "First puking, now kissing?"

"Be safe, Sunny," Freddie said, and there was so much fear and relief mingling in the words that my chest constricted, my throat ached, my hands shook. "I'll be waiting."

Taking the comm from me before it fell from my trembling fingers, Rax told Freddie, "We're leaving in five. I'll keep her safe."

Rax helped me to my feet, and suddenly, the only thing I wanted to do was get on the shuttle, put my head in my hands, and weep. But Makenna cut us off halfway there.

Dropping to her knees, she took Sai's face between her hands. "Are you all right? Did they hurt you?"

He shook his head, trying to be stoic, but his eyes shone like glass.

Makenna crushed him to her chest, holding him close while she looked up at me and asked, "Are you okay, Sunny?"

I squinted at her, less in disapproval that she'd lied to all of us—including Chan—for weeks (well, maybe a bit in disapproval), but more to focus my swimming vision. "I'm fine," I lied.

After giving Sai a kiss on his head, she rose to her feet. "Thank you," she said, her voice cracking, "for protecting Sai. Thank you."

"No problem," I said with a shake of my head, the motion making me so dizzy the ground heaved beneath my feet. "But I think I need to lie down."

Grabbing my elbow to steady me, Makenna said, "You look like you're about to fall over. Let's get you both to the shuttle."

Despite my aching head, blurry vision, and rubbery, adrenaline-wrecked muscles, I strode upright past the FFK. They were all on their knees, all cuffed the same way I'd spent the last forty-eight hours. And for a moment, for all but Reya, I let myself appreciate the symmetry.

"Sunny," Sai shouted, entering the shuttle in front of me. "There's food!" He ran back to his seat, digging into a plate of soft bread and a creamy-looking dip my crew had brought for him. "It's my mom's hummus," he said, tears streaming freely down his cheeks. "They brought my mom's hummus."

I sank onto my seat, my cave-sore ass soothed by the soft cushion, my cave-hidden heart soothed by the knowledge that Sai was safe and eating and heading back home to his moms. That I was heading back home to Freddie. The relief was so potent, I was a breath away from joining him in letting myself cry. But Morgath stepped onto the shuttle behind me, his head ducked, his broad shoulders hunched. "Uh, hi, Sunny," he said. "I'm sorry about—"

"A sonic cannon?" I scowled up at him. "Really?"

"I'm a dingus." He ducked his head so thoroughly his chin touched his chest. "But she had her arm around your throat. I didn't trust that she wouldn't..." His hands curled into fists at his sides. "I couldn't let her hurt you."

I softened, not even my raging headache letting me stay

upset with him. "I understand. Thank you, Morgath. Thank you for coming. Thank you for saving our lives."

Kneeling in front of me, which still put his face above mine, he said, "I'm sorry it took us so long. It was hard to follow their ship through the jump. We kept losing the signal."

"So the laser-tracker thing worked?" Sai asked around a mouthful of bread, coming to sit beside me.

Ruffling Sai's hair, Morgath said, "Totally. And I'll tell you all about it once we're in the air."

SAI SLEPT through the entire trip, his head on my lap while I ran my fingers gently through his hair, just like I used to with Jonathan. It wasn't something I ever imagined I'd be able to do again, but I let myself have the comfort. I tried not to push away the memories but to sit with them, even though they stung. But when we docked with the *Ignisar*, when I disembarked the shuttle to find Freddie standing outside the airlock, waiting for me with a hand-written sign that read *Welcome Home*, it was more than just my memories that stung.

I used to think he made me weak. But seeing him now, watching the smile streak across his face while he swiped a knuckle under his eye, I couldn't believe how wrong I'd been. He'd never made me weak. He made me feel. He made me whole. He made me strong.

This ship had been my home for the last five years, but now, I realized as my eyes filled with tears, he was my home.

After the airlock finished cycling, the doors slid open, and in my torn jumpsuit and dirty bare feet, I ran to him. His arms came around me, the warmth and pressure of his embrace almost convincing my body that it was safe again. But then my heart froze in my chest as Lena and Sonia raced around the corner, falling to their knees in relief at the sight of their son.

I didn't know, hadn't realized how hard it would be, seeing the relief I'd never been lucky enough to feel on Lena's and Sonia's faces, the joy and fear and love and absolute relief as they took Sai into their arms and held him, kissed him, cried with him. It was unbearable. I wasn't strong enough for this. "I can't," I whispered into Freddie's chest. "I can't be here. It's too much."

He kissed my head, ushering me toward the elevator, telling me, "I've got you, sweetheart. I've got you."

I didn't know how long I'd spent sobbing in his arms, trembling on his bed, his hand brushing over my hair and running up and down my back in long, soothing strokes. I only knew that once I finally calmed enough to ask, "Can you do me a favor?" he hopped out of bed without hesitation.

Five minutes later, he returned from my pod, helping me out of my filthy jumpsuit, helping me into the shower, helping me wash my hair and my body, drying me off. And then he slipped my favorite nightshirt over my head and pulled my favorite Venusian wool socks up my legs while I braced myself on his shoulders.

I was still shivering, still cold, so he curled up with me again on his bed, holding me close, surrounding my body with his. It took some time before I was finally warm, but only a moment longer before I fell asleep.

When I woke sometime later, still held tightly in his arms, still warm, everything was different. The sadness had faded. The pain had ebbed. And I felt safe. I felt exhausted and sore and warm and safe.

Rolling over to face him in the dim light of his pod, I placed my hand over his heart and said, "I love you, Freddie. I'm so sorry I left."

"I love you too, Sunny." His hand rose to cover mine. "And I'm not sorry. You saved him. You brought him home to his moms, and you brought yourself home to me. You are the bravest being I have ever known."

Raising my gaze to his, my chest so full of love for him everything inside it ached, I said, "You mean so much to me. I never told you how much, and I regretted it. Sitting in that cave, wondering if I'd ever see you again, I regretted that I didn't tell you, that I might have missed my chance to make sure you knew. Because you mean everything to me, Freddie. Your heart" —I moved our hands so I could kiss his chest, his steady heart-beat thumping against my lips—"means everything to me. I'm so sorry for hurting it. I'm so sorry that what I did to keep the worst thing that ever happened to me from happening to someone else"—my voice cracked, my eyes filling with hot, guilty tears—"must have felt a lot like the worst thing that ever happened to you. I never wanted that. I never wanted to hurt you like that."

"Oh, sweetheart." He brushed my tears off my cheeks, kissed them off my eyelashes, my lips. "Of course you didn't. You mean everything to me too. And you have nothing to be sorry for, unless"—he reconsidered—"you do it again."

"I won't," I said with a watery laugh. "I promise."

"Good. Then it's like I said. Don't be sorry. Just be in my arms."

And then he kissed me, and I kissed him back. When I fell asleep again, nestled against him, surrounded by his safe embrace, I didn't wake up for another fifteen hours.

EPILOGUE

"CHEERS." I held my glass out to Chan, and he clinked it with his. But there, in the bar above the main deck atrium, in the amber light of sunset sim, he wore the same distant expression he'd worn since I'd returned to the ship two weeks ago. "Darling, what's wrong?" I asked, resting my hand over his.

"I don't know, Sunny." He stared down into his drink. "I thought… I let myself think that maybe, this time, it was real. It was really happening. And maybe I wouldn't be alone anymore."

"Makenna?" I guessed, and he gave me a nod.

Makenna had disembarked with the senator and her family last week, taking a piece of my heart with them in the shape of a ten-year-old boy. Maybe they'd taken a piece of Chan's as well.

"I'm sorry, Chan."

His shoulders rose and fell, his hoverchair humming softly. "I should have known it was all a trick. She seemed *way* too into me. She didn't even flinch when I accidentally asked her if her eyelashes were real."

Deciding it would be best not to comment, I only gave his hand a squeeze.

"I got carried away," he said, straightening with a sudden and fierce determination. "It won't happen again."

Chan cared about Makenna, and he'd thought she'd cared about him too. It was just like the conversations I'd had with Tig since I'd returned to the ship. They both felt betrayed by someone they'd thought they could trust, someone they thought they could love. Maybe every one of us—Chan, Tig, Rax, Morgath, Freddie, me...maybe even Elanie—spent far too much time on this ship, seeing the best and worst of love played out in real time in our every waking moment. When we finally risked the hope that we might have a love of our own, it was devastating when it all fell apart.

"I understand," I said, but inwardly I promised him, *I will make sure it happens again for you, if it's the last thing I do.*

After we shared another silent, pensive glass of Venusian whiskey, Chan turned to me with a solemn expression. "Sunny, would you ever consider telling me what happened to you? Not what happened on Kravax, but before. I know something happened, something awful, something you never talk about. But I'm your friend." He squeezed my hand now. "I'm here for you. Always. You can talk to me, if you ever need to."

This caught me so off guard I couldn't think of what to say, how to say it.

"I'm sorry." He turned away, his cheeks flushing red with embarrassment. "I shouldn't have asked. That was rude of me."

But as the sun set over the treetops, casting long pink and purple shadows across our table, I realized he was right. Chan was my friend. One of my best friends. He loved me. I could tell him about Jonathan.

And so I did.

He didn't say a word, no stranger to loss, but his hand continued to hold mine as pools of silver lined his eyes. We sat together in silence until the first twinkling of simulated starlight pierced the darkening dome suspended over the atrium.

"Chan?" I said after taking another sip of whiskey. "Will we be okay?"

"I suppose," he replied. "We carry on, don't we? What else can we do?"

"What else can we do?" I repeated softly, distantly, feeling the truth of it in my bones. Tilting my glass his way, I said, "If it's any consolation, even with the eyelash comment, I think your game is improving."

"You do?" His eyebrows climbed toward his hairline. "I've really been working on it. I've been reading romance novels."

Smiling at him, I said, "Absolutely."

We'd been so busy over the last few weeks that Freddie and I had barely spent a single moment alone. After the press interviews, the sentencing trials for the FFKs, and the fallout and restructuring of LunaCorp after Proposition 2126 passed the KU Senate by a wide margin, life aboard the ship, I hoped, was returning to normal.

<What are you up to?> Freddie commed while I walked back from the airlock to the staff pods.

<Just welcoming that adorable pop band from New Earth Korea aboard. I'm headed up to twelve now.>

<Adorable? How adorable?>

I grinned. <Extremely. But nowhere near as adorable as you when you get jealous.>

<Did you chat with Sai today?>

My smile grew while I stepped into the elevator. <I did. He's starting middle school next week. He's nervous.> Sai and I had a standing video chat every week, something I hoped would continue so I could watch him grow—with the ultimate end goal of becoming his campaign manager when he ran for KU President, of course.

<Aww. Poor kid. He'll do great.>

<That's exactly what I told him.>

<We received a digcard today,> Freddie commed while the elevator doors opened on the staff deck. <An invitation to Garran and Kasa's handjoining.>

"*What*?" I screamed, making the Blurvan across the hall spin around so fast his lower half kept going before springing back with a rippling wobble. Wincing, I whispered, "Sorry," to the Blurvan, then commed, <Really? That's wonderful. When?>

<Next year, on Argos. We could take a holiday. Maybe combine the joining with a visit to Tranquis. If you wanted to, that is.>

My pace slowed. <You want to visit Tranquis?>

After a brief pause, he said, <I thought maybe I could—only if you're ready—meet your parents.>

<You want to meet my parents?>

<I do,> he replied.

I was a second away from saying several nauseatingly sweet —and a few suitably filthy—things to him when Elanie stormed toward me, her eyes red and swollen and...*are they wet?*

<I do too,> I commed him quickly. <It's a wonderful idea, and I want to come kiss you for thinking of it. But something's up with Elanie. This may take a minute.>

<Comm me if you need backup.>

"Out of my way, Sunny," Elanie barked when I stepped into her path, my arms stretched out wide.

"No," I said sternly. "Not until you tell me why you're so upset."

Slowing to a halt, she stared at me for a long moment. Then she hung her head, buried her face in her hands, and started to sob.

I took her by the elbow, spun her around, and walked her back to my pod. "What in the worlds is going on?" I demanded after depositing her on the edge of my bed. "Why are you crying?"

Through her tears, she said haltingly, "He...he told me... He said he thought I was...b-beautiful."

I frowned. "Who? Who told you that? And why are you crying over it?"

Blowing her nose on the tissue I handed to her, she blurted out, "His name is Blake. He was the bionic staring at me at the New Year's party. I said hello to him in the hallway *one time*," she said, holding up a finger. "And now he won't leave me alone. He keeps smiling at me whenever I see him, waving at me, asking me how my day is going. Why is he torturing me like this?"

"Torturing?" Something was wrong. This wasn't like Elanie at all. She was distressed. She was crying. She was...*emotional.* I stumbled back a step, running ass-first into my dresser. "Elanie," I gasped. "Good gods, have you upgraded?"

"Whatever," she cried, throwing her hands into the air, the tissue landing in a crumpled ball somewhere on my floor. "Who even cares? It's all so ridiculous."

"You upgraded without telling me? Why? Why didn't you tell me?"

"I don't know." Her shoulders slumped, her arms hanging limply from her sides. "But I hate it. I can't think straight. Everything hurts." She squeezed her belly. "And I feel so puffy all the time."

"That sounds about right," I said, oozing sympathy because puberty was one thing. Puberty as a twenty-eight-year-old bionic was something else entirely.

"It's just, you and Freddie seemed so happy," she said, cutting me off. "So I thought maybe I could be happy too. Well, guess what? Joke's on me. I've never been so miserable in my entire existence!"

Joining her on the bed, I tucked a strand of her hair behind her ear. "It's all right, Elanie. It will be all right, I promise. We just need a plan. All this requires are some anti-nox tabs, a lengthy conversation, and a *lot* of food. Would you like to get some ice cream?"

After picking the tissue up off the floor so she could blow her nose into it again, she looked at me, sniffled, and said, "That sounds really good."

"I know, darling." I pulled her in close. "It always does."

One hour and two scoops later, I stepped into the elevator and pressed the button for deck sixteen. Freddie had been waiting for me on twelve, but I hadn't been to the pool on sixteen once since Makenna reversed the trick that had drained it dry. The pool that now was silent and blue and beautiful, with starlight through the flexGlass ceiling shimmering across the water.

Stripping down to my underwear, I dove headfirst into the deep end. After coming up for air, I opened my *Squee* app and sent a message.

<Hello, Joshua. Any chance you're available for a date at the pool on sixteen? Say, nowish?>

Even though we were openly dating, sometimes we still liked to play.

In the space of two heartbeats, he responded, <Good evening, Phoebe. I'm on my way.>

I was floating on my back when he arrived, turning to lock the door behind him before walking to the edge of the pool. Staring down at me, he said, "Sunastara Nex, you are the most beautiful woman I have ever laid eyes on. How in the worlds did I get so lucky?"

Rolling over onto my belly, I swam to him, close enough to pull his shoelace free of its tight little bow. “Come swim with me.”

I loved watching him undress, shedding his suit coat, his tie, his pants. The professional costume of Freddie the L&C fell to the ground to reveal the soft skin and long limbs of Freddie the man. Freddie, who’d loved me even when I’d pushed him away. Even when I’d refused to let myself be loved. Even now, when I loved him back so much it sometimes hurt. Freddie, who saw me for the broken woman I was, and, instead of running, he stayed, waited, helped put me back together.

After kicking off his boxers, he dove into the pool with predictable grace. And when his head emerged, I reached behind my back, unhooked my bra, tossed it onto the deck, and said, “Come here.”

Instead of swimming the short distance between us, he dove under the water. When he reached me, his fingers curled into the waistband of my underwear, sliding them over my hips, down past my knees, off one foot and then the other. After coming back up for air, he pushed me back to the edge of the pool, setting my underwear on the deck with a wet slap.

When he kissed me, his tongue slipping between my lips, his hands cupping my ass, sliding to my hips, he lifted me out of the water. Placing me on the edge, he hooked my legs over his shoulders and nestled between them. “Beautiful,” he said while I slid my fingers into his hair. “So beautiful.”

I grinned down at him. “Who are you speaking to, darling?”

Not taking his eyes from between my legs, he said, “Both of you.”

I laughed, then sighed, then panted and writhed and cried out his name as he kissed and licked and sucked until my body went taut, my fingers gripping his hair, holding him in place while flashes of white heat pulsed through me, brighter than the stars shining above us.

I was still hovering somewhere on the outer edges of consciousness, lost to pleasure, when he pulled me back into the water with him. But my body knew what to do, my legs wrapping around his waist, my hand reaching down, guiding him to my entrance, my arms clinging to him as he thrust up into me. My chest pressed against his so tightly I felt each beat of his heart across the skin and bones that separated us.

Sometime later, after he found the edges of his consciousness too, I kissed his shoulder and asked, "Do you remember that poem you read to me?"

"I do," he said, his lips brushing along the skin of my neck.

Looking up through the flexGlass into the infinity of time and space above us, where stars burned and expanded and collapsed, where planets spun and revolved around their suns, where it was the fate of all objects to push inexorably away from one another—except for us—I said, "Fredrick Caruthers the Third, I vow to love you forever under these stars that formed us, so long ago."

He kissed me deeply, fiercely, and then softly as we floated together in the water, staring up at the stars. And I smiled, thinking about luck. Despite the odds, despite the gravity of our pasts conspiring to keep us apart, we'd held on. And even though we'd been lost once, we'd found each other, and now we were both finally home.

Thank you so much for reading. For more information on the author, please visit jesskhardy.com

# ACKNOWLEDGMENTS

This story started with two thoughts:

1. Love Boat in space
2. The pleasure pods will malfunction.

This is a funny story. It's a romantic story. But it's also a heartbreaking story. I only hope I was able to tell it with the honesty and care it deserved. In light of this, and for countless other reasons, there are many wonderful people I need to thank for helping Sunny's story get told.

First, thank you to Paul. I don't know where you are, and I hope you're okay. And I miss you.

To Angela Wren Crocker, my dear friend, my twin Eeyore, meme wizard, and Pedro superfan. Thank you for being such a damn good writer because it inspires me to be better. Thank you for your support and humor and for making me realize that we are never too old to find a new best friend. I love you.

To J Calamy, thank you for getting me, for being my Gen X touchstone, for Graves, and for your friendship.

To Livy Hart, thank you for reading, for cheerleading, for writing the funniest romcoms out there, and for being such a phenomenal human being.

To Sarah T. Dubb, thank you for always being there for me, for your friendship, and for your amazing editorial eye.

Thank you to my husband and son, sisters, brother, and parents. Thank you for your love and support and for being the most important people in my life.

Lastly, thank you from the bottom of my heart to every single being who reads this book. I hope you will join me for more adventures aboard the *Ignisar*. I mean, we all have to see what happens to Elanie as she goes through bionic puberty, right? ;)

ABOUT THE AUTHOR

A Montana transplant hailing from the suburbs of Chicago and about twenty other places, Jess K Hardy is a lover of mountains and snow, long nights and fireplaces. She has been a sandwich artist, a student, a horse trainer, a physical therapist, a wife, a mother, and also a writer. She writes contemporary and speculative adult romance.

ALSO BY JESS K HARDY

COME AS YOU ARE (BLUEBIRD BASIN BOOK 1)
LIPS LIKE SUGAR (BLUEBIRD BASIN BOOK 2)
WISH YOU WERE HERE (BLUEBIRD BASIN BOOK 3)
THE CURSE OF NONA MAY TAYLOR

www.ingramcontent.com/pod-product-compliance
Lightning Source LLC
LaVergne TN
LVHW010309070526
838199LV00065B/5500